A Bride Worth Keeping

Providence Ridge Book #1

VIVIAN BELLE

STERLING RIDGE PRESS LLC

A Bride Worth Keeping © 2026 by Vivian Belle

All rights reserved. No part of this book may be reproduced, distributed, or transmitted in any form or by any means, including photocopying, recording, or other electronic or mechanical methods, without the prior written permission of the author, except in the case of brief quotations embodied in critical reviews and certain other noncommercial uses permitted by copyright law.

This is a work of fiction. Names, characters, places, and incidents either are the product of the author's imagination or are used fictitiously. Any resemblance to actual persons, living or dead, events, or locales is entirely coincidental.

Unless otherwise indicated, all Scripture quotations are taken from the Holy Bible, King James Version.

Cover designed by Sterling Ridge Press

Published by: Sterling Ridge Press, www.sterlingridgepress.com

ISBN: 978-1-966093-49-7
Printed in the United States of America

First Edition: A Bride Worth Keeping 2026

For permissions, contact: support@vivianbelle.com or visit www.vivianbelle.com

Dedication

Trust in the LORD with all thine heart;
and lean not unto thine own understanding.
In all thy ways acknowledge him, and he shall direct thy paths.
Proverbs 3:5–6

Contents

Chapter 1

"**Y**ou simply must come to the Ashford luncheon next week," Caroline Webb said, leaning forward in her chair with the bright, uncomplicated confidence of a woman whose biggest concern that morning had been choosing between two perfectly good hats. "Mrs. Ashford asked about you specifically, and I told her I would do my very best to convince you."

Opal set her teacup in its saucer with care, the thin Haviland porcelain clicking softly against itself. The parlor windows stood open to the mild September afternoon, letting in a whisper of warm air that carried the faint sweetness of the magnolia trees along the front walk. Somewhere beyond the iron fence, a carriage rolled past on Franklin Street, its wheels grinding over brick in a slow, steady rhythm.

"That was kind of Mrs. Ashford," Opal said. "Please give her my regards when you see her."

Caroline's smile faltered just slightly, the way it always did when Opal offered pleasantries instead of promises. She was twenty-two, the same age as Opal, with round cheeks and a generous mouth that seemed built for enthusiasm. Her visiting dress was a cheerful blue lawn with ivory lace at the collar, and she sat in the Bennett parlor as though she belonged there, which in many ways she did. She had been coming to this house since they were both twelve years old, sharing lemonade on the porch in summer and whispering over needlework in winter while their mothers talked in the morning room.

That was before, of course. Before the accident that took both of Opal's parents in a single afternoon two years ago and left her alone in a house that no longer felt like hers.

"Opal." Caroline tilted her head, her expression shifting into something softer and more careful. "You haven't accepted a single invitation in months. Not the Ashford luncheon, not the Mercer tea, not even the church picnic last Sunday, and you know Reverend Hollis always saves you a seat near the oak tree because you like the shade."

"I've been occupied with household matters."

"You've been hiding."

Opal smoothed her skirt across her knees, a pale gray muslin that was perhaps too somber for a Wednesday afternoon in early September, though it suited her mood well enough. The fabric was cool beneath her fingers, freshly pressed by the maid that morning.

"I'm not hiding, Caroline. I've simply had a great deal to manage."

Caroline studied her for a moment with those wide, earnest eyes, then seemed to decide against pressing further. She reached for a shortbread biscuit from the tray between them and took a delicate bite. "Well, you will be pleased to know that I have news of my own. Wonderful news, actually, and I have been waiting all week to tell you in person rather than sending a note, because some things deserve to be said face-to-face."

Something in Caroline's voice shifted, rising toward the kind of trembling joy that could only mean one thing.

"Thomas Porter proposed," Opal said quietly.

Caroline's whole face lit up like a lantern. "Last Saturday evening. In his mother's garden, under the arbor. Oh, Opal, I wish you could have seen his face. He was so nervous he nearly dropped it in the rosebush."

A genuine smile found its way to Opal's lips, the first real one she had managed in days. She reached across the small tea table and took Caroline's hand. "I am so happy for you. Truly. Thomas is a good man, and he has loved you since we were sixteen."

"Longer than that, if you believe his mother." Caroline laughed, squeezing Opal's fingers. "We are planning a spring wedding. April, if the church is available. And I want you there beside me, Opal. I want you to stand with me."

"I would be honored," she said, and meant it with every part of herself that was still capable of meaning anything at all.

The warmth in Opal's chest tightened into something more complicated, a sweetness threaded with an ache she couldn't afford to show. Caroline's life was unfolding along the lines it was meant to follow: courtship, engagement, a wedding, and eventually a home of her own. It was the life their mothers had imagined for both of them, sitting in this very parlor over cups of tea, planning a future that seemed as solid and sure as the brick walls around them.

Opal wanted that life. She had always wanted it. Not the trappings of it, not the society wedding or the fine house, but the substance: a man who looked at her the way Thomas looked at Caroline, with that particular mixture of wonder and steadiness that said I choose you, and I will keep choosing you, and nothing about that choice frightens me. Her parents had shared that kind of love. Her father had looked at her mother across the supper table with quiet, constant warmth, and her mother had looked back with the calm assurance of a woman who knew she was treasured. Opal had grown up inside that love the way a child grows up inside a house, assuming it would always be there, never questioning.

The life Caroline was stepping into felt as distant as a country Opal could see from a high window but could never reach. Not because she didn't want it. Because the man who controlled her future had decided that her wants and desires didn't matter.

Caroline beamed and launched into a breathless account of wedding details: the fabric she was considering for her dress, the flowers Thomas's mother had suggested, and the question of whether the reception should be held at the Porter home or in the church hall. Opal listened and nodded and asked the right questions at the right moments, and if her mind drifted now and then toward darker rooms in this house, she pulled it back with the discipline of long practice.

"Oh, and speaking of weddings," Caroline said, pausing mid-thought as though something had just surfaced, "did you hear about the Henderson girl? Mary Henderson, who was two years behind us at the academy? Mother told me last week that she answered one of those matrimonial advertisements in the newspaper and went off to Oregon Territory to marry a wheat farmer she'd never laid eyes on." Caroline's tone held equal parts scandal and fascination. "Can you imagine? Getting on a train to marry a perfect stranger. Mother was horrified, of course, but Mrs. Henderson told her Mary's letters have been nothing but cheerful." She shook her head with a small laugh. "I suppose when a woman decides she wants a home of her own badly enough, she'll cross a continent to get one."

Opal lifted her teacup and said nothing.

"You know," Caroline said after a pause, setting her teacup down with a thoughtful expression, "Reverend Hollis spoke last Sunday about God's provision in seasons of loss. About how He places people in our lives to guide us through the valley, even when we cannot see the path ourselves." She glanced at Opal with a look that was both tender and slightly pointed. "I think Mr. Hawthorne has been that kind of provision for you, Opal. I know you find his attention... persistent. But he has managed your father's affairs so faithfully, and he has kept this house exactly as it was, and I think your father would be grateful to know someone was looking after you."

Opal's fingers tightened around the handle of her teacup, a small contraction she hid by lifting it to her lips.

"Mr. Hawthorne has certainly been attentive," she said, and the words tasted like ash.

"And Edward is quite well-regarded, you know. Mother says he will be a fine match for someone, and everyone assumes..." Caroline trailed off, reading something in Opal's expression that made her reconsider. "Well. I only mean that you are not as alone as you seem to believe. You have people who care about you and want the best for you."

"I know," Opal said. She set the cup down and folded her hands in her lap, every finger still and composed. "And I am grateful for your friendship, Caroline. More than I can say."

It was the truth. Caroline was kind, loyal, and entirely incapable of imagining that a man like Charles Hawthorne could be anything other than what he appeared: a distinguished gentleman fulfilling a solemn duty to his late partner's only child. Caroline saw the public face, the generous guardian, the concerned family friend who attended every church function and spoke of Opal's welfare with such convincing tenderness that half of Richmond believed he was practically a saint.

Opal saw the private one. The man who sat behind her father's desk as though it had always been his. The man who controlled every dollar of her inheritance, reviewed every household expense, and had quietly replaced half the servants with people who reported to him. The man who had committed his own wife to an asylum three years ago with nothing more than a doctor's signature and the sympathetic nods of their social circle.

But these were not things she could say to Caroline Webb over shortbread and tea on a Wednesday afternoon. So she smiled and asked about the wedding flowers, and Caroline, satisfied that she had planted a seed of encouragement, returned to happier subjects.

They had just begun discussing the merits of white roses versus gardenias when a quiet knock interrupted them. Mary Simmons stood in the parlor doorway, her expression carefully neutral in the way it always was when she carried messages she understood the weight of better than she let on. Mary was young, with a plain face and steady hands, and the particular talent of appearing to see nothing while observing everything.

"Miss Bennett," Mary said, her voice even and unhurried. "Mr. Hawthorne has arrived. He requests your presence in the study immediately."

The word sat in the air like a stone dropped into still water. Immediately. Not at your convenience. Not when your guest has departed. Immediately.

Opal set her napkin beside her plate and rose from her chair with the same smooth, unhurried composure she had spent years perfecting. "Thank you, Mary. Please let Mr. Hawthorne know I will be along shortly."

Mary dipped her chin and withdrew, her footsteps fading down the hallway toward the rear of the house.

Caroline was already gathering her gloves and parasol, entirely unbothered. "I should let you attend to your business. Mr. Hawthorne is always so conscientious about keeping you informed of affairs, isn't he? You really are fortunate, Opal. So many young women in your position would have no one at all."

"Yes," Opal said softly. "Fortunate."

She walked Caroline to the front door, accepted her friend's warm embrace and her cheerful promise to send a note about the Ashford luncheon, and stood on the porch watching as Caroline's hired carriage pulled away down Franklin Street, the blue of her dress visible through the window like a bright flag of ordinary happiness disappearing around the corner.

Opal turned back into the house.

The central hallway stretched before her, long and dim, the dark oak floors gleaming beneath the patterned wool runner. The coatrack by the door held only her shawl and a single umbrella. The narrow table along the wall still bore the silver card tray her mother had placed there years ago, though the cards it collected now were from Hawthorne's associates rather than her parents' friends.

Opal moved through the hall toward the rear of the house, and with each step she catalogued the small erosions she had learned to read like weather signs. The arrangement of furniture in the dining room had been altered last month without her being consulted; the chairs pulled back from the table as though someone had measured the spacing with a ruler. The vase on the hall table held fresh flowers, but they were not the roses her mother preferred. They were hothouse lilies, stiff and waxy, placed there by Mary on Hawthorne's standing order.

Her father's study door was closed. Thomas Bennett had never closed that door during daylight hours. He had believed an open door invited conversation, that a man who shut himself away from his household was a man who had forgotten what mattered most. Opal could still picture him there on winter evenings, seated at his desk with his reading glasses perched on his nose and the door standing wide, calling out to her as she passed: Come in, sweetheart. *Tell me what you read today.*

She stopped outside the closed door, drew one slow breath, and knocked.

"Come in."

Opal opened the door and stepped inside.

Charles Hawthorne sat behind her father's walnut desk as though he had been born to it. He was fifty-nine years old, tall and broad-shouldered, with iron-gray hair combed back from a high forehead and a neatly trimmed beard that gave him the appearance of a judge or a senator. His suit was dark and finely tailored, his watch chain glinting against his waistcoat, and his hands rested on the desk's surface with the easy authority of a man who had never questioned his right to occupy any space he chose. The room smelled of his sandalwood cologne and cigar smoke, scents that had long since replaced the mild, homey fragrance of her father's pipe tobacco.

Edward Hawthorne stood near the window, half-turned toward the glass as though he found the view of the garden absorbing. He was twenty-five, fair-haired, and built along softer lines than his father. His expression held the particular blankness of someone who had trained himself not to react.

"Opal, my dear." Hawthorne rose from the desk chair with a courtesy so practiced it moved like clockwork. He gestured to one of the leather armchairs facing the desk. "Please, sit down. I apologize for the interruption to your afternoon. I know you were visiting with the Webb girl."

Opal lowered herself into the chair and settled her hands in her lap. The leather was warm from the afternoon light that filtered through the half-drawn curtains. Behind Hawthorne, on the wall, her father's framed business license hung beside a watercolor of the textile mill, artifacts of a partnership that had once been built on trust.

"I hope you are well, Mr. Hawthorne," she said, because two years of this had taught her that politeness was the only shield she owned.

"Well enough, though I confess I have been concerned." He lowered himself back into the chair with a slow exhale, and his gaze settled on her with the patient weight of a man who had all the time in the world. "You declined the Ashford invitation again. And the Mercer gathering last week. And the church social before that."

She kept her face still. She had not told him about the Ashford invitation. Mary, then. Or perhaps Mrs. Ashford herself, dropping a word in his ear at services, seeking reassurance that poor dear Opal was managing.

"I have been feeling a bit tired," Opal said. "The summer heat is difficult this year."

"September is cooler. And yet here you sit." He steepled his fingers on the desk, the gesture so familiar she could have drawn it from memory. "Opal, I have been patient. I believe you would agree that I have been extraordinarily patient. After your father's passing, God rest him, I took on the management of his affairs and the care of his household and his daughter without a single complaint. I have preserved this house. I have maintained your stipend. I have ensured that your reputation in this community remains exactly what your parents would have wished."

"And I am grateful for your stewardship, Mr. Hawthorne," Opal replied, meeting his eyes with the careful steadiness of a woman walking a ledge.

"I am glad to hear it." He studied her for a moment, then leaned back in the chair. "Because gratitude, Opal, ought to be expressed through cooperation. And I find that your cooperation has been... lacking."

The air in the room shifted. Opal felt it the way a person feels the barometric pressure drop before a storm, a tightening across the skin that has nothing to do with temperature.

"Edward," Hawthorne said, without looking at his son, "tell Miss Bennett about Friday evening."

Edward turned from the window. His gaze moved to Opal, and something crossed his face that she had seen before and learned not to mistake for sympathy. It was irritation, the tight-lipped displeasure of a man who resented being made to perform a scene that should have been settled weeks ago. She remembered the last time Edward had visited the parlor alone, three months ago, when she had declined his invitation to walk in the garden. He had stood in the doorway and looked at her the way a clerk looks at a ledger entry that refuses to balance, and said, with a thin smile that never reached his eyes: *You make things more difficult than they need to be, Opal. For everyone.*

He opened his mouth to speak, but Hawthorne continued as though the instruction had been merely rhetorical.

"I am hosting a formal dinner and dance at my estate this Friday evening," Hawthorne said. "A celebration, one might say. Edward will be proposing to you formally, in the company of our families' closest friends and associates." He paused, letting the words settle. "A carriage will be sent to collect you at five o'clock sharp. I trust you will have Mrs. Jennings help you dress appropriately for the occasion."

The room went silent. Even the muffled sounds of the street outside seemed to recede, as though the house itself were holding its breath.

Opal kept her voice level. "Mr. Hawthorne, I appreciate the sentiment, but I believe we have discussed this matter before, and I have expressed my wish for more time to consider—"

"You have had two years of time." The warmth vanished from his voice like a candle snuffed between two fingers. "You have had every advantage, every kindness, every opportunity to come to the sensible conclusion on your own that I had hoped you would. Your father was a reasonable man, and I assumed his daughter had inherited his good judgment." He leaned forward, his hands flat on the desk, the gold of his signet ring catching the light. "It appears I was mistaken."

"Father—" Edward said, and the single word carried not the weight of protest but of impatience, the tone of a man who wished his father would stop negotiating and simply settle the matter.

Hawthorne silenced him with a glance so sharp it could have cut glass. Edward pressed his lips together and turned back to the window, his jaw tight. But not before his eyes swept past Opal with a look she recognized. She had seen it on his father's face a hundred times, that particular blend of entitlement and annoyance directed at a woman who wouldn't cooperate with plans made for her benefit. Edward wore it less skillfully than his father, the way a son wears a coat he has not yet grown into, but the fit was close enough. Close enough to tell Opal everything she needed to know about what life with Edward Hawthorne would look like: not a partner but a manager, not a husband but a smaller, paler copy of the man already controlling her life, irritated by her resistance and entirely unable to see why she might resist at all.

Hawthorne returned his attention to Opal. "I have had some troubling reports about your behavior, Opal. Your withdrawal from society, your refusal to attend functions, and your increasing isolation within this house. These are not the habits of a healthy young woman."

"I have been in mourning—"

"Mourning has a season." His voice hardened. "Yours has stretched beyond what anyone would call appropriate, and the Richmond community has noticed. People are talking, Opal. They are asking questions about your state of mind, your emotional stability, and your fitness to manage even the simplest social obligations." He paused, allowing those words to do their slow, poisonous work. "It reminds me, I must confess, of Adelaide."

The name landed like a slap.

Adelaide Hawthorne. His wife. A woman Opal remembered as gentle and soft-spoken, with nervous hands and a way of looking at doorways as though she expected someone to walk through them and tell her what she had done wrong. Three years ago, Adelaide had been sent to the Virginia Sanitarium outside of Richmond for what Charles described publicly as a rest cure. It was a period of recovery from the pressures of her social obligations and the strain of her delicate constitution.

She had not come home.

And Edward had not objected. Opal remembered that, too. She remembered standing in the Hawthorne parlor at a reception weeks after Adelaide's commitment, watching Edward accept condolences about his mother's health with the same bland courtesy he used for everything else, and offering his own summary to a concerned neighbor with a shrug so slight it was barely visible: She's well looked after. Better than she managed here, I'm told. He had said it the way a man comments on the boarding of a horse. Practical. Settled. Done.

"Adelaide was a fragile woman," Hawthorne continued, his tone shifting to one of practiced, mournful concern. "Too fragile, I'm afraid, for the demands of ordinary life. The Virginia Sanitarium has provided her with excellent care, the very best available, and I visit her regularly. The physicians there are wonderfully attentive to women who find themselves overwhelmed by circumstances they simply cannot manage on their own."

Opal's hands were perfectly still in her lap. Her face revealed nothing. But beneath the gray muslin of her skirt, her fingernails pressed into her palms hard enough to leave marks.

"I would hate," Hawthorne said softly, "to see a similar pattern in someone I care for so deeply."

The threat hung in the room like smoke, too thick to ignore, too diffuse to grasp. He would never say it plainly. He would never have to. A doctor's signature. A concerned guardian's testimony. An unmarried woman with no family, no allies, and no legal standing of her own, exhibiting signs of nervous distress and emotional withdrawal. It would take so little. A few quiet conversations, a few sympathetic nods, and Opal Margaret Bennett would follow Adelaide Hawthorne into the kind of care from which women didn't return.

And Edward would shrug. Edward would tell the neighbors she was well looked after. Edward would move on with the same bland efficiency he had shown when his own mother was erased from polite society, because Edward didn't resist his father's machinery. He operated it.

"Furthermore," Hawthorne said, straightening a stack of papers on the desk with the air of a man tidying up after a productive meeting, "I have been reviewing the household accounts. Mrs. Jennings is getting on in years, and I wonder whether it might be time to consider her retirement. A woman of her age, the demands of maintaining a house of this size... it would be a kindness, really, to relieve her of the burden."

Mrs. Jennings. The one person in this house who still looked at Opal and saw Thomas Bennett's daughter rather than Charles Hawthorne's problem.

Opal drew a breath so slow and controlled it might have been measured with a metronome. She met Hawthorne's eyes and held them. "You have given me a great deal to consider, Mr. Hawthorne. May I be excused to reflect on your words?"

He regarded her for a long moment, his expression calculating, weighing whether her composure was compliance or resistance. Then he smiled, the kind of smile that never quite reached his eyes.

"Of course, my dear. Take the evening. Reflect. Pray, if you wish," he settled back in the chair. "Friday. Five o'clock. I will send the carriage."

Opal rose from the chair, inclined her head in a gesture that could pass for deference, and walked out of the study. She closed the door behind her with a quiet, precise click. She moved through the hallway, past the staircase where her parents' portrait watched from the landing wall, past the parlor where Caroline's empty teacup still sat on the tray, and up the stairs with measured steps that gave nothing away to anyone who might be listening or watching.

She reached her bedroom and shut the door.

For a moment she stood motionless in the center of the room, her back to the door, her hands at her sides. The afternoon light came through the two front windows in long, warm bars that fell across the braided rug and the edge of her bed with its crocheted coverlet. Outside, Franklin Street continued its quiet, respectable business: carriages rolling past, a woman walking with a parasol, and a delivery wagon turning the corner toward the alley. The world beyond her windows moved along its ordinary course without the slightest awareness that inside this room, inside this house, a man had just offered a woman the choice between a cage and a smaller cage.

She sat on the edge of her bed. Her hands were trembling now, a fine vibration she couldn't stop, and she pressed them flat against her knees until the trembling turned to stillness.

The anger inside her felt like a living thing, white-hot and righteous, coiled so tight in her chest she could barely breathe around it. For two years she had endured this. Two years of careful deflection and polite compliance, of smiling when she wanted to scream, of playing the grateful orphan while the man who was supposed to protect her inheritance dismantled her life one small piece at a time. She had believed, foolishly, that patience would be enough. That if she waited quietly and managed carefully and didn't provoke him, she could hold on until she turned twenty-five, when the trust dissolved and she could finally reclaim what her father had left her.

She understood now, with a clarity as cold and bright as January ice, that she would never reach twenty-five years of age as a free woman to do as she pleased. Hawthorne had no intention of waiting. He had named the Hartwell Sanitarium aloud in her presence and had spoken Adelaide's name with the casual familiarity of a man referencing a tool he had used before and wouldn't hesitate to use again. He had threatened Mrs. Jennings. Furthermore, he had set a date. Friday. Two days from now.

Two days.

Opal's gaze fell on the small bookshelf beside her bed, and she reached for the worn leather volume that sat on its top shelf, the one object in this house that still felt entirely hers. Her father's Bible. The leather was soft with years of handling; the pages edged in gold that had worn to a warm amber, and when she opened it, it fell naturally to the Psalms, where her father had kept a thin silk ribbon as a marker.

Her eyes found the forty-sixth Psalm, a passage she had read so many times the words rose to meet her like old friends.

"God is our refuge and strength, a very present help in trouble. Therefore will not we fear, though the earth be removed, and though the mountains be carried into the midst of the sea."

She closed her eyes and pressed the open book against her chest, and she prayed. Not the composed, carefully worded prayers she offered at church or at the dining table. This was something rawer, stripped of all formality, the kind of prayer that comes from a place beyond words.

"Lord, I am afraid. I am so afraid. I do not know what to do. I cannot fight this man with his own weapons. I cannot wait him out. I cannot stay and survive what he is planning. Show me a way. Please. Show me a door I cannot see."

The room was quiet. The clock on her writing desk ticked softly. A breeze stirred the lace curtains, carrying the faint floral scent of the magnolias below. From somewhere down the street came the distant sound of children's voices, high and bright, calling to each other in the last warmth of the afternoon.

Opal opened her eyes. She rose from the bed and crossed to the window, still holding the Bible against her ribs, and looked out over Franklin Street. Below her, Richmond moved through its Wednesday rhythms: a man tipping his hat to a neighbor, a woman adjusting the parcels in her arms, and two girls walking arm in arm toward the park at the end of the block. All of them free. All of them going about the ordinary business of their ordinary lives without a thought for the young woman watching from the second-floor window of the Bennett estate, the one who looked so composed and fortunate and well-provided-for.

As she stood watching the street below, something shifted inside her, the way bedrock shifts beneath soil, slow and deep and irreversible. Her fear had not disappeared. It hardened. It became the foundation for something else, something that had been building in her for months.

She wouldn't marry Edward Hawthorne.

She wouldn't be sent to the Virginia Sanitarium.

She wouldn't let this man silence her the way he had silenced Adelaide.

Opal set her father's Bible on the writing desk, smoothed its open pages with steady fingers, crossed the room to the bell pull near her door, and rang for Mrs. Jennings.

Chapter 2

The door clicked shut, and for a moment Mrs. Jennings stood with her back pressed against the wood, studying Opal with the assessing eye of a woman who'd dressed this child for her christening. She would know her moods in the dark by the sound of her breathing alone.

Clara Jennings was fifty-nine years old, built sturdy and compact the way a well-made kitchen table is built. She carried herself with the quiet authority of a woman who'd run a fine household for three decades without ever once raising her voice above the level required to be heard clearly in the next room. Her dress was plain dark cotton, neat as a pin, with a white apron tied at her waist. Her hands were reddened from years of kitchen work, the knuckles swollen slightly in the way that came with age and hot water and the daily business of keeping a house alive. Her face was lined, her gray hair pinned back in a tight, practical bun, and her eyes were the sharp, assessing brown of a woman who missed very little and forgot even less.

"You rang, Miss Opal?" Her voice was carefully ordinary, but her gaze moved across Opal's face with the swift efficiency of someone checking for fever, tears, or trouble. She'd heard the front door close behind Miss Webb. She'd seen Mary Simmons carry the message to the parlor. She knew Mr. Hawthorne was in the study, and she knew what his unscheduled visits usually meant, and every one of those facts was written in the careful steadiness of her expression.

"Close the curtains, please," Opal said quietly. "And come sit with me."

Something shifted in Mrs. Jennings's face. In all their years together, through childhood illnesses and scraped knees and the terrible, hollow months after the funeral, Opal had never asked her to close the curtains in the middle of the afternoon. Mrs. Jennings crossed the room without a word, drew the lace panels together so the light softened to a pale haze, and then settled herself on the edge of the rocking chair near the bed with her hands folded in her lap and her back straight, waiting.

Opal sat on the edge of her bed, facing her. The crocheted coverlet her mother had made lay smooth beneath her palms, each careful stitch a small act of love preserved in cotton thread.

"He's set a date," Opal said.

Mrs. Jennings didn't move. Her hands stayed folded. Her eyes stayed fixed on Opal's face. "Tell me."

So Opal told her. She told it the way she'd tell a report of accounts: clearly, precisely, and without decoration. She described Hawthorne's announcement of the Friday dinner and dance. Edward's proposal, planned and public, in front of Richmond's finest families. The carriage arriving at five o'clock sharp. She described Hawthorne's shift from paternal concern to cold instruction, and she watched Mrs. Jennings's jaw tighten with each new detail, though the older woman said nothing and made no sound.

When Opal reached the part about Adelaide, Mrs. Jennings's composure cracked. Not dramatically. Just a small, sharp breath drawn through her nose.

"He said that?" Mrs. Jennings's voice was very low. "He spoke her name? To your face?"

"He spoke of the sanitarium as though he were recommending a hotel," Opal said. "He mentioned the excellent care. The attentive physicians. Women who find themselves overwhelmed by circumstances they simply cannot manage."

Mrs. Jennings's hands gripped each other in her lap, the knuckles going white. She'd known Adelaide Hawthorne. She'd served tea to Adelaide Hawthorne in the parlor years ago, when Adelaide still came to social calls with that nervous, flickering smile and those restless hands. She'd watched Adelaide grow quieter and thinner and more careful with every visit, until the visits stopped entirely, and then the word came through the servants' network, the way all real information traveled in Richmond's great houses: Mrs. Hawthorne had been sent away. For her health. For a rest.

"And Mrs. Jennings," Opal continued, keeping her voice steady, "he mentioned the household accounts. He said you were getting on in years. That perhaps it was time to consider your retirement."

The older woman's chin lifted. A flush of color rose along her weathered cheeks, not embarrassment but anger, the deep, banked kind that burns slow and hot. "He wouldn't dare dismiss me without cause. Your father hired me. This is the Bennett household."

"It's his household now," Opal said gently. "In every way that matters. He pays the wages. He reviews the accounts. Mary and every other hired hand report to him. The only reason you're still here is because dismissing you without explanation would raise questions he doesn't want asked." She paused. "But if I refuse Edward on Friday, he won't need to worry about questions anymore. He'll have his answer about my character, and everything that follows will be framed as necessary measures for an unstable young woman who couldn't be reasoned with."

The room was quiet. From somewhere below, they could hear the faint sounds of Mary moving through the first-floor, closing windows against the cooling afternoon.

"Whatever shall you do?" Mrs. Jennings asked.

Opal met her eyes. "I can't fight him, Clara."

The use of her Christian name, so rare between them despite the closeness of their bond, made Mrs. Jennings blink.

"I've thought about it from every direction," Opal continued. "I can't challenge the trust. I've no attorney of my own, no funds to hire one that he wouldn't learn about within the week. Richmond is too small at the top, and his reputation is too solid. I can't appeal to society. To them, he's the generous guardian who's kept the Bennett household running and the Bennett girl clothed and fed out of nothing but Christian duty. I'm the one who's withdrawn, who's refused invitations, and who won't attend functions. They already think I'm fragile." She folded her hands together, one over the other, pressing hard. "I can't confide in Caroline or anyone else. Anything I share will reach him. I can't refuse Friday's proposal and simply endure what follows. And I can't wait until I'm twenty-five, because he won't let me reach twenty-five. Not free."

Each option laid out and dismissed, each door closed with the quiet finality of a lock turning. Mrs. Jennings listened to all of it, her face grave, her hands still gripping each other in her lap.

"I have to leave," Opal said. "Before Friday."

Mrs. Jennings closed her eyes. For a long moment she sat perfectly still in the rocking chair, and Opal could see the war being fought behind that lined, steady face: the terror of what Opal was proposing against the terror of what would happen if she didn't. When she opened her eyes again, they were bright with unshed tears, but her voice was level.

"Where?"

"I need distance," Opal said. "A city large enough that one woman can disappear into the crowd. Somewhere with respectable work for a woman of education, and far enough from Richmond that his name carries no weight." She pressed her palms flat against her knees. "I'll take the train to Washington and purchase a westbound ticket. Beyond that, I'll decide once I'm moving and can think more clearly."

Mrs. Jennings studied her. "Chicago," she said, not as a question but as a practical assessment, the way she might name the right cut of fabric for a particular job. "It's the largest city on the western rail lines. Far from Virginia. Full of people from everywhere, and no one pays much mind to one more."

"Chicago is a possibility," Opal agreed. "Perhaps the likeliest one. But I don't want to lock myself into a single plan before I've had time to see what's ahead of me. I'll know more once I'm on the train and can read the situation with a clear head." She paused. "I've learned the cost of rigid plans in this house. I'd rather stay nimble."

Mrs. Jennings nodded slowly. There was approval in the gesture, the recognition of a woman who understood that the best-laid plans mattered less than the ability to adapt when circumstances shifted.

"You've thought this through."

"I've been thinking about it for quite some time, to be honest," Opal admitted.

"Do you have any money saved?" Mrs. Jennings asked.

"Just over two hundred dollars." Opal kept her voice low. "I set aside small amounts each month from my stipend. I've been skipping the dressmaker, declining invitations that would require new clothes, and making do with what I have."

Mrs. Jennings nodded slowly. "And your mother's jewelry?" Mrs. Jennings asked. "The pieces she gave you herself, not the ones locked in his safe?"

"The pearl brooch. The garnet ring. The cameo. The little gold locket with Papa's hair in it." Opal's voice caught slightly on the last item, and she steadied it. "A few others. I won't sell the locket. But the rest, once I'm settled and far from anyone who'd recognize them, I can sell to a jeweler or a broker. That should give me enough to see me through until I've found steady work."

"Then that will have to be enough," Mrs. Jennings said, and her voice carried the firmness of a woman who had run a household on less than what she wanted and made it stretch every time. "It's enough to get you out of this house and onto a train and into a room of your own somewhere he can't reach. The rest you'll sort as it comes."

"I will take two trunks," Opal said, her mind moving now through the practical geography of departure. "The ones in the attic storage, the brown leather pair Mother used when we traveled to the mountains. My carpetbag for the journey itself and my satchel for documents and money. Everything important stays on my person."

"You'll need practical clothes," Mrs. Jennings said. "Not your silks and visiting dresses. Sturdy fabrics. Things that travel well and don't show dirt. Your gray wool, the brown serge, and your dark blue cotton. Undergarments, stockings, your warmest shawl. A good pair of boots."

Opal nodded. The list was taking shape between them like a shared piece of needlework, each woman adding stitches where they were needed.

"When?" Mrs. Jennings asked.

"Friday, before dawn. We have tomorrow, Thursday, to prepare. I'll sort what to pack while you're going about your usual work so Mary doesn't notice anything out of the ordinary. I'll organize my documents and papers Thursday evening after Mary retires." She paused. "I'll need a carriage. Not from Mr. Hawthorne's livery. From someone he doesn't know."

"I know a man," Mrs. Jennings said without hesitation. "Jacob Furlow. He runs a small carriage service near Shockoe Bottom. I've hired him before for market errands when the household cart was occupied. He's quiet, and he doesn't ask questions, and he's never set foot in Mr. Hawthorne's circle." She straightened her shoulders. "I'll send word tomorrow morning and ask for a carriage in the rear alley by four o'clock Friday morning. You can make your exit through the kitchen door."

The kitchen door. The servants' entrance.

"And your ticket," Mrs. Jennings continued, practical as a compass needle pointing north. "You mustn't buy it beforehand. A clerk might remember. You'll purchase it at the station Friday morning, first thing. One of many passengers in the early crowd. Anonymous."

"Agreed."

"I'll go about Friday as any other day. I'll tell Mary I looked in on you at breakfast and you'd asked not to be disturbed... a headache, perhaps, and you're resting. Mary won't question it." A thin, bitter edge sharpened her voice on those last words, and she pressed her lips together as though catching it. "When Mr. Hawthorne's carriage arrives at five and you aren't here, I'll be surprised. Concerned. I'll say I assumed you were in your room."

"Clara—"

"I know what it will cost me." Mrs. Jennings's voice was quiet and absolutely steady. "I've known for a long time what it would cost if this day came. He'll suspect me. He may dismiss me on the spot. He may do worse." She looked at Opal with those sharp, loving eyes, and what lived in her expression wasn't fear but the fierce, settled calm of a woman who'd already made her peace with a hard thing. "Your mother would expect me to keep you safe. Your father trusted me with the most precious thing he had in this world. I'll not fail them now."

Opal's throat ached. She pressed her lips together hard and looked down at her hands, at the smooth, uncallused fingers that would need to learn new work in a new place and leave her childhood home behind.

"We should pray," Mrs. Jennings said softly.

Opal nodded, not trusting her voice. She reached across the space between them and took Mrs. Jennings's rough, warm hands in her own, and they bowed their heads together in the fading afternoon light of the bedroom where Opal had said her prayers every night since she was old enough to fold her hands.

"Lord," Mrs. Jennings murmured, her voice low enough to stay inside these four walls and no further, "we come to You with frightened hearts and willing hands. We don't know if what we're planning is the path You'd choose for us, but we know that staying is a path that leads to darkness. We believe You are a God who opens doors when every window is shut tight. Guide this girl. Protect her. Give her courage for the journey and wisdom for the road. And if it be Your will, Lord, let her find safety and kindness wherever she lands." Her grip tightened on Opal's fingers. "And watch over this house when she's gone from it. Amen."

"Amen," Opal whispered.

They sat together in the quiet for a moment longer, hands clasped, heads bowed, and the silence between them was full of everything that couldn't be said aloud. Thirty years of service. A christening gown sewn by hand. A little girl carried on sturdy hips through the garden while her mother cut roses. A frightened twenty-year-old held upright at her parents' funeral by the arm of the only person in the room who loved her without condition or calculation. All of it lived in the space between their joined hands, and both of them knew that after Friday, this space would exist only in memory.

Mrs. Jennings released Opal's hands and stood. She straightened her apron with two brisk pulls, the way she always did when shifting from feeling to function, and cleared her throat. Then she took

Opal's face in both her reddened, kitchen-roughened hands and kissed her forehead the way she'd done when Opal was small and frightened of thunderstorms.

"Your mother would be so proud of you," she said. Her voice cracked on the last word, just slightly, and she pressed her lips together and blinked twice, hard. "Now. I've got arrangements to make, and you've got packing to start, and neither of us has time for what we're feeling. We'll feel it later. Right now we work."

Opal nodded. Her eyes burned with tears, but she held steady because Mrs. Jennings was holding steady, and that was the gift they gave each other: the permission to be strong by being strong together.

Mrs. Jennings crossed to the door and slipped out into the hall-way.

Opal stood in the center of her bedroom. The light behind the closed curtains had shifted toward the amber warmth of late afternoon, casting the room in a soft, hazy glow that touched the edges of familiar things. It made them look, for just a moment, like objects in a painting rather than the furnishings of a life. The sampler by the door. The rocking chair she'd dragged from her parents' bedroom after the funeral. The writing desk where she'd sat on a hundred quiet evenings composing letters to friends. The small watercolor of the James River that her mother had painted, hanging above the desk in its modest frame, the brushstrokes still visible where Margaret Bennett's steady hand had captured the light on the water. One September afternoon, not so different from this one.

She'd always imagined leaving this room as a soon-to-be bride. Walking down the front staircase on her father's arm while the hall filled with flowers and laughter and the bells of St. Paul's rang across the rooftops of Franklin Street. That girl, the one who'd chosen this wallpaper at sixteen and stitched that sampler at twelve and knelt beside this bed every night to pray, had never once imagined she would leave through the kitchen door before dawn, carrying everything she cared to take with her in two trunks and a carpetbag, running from the man her father had trusted with her future.

But that girl had also never imagined burying both parents at such a young age or being held captive in her own home by a man who smiled for Richmond while he tightened his grip in private. The world had changed, and the girl had changed with it, and the woman who stood here now wasn't the same person who'd picked out ivory wallpaper with small blue flowers and thought it was the prettiest pattern she'd ever seen.

Opal crossed the room and opened her wardrobe. The brown serge dress hung near the back, sturdy and plain, the kind of garment a woman wore when she had work to do and no one to impress.

She lifted it from its hook and laid it across the bed.

Chapter 3

Opal stood at her dressing table in the thin glow of a single candle, her fingers working the buttons of her chemise. The candle flame wavered slightly, throwing soft, unsteady shadows across the ivory wallpaper with its small blue flowers. The room looked almost the same as it always did: the bed neatly made with her mother's crocheted coverlet, the sampler hanging by the door, the writing desk cleared of papers, and the rocking chair tucked into its corner. She'd arranged everything deliberately, leaving the surfaces tidy and undisturbed, so that anyone glancing in would see a room whose occupant had simply stepped out. The wardrobe, if opened, would tell a different story.

Thursday had been the longest day of Opal's life. Twenty-four hours of performance so careful it had left her jaw aching from the effort of keeping her expression steady. She'd sat at the breakfast table while Mary served toast and preserves and coffee, and she'd eaten every bite as though nothing in the world concerned her beyond the weather and whether the preserves were strawberry or fig. She'd answered Mary's questions about whether she'd like the parlor dusted before or after luncheon, and she'd said after, please, in a voice so ordinary she'd nearly convinced herself. She'd watched Mrs. Jennings move through the house with her usual brisk competence, carrying linens and polishing silver and betraying nothing—not a tremor, not a glance, not a single break in the rhythm of thirty years of flawless service.

And in stolen moments, when Mary was occupied on the first floor or out in the yard beating rugs, Opal had added items to the two brown leather trunks that were hidden in a spare bedroom. A dress folded quickly, a pair of stockings tucked between layers, her father's Bible wrapped in a cotton chemise for protection. Each addition had felt like a small act of theft, though everything she packed belonged to her. She was stealing herself, piece by piece, out of Charles Hawthorne's keeping.

By late Thursday night, the trunks were full, latched, and waiting. Mrs. Jennings had carried them down to the kitchen in the dark of night, one at a time, navigating the back stairs with the practiced silence of a woman who'd been moving through this house without being heard for decades.

Opal pulled her corset into position and began working the laces herself. Her fingers moved the laces through the eyelets with a competence born of months of quiet practice, pulling snug but not tight, because she needed to breathe today, needed to move freely, and needed her ribs to expand when fear tried to press them flat.

Her petticoat came next, and she smoothed it carefully over her hips before reaching for the small folded bundle she'd prepared the night before. The hidden pocket was sewn into the inside of the upper petticoat, flat against her left hip, stitched there by her own hand yesterday. Into this pocket she placed her banknotes, folded tight and bound with a scrap of ribbon.

Into a second pocket on the right, she tucked a flannel-wrapped bundle. Her mother's pearl brooch. The garnet ring. The cameo with its carved ivory profile. The small gold locket that held a curl of her father's hair, clipped by her mother years ago and presented to Opal the Christmas before the accident. A pair of garnet earrings. A thin gold chain.

The flannel bundle settled against her hip, warm and solid. Her entire fortune, such as it was, now rode against her body where no pickpocket could reach and no porter could misplace it. The rest of her life fit in two trunks, a carpetbag, and a leather satchel.

She stepped into her traveling skirt, the dark brown wool serge, and fastened the waistband with steady fingers. The fitted bodice buttoned up the front, high-collared and long-sleeved, plain enough to attract no attention and sturdy enough to endure days of travel without showing wear. The skirt cleared the ground by a good inch and a half, shorter than fashion dictated for ordinary dress but correct for a woman who'd be stepping on and off train platforms and navigating station crowds. She pinned a small watch to her bodice and checked its face in the candlelight. She had perhaps ninety minutes before Mary's morning routine began.

She sat on the edge of the bed and pulled on her stockings, then picked up her boots, the sturdy black leather lace-ups with low heels and thick soles that she'd chosen for walking, not for looks. She didn't put them on. She held them in one hand, the leather cool and stiff against her palm.

Opal blew out the candle. The room dropped into darkness, and the familiar shapes of her childhood dissolved into shadow. She picked up her carpetbag with its dark floral tapestry and leather handles, slung her satchel over her shoulder so its strap crossed her body and the bag rested at her hip, and moved toward the door.

The hallway was black. No gaslight, no candle, no moonlight through the narrow window at the end of the corridor. Opal stood still for a moment, letting her eyes adjust. She knew this house the way she knew her own body, every board that creaked, every threshold that caught, every place where the runner ended and bare wood began. She'd walked these floors ten thousand times in daylight. She could walk them once more in the dark.

She turned left, away from the central hall, away from the main staircase, toward the narrow back passage that connected the family bedrooms to the rear stairs. The back stairs were steep and narrow, and she descended them one careful step at a time, testing each tread with her weight before committing, her free hand trailing along the wall for balance. Her carpetbag bumped softly against her leg with each step. Her boots dangled from her other hand, the leather laces whispering against each other.

Halfway down, she paused. Above her, the house was silent. Mary's room was directly overhead. Opal stood on the dark stairs and listened with every nerve she possessed. Nothing. No creak of bedsprings. No shuffling of feet on bare boards. Nothing but the deep, held stillness of a sleeping house and the distant tick of the parlor clock filtering through walls and closed doors.

She kept moving.

When her stockinged feet found the brick of the kitchen floor, the cold shot through the thin cotton like a slap. The room was dark except for a bit of faint moonlight; the cookstove unlit, and without its fire, the kitchen held a strange, bereft chill. It felt wrong in a space so usually full of warmth and life and the smell of Mrs. Jennings's cooking.

A shadow moved near the back door, and Opal's breath caught before her mind registered what her eyes already knew.

Mrs. Jennings stood at the kitchen door in her dark dress and her good shawl, her posture as straight and steady as a fence post. She held a cloth-wrapped parcel in both hands, tied with kitchen string, and her face in the dimness was composed.

"The carriage is waiting," Mrs. Jennings whispered. "Your trunks are loaded."

Opal crossed the brick floor to her, and Mrs. Jennings held out the parcel. "Sandwiches. Seedcake. Two apples. Enough to see you through today and into tomorrow if the trains don't offer anything decent, which in my experience they never do." Her chin lifted slightly. "And I wrapped the sandwiches in waxed paper, not newspaper, because you'll not eat food that's been sitting against yesterday's ink."

Opal took the parcel and tucked it into her carpetbag, her throat too tight for speech. Mrs. Jennings watched her, and then she did the thing that Opal had been bracing for and dreading since Wednesday afternoon.

She reached out with work-roughened hands that had bathed Opal as an infant and braided her hair for church and pressed cool cloths to her forehead during every childhood fever, and she took Opal's face between her palms and held her there.

"Now you listen to me," Mrs. Jennings said. "You are Thomas and Margaret Bennett's daughter. You are brave, and you are kind, and you are smarter than that man has ever given you credit for. You go out that door and you don't look back, and you find a life that's worthy of the girl your mother raised."

Opal's vision blurred. She blinked once, hard, and felt the tears spill but didn't wipe them.

"I can't write to you," she whispered.

"I know."

"If he questions you—"

"I know what to say and what not to say." Mrs. Jennings's thumbs brushed the tears from Opal's cheeks with brisk tenderness. "You worry about yourself. Let me worry about me."

Opal set down her bags and wrapped her arms around Mrs. Jennings. The embrace was fierce and brief because, in their hearts, both of them understood that if they held on too long, neither would be able to let go.

Mrs. Jennings released her first. She stepped back, straightened Opal's collar with a quick, practical gesture, and nodded once.

"Go," she said. "God keep you, child."

Opal quickly slipped her boots on and laced them. She grabbed her bags and looked at Mrs. Jennings one more time, standing alone in the dark kitchen of the house she'd given her life to, and she burned that image into her memory: the straight back, the steady eyes, the hands clasped at her waist, and the chin held level. Then she turned, opened the kitchen door, and stepped out into the alley.

The September air touched her face, warm and thick with the scent of boxwood hedging and old brick and the faintly sweet smell of overripe figs from the tree her mother had planted against the carriage house wall. The sky above the alley was a deep, midnight blue, the last true darkness before dawn began to thin it. The carriage was there: a plain hired hack, dark-painted, unremarkable, the horse standing quiet in its traces. The driver, a heavyset man in a slouch hat, sat on the box with the incurious patience of someone who'd been paid not to ask questions and saw no reason to volunteer conversation.

Her trunks were secured on the luggage rack behind. Opal climbed into the cab, settled her carpetbag on the seat beside her, and her satchel on her lap. The driver clicked his tongue at the horse without waiting for instructions. The carriage rolled forward, the wheels grinding softly over the alley's packed earth, and the kitchen door grew smaller behind her until the carriage turned onto the cross street and the Bennett estate disappeared.

Richmond passed by in pieces. Franklin Street, with its iron fences and dark magnolias, the houses of people she'd known all her life standing shuttered and asleep. The corner where she and Caroline had walked to church on Sundays, arm in arm, discussing nothing more consequential than hymn selections and whether the Mercer girls' new hats were pretty or ridiculous. The steeple of St. Paul's rose like a dark finger pointing toward heaven. The Capitol dome, barely visible, was a shadow among shadows.

The streets were nearly empty. A milk wagon rattled past, heading in the opposite direction, its bottles clinking softly in their wooden crates. A lamplighter moved along the far sidewalk, reaching up to extinguish the gas lamps one by one. A man in work clothes walked with his head down, his hands in his pockets, heading toward the commercial district. None of them looked at the plain hired carriage carrying a young woman in brown wool through the quiet streets of the city she was leaving forever. She was already invisible. She was already gone.

Opal pressed her gloved hands flat against her left and right sides, feeling through the layers of wool and cotton and linen the firm, reassuring shape of her banknotes and jewelry. Her entire future in pockets sewn by her own hand. The solid feeling of them steadied something in her that prayer hadn't quite reached this morning. She had money. She had a plan.

The carriage pulled up to Elba Station just as the sky turned a deep purple. The RF&P depot was already alive with activity: porters moving between the platform and the baggage area, passengers emerging from hired carriages and private conveyances, a newsboy setting up his stand near the entrance, and the distant sound of steam and iron from the rail yard where locomotives were being prepared for the day's runs.

Opal paid the driver his fare and a modest tip, and he accepted both with a nod and not a word. A porter, a young man with broad shoulders and a cap pulled low over his forehead, helped transfer her trunks to a luggage cart and asked where she was headed.

"Washington," she said. "Please check them through."

He chalked a destination mark on each trunk, gave her a claim ticket, and wheeled them away toward the baggage car.

She turned and walked into the station.

The ticket window was staffed by a clerk with spectacles and ink-stained fingers who looked as though he'd been selling tickets since before the war and had long since ceased to notice the faces attached to the hands that pushed money across his counter. Opal asked for a single first-class coach ticket to Washington, D.C. She paid in cash. The clerk counted her money, stamped a rectangle of heavy cardstock, slid it across the counter, and was already looking past her to the next customer before she'd picked it up.

No name asked. No questions. No second glance.

She purchased a newspaper from the boy near the entrance, tucked it under her arm, and walked through the station toward the platform. Her boots clicked on the stone floor, one sound among many, and the noise and movement of the station flowed around her like a current. Porters calling out. A child crying somewhere near the waiting room. Two men in business suits arguing about a connection to Norfolk. A woman in a feathered hat adjusted her luggage with sharp, impatient gestures while her husband stood by looking helpless.

All of it ordinary. All of it anonymous. For two years, Opal had lived under Hawthorne's observation. She'd measured her words, moderated her expressions, censored her correspondence, and performed normalcy as though her life depended on it. And now she stood in a crowded train station, one traveler among dozens, and not a single person in this building knew her name or cared where she was going.

She breathed in. The air tasted of coal smoke, damp stone, and coffee from a vendor's cart, and it was the sweetest breath she'd drawn in two years.

The train waited at the platform, the locomotive breathing slow, rhythmic clouds of steam that drifted along the length of the coaches and softened the outlines of everything they touched. Opal found the ladies' car, gave her ticket to the conductor at the door, and climbed the narrow steps into the coach. The interior was paneled in dark wood; the seats upholstered in a serviceable green fabric, and the windows large enough to watch the world pass. She chose a seat on the left side, facing forward, and settled herself: satchel on her lap, carpetbag at her feet, her back straight against the upholstery, and her gloved hands folded over the satchel's clasp.

The car filled around her. Two older women took seats near the front, speaking in low, comfortable voices about someone's daughter in Baltimore. A young mother with a sleeping infant settled across the aisle. A woman, Opal's age, sat three rows ahead, already absorbed in a novel, her bonnet pushed back on her forehead as though she'd forgotten she was wearing it.

The conductor passed through, checking tickets, his punch clicking through cardstock with a sound like a small, decisive heartbeat. He glanced at Opal's ticket, punched it, handed it back, and moved on without a word.

The whistle blew. Two sharp blasts cut through the station noise and silenced every conversation in the car for a single held breath. The train shuddered. Metal groaned against metal. And then, with a slow, gathering lurch, the coaches began to move.

Opal pressed her shoulder blades against the seat back and watched through the window as the platform slid away. First the station, its brick walls and iron canopy receding like a door swinging shut. Then the rail yard, a tangle of tracks and switching towers and idle rolling stock. Then the commercial buildings along the river, their windows catching the first pale light. Then the neighborhoods, rows of houses with shuttered windows and quiet yards, chimneys just beginning to trail the thin smoke of morning fires. Then the outskirts, where the city thinned into open land and scattered farmhouses and the long, gentle roll of Virginia's hills.

Richmond grew small in the window. Then smaller. Then it curved away behind a line of trees and a bend in the track, and it was gone.

Opal sat very still. The train rocked gently beneath her, its rhythm settling into the steady, repeating pulse of wheels over rail joints, and the Virginia countryside opened outside her window in long, green swells of pasture and timber. She watched it without seeing it.

She'd done it. She was on a train moving north, and no one in this car knew who she was. By the time Charles Hawthorne's carriage arrived at the Bennett house at five o'clock this evening to collect her, she'd have purchased a westbound ticket in Washington D.C., to a city where she could disappear.

The grief found her somewhere just past Fredericksburg.

It didn't announce itself. It arrived the way weather arrives on the Virginia piedmont, gathering at the edges of the sky and moving in quietly until it covered everything. She was watching the countryside scroll past her window, the farms, and fences, and small-town stations blurring into a green-and-brown wash, and then her throat tightened and her vision swam, and the tears were there, sliding down her cheeks, and she let them come.

She didn't make a sound. She turned her face toward the glass and let the tears fall without wiping them. She cried for everything she was leaving behind: her parents' graves in Hollywood Cemetery that she wouldn't visit on the anniversary of their deaths next month. Mrs. Jennings standing alone in a kitchen, composing her face for a day of lies that might cost her everything. The house on Franklin Street with its magnolia trees and its parlor clock and its gas-lit hallways where she'd learned to walk and read and pray.

The tears lasted perhaps ten minutes. Then they were done, the way a brief summer rain is done, leaving the air cleaner. Opal drew a slow breath, pressed her handkerchief to her cheeks beneath the cover of adjusting her bonnet, and straightened in her seat.

The train carried her north through the September morning, and the Virginia hills rolled past like pages turning in a book she'd already finished reading.

Chapter 4

S he woke to a landscape she didn't recognize.

The train swayed beneath her in its steady, iron-wheeled rhythm, and for a disoriented moment Opal couldn't place herself. Her neck ached from the angle she'd slept at, bent sideways against the window frame with her linen duster wadded beneath her cheek as a pillow. Her mouth was dry, her hair had loosened from its pins on one side, and the light coming through the glass was wrong. Too bright. Too wide. Too golden.

She straightened carefully, wincing at the stiffness that had settled into her spine, and looked out the window.

Virginia was gone.

The rolling green hills, the dense stands of oak and hickory, the neat fences, and the familiar red clay were nowhere to be seen. In their place, the land had opened like a hand unclenching. Fields stretched away from the tracks in every direction, broad and golden under a September sky so pale and vast it seemed to belong to a different country entirely. Wheat stubble glinted in the afternoon light. Corn stood in tall, drying rows, the tassels browning at the tips. A farmhouse sat far back from the tracks, small and solitary against all that space, with a barn and a windmill and a thread of smoke rising from the chimney into air so clear it looked like glass.

Ohio. She was in Ohio, or perhaps western Pennsylvania. She'd changed trains in Washington, D.C., after purchasing her west-bound ticket on the Baltimore & Ohio.

The ladies' car held perhaps a dozen passengers. Two women in traveling suits sat near the front with their heads together over a shared book. An older woman across the aisle knitted steadily, her needles clicking in counterpoint to the rhythm of the wheels. A girl of perhaps fifteen sat three rows ahead, her face pressed to the window, watching the farmland pass with the rapt attention of someone seeing it for the first time. Opal understood that expression. She was wearing one very much like it.

She reached into her carpetbag at her feet and found the cloth-wrapped parcel from Mrs. Jennings. She ate an apple slowly, looking out the window, and tried to think clearly about what lay ahead.

Chicago. She'd never been to Chicago. She'd never been any-where beyond Virginia. Everything she knew about Chicago came from newspapers and her father's occasional business talk at the dinner table: a city of industry and commerce, rapidly growing, and full of people from everywhere.

She'd need to find a respectable boarding house as soon as she arrived. Then present herself to potential employers as a woman of education and modest means seeking honest work. A governess position, perhaps. A seamstress, more likely. Her needlework was genuinely skilled, her stitches fine and even, and sewing was one of the few accomplishments from her Richmond education that translated directly into wages. She could mend. She could alter.

And then what? Three years of quiet survival until she turned twenty-five, claimed her inheritance, sold her share of the company, and finally, irrevocably, severed herself from everything connected to the Hawthorne name. Three years of rented rooms and careful spending and the constant, low-grade vigilance of a woman who couldn't afford to be found. The arithmetic wasn't generous. Two hundred dollars, minus what she'd already spent on train fare and meals, left her perhaps a hundred and sixty dollars to stretch across however long it took to find steady work. A boardinghouse in a city the size of Chicago might cost a dollar a night, seven dollars a week if she could negotiate a rate. A seamstress earned four dollars a week, perhaps five. Even with the jewelry she hadn't yet sold, the margin between solvency and destitution was thinner than she liked to examine too closely.

It was a survivable plan. Sitting on this train, watching farmland roll past like a painting being slowly unfurled, it also felt like a plan built entirely around the shape of what she was running from, with very little thought given to what she was running toward.

"Lord, I'm here. I left, like I believed You wanted. I'm on this train, and I don't know what's ahead of me, and I'm asking You to show me, because I can't see it on my own."

The prayer formed in her mind the way prayers had been forming for the past two years: not as a formal address, not as the composed petitions she'd offered at church or at the Bennett dining table with her hands folded and her eyes properly closed, but as the running, honest, slightly desperate conversation of a woman talking to someone she trusted enough to admit she was frightened. She didn't close her eyes. She didn't fold her hands. She sat in her coach seat with her satchel on her lap and the apple core wrapped in her handkerchief and the vast, unfamiliar countryside scrolling past her window, and she talked to God the way she'd talk to her father if he were sitting beside her: plainly, without ceremony, trusting that He was listening even if He wasn't answering in any way she could hear.

Was leaving right? Was it obedience or just fear? Am I running toward something, or am I only running away? Is Mrs. Jennings safe?

No voice answered. No sign appeared. The train rocked onward. The knitting needles across the aisle clicked their quiet rhythm. The afternoon light poured through the window and warmed her lap.

She reached into her satchel for something to occupy her hands and her thoughts, and her fingers found the newspaper she'd purchased at Elba Station.

The front page held national dispatches: a report on tariff negotiations in Congress, an account of railroad expansion into the Dakota Territory, and something about a labor dispute in a Pennsylvania coal town. She read the words without absorbing them. The world described in newsprint felt distant and impersonal, events happening to people she didn't know in places she'd never been, and her mind kept sliding off the sentences the way water slides off oiled cloth.

She turned pages. A market report on cotton and grain prices. A society column from Baltimore. A piece about improvements to the Chesapeake & Ohio Canal that someone had written with more enthusiasm than the subject warranted. A column of shipping notices. She was reading the way a person reads when they're reading to keep from thinking: mechanically, without expectation, turning pages because turning pages was something to do with her hands that wasn't wringing them.

The classified notices occupied the back pages in dense columns of small type, organized by category. Situations wanted. Rooms to let. Land for sale. Farm equipment. Livestock. Domestic help. Legal notices in a language so compressed it was nearly a code. She scanned them with the mild, detached curiosity of someone browsing a shop window with no intention of buying.

The matrimonial column ran along the bottom of the third-to-last page, set apart by a thin ruled border and a small header in bold type. She'd seen such columns before in Richmond papers, though she'd never read them with any attention. They were a feature of the back pages, tucked between the patent medicine advertisements and the notices for lost dogs.

She read them now with nothing better to do.

Prosperous farmer, 42, seeks stout, healthy woman willing to share labor of 160-acre homestead. No objections to children. Must be willing to milk. Write care of this paper.

Widower, 38, Kansas, good land, steady income. Seeks Christian lady to manage house and four children ages 3–10. Send photograph and character reference.

Miner, Silver Creek, Colorado. Good wages, own cabin. Want a wife. Any respectable woman willing to relocate may apply. Age and appearance no matter if willing to work.

Gentleman of means, 55, recently settled in Nebraska Territory. Seeks young, healthy, attractive bride of good moral character. Must be accomplished in domestic arts and of cheerful disposition. No invalids or widows with children, please.

Opal read through them with a growing heaviness she couldn't quite name. The men behind these advertisements were not wicked. Most of them were probably decent enough, lonely, overworked, and genuinely in need of companionship as much as help. But the language reduced marriage to a transaction, wives to a list of specifications, and the future these ads described was a life of labor in someone else's house under someone else's authority, and she'd just left exactly that.

She was about to turn the page when her eye caught on an advertisement set slightly apart from the others, distinguished less by its placement than by its tone.

Christian man, 28, of honest reputation and steady employment, seeks a godly woman willing to build a life together in Silver Springs, Montana Territory. I own land and work it faithfully. I attend worship services and live by the Word as best I can. I will not pretend this country is easy. The winters are long, the nearest city is far, and the work never ends. But the land is beautiful, the people are good, and I believe God blesses the labor of willing hands. I seek not a servant but a partner — a woman of faith and courage who desires a true home built on shared work, shared prayer, and mutual respect. If this speaks to your heart, write to Mr. E. Callahan, care of the postmaster, Silver Springs, Montana Territory.

Opal read it through once. Then she went back to the beginning and read it again, more slowly, the way she'd read a passage of Scripture that snagged on something she couldn't immediately identify.

The sentences were complete and grammatical, which by itself set the advertisement apart from most of its neighbors. But it was more than penmanship. The man who'd written this had chosen his words with care. He hadn't listed requirements the way the others had, hadn't described the kind of woman he wanted the way a person described a horse they were hoping to purchase. He'd described himself: his faith, his work, his land, and the honest difficulty of the life he was offering. And he'd described what he was looking for in language that sounded less like a contract and more like an invitation. Not a servant, but a partner. A woman of faith and courage. A true home built on shared work, shared prayer, and mutual respect.

Her father would have liked this man. The thought arrived unbidden and so specific it startled her. Thomas Bennett, who'd judged men by their handshake and their willingness to speak plainly, who'd valued integrity over polish and substance over show, who'd treated her mother as his equal in everything that mattered. He would have read this advertisement and nodded and said, That's a man who means what he says.

She read it a third time. Montana Territory. She knew it was west, far west, past the plains and the prairies and into the mountains, a territory that hadn't yet achieved statehood, wild and remote. Silver Springs. She'd never heard the name. It probably wasn't even a proper town, just a cluster of buildings and a post office at the end of a wagon road. The kind of place that existed on maps as a dot and in reality as a handful of stubborn people trying to make something out of nothing.

The train swayed. The knitting needles across the aisle clicked. Outside, the farmland had given way to a stretch of low, wooded hills, the trees just beginning to show the first faint blush of autumn color at their edges.

Opal folded the newspaper carefully, pressing the crease flat with her thumbnail. She slid it into her satchel, tucking it between her writing paper and the oilskin toiletry pouch, and latched the clasp.

Chicago was the plan. Chicago was practical, anonymous, and reachable. Chicago was a boardinghouse and three years of careful invisibility until the trust matured and she could reclaim what was hers. It was a plan built on caution and the reasonable assumption that a woman alone in the world should choose the safest path available to her.

Montana wasn't safe. Montana was wilderness and a territory she knew nothing about, at the end of a rail line that stretched into country most people in Richmond would call uncivilized. Answering a stranger's advertisement in a newspaper was something women did when they had no other choice, no education, no resources, and no options. Opal had options. Opal had a plan.

She leaned her head against the window and watched the hills roll past, gilded with the low, amber light of late afternoon. A hawk circled above a distant field, riding a current of air she couldn't feel, turning slow, patient spirals against the pale sky. The land kept opening. The horizon kept pulling back, as if the country itself were making room for her.

She thought about three years in a rented room in Chicago. She thought about hiding. She thought about a man in Montana who'd written the word partner in a newspaper advertisement.

Chapter 5

The train ground to a halt with a shriek of iron that Opal felt in her teeth.

Steam billowed past the windows in thick, gray sheets, blotting out the platform for a long moment before thinning into wisps that drifted upward. The conductor's voice carried through the car, clipped and practiced: "Chicago. Union Depot. All passengers for Chicago, this is your stop. Watch your step on the platform, ladies and gentlemen."

Opal gathered her satchel and carpetbag. Her brown wool suit was wrinkled beyond any hope of pressing. Her linen duster carried a fine layer of rail dust in every crease, and her hair had been re-pinned so many times that the pins themselves seemed to have given up cooperating. She was stiff in places she hadn't known could stiffen; her mouth tasted of stale coffee purchased from a platform vendor somewhere in Indiana, and the skin of her face felt tight and gritty from coal soot that no amount of dabbing with a handkerchief could fully remove.

She stepped down from the ladies' car onto the platform, and Chicago hit her like a brick wall.

The noise came first. Not the single, identifiable sounds she was accustomed to—the clip of a horse on cobblestone, the chime of a parlor clock, the measured tick of a quiet house—but a roar. A continuous, layered, unstoppable roar made of locomotive whistles and hissing steam and iron wheels grinding on iron rails and the voices of what seemed like a thousand people all talking at once. Porters shouted. A baggage cart rattled past close enough that she stepped sideways to avoid it. Somewhere deeper in the station, a child was wailing with the full-throated commitment of the very young and very unhappy. The air smelled of coal smoke and machine oil and damp stone and something else, something sharp and sour and organic that she couldn't identify.

She stood on the platform with her bags clutched to her chest and let the crowd flow around her the way a stream flows around a boulder. For one long, airless moment, she understood with perfect clarity that she was standing in the largest city she had ever seen, and she was out of her element.

She drew a breath. Then another. Then she straightened her shoulders, adjusted her bonnet, and found the nearest person in a uniform and asked for help.

The porter was a broad-shouldered man with a waxed mustache and the patient, slightly worn expression of someone who spent his days answering the same questions from an endless rotation of bewildered faces. Opal asked him three things: where she could arrange for her trunks to be held for pickup, where she might find a respectable boardinghouse suitable for a woman traveling alone, and where the ticket office was located.

He answered all three with the brisk efficiency of a man who could do this in his sleep. Her trunks could be held at the baggage office near the south entrance for a small daily fee. For lodging, he recommended Mrs. Peabody's boardinghouse on Dearborn Street, three blocks north, clean and decent, catering to respectable women and commercial travelers. And the ticket office was just inside the main hall, to the left past the newsstand.

Opal tipped him and made her way through the crowd toward the main hall.

The ticket office was a long wooden counter behind iron grill-work, staffed by three clerks processing a steady line of passengers. When she reached the window, the clerk, a thin man with spectacles and ink on his cuffs, looked at her with polite disinterest.

"Where to, ma'am?"

"I'd like some information, please. What is the route to Montana Territory from Chicago?"

He didn't blink. "Montana Territory, you'd want the Chicago, Milwaukee and St. Paul line to St. Paul, Minnesota. From St. Paul, you'd connect to the Northern Pacific Railway. That takes you through to Livingston, Montana Territory. Livingston's the main stop."

"And the cost?"

"Coach class to St. Paul runs about twelve dollars. St. Paul to Livingston, another thirty-five to forty, depending on connections. Call it fifty dollars all told, give or take."

Fifty dollars. The number settled into the arithmetic she'd been running in her head since Fredericksburg. She'd started with two hundred. The ticket to Washington had cost three dollars. The Baltimore & Ohio fare to Chicago, another eighteen. Meals along the way, two dollars and change. The porter's tip. The daily fee on her trunks. She was somewhere around a hundred and seventy dollars now, and fifty of that would vanish the moment she bought a ticket west. A hundred and twenty dollars to arrive in a territory she'd never seen, with no employment secured and no certainty that Mr. Callahan's advertisement was anything more than words on paper.

"When does the next train depart for St. Paul?"

"Day after tomorrow. Ten o'clock sharp, Track Seven. You can purchase your ticket any time between now and departure."

"Thank you." She stepped away from the counter without buying anything.

The walk from the depot to Mrs. Peabody's boardinghouse took her through streets that bore no resemblance to anything she'd known. Richmond was a city, yes, but Richmond was a city that moved at the pace of its own history, measured and conscious of itself. Its tree-lined avenues and brick facades carried the composed dignity of a place that had been important for a long time and intended to remain so. Chicago had no interest in dignity. Chicago was building itself as fast as humanly possible and didn't care who noticed.

She walked along Dearborn Street through a canyon of buildings that seemed to compete for height, new masonry structures rising four and five stories alongside older wooden buildings that still bore the scars of hasty post-fire construction. The sidewalks were crowded with people moving in every direction: men in suits and bowler hats striding toward offices, women in working dresses carrying parcels, and newsboys hawking papers on corners. A police officer stood at an intersection with his arms folded and his whistle hanging from a chain at his chest. Horse-drawn wagons and hired carriages clogged the street itself, their drivers shouting at each other with a cheerful hostility that seemed to be the city's primary form of communication. Above it all, the constant percussion of construction: hammers, saws, the clang of steel being fitted to steel, and the shouts of workmen on scaffolding.

And the smell. Coal smoke from a thousand chimneys mixed with horse manure baking in the September warmth, mixed with the sharp, chemical tang of industry, mixed with something worse beneath it all. Something thick and foul and organic that she traced, after another block of increasingly shallow breathing, to the Chicago River. She crossed a bridge, and the stench rose to meet her like a living thing: sewage and stockyard waste and rotting vegetation and the particular, unmistakable reek of water that had been asked to carry more than water should ever have to carry. She pressed her handkerchief to her nose and walked faster, and not a single person around her seemed to notice the smell at all, which told her everything about what it meant to live here.

Halfway to the boarding house, she passed a church. It was a modest brick building wedged between a dry goods store and a tobacconist, with a wooden cross above the door and a chalkboard sign on the sidewalk announcing Sunday services at ten and Wednesday prayer meetings at seven. Opal slowed as she passed it. The doors were propped open, and through them she caught a glimpse of wooden pews, a plain altar, and the particular quality of light that lived inside churches regardless of their size or denomination: filtered, quiet, and still.

She didn't go in. She noted its location the way a sailor notes the position of a lighthouse, filed it away as a fixed point in an unfamiliar sea, and kept walking.

Mrs. Peabody's boardinghouse was a narrow, three-story wooden building with a clean front step and curtains in the windows. The woman who answered Opal's knock was perhaps fifty, built solid as a church pew, with iron-gray hair pulled back under a plain cap and the direct, measuring gaze of someone who'd made a living reading strangers at a glance. She looked at Opal the way a shopkeeper looks at merchandise: assessing quality, condition, and likely cost.

"Room and meals is a dollar a night," she said before Opal had even spoken a word. "Breakfast at seven, supper at six, no exceptions. No gentlemen callers past the front parlor. Hot water for bathing on Wednesdays and Saturdays. Payment in advance, one night at a time, or by the week. It'll be quieter if you take a room on the third floor, noisier but warmer on the second."

"Third floor, please," Opal said. "I'm not certain how long I'll be staying."

Mrs. Peabody accepted this with the practiced indifference of a woman who heard the same answer several times a week. She took Opal's dollar, produced a key from the pocket of her apron, and led her up two flights of narrow stairs to a room at the end of the hall.

The room was small, clean, and utterly without personality. An iron-frame bed with a white coverlet. A washstand with a chipped pitcher and basin. A wooden chair beside a small writing desk. A narrow window that looked down onto the street below, where the city continued its relentless noise. The walls were papered in a faded pattern of brown leaves on cream, and the floor was bare wood, scrubbed to a pale, exhausted smoothness.

Opal set her carpetbag on the bed and her satchel beside it. She stood in the center of the room and listened to the city pushing against the window glass, carriage wheels and shouting voices, and the distant, rhythmic clang of construction, and she felt her hands begin to shake.

Not from cold. Not from hunger. From the sheer, staggering weight of where she was and what she'd done. She was alone in a room in a city of six hundred thousand strangers, and not a single person here knew her name. She'd wanted this. She'd planned for this. She'd prayed for this. And now that she was standing in it, the anonymity she'd craved felt less like freedom and more like falling, the kind of falling where the ground isn't visible and the only thing certain is that it's still coming.

She sat down on the bed. The springs protested with a thin squeal. She pressed her hands flat against her knees and held them there until the trembling stopped.

She asked Mrs. Peabody about having her trunks collected.

"My nephew runs errands for me when he's not being useless. Give me your claim ticket and fifty cents, and he'll have them here before dark."

Opal fished the claim ticket and two quarters from her satchel and handed them to the woman.

Mrs. Peabody tucked them into her apron pocket and turned to go, then paused in the doorway. Her gaze lingered on Opal's face for just a moment longer than necessary, reading something there that she chose not to name aloud. Then she pulled the door shut behind her.

Through the window, the late afternoon light slanted across the rooftops, catching the smoke from a dozen chimneys and turning it amber. She could hear the couple in the next room arguing about something, their voices muffled but sharp through the thin walls, and below that the constant, grinding murmur of the city.

She opened her satchel, took out the newspaper, and unfolded it. Mr. E. Callahan's words looked back at her in their small, steady column of print.

I seek not a servant but a partner—a woman of faith and courage who desires a true home built on shared work, shared prayer, and mutual respect.

Chapter 6

The book lay open in her lap, the same page she had been staring at for twenty minutes without reading a single line. Opal sat cross-legged on the boardinghouse bed with her back against the iron headboard, her stockinged feet tucked beneath the hem of her skirt. The words on the page might as well have been written in Greek for all the good they were doing. Through the thin walls, the couple next door had resumed their argument from yesterday, their voices rising and falling in a cadence that had become as familiar as the streetcar bells.

Today had begun with purpose. She had dressed carefully and eaten breakfast at Mrs. Peabody's table alongside a telegraph clerk and two sisters traveling to see family in Milwaukee. She'd walked out into Chicago with the specific intention of finding the shape of the life this city could offer her. She had walked for hours. She had studied hiring notices posted in shop windows along State Street and paused outside a dressmaker's establishment on Wabash Avenue, where a small card in the glass read EXPERIENCED

SEAMSTRESS WANTED — INQUIRE WITHIN. She had stood before that card for a long time, reading it over and over. She had not gone inside.

She had eaten a bowl of soup at a lunch counter on Clark Street, seated between a woman in a threadbare shawl who ate without looking up and a man who read his newspaper with one hand and spooned broth with the other. Neither of them glanced at her. She had watched women her age and older moving through the streets with a brisk, closed-off efficiency that spoke of long hours and low wages.

Now it was late afternoon, and she was back where she had started, sitting on this bed with a novel she couldn't concentrate on.

Opal closed the book and set it aside. She rose from the bed and crossed the small room to the window.

The street below was busy with the particular restless energy that seemed to fill Chicago at every hour. A young couple on the sidewalk, the woman's arm looped through the man's elbow, her head tipped back in laughter at something he had said. They moved through the crowd as a single unit, connected and easy, and watching them produced a sensation in Opal's chest that she could only describe as absence. Not envy, exactly. Something hollower. The awareness that there was no one in this city, or in any city on this continent, who would loop their arm through hers and walk with her as though they belonged to each other.

In the alley between buildings, two figures sat hunched against the brick, bundled in coats too heavy for September. She couldn't tell if they were men or women. They didn't move.

A police officer walked past at a clip, his nightstick swinging from his belt, and a man burst from a shop entrance three doors down and disappeared around the corner at a dead run, coattails flying.

Chicago was alive the way a machine is alive. Turning, grinding, producing, consuming. She could live in this city for three years, paying her rent on time, eating at lunch counters, sewing seams for four dollars a week in a shop that smelled of sizing and sweat, and at the end of those three years she would walk out the same way she walked in. Unremembered. Unclaimed.

She had left Richmond to escape being managed and diminished. Was this so different? A different kind of cage, certainly. One with no lock and no keeper. But a cage could also be a room no one came looking for you in, a street where no one called your name, or a city where your disappearance would register as nothing more than an unpaid week at the boardinghouse and an empty chair at supper.

Opal turned from the window. Her gaze fell on the nightstand, where the newspaper sat folded to the same page it had been folded to since yesterday.

She picked it up, sat down on the bed, and read the advertisement again.

Christian man, 28, of honest reputation and steady employment, seeks a godly woman willing to build a life together in Silver Springs, Montana Territory. I own land and work it faithfully. I attend worship services and live by the Word as best I can. I will not pretend this country is easy. The winters are long, the nearest city is far, and the work never ends. But the land is beautiful, the people are good, and I believe God blesses the labor of willing hands. I seek not a servant but a partner — a woman of faith and courage who desires a true home built on shared work, shared prayer, and mutual respect. If this speaks to your heart, write to Mr. E. Callahan, care of the postmaster, Silver Springs, Montana Territory.

Each time she read it, she noticed something new. This time it was the phrase I will not pretend this country is easy. A man who began his appeal for a wife by admitting the difficulty of what he was offering. A man who assumed the woman reading his words was intelligent enough to deserve honesty rather than flattery. Her father had been that kind of man. The kind who believed that respect began with the truth, even when the truth was inconvenient.

She also noticed what Mr. Callahan didn't say. He didn't describe the kind of woman he wanted in terms of her appearance, her age, her cooking ability, or her willingness to bear children. The advertisements above and below his were blunt about such things. Stout, healthy woman willing to share labor. Young, healthy, attractive bride of good moral character. No invalids or widows with children, please. Mr. Callahan's advertisement described a life and asked if someone wanted to share it. The distinction was small on paper. In practice, it was everything.

She set the newspaper down and pressed her hands flat against her knees. She thought about the dressmaker's shop on Wabash Avenue. She could go back tomorrow. She could walk in, present herself, and ask about the position. She sewed well. Her stitches were fine and even, her eye for proportion was good, and she learned quickly. But the woman behind the counter would ask for references. Where had she worked before? Who could vouch for her skill, her character, and her reliability? And Opal would have to lie or deflect, and either choice would mark her as someone with something to hide.

She could try a governess position. Her education qualified her easily. But governesses lived in the households of their employers, subject to their schedules, their scrutiny, and their authority. She would be trading one form of dependence for another, and this time without even the legal protections of kinship or inheritance.

"Lord, I don't know what to do. I've turned this over and over until there is nothing left to turn, and I still can't see. I can't tell if this peace I feel when I read that man's words is You speaking or just me wanting something so badly that I'm calling it holy because I'm too frightened to call it foolish."

The knot in her chest was a living thing. She breathed around it the way she had learned to breathe around grief, in careful, measured pulls that kept the worst of it from rising into her throat.

"I'm alone. I know You say I'm not, and I believe that, I do, but I'm sitting in a room that belongs to someone else in a city that's always in motion, and a stranger's advertisement in a newspaper keeps drawing me in. In my heart, I do not believe I could survive three years living in this wretched city. That is what I have, Lord. That is everything. I'm about to do something I cannot take back, and I am doing it with nothing but a feeling I can't explain and a faith I'm not sure is strong enough for what I'm asking it to carry. Please watch over me and guide me through what I'm about to do."

She reached for her satchel and removed her writing supplies.

She walked to the small table by the window and sat down. Opal uncapped her ink bottle and smoothed a sheet of cream stationery flat beneath her hand. The lamp on the nightstand threw just enough light to write by, and she positioned the paper so the glow fell across it evenly.

She wrote slowly. Each word chosen and weighed.

Dear Mr. Callahan,

My name is Opal. I am a Christian woman, educated and of good character. I have read your advertisement, and I am writing because your words describe a life I believe I could share with earnest willingness and honest labor.

I am capable of hard work and eager to learn what I do not yet know. I value faith, honesty, and mutual respect above all else in any partnership, and I would bring those qualities to yours without reservation.

I expect to travel from Chicago to St. Paul by rail and from there by the Northern Pacific Railway to Livingston, Montana Territory. From Livingston, I will seek passage to Silver Springs. Weather and connections permitting, I hope to arrive by the end of September.

If you have already made other arrangements, I ask only that you leave word at the post office in Silver Springs so that I may know upon arrival.

Respectfully yours,
Opal

She read the letter through twice. Six sentences. No surname. No return address.

She folded the letter, slipped it into an envelope, and addressed it in her neatest hand: Mr. E. Callahan, care of the Postmaster, Silver Springs, Montana Territory.

Then she stood, washed her face and hands at the basin, put on her bonnet and gloves, grabbed her satchel, and picked up the letter.

Mrs. Peabody was in the front hall when Opal came down the stairs. She glanced up from the ledger she was reviewing at the hall table.

"Where might I find the post office, Mrs. Peabody?"

"It's on Dearborn. You've got forty minutes until they close."

"Thank you. And Mrs. Peabody, one other question. Where might I find a reputable jeweler?"

Mrs. Peabody studied her for a moment with an expression that shifted from professional neutrality to something quieter and more understanding.

"Mr. Hirschfeld on Wabash Avenue," she said. "Between Adams and Jackson. He's a goldsmith and estate dealer, honest as they come in that line of work, and he's discreet. Tell him I sent you." A brief pause. "He'll give you a fair price. Some won't. He will."

"Thank you, Mrs. Peabody."

She mailed the letter first. The post office was a stone building with tall windows and a flag that hung limp in the still air. Inside, a clerk with rolled sleeves and bags under his eyes accepted the letter, weighed it, and quoted the postage. Opal paid. The clerk tossed the letter into a canvas sorting bag behind the counter without ceremony.

Then she walked to Wabash Avenue.

She'd done the arithmetic twice before writing the letter. A hundred and sixty-seven dollars remained from her original two hundred, after trains and meals and two nights' lodging. The ticket to Montana would cost fifty. She would arrive in Livingston with a hundred and seventeen dollars, and still need to pay for transportation to Silver Springs and food. Perhaps another twenty dollars or so. All this sounded reasonable until she considered that she was traveling to meet a stranger on the strength of a newspaper advertisement, and if Mr. Callahan proved to be anything other than what his words suggested, less than a hundred dollars was all that stood between her and destitution.

She needed more money.

She found Mr. Hirschfeld's shop between a stationer and a hat-maker, a narrow storefront with gold lettering on the window and a display of pocket watches and brooches behind the glass. A bell rang when she opened the door.

Mr. Hirschfeld was a small, neat man with silver-rimmed spectacles and careful hands. He greeted Opal with the courteous reserve of a man who understood that women who came to sell jewelry often came with stories they didn't wish to tell, and he didn't ask for hers.

She unwrapped the flannel bundle on his counter and presented two pieces: the pearl brooch and the garnet ring.

Mr. Hirschfeld examined the brooch first, turning it under a magnifying lens with the slow, appreciative attention of a man who knew quality when he held it. The pearls were genuine and well-matched. The setting was gold, finely worked.

The garnet ring received the same careful inspection. The stone was a deep, clear red, well-cut, set in a band of yellow gold with small seed pearls on either side. He held it up to the light from the shop window, and for a moment the garnet caught the sun and burned like a small, contained fire in his fingers.

Mr. Hirschfeld named his price. Opal countered gently with a number seven dollars higher. He studied her over his spectacles with something that might have been respect, adjusted his offer by five, and she accepted.

He counted banknotes onto the counter. She folded them into her petticoat pocket alongside her other funds. The pearl brooch and the garnet ring now belonged to a small, careful man on Wabash Avenue who would clean them and set them in his display case and sell them to someone who would never know that the pearls had rested at Margaret Bennett's throat on Easter Sundays or that the garnet had caught the light of a hundred Richmond dinners on a hand that had also braided a daughter's hair and pressed wildflowers between the pages of books.

She had traded pieces of her mother's life for passage to her own. The thought arrived without sentiment, clean and factual, and she let it stand. Her mother would have understood. Margaret Bennett had been a practical woman beneath the refinement, and she would have said, without hesitation, that jewelry locked in a pocket was worth less than a daughter with a future.

Opal thanked Mr. Hirschfeld, who wished her well with the same quiet courtesy he'd shown throughout, and walked to the rail depot next.

The ticket window was staffed by a different clerk than the one she had spoken to yesterday. This man was older, with a thick mustache and a distracted manner that suggested he was counting the minutes until his shift ended. Opal asked for coach passage to St. Paul on the morning train, with a connecting ticket on the Northern Pacific Railway to Livingston, Montana Territory. The clerk quoted the fare. She counted out the bills and coins. The clerk processed the tickets, stamped them, and slid them across the counter.

"Train departs at ten o'clock sharp, Track Seven," he said. "Connection in St. Paul is same-day... the four-fifteen westbound."

Opal tucked the tickets into her satchel beside her documents.

The walk back to the boarding house took several minutes. The sky was going dark, and the gas lamps along the street threw pools of amber light across the sidewalk. She passed the church she had noted yesterday; its doors closed now, its chalkboard sign unreadable in the dim. She passed the dry goods store, the tobacconist, and the narrow alley where the ragpickers sorted their day's collection into piles.

She entered the boarding house, climbed the stairs, unlocked her door, and stepped into the room.

She opened her trunk, retrieved her father's bible, and opened it to Proverbs 3.

"Trust in the Lord with all thine heart; and lean not unto thine own understanding. In all thy ways acknowledge him, and he shall direct thy paths."

Chapter 7

The cold found her before her boots hit the platform. A sharp, dry bite that had nothing in common with any September she had ever known. Opal steadied herself on the last iron step, her carpetbag in one hand and her satchel strap crossing her chest, and drew a breath that tasted like nothing she could name. Thin. Clean. Almost metallic, as though the air itself had been scrubbed of everything soft and damp and familiar and replaced with something leaner and harder.

The rail yard spread out to her left in a confusion of iron and steam, locomotives hissing on parallel tracks, and yard workers shouting to each other in a language of numbers and signals she couldn't decipher. Coupling cars slammed together somewhere behind the train she had just left, a sound like a gunshot followed by a groan of protesting metal. Freight handlers moved between the platform and a row of waiting wagons, carrying crates and barrels with the rough efficiency of men who got paid by the load. The air smelled of coal smoke, hot grease, and the sharp mineral scent of the mountains that rose on every side of this town like the walls of a vast room.

She pulled her cloak tighter and looked up.

The sky was the problem. Or rather, the sky was the revelation. It was too large. That was the only way she could think to describe it. In Virginia, the sky had always been a reasonable thing, framed by trees and rooftops and the gentle roll of hills that kept the world contained and human-scaled. Here the sky went on until it simply ran out of room. A pale, enormous bowl of blue that stretched from the jagged line of mountains in the south to the jagged line of mountains in the west to more mountains in the east, all of them carrying white on their upper reaches. Snow. In September.

She had seen the Blue Ridge Mountains from a distance. She'd found them lovely and impressive and sufficiently dramatic for a Virginia girl's sense of grandeur. These mountains were not the Blue Ridge. They were massive and ancient and so much bigger than anything she had been prepared for.

A porter passed, wheeling a luggage cart. Opal stopped him, gave the claim numbers for her trunks, and asked that they be held at the baggage office until she could arrange for their collection. The man chalked her tickets, nodded, and moved on without a second glance. She was one of perhaps forty passengers who had stepped off this train, and the platform was a tangle of bodies sorting themselves into destinations. Two men in wide-brimmed hats and leather chaps pushed past her. A family with three children and more luggage than seemed survivable clustered near the depot entrance, the mother counting bags while the father argued with a driver about rates. A group of well-dressed men and women followed a guide toward a waiting wagon with "PARK EXCUR-SIONS" painted on its side in red letters.

She gathered herself and walked into the depot. The ticket counter was a long wooden surface with a grille above it and a harried-looking man behind it sorting through a pile of telegrams. He was middle-aged, with a weathered face, and he glanced up at Opal. She watched him register her traveling suit, her bonnet, and her gloves.

"I need passage to Silver Springs," Opal said. "Can you tell me the schedule for the stage route?"

The agent set down his telegrams. "No stage to Silver Springs, ma'am. That's a Star Route. The mail hack runs out of McAdams' livery on Second Street. He carries passengers when he's got room, but it's not a daily service." He consulted a schedule tacked to the wall behind him. "Next departure is Monday morning, seven o'clock sharp."

Monday. Two full days. Opal absorbed this without changing her expression.

"The mail hack," she said. "What sort of vehicle is it?"

"Covered wagon with a bench seat. Carries the U.S. mail, any freight that's contracted, and passengers. Road's decent this time of year, mostly. Depending on weather."

"And how long is the journey to Silver Springs?"

"Day and a half, give or take. You'd overnight on the road and arrive Tuesday afternoon if the weather cooperates." He paused, and something in his manner shifted. "Ma'am, have you ever been out on the territory before?"

"No. I have not."

He rubbed the back of his neck. "Well, I don't mean to discourage you, but I want to make sure you know what you're heading into. Silver Springs isn't what you'd call a proper town. There's a mercantile that handles the post, a saloon with a few rooms to let upstairs, and maybe twenty or thirty families spread out in the valley and up the draws. No hotel. No dedicated boarding house." He let that settle. "It's good country, mind you. Good people, most of them. But it's remote. The nearest telegraph is right here in Livingston. The nearest railroad is right here in Livingston."

He said this last part with the gentle emphasis of a man offering a woman one last chance to reconsider.

"Thank you," Opal said. "I appreciate your honesty. Where can I secure my passage on Monday's departure?"

He gave her the address of McAdams' livery, where she could book her seat and arrange for her trunks. He also recommended a boardinghouse on Main Street, three blocks north of the depot. "Mrs. Calloway's place. Clean, decent, and she doesn't put up with nonsense. Tell her Jim Harlan sent you."

Opal thanked him again and stepped away from the counter. She stood in the depot for a moment, amid the noise of travelers and the scratch of the telegraph key in the back office, and let the ticket agent's words arrange themselves into their true shape.

Silver Springs wasn't a town. It was a settlement. A mercantile, a saloon, and scattered families. No boardinghouse. No telegraph. No railroad.

She had written a letter to a stranger, purchased a ticket across the continent, and committed her entire future to a community that might not have enough buildings to qualify for a post office if the mercantile closed.

She stepped out of the depot into the afternoon.

Livingston's commercial district ran along a wide main street that was all hard-packed dirt and horse traffic. The boardwalks on either side were raised a good eight inches above the road surface, built to stay above the mud that would come with rain or snowmelt. The buildings lining the street were timber-framed with false fronts that made single-story structures look taller. Their facades painted in practical colors and hung with hand-lettered signs: GENERAL MERCHANDISE. HARDWARE & MINING SUPPLIES. LIVERY AND FEED. MEAT MARKET. A barbershop with a striped pole. A watchmaker's window displaying pocket watches on velvet trays. A saloon with its doors propped open, spilling the sound of a badly tuned piano onto the sidewalk.

Everything looked new. Not new the way a Richmond building looked new, with its careful brickwork and architectural ambitions. New the way a thing looks when it was built quickly by people who needed it built now and would worry about appearances later. The lumber was still pale in places, not yet weathered to the gray that would come with a few Montana winters. The signs were crisp.

Livingston buzzed with a confident, scrappy energy that Richmond would never have recognized. Men moved along the boardwalks with purpose; their boots loud on the planking. Women were visible but scarce, and the ones Opal saw moved with a practical briskness that suggested they had places to be and no intention of lingering. Two women in plain wool dresses and heavy shawls came out of the general store carrying parcels, their hair pinned simply beneath no-nonsense bonnets. They looked at Opal as they passed. One of them gave her a quick, appraising glance that took in her Eastern traveling suit, her fine bonnet, and her gloves, then offered a brief nod. The other woman looked away.

A gust of wind funneled between the buildings and caught Opal squarely in the face. She pulled her cloak tighter with her free hand and kept walking. If this was September, what was January?

She found Mrs. Calloway's boardinghouse at the end of the third block, a two-story frame building with a steep-pitched roof and a front porch where two rocking chairs sat empty in the wind. A painted sign above the door read ROOMS AND MEALS in clean black letters. Opal climbed the porch steps and knocked.

The woman who opened the door was built along sturdy lines, with broad shoulders, capable hands, and the kind of face that suggested she had heard every excuse, endured every inconvenience, and stopped being surprised by either about twenty years ago. Her hair was dark, going silver at the temples, pinned in a thick coil at the back of her head. Her apron was clean. Her eyes were sharp.

"Mrs. Calloway? Jim Harlan at the depot recommended I inquire about a room. I'd like lodging for two nights."

Mrs. Calloway looked her over the same way the women on the boardwalk had, that quick, thorough assessment that frontier women seemed to perform as naturally as breathing. Whatever she concluded, she stepped aside and held the door.

"Dollar a night, meals included. Breakfast is at six-thirty, and supper's at six. I don't hold plates for latecomers. Your room is upstairs, second door on the left. There's water in the pitcher and clean towels on the stand." She led Opal through a front hall that smelled of wood smoke and roasting meat and up a staircase that creaked on every other step. The room was small, neat, and warm, heated by a stovepipe that ran through the wall from the room below. A quilt in a log cabin pattern lay folded at the foot of the bed.

"I have two trunks at the depot baggage office," Opal said. "Is there someone who could collect them?"

"My boy can fetch them after supper. Give me your claim tickets and two bits, and he'll have them here before dark."

Opal handed over the tickets and the coins. Mrs. Calloway tucked them into her apron pocket and turned to go, then paused in the doorway.

"Where ya headed?"

"Silver Springs."

"You have people there?"

"I'm going to meet someone," Opal said.

Mrs. Calloway studied her for a moment. "You'll be takin' the Star Route. The driver's Hank Meecham. He's been running that route for four years, and he knows this territory better than most men know their own homes. You'll be in good hands." She folded her arms. "Dress warm. Warmer than you think you need to." She let that sit. "Supper's in two hours. You look like you could use a hot meal and a good night's rest."

"Thank you, Mrs. Calloway."

The woman nodded once and pulled the door shut behind her.

Opal walked to the window, where she saw Main Street below, the boardwalks and the false-front buildings, and the wide dirt road where a freight wagon was rolling past with its load of lumber stacked high and roped down tight. Beyond the rooftops, the mountains filled the southern sky, enormous and snow-touched, their peaks catching the afternoon light in a way that turned the white to a color she had no name for. Something between gold and silver and the palest shade of blue. It was the most beautiful thing she'd ever seen.

Chapter 8

Hank Meecham stopped the wagon without warning.

Opal had been bracing herself for so many hours that the stillness felt wrong. Her spine hummed with the memory of ruts and jolts, her teeth ached from the miles of clenching her jaw, and her fingers were locked around the edge of the bench seat in a grip that had long since passed from voluntary to involuntary. The backs of her legs burned from the effort of keeping herself upright on a wooden plank that seemed personally committed to throwing her sideways at every dip in the road.

Hank climbed down from his seat without a word. He landed heavily, his boots hitting packed earth. He walked to the lead pair of horses and began unbuckling the harness on one of them.

Opal sat on the bench and watched him work. The wagon had stopped on a low, flat bench of ground above a river that she could hear more than see, a rushing, insistent sound that filled the valley like a second wind. Cottonwood trees rose around her, their trunks pale and smooth, their leaves a dry, papery gold that caught the late afternoon light and held it. The air here was different. Damp. Layered with the mineral scent of moving water and the sweet decay of fallen leaves turning soft along the riverbank.

She gathered her skirts and climbed down carefully, one hand on the wagon's iron rail. Her boots met the ground, and her knees protested, stiff and unreliable, and she stood beside the wagon for a moment, letting her legs remember what solid earth felt like. Her lower back ached in a way she had never experienced, a deep, structural soreness that told her the human body wasn't designed to spend nine hours on an unpadded bench behind a team of horses.

"Can I help with anything?" she asked.

The driver glanced at her over the horse's back. He was a lean man, weathered to the color of old leather, with a salt-and-pepper beard trimmed short and hands that looked like they had been carved from the same wood as the wagon. He had spoken maybe thirty sentences since they left Livingston, and most of those had been to the horses.

"Best stay clear of the team till they're settled." He turned back to the harness. "There's a flat rock yonder that'll do for sitting. I'll have a fire going directly."

Opal found the flat rock. It was wide and smooth. She sat down and pulled her cloak tight around her shoulders and watched the driver work.

He moved through the process of making camp with the same wordless efficiency he had shown all day. The horses were unhitched, watered at the river's edge, and picketed on a grassy stretch where they could graze. He gathered wood from a deadfall cottonwood, selected a fire site that was sheltered from the wind by a low bank of earth, and built a fire with the quick, practiced motions of a man whose hands knew this task so well his mind could be elsewhere entirely. Kindling first, arranged in a precise cone. A match struck on his boot heel. The flame caught, crackled, and climbed. He fed it larger pieces until the fire settled into a steady burn; the smoke rising in a thin blue column that leaned slightly south.

Every action was purposeful, and none of it required her. Opal sat on her rock and felt the particular helplessness of a woman whose entire catalog of useful skills had been written for a different world. She could manage a household of six servants. She could plan a dinner party for twenty. She could embroider a handkerchief so fine it looked like frost on linen. She couldn't build a fire. She couldn't unhitch a horse.

The fire grew. Its warmth reached her in slow waves, pressing against the cold that had settled into her bones during the long hours on the wagon. She held her hands toward it and felt the heat work into her fingers, loosening the stiffness that the cold and the gripping had left behind.

Hank brought provisions from a wooden box secured beneath the wagon seat: a tin of pilot bread, a paper-wrapped slab of dried beef, a small cloth bag of coffee beans, and a dented tin coffeepot blackened with years of fire residue. He filled the pot from the river, measured coffee into it with a cupped palm, and set it on a flat stone at the fire's edge. Then he sat down on a section of log across the fire from Opal and began slicing the dried beef with a folding knife, laying strips across a piece of pilot bread with the unhurried precision of a man for whom this meal was neither special nor inadequate. It was simply what there was.

Opal opened the cloth bundle she'd retrieved earlier that Mrs. Calloway had packed for her that morning: biscuits wrapped in a clean napkin, a wedge of hard cheese, strips of dried venison, and two apples. She ate a biscuit and a piece of cheese and watched the coffee pot. The water was beginning to steam, a faint curl of vapor rising from the spout.

"How far are we from Silver Springs?" she asked.

"Fifteen miles, give or take." He chewed his beef and bread with methodical patience. "Road gets rougher on the pass. Mountain road, narrow in places. Good footing when it's dry going up, worse when it's not."

"Tell me about this pass."

"Six thousand feet at the top. Grade's steady but long. Team handles it fine if the road's clear." He glanced at her briefly, then back at the fire. "You'll want to walk the steep stretches. Lightens the load for the horses."

Opal nodded.

Walking. In her traveling boots, on a mountain road. She looked down at the boots in question, the sturdy black leather lace-ups she had chosen for durability back in Richmond. They had seemed so practical at the time. Here, beside a fire built by a man who struck matches on his boot heel, they seemed like something from a different century.

The coffee came to a boil with a violent rattle of the lid. Hank lifted the pot from the stone with a folded rag, let it sit for a minute, then poured two cups. He handed one to Opal. The tin was hot, even through her gloves, and she wrapped both hands around it and brought it close to her face. The steam rose against her skin, warm and bitter-smelling, and she breathed it in before she drank.

The coffee was black and strong enough to stand a spoon in. It tasted faintly scorched, nothing like the smooth, carefully prepared coffee Mrs. Jennings had served in porcelain cups in the Bennett kitchen. But the heat of it spread through her chest and into her arms and down to her cold-stiffened fingers. The simple comfort of holding a warm cup in cold air was so immediate and so complete that she closed her eyes for a moment and just let herself feel it. Warm hands. Warm chest. The fire crackling. The river running its constant, unhurried conversation with the stones.

"Thank you for the coffee," she said.

Hank nodded once and drank from his cup, his eyes on the far bank of the river where the cottonwoods caught the last of the light in their gold leaves.

They ate the rest of the meal without much conversation. Opal finished her biscuit and cheese and one of the apples, wrapping the second in her napkin for tomorrow. Hank cleaned the tin pot with river water and sand, then stowed his remaining provisions. He checked each horse, running his hand along their legs and flanks, adjusting the blankets he had thrown over their backs against the cold. One of the horses, a stocky bay with a white blaze, nosed his shoulder as he worked, and Hank scratched behind its ear with a rough gentleness that told Opal more about him than any conversation had. He murmured something to the animal she couldn't catch, his voice lower and warmer than anything he'd offered her all day, and the bay leaned into his hand the way a dog leans into its owner's palm.

When he came back to the fire, he stood instead of sitting. He was looking south, toward the mountains that filled the valley like a wall.

Opal followed his gaze. The peaks that had been sharp and clear all afternoon had lost their edges. Where she'd been able to see individual ridgelines and the dark bands of timber that climbed toward the snowline, the upper slopes now blurred behind a veil of cloud that was thickening. The sky above the mountains had taken on a textured, rippled look, like the underside of a washboard. The clouds were moving from the southwest in a steady, purposeful drift that was different from the scattered, aimless clouds she had watched all day.

The wind gusted. It had been steady from the north since morning, a persistent push. Now it shifted, coming in pulses from different directions, uncertain of itself. The smoke from their fire, which had been climbing in a tidy column, flattened for a few moments and slid sideways along the ground before recovering.

Hank watched the sky for a long time. Then he looked at the smoke. Then at the mountains again. His jaw worked slightly, the way a man's jaw works when he's questioning something he doesn't like the answer to.

"That sky's building something," he said. "I want through the pass before it gets here. We leave before light."

"How early?"

"Four. Maybe sooner, depending on how the wind acts through the night." He picked up a stick and pushed a log deeper into the fire, sending a shower of sparks upward. "It may amount to nothing. Weather in these mountains lies as often as it tells the truth. But I don't gamble with the mail, and I don't gamble with that pass."

He said it the way a man states a policy he'd never had reason to question. Then he unrolled his bedding near the wagons off-side wheel, positioned where he could see the horses and quickly reach the brake in the dark if something spooked them in the night. He pulled a heavy wool blanket up to his chin, tipped his hat over his eyes, and within minutes his breathing changed. Opal remained by the fire. She wasn't ready to sleep, and she wasn't sure sleep would come if she tried. Her body was exhausted in ways she had no experience measuring, sore in muscles she hadn't known she possessed, but her mind was restless, turning over everything the day had given her and everything tomorrow might demand.

The valley had gone dark. Not the gradual, negotiated darkness of a Virginia evening, where gaslights and parlor lamps pushed back the night by comfortable degrees. This was absolute. The sun dropped behind the western ridge, and the darkness arrived like something physical, a presence that poured into the valley and filled it from the ground up. The fire made a small, bright room in the middle of all that black, and beyond its reach there wasn't a thing. No light. No shape. No reference point except the sound of the river and the occasional stamp of a horse's hoof on hard ground. She thought of Mrs. Jennings. Was she still in the Bennett house, or had Hawthorne dismissed her by now? Was she sleeping in her narrow room behind the kitchen, or had she been sent away with a week's wages and a cold reference? The not-knowing was its own kind of wound, and Opal pressed against it gently, the way a person presses a bruise to test whether it still hurts. It did. It would for a long time.

And then she looked up.

The stars were so thick they seemed to have weight. They filled the sky in a density she'd not known was possible, layered and luminous.

She lay back on the bedroll the driver had spread for her near the fire, a canvas ground cloth with a wool blanket folded double, and stared upward. The stars didn't twinkle the way they did in Richmond. They burned. They were steady and clear and so close she had the irrational thought that if she reached high enough, her fingers would come back dusted with light. The Milky Way ran overhead in a broad, pale river of its own, and she traced it with her eyes as she thought of the Psalms her father had loved. *The heavens declare the glory of God; and the firmament sheweth his handiwork.* David had written those words in a wilderness not so different from this one. A shepherd lying on hard ground, watching the same stars wheel overhead, feeling the same immensity pressing down on him and somehow, instead of being crushed by it, finding comfort. Finding God in the largeness rather than despite it.

From somewhere on the dark mountainside to the east, a sound rose.

It began low, a deep, resonant note that seemed to come from inside the earth itself. Then it climbed, rising in pitch until it became a high, eerie whistle that lifted and lifted and broke into a series of rough, guttural grunts before falling away into silence. The sound carried across the valley and bounced off the far ridge and came back as a faint, distorted echo of itself, layered and strange.

Opal's whole body went still. Every nerve she possessed locked onto that sound and held. She had never heard anything like it. It wasn't a domestic sound, not a barnyard animal, not a dog or a bird or anything she had a name for. It was wild in a way that the word wild didn't adequately describe. Beautiful and unsettling in the same breath, like hearing a language she would never learn but could somehow feel the meaning of.

The driver didn't stir. His hat remained over his eyes. His breathing didn't change. Whatever the animal was, Hank Meecham considered it no threat, and Opal took what comfort she could from the steady rise and fall of his chest beneath the wool blanket.

The animal called again, farther away this time, the whistle thinner and the grunts trailing off into the dark like a conversation moving to another room. Then silence.

Opal lay still on her bedroll and looked at the sky. The largeness of it pressed against her. It was the feeling of being held inside something so much bigger than herself.

Lord, I feel so very small tonight. I'm lying beside a river, under a sky I've never seen before, in a breathtaking territory. And I don't know if I've been faithful or foolish for coming here. I left everything I knew. I sold my mother's jewelry. I wrote to a stranger and bought a ticket to a place that barely exists on a map, and now I'm sleeping on the ground beside a river, and tomorrow I'll climb a mountain pass in my Richmond boots, and later I'll arrive in a town that isn't a town to meet a man I've never seen. And all I have is this feeling, Lord. This quiet, persistent feeling that won't let me go, like a hand on my shoulder turning me west. I'm choosing to believe that hand is Yours. Please don't let me be wrong.

The fire popped. A log shifted, settling, and a new curl of flame licked up from the coals and threw a brief wash of orange light across the underside of the cottonwood branches overhead. The leaves caught the light and released it, gold and shadow, gold and shadow, a quiet rhythm.

The cold worked through the blanket in slow degrees. She felt it along her hips first, where the hard ground pressed up through the canvas, then along her shoulders and the backs of her arms. Her face was tight with wind and dust, her lips dry and cracked at the corners. Her hair felt heavy and gritty against the folded cloak she was using as a pillow. Every part of her body registered a complaint of some kind, and none of them were complaints she had ever had before. She'd never slept on the ground. She'd never been this far from a locked door and a roof she trusted.

She pulled the blanket higher and turned onto her side, facing the fire. The coals glowed red and orange beneath a thin crust of white ash. Beyond the fire, the darkness was complete. Beyond the darkness, the river. Beyond the river, the mountains.

She closed her eyes. The river kept its steady, insistent voice, water over stone, and she listened to it until she drifted off to sleep.

Chapter 9

Nolan Ridgeway pulled his horse to a halt on the ridge above the homestead and studied the sky.

He did it the way a man checks a pocket watch, without deciding to, because the sky was the clock he lived by and he'd been reading it since before he could saddle a horse on his own. He turned the gelding west and let his eyes move along the horizon, reading the clouds the way another man might read a letter. The peaks above Paradise Valley had lost their edges. Where this morning they had stood clean and sharp against a blue so deep it looked poured, they were now soft, blurred, the upper ridgelines disappearing into a bank of gray that was thickening as he watched. The light had gone flat, too, losing the warmth it had carried all afternoon and turning the valley below into something pale and washed out, like a painting left too long near a window.

He sat with it for a moment. The gelding, a stubborn buckskin named Cob who had been Nolan's primary saddle horse for three years, shifted beneath him and stamped once, his ears swiveling forward toward the homestead below where he knew hay and rest were waiting. Boone stood ten yards ahead on the trail, tongue out, watching Nolan with the patient expectation of a dog who had learned that when his master stopped moving, there was usually a reason, but that the reason was rarely interesting enough to sit down for.

"All right," Nolan said to neither of them in particular, and nudged Cob forward with his knees.

The trail dropped through a stand of lodgepole pine and opened onto the broad, grassy slope that ran down to the homestead from the east. From here, Nolan could see the whole property laid out below him in the fading light: the house and barn sitting on the bench of land above the creek, the corral with its heavy pine rails, the woodshed with its growing stack of split timber, the chicken coop near the kitchen door, the smoke from the chimney rising in a thin gray thread that leaned south instead of climbing straight. He noticed the lean. South meant the wind was pushing from the north, which confirmed what the clouds were already telling him.

He counted what he could see as he rode. Four horses in the corral, standing hip-shot and lazy near the water trough. The milk cow was in the small pasture behind the barn, working at the grass with the single-minded patience that cows brought to everything they did. The chickens had already gone in for the night, which meant Elizabeth had closed the coop early. She'd been watching the sky, too.

The south pasture gate came into view as the trail curved, and Nolan fixed his eyes on the fence post he'd been meaning to reset for two weeks. It was leaning a good six inches off plumb where the freeze-and-thaw cycle had worked the base loose in the ground.

Not dangerous yet. Another hard frost and it would be. He'd need to dig it out and reset it before the ground went solid for the winter, which gave him maybe three weeks if the weather cooperated and less than one if it didn't. He added it to the list he kept in his head, the one that never got shorter no matter how many hours he worked.

Cob picked his way down the last stretch of trail and crossed the yard at a walk, hooves quiet on the packed earth. Boone trotted ahead and disappeared around the corner of the barn, off to check whatever needed checking in a dog's estimation of the world. Nolan swung down from the saddle in front of the barn doors and landed with the careful stiffness of a man who had been riding since before first light and whose body was reminding him of every mile. His right shoulder caught as his boots hit the ground, that familiar hitch from the fall two winters ago, and he rolled it once without thinking about it and led Cob inside.

The barn was dim and warm with the smell of hay, horses and old wood. The air thick with the particular sounds of a building that held living things. The other horses lifted their heads from their stalls as Nolan led Cob in, ears forward, nostrils working. The bay mare nickered softly. Cob answered with a low sound in his chest, and Nolan ran a hand down the gelding's neck as he cross-tied him in the aisle.

"Long day," he said, loosening the cinch. "You earned your supper."

He pulled the saddle and the sweat-damp blanket beneath it and carried them to the tack room, settling the saddle on its rack and draping the blanket over the rail to dry. The tack room smelled of leather and neatsfoot oil, and the light from the open barn door caught the row of bridles hanging on their pegs along the back wall. Four bridles for four horses. And one more, hung on the end peg where it had been since his Uncle Josiah died, the leather going stiff from disuse; the bit tarnished. His uncle's bridle. Nolan had cleaned it once, about a year after the funeral, and then hung it back up and hadn't touched it since.

He turned back to Cob and picked up the brush.

"Counted twenty-three head on the upper bench," he told the horse as he worked the dust and dried sweat from the buckskin's coat in long, firm strokes. "Two heifers I couldn't find. Might be in the draw north of the spring, or they've drifted further than I like." Cob stood with his head low, eyes half-closed, leaning into the brush the way he always did. "Need to get them down before this weather moves in. Ground's still soft enough to hold tracks, so that's something."

He checked each hoof, cleaning them with the pick, and ran his hands down Cob's legs, feeling for heat or swelling. Everything was sound. He gave the gelding a measure of oats in his feedbox and forked hay into the stall, then moved down the aisle doing the same for each horse. He topped the water trough from the barrel near the door, checked the milk cow's stall, and forked fresh straw where the bedding had gone flat.

The barn filled with the sound of horses eating, that steady rhythmic grinding that was one of the most contented sounds Nolan knew. He stood in the aisle for a moment with the pitchfork in his hand and let the quiet settle around him. The light through the barn door was turning copper as the afternoon gave its last effort, and the air had that weighted stillness that came just before the temperature dropped for the night.

He set the pitchfork against the wall, gave Cob a final pat on the neck, and stepped out of the barn into the evening air.

The cold found him immediately, sharper than it had been an hour ago, and he turned up his collar as he crossed the yard toward the woodshed. He loaded an armload of split logs against his chest, steadying the top piece with his chin, and started toward the house. Halfway across the yard, he heard Elizabeth singing. Her voice carried through the kitchen wall and out into the cold, clear, and sweet in the way that young voices are when they don't know anyone is listening. It was one of the old hymns their mother used to sing while she worked, and the sound of it stopped him for a half step on the hard-packed earth. He stood there with the firewood heavy against his chest and the wind pressing at his back, listening, and the muscles in his chest tightened around his ribs.

He walked the rest of the way to the house, climbed the porch steps, and pushed through the front door with his shoulder.

The main room wrapped around him like a warm hand. The cookstove was radiating heat, and the smell of venison stew and fresh bread filled the space with a richness that his empty stomach answered before his mind caught up. The lamp was lit on the table, casting a steady yellow glow across the room. Elizabeth stood at the stove with a wooden spoon in one hand and a dishcloth over her shoulder. Her braids pinned up, and a smudge of flour on her left cheek.

"You're late," she said without turning around.

"Rode the upper bench."

"I figured. You smell like you slept in the barn."

She turned then, and her face broke into the quick, bright smile that had been lighting up this kitchen since she was old enough to reach the table. Elizabeth Ridgeway was eighteen years old, sturdy and fresh-faced, with the kind of energy that made a room feel smaller and warmer the moment she walked into it. She had their mother's light brown hair and their father's blue eyes, and she moved through the house with the brisk purpose of a woman who had been running it since she was fifteen and intended to keep running it whether anyone asked her to or not.

"Wash up," she said. "Supper's been ready for twenty minutes."

Nolan stacked the firewood in the box beside the stove and went to the basin near the kitchen door. He poured water from the pitcher, scrubbed his hands, face, and the back of his neck. The water was cold enough to make his skin tighten, and he could feel the day's grime lifting as he worked the cloth across his jaw. He dried off with the towel hanging on the nail and took his seat at the table.

Elizabeth had the table set: two bowls of stew, a loaf of bread, a crock of butter, and two cups of coffee so strong the smell alone could have kept a man upright through another four hours of fence work. She settled into her chair across from him, bowed her head, and waited.

Nolan said the blessing. It was short, the way all his prayers were, and it covered the essentials: thanks for the food, thanks for the day, a request for safety and provision. He said amen, and Elizabeth echoed it, and they ate.

The stew was good. It was always good. Elizabeth had a gift for making simple things taste like more than they were, stretching a modest cut of venison and whatever the garden had left into something that warmed a man from the inside out. Nolan ate steadily, his attention on the food and the warmth spreading through his tired body, while Elizabeth talked.

"The bread turned out better today," she said, pulling a piece from the loaf and passing the rest to him. "I moved the dough right up next to the stove this morning and covered it with wool instead of cotton. You should have seen the rise in it. Doubled in half the time."

Nolan tore off a piece and chewed. She was right. The crumb was lighter than usual, soft and even, with a good crust. "It's good," he said.

"It's better than good. It's the best batch I've made since August." She pointed her spoon at him. "Don't you go expecting this all the time; you should know I can't promise the wool trick works twice. Bread has a mind of its own."

"Sounds like someone else I know."

Elizabeth's eyes widened, and a laugh broke out of her so sudden and bright that it filled the kitchen like lamplight fills a room when you turn the wick up. "Did you just make a joke?"

"No."

"You did. You absolutely did. I'm marking this day on the calendar."

Nolan took another bite of stew in an attempt to suppress his grin.

"Oh, and I fixed the garden rail," she said. "Two nails and a hammer. Took me all of five minutes. I don't know why you made it sound like it needed an act of Congress."

"I said I'd get to it."

"You did say that on Friday. Today is Monday."

He nodded and continued to eat.

"Chickens are laying less, too," she said, her voice shifting from teasing to thoughtful. "Only got four eggs this morning. Three yesterday. The days are getting shorter and they know it."

Nolan nodded. He'd expected as much. The hens would slow through October and nearly stop by November, picking up again when the light returned in late winter. It meant rationing eggs through the cold months, which Elizabeth already knew and was already planning for, because she planned for everything the way their mother had planned for everything, with a quiet competence that kept the household running.

"I watched a hawk from the porch this afternoon," Elizabeth said after a moment, her voice going softer. "A red-tail. It was circling over the south meadow for the longest time, just riding the wind in those big, slow turns. It never flapped its wings. Not once. It just held them out and let the air carry it." She looked down at her stew. "I stood there watching it for probably ten minutes. I know that sounds foolish."

"Doesn't sound foolish."

She glanced up at him. "I just think about what it must be like. To see everything from that high up. The whole valley, all at once. Every trail, every creek, every little moving thing." She paused. "Must be something."

Nolan looked at his sister across the table, at the flour still on her cheek and the light in her eyes, and the way she held her bread with both hands, the way she'd done since she was a little girl. Something stirred in him that he didn't have a word for. She was eighteen years old. She should be going to dances and having supper with friends her own age and seeing something of the world beyond this valley. Instead, she was here. Mending fences and baking bread and watching hawks because the hawks were the most interesting company available to her on a Monday afternoon miles from the nearest neighbor.

He took a drink of his coffee and set the cup down. "Maybe it is."

"Mrs. Hanscombe asked after you when I was in town last week," Elizabeth said, tearing a piece of bread and spreading butter across it with her thumb. "She wanted to know if you'd be coming to the gathering next month."

"Depends on the weather."

Elizabeth looked at him over her bread. "It's four weeks away, Nolan."

"Weather can change in four weeks."

"Weather can change in four hours. That doesn't stop most people from making plans."

He took another bite of stew and said nothing. Elizabeth watched him for a moment with those clear, knowing eyes that saw too much and said just enough, and then she let it go. She moved on to the price of flour at the mercantile and whether they should add another order of salt before the supply wagon made its last run of the season. The moment passed the way such moments always passed between them, gently and without a seam.

After supper, Nolan pushed back from the table and stepped out onto the porch.

The night had come down while they ate, and the air hit his face with a cold that had edges to it, sharp and damp, different from the dry chill of an ordinary September evening. He leaned against the porch post and looked west. The stars were visible only in patches between the clouds that had spread across the sky like a wool blanket pulled slowly over a bed. The mountain peaks were gone entirely, swallowed by a darkness that had nothing to do with the hour. The wind came in gusts, pushing against the barn door so that the latch rattled, and somewhere in the corral one of the horses snorted and shifted.

He could smell it now. That wet stone smell, heavy and mineral, the way the air thickened and pressed down when the mountains were about to deliver something. Rain first, probably. Then cold behind it. Maybe snow on the upper elevations, depending on how low the temperature dropped overnight. He watched the clouds for a long moment, reading their thickness and their speed, and the direction they were traveling. Just as his father had taught him to do when he was barely tall enough to see over the porch rail. His father had called it listening to the sky. Nolan had never heard a better name for it.

Boone appeared at the bottom of the porch steps, his ears pricked forward, his nose working the wind. The dog looked up at Nolan as if confirming what they both already knew, then circled twice and settled onto the porch boards with his chin on his paws, positioned where he could watch the yard and the barn and the trail beyond.

The door opened behind him, and Elizabeth stepped out carrying two cups of coffee. She handed one to Nolan without a word and leaned against the opposite porch post, wrapping both hands around the warmth of her cup. For a moment, they stood together in the cold and said nothing, and the silence between them was the comfortable kind, the kind that comes from years of sharing the same roof and the same work and the same losses until you don't need to fill every quiet space with sound.

"Storm's coming," Elizabeth said at last, watching the sky.

"Looks like it."

"How bad?"

Nolan considered. "Can't say yet. Could blow through in a day. Could settle in for three." He took a drink of coffee. "Either way, I want to ride out at first light and push the herd down from the upper bench. Get them closer where I can reach them if it sets in."

Elizabeth nodded as if she'd been expecting this, which she probably had. She'd been watching the same sky all day from the same valley with the same instincts, bred into her the same way they'd been bred into him.

"I'll go with you," she said. "The house chores can wait a day."

"Take the bay. Not the gray."

"I know. She spooks in the wind." Elizabeth took a long sip of her coffee and stared out into the darkness, where the outline of the barn was just barely visible against the deeper black of the hillside beyond. "I'll pack enough food for midday. We should be back before dark if we leave early enough."

"Before dawn."

"Before dawn," she agreed, and there was no complaint in it, only the straightforward acceptance of a woman who had been rising before dawn since she was old enough to reach the stove.

She finished her coffee as the wind picked up again, pressing her skirt against her legs and sending a loose strand of hair across her face. She tucked it behind her ear and looked at her brother for a moment, studying him the way she sometimes did when she thought he wasn't paying attention, with a quiet concern she had learned to keep off her face but not entirely out of her eyes.

"Good night, Nolan."

"Night."

She slipped back inside, and he heard her bedroom door close a moment later. Nolan stayed on the porch a little while longer, finishing his coffee, listening to the wind work its way through the valley. Boone sighed at his feet, a long, slow exhale that sounded almost human in the dark.

When the cold had worked through his thick shirt and into his shoulders, Nolan went inside and latched the door behind him.

The main room was quiet in the way that only a house at the end of its day can be quiet, when the work is done and the fire is settling and the people who live there have said everything they are going to say until morning. The stove ticked softly as the metal cooled. The lamp still burned on the table, its flame steady and small, casting a circle of light that reached the two chairs pushed in on either side.

Nolan sat down in the rocker, the wood creaking beneath his weight the way it had creaked beneath his father's weight and his uncle's weight before his. He picked up the Bible and let it fall open in his hands. The spine was soft with use, and the pages settled naturally to Proverbs, where a thin ribbon marked his place.

Trust in the Lord with all thine heart, and lean not unto thine own understanding. In all thy ways acknowledge him, and he shall direct thy paths.

He sat with the passage for a moment, the Bible open on his knee, his thumb resting against the page. The words were as familiar to him as the sound of the creek or the weight of an ax handle. His mother had read this passage aloud at the kitchen table when he and Elizabeth had been children. He could still hear her voice in the cadence of the sentences, steady and certain, the voice of a woman who believed what she read and lived as though she meant it.

He closed the book and set it on the side table. He bowed his head and folded his hands, and he prayed.

Lord, keep the stock safe tonight. Keep Elizabeth well. Let the weather hold long enough to get the herd down.

He sat for another moment with his head bowed and his hands still folded, not because he had more to say but because there was a stillness in prayer that he could find nowhere else. The world stopped asking things of him when he prayed. The list went quiet. The work could wait. For a few seconds, he was just a man sitting in a chair in a warm room, and that was enough.

He rose from the rocker and banked the stove for the night, closing the damper until the flames died back to a bed of coals. He blew out the lamp, and the room went dark except for the faint orange glow breathing through the stove's draft slots.

He stood in the dark and listened to the wind.

Tomorrow he and Elizabeth would ride out before the sun came up, and they would do the work that needed doing, the way they always did.

He walked to his bedroom and closed the door.

Chapter 10

The front wheel dropped into a rut so deep the whole wagon pitched forward, and Opal's jaw snapped shut hard enough to send a sharp ache through her back teeth. She grabbed for the bench rail with both hands as the rear wheels followed, slamming down into the same trench and launching her an inch off the seat before the road caught the wagon again and shook it level.

The town of Providence Ridge was already behind them. Hank had stopped to swap mail sacks at the mercantile and water the horses at the livery trough. She had not climbed down. Her legs ached too deeply to trust them, and the cold had settled into her joints during the hours since the predawn departure, a raw, biting cold that worked through her wool cloak, gloves and petticoat as though none of them existed.

The sky had closed over them like a wool blanket pulled across a bed, heavy and gray and uniform, pressing the mountains into flat silhouettes that lost their upper ridgelines in cloud. The timber thickened on both sides of the road. Lodgepole pine grew in dense, straight columns that blocked the wind in stretches, then opened into clearings where it hit the wagon broadside and made the canvas snap against its frame.

"How much farther to Silver Springs?" Opal asked.

Hank kept his eyes on the road. "Six hours, if this road behaves. Eight if it doesn't."

"And Silver Springs itself. I was told there is only a saloon with available rooms. Is that correct?"

He glanced at her briefly, then back at the team. "There's rooms above the saloon," he said. "Wouldn't recommend them for a lady."

"Is there nothing else?"

"Some families take boarders now and again. The mercantile owner might know of someone." He shifted the reins to one hand and tugged his hat lower against a gust of wind. "Silver Springs isn't built for visitors, ma'am. It's built for people who already live there."

Opal pressed her hands together in her lap, and the rain began before she could form words to respond.

It came hard and fast and without mercy. Not a building storm that gave warning, but a wall of cold rain that struck the wagon like a thrown bucket and didn't stop. The drops hit the canvas overhead in a roar that swallowed every other sound, hammered the bench planks between her and Hank, and drove sideways into her face with a force that made her flinch and turn her head. Within seconds her cloak was soaked through. The wool went heavy against her shoulders, pulling at her neck, and the cold water found every seam and gap: her collar, her cuffs, the space between her bonnet and the back of her neck where it ran in a steady stream down her spine.

Soon the road surface changed. Where it had been packed earth, rutted but solid, it became slick clay that shone with a dull gleam under the flat light. The horses' hooves lost their rhythm. Instead of the steady four-beat cadence Opal had grown accustomed to, the sound became irregular, punctuated by the scrape and catch of iron shoes sliding on wet ground before finding purchase again. The wagon swayed in unpredictable ways that kept her grip tight on the bench rail.

The terrain changed, too. The road was no longer level. It ran along the side of a long, rising slope, cut into the hillside so that the uphill bank rose on their left and the ground fell away on their right into a shallow ditch and then a grassy bench that sloped toward the tree line below. The road tilted enough that Opal could feel the wagon leaning. Water ran in sheets across the road surface from the cut bank above, carrying mud and small stones that collected in the ruts and made the footing worse with every passing minute.

She gripped the bench with both hands and braced her boots against the footboard.

Hank was quiet. Not the easy quiet of a man who simply had nothing to say, but a tight, watchful silence that changed the air between them. His shoulders had shifted forward, drawn close to his body, and he held the reins with a tension she had not seen in him before. His hands were low and his forearms rigid, and he worked the leather with small, constant adjustments, reading something in the pull of the horses that Opal couldn't feel but could see in the hard set of his jaw.

The horses felt it too. The lead pair tossed their heads against the harness, ears flat, their steps uncertain. The team no longer pulled with the steady, resigned patience that had carried them up from the valley. They pulled in short, nervous surges, fighting for footing that kept shifting beneath them.

"Should we stop? Could I get down and walk?" Opal asked.

"Can't stop on this grade. She'll bog down and we'll never get her moving again." His voice was clipped, stripped of everything but the words themselves. "Hold the bench rail. Brace your feet flat on the boards. Don't let go for anything."

Her memory flashed to the night before. Hank had stood and looked south at the mountains and said the sky was building something. He had wanted through the pass before it arrived.

They had not made it. Whatever the mountains had been building was here now, falling on them in sheets of cold rain, and they were caught in it.

Opal braced her feet. She held the rail. The wood was wet and cold beneath her fingers and she gripped it until her knuckles ached. The rain thickened. The wagon swayed on its springs with a loose, sickening motion that turned her stomach. The road narrowed further, and the downhill edge crumbled in places where water had undercut it, leaving gaps that the wheels passed over with a sickening lurch.

Ahead, a shallow drainage cut across the road where runoff had carved a channel, maybe two feet wide and eighteen inches deep, with water running fast and brown through the bottom. Someone had laid rough planks across the worst of it, a field repair that in dry weather would have been adequate. In this rain, the planks were dark with water, and the channel had deepened into a rushing stream that undercut the road surface on both sides.

Hank angled the team toward the best line of crossing he could find, pulling the leaders slightly uphill to keep the wagon's weight on the high side. The lead horses picked their way through the water, hooves splashing, nostrils wide. The front wheels crossed the planks with a hollow, wet thud. For a moment, Opal thought they were through.

Then the rear wheel on the downhill side dropped.

It dropped hard and sudden, and the entire wagon lurched sideways with a violence that threw Opal's weight against the rail she was holding. She felt her fingers slip on the wet wood. She grabbed again, caught the edge with her right hand, lost it with her left. The bench tilted beneath her; the angle changing so fast that her body couldn't adjust, and she was sliding.

Hank shouted. One sharp, raw syllable directed at the team cut through the rain and the noise of groaning wood. The horses surged forward, but the wagon didn't follow. It continued to slide, the downhill wheels plowing through clay that had no grip to give, and then the dropped wheel caught on something solid buried in the channel, a rock or a root or the edge of the plank itself, and the catch while the rest of the wagon was still moving sideways created a wrenching, twisting force that Opal felt in her bones.

Wood cracked with a sharp splintering sound. Harness chains snapped taut with a metallic shriek. The bench tilted even more beneath her, sudden and absolute, and Opal's hands found nothing to hold. She felt herself leave the bench and then something struck her left leg below the knee, a blow so sharp and enormous that it swallowed every other sensation in her body, and the world became a single point of white-hot wrongness that shut out every-thing else.

Then she hit the ground. Mud and cold and wet grass against her face, and the smell of crushed earth filling her nose and mouth. Rain on her skin. The sound of horses screaming, high and raw and desperate, and beneath that the groan of settling wood and the smaller sounds of things still breaking, still shifting, still falling into the positions where they would finally stop.

The sounds began to thin. The edges of what she could hear and see and feel narrowed inward, as if someone were drawing a curtain around her from all sides at once, leaving less and less of the world visible, less and less of the cold and the rain and the terrible sound of the horses, until what remained was just the rain itself, steady and impersonal, falling on her face.

Then nothing.

Chapter 11

The last heifer fought him all the way down the draw. She was a red-and-white crossbreed with a wild eye and the particular stubbornness of an animal that had decided, somewhere in the deep and unreachable machinery of her bovine brain, that downhill was a direction she wouldn't go. Nolan pressed Cob forward on the uphill side, cutting the angle, while Boone worked the far flank with the low, efficient crouch that made him worth three hired hands in rough country. Elizabeth held the bay steady on the opposite ridge, blocking the escape route the heifer was eyeing.

The rain fell in sheets that came sideways on the gusts and then straightened when the wind paused, a cold, relentless pour that had soaked through Nolan's hat and any clothing not covered by the buckskin he wore for warmth. His hands were stiff on the reins. The leather was slick, and the cold had worked into his knuckles and settled there with a dull, grinding ache.

The heifer made one more break toward the north, and Boone cut her off with a bark that turned her back toward the draw. She bawled once, loud and offended, and then gave up the fight and trotted downhill toward the rest of the herd bunched in the creek bottom below.

Nolan pulled Cob to a halt and counted. Twenty-three heads. He was still missing two, the same two he hadn't found yesterday on the upper bench. They had either drifted into the timber north of the spring or crossed the ridge into the next drainage, and either way he wasn't going to find them today. Not in this weather. Not with the temperature dropping the way it was, the kind of drop he could feel in his teeth and in the ache behind his eyes and in the way Cob kept turning his hindquarters into the wind.

Elizabeth rode up beside him. Her braid hung heavy and dark against her back, plastered flat by the rain. Her cheeks were raw with cold, but her eyes were clear and alert, and she sat on the bay with the easy balance of a girl who had been in a saddle for years.

"That's twenty-three," she said, raising her voice above the rain.

"Twenty-three."

Elizabeth looked at the sky, which wasn't so much a sky anymore as a low, uniform ceiling of gray that pressed down on the valley like a hand on a lid. The surrounding mountains had vanished almost entirely. Where the upper ridges and timber slopes should have been, there wasn't a thing but low-lying clouds.

"We should head back," she said.

Nolan nodded as he turned Cob south, and Elizabeth fell in beside him on the bay. Boone trotted ahead, tongue out, coat soaked flat to his body, looking like a half-drowned wolf with the disposition of a saint. The trail they followed was a stock path that ran along the bench above the mountain road. From this elevation, the road was visible below as a ribbon of mud cutting across the hillside, winding through a stretch of open meadow before it entered the timber and began another climb toward the pass road that eventually led to Silver Springs.

Nolan's gaze caught on something in the landscape below that didn't belong. A pale shape, lying on its side near the road. A dark tangle beside it. The shapes of horses, three of them standing motionless in the rain with their heads low and a fourth on the ground, and a stillness over all of it that was wrong.

Nolan reined Cob to a halt, and Elizabeth stopped beside him. She followed his gaze down the slope.

"Is that the mail hack?" Elizabeth's voice was tight.

Nolan didn't answer. He was already reading the scene the way he read weather, piecing together what had happened from the evidence the ground was giving him. The pale shape was canvas, the covered top of the mail wagon, on its side in the shallow ditch at the road's edge. One wheel pointed upward, and even from this distance he could see it turning slowly in the wind. The three standing horses were hitched to the broken wagon tongue, held in place by the dead weight of the overturned wagon behind them. The fourth horse was down in the mud.

"Stay with the cattle," he said.

"Nolan."

"Stay here."

He put his heels to Cob, and the gelding lunged downhill through the wet grass, his hooves cutting furrows in the soft earth as he drove toward the road. Boone shot ahead like a brown arrow, belly low to the ground, reading his master's urgency and answering it. Behind him, Nolan heard the bay's hooves and knew without looking that Elizabeth hadn't stayed.

The slope leveled out where it met the road, and Nolan pulled Cob up short near the wreckage. He was out of the saddle before the horse had fully stopped, boots hitting the mud with a thick, wet sound.

Up close, the damage was worse than it had looked from the bench above. The rear axle had snapped clean, and the bed had twisted as it went over, cracking the sideboards and throwing the contents sideways. Mail sacks had spilled from the back, scattering pieces of mail everywhere. The canvas cover was torn, and the iron rim of the upturned wheel groaned as the wind pushed it through another slow, aimless rotation.

Hank Meecham lay facedown in the road, ten feet from the wagon. His hat was gone. His coat was spread around him in the mud, and one arm was bent at an angle that living arms do not hold. He wasn't moving. The rain fell on his back and pooled in the folds of his coat and ran in small rivulets into the ruts beside him.

Nolan crouched beside the man and pressed two fingers to the side of his neck. The skin was cold, with no pulse beneath it. He turned Hank's head just enough to see the wound above his left temple. The injury was severe.

Nolan rose and removed his hat, holding it against his chest for a moment, looking down at the man who had driven the Star Route for years. Hank had carried mail through mud and snow and wind without missing a run. He'd drunk coffee in the mercantile in Providence Ridge with him as he told stories about the road with the dry, understated humor of a man who knew this country and respected it. Hank deserved better than a ditch in the rain. He would get a proper burial when the weather allowed and the marshal could organize recovery.

Nolan put his hat back on and turned to face what needed facing.

Elizabeth had dismounted and was standing nearby, her face white beneath the rain. Her eyes were on Hank, and her jaw was set in a hard line that Nolan recognized as the expression she wore when she was keeping something down by force of will.

"He's gone," Nolan said. "Nothing we can do for him."

Elizabeth nodded once, a small, tight motion.

Nolan turned his attention to the horses. The three standing animals were shaking, their coats dark with rain and sweat, their nostrils wide. The traces were tangled around the broken wagon tongue, and the lead horse had a shallow gash along its shoulder. The fourth horse on the ground was dead, its neck bent wrong. Killed in the fall. Nolan moved to begin freeing the surviving horses from the tangled harness when he heard the sound.

It was low and weak, a moan that barely rose above the noise of the rain.

Nolan moved fast, rounding the wagon to see a woman lying in the mud at the road's edge. Her cloak was soaked through, the wool gone heavy and dark, spread around her in the clay. Her bonnet was gone, and her hair, brown and long, had come loose from its pins and lay plastered to her face and neck in wet strands that the rain kept rearranging. A bruise was darkening along her left cheekbone where she had struck the ground, and a thin cut above her right eyebrow had bled and been washed pale by the rain, leaving a faint pink trail across her temple. Her dress beneath the cloak wasn't frontier clothing. Even soaked and muddied beyond recognition of its original quality, he could see that the cut and the fabric were Eastern, the kind of traveling suit a woman from a city would wear, well-made and entirely wrong for this country.

Her left leg was bent below the knee at an angle that made his stomach tighten.

He crouched beside her and pressed two fingers to her throat, where a pulse met him, thin and too fast but present. Her breathing came shallow and uneven, the short, labored rhythm of a body working hard to keep itself alive. Her skin beneath his fingertips wasn't cool but cold, the waxy cold he had felt on calves pulled from icy creeks. The kind of cold that meant the body was losing its fight with the temperature and wouldn't win it without help. Her hands were ungloved, her fingers white and curled, and the nails tinged with blue.

She was small. That registered even as he assessed the injuries: a small woman, fine-boned, with a face that even in unconsciousness held a composure that struck him as odd. Most people in severe pain lost all control of their features, but this woman's face, bruised and bleeding and slack, looked as though some part of her was still holding herself together even now.

"Nolan," Elizabeth said as she came up beside him.

"She's alive." He didn't look up because he was examining the woman's leg. Below the knee, the bone had shifted visibly beneath the skin, but the skin itself wasn't torn, which meant a closed fracture. That was better than the alternative, though better was a word that lost most of its meaning when you were kneeling in freezing mud miles from home and thirty miles from the nearest doctor. Her body was spending everything it had fighting the cold and the break in her bone, and the combination would kill her before the day was done if he didn't get her warm, dry, and sheltered soon.

"How bad?" Elizabeth knelt beside him, her hands already reaching to brush the wet hair from the woman's face with a gentle, instinctive touch. Something in Elizabeth's expression shifted when her fingers met the woman's skin and felt the depth of the cold in it.

"Leg's broken. She's half-frozen."

Nolan stood and let his mind work through the options the way he worked through a fence problem or a failing piece of equipment, testing each solution against the constraints and discarding the ones that didn't hold. Riding to Providence Ridge for help meant at least an hour and a half round trip in this weather, even if he pushed his horse as fast as it would go. Attempting to take the woman to Livingston was out of the question; she'd most likely die before they made it.

"We're taking her home," he said. "I'll need your help with the leg. When I lift her, you hold it steady. Keep it as straight as you can and don't let it twist."

Elizabeth nodded. She was pale, and her hands were shaking, but when she positioned herself beside the woman's injured leg, her grip was firm and her eyes were focused.

Nolan slid one arm beneath the woman's shoulders and the other beneath her hips. She moaned when he shifted her weight, a sound so small and raw that Elizabeth flinched, but the woman didn't open her eyes. She was somewhere deep beneath consciousness, and the pain was finding her even there. He lifted her, and she weighed almost nothing in his arms, a hundred pounds at most, soaked through and limp. He had carried downed calves that weighed more than this woman did. She cried out as her body left the ground, a sound that cut through the rain and made his chest ache.

Elizabeth kept the leg steady, her face white, her jaw locked, and her eyes fixed on the injured limb as they moved together toward Cob. The gelding stamped and shifted when Nolan approached with the limp figure in his arms, nostrils flaring, but he held. Nolan had trained him for difficult work, and Cob's nerves ran deep beneath a stubborn, reliable core that steadied when lesser horses would have bolted.

Elizabeth guided the injured leg with both hands as Nolan eased the woman up and across Cob, positioning her upper body against the horse's upper back, where the warmth of the animal's blood and muscle would do her some good. Cob shifted beneath the unfamiliar weight, his ears pinning back, but Nolan spoke to him low and firm, and the gelding settled.

He shrugged out of his heavy buckskin coat, the icy rain hitting his shirt and soaking through to his skin instantly, which made his jaw clench. He spread the coat over the woman's body and tucked it around her shoulders and chest, layering it over her soaked cloak so that the buckskin's weight and the residual heat trapped in its lining pressed against her. The coat swallowed her, and the sight of her small, bruised face above the collar, her lashes dark with rain against that too-pale skin, did something to the back of his throat.

Elizabeth unwound her wool scarf and wrapped it around the woman's head and neck, tucking the ends in against her chest with hands that were gentle and quick despite the cold that had turned her fingers red.

"Unhitch the three standing horses," Nolan said, keeping one hand on the woman's back, steadying her against any shift in the horse's weight. "Cut the traces if you have to. They'll drift back toward town on their own."

"What about..." Elizabeth glanced toward the road where Hank lay.

"I'll send word to Marshal Sutter when we can. There's nothing more we can do for him now."

Elizabeth pressed her lips together, then turned and hurried back to the wrecked wagon. Nolan watched her from his position beside Cob, his hand firm against the woman's back, feeling the faint rise and fall of her breathing through the layers of wet wool and buckskin. The rain ran down his bare forearms and dripped from his elbows, and the cold was settling into him now with a deep, insistent grip that he did his best to ignore.

Elizabeth moved among the frightened horses with the calm authority of a girl raised around animals, working the harness buckles with hands that were stiff with cold. She talked to the trembling animals in a low, steady voice that calmed them while she worked. The lead horse flinched when a trace fell away, and Elizabeth caught its bridle and held it for a moment, murmuring something Nolan couldn't hear, before she released it. While she worked, Nolan's eyes found the two trunks lashed inside the overturned wagon bed, shifted during the roll but still secured by the ropes that had held them. The woman's belongings, clearly. When the weather cleared, he or someone from town would need to come for the trunks, the mail sacks, and the driver. The wreck site would need to be cleared, but all of that belonged to a future that could wait.

Within minutes the three horses were free, and they stood for a moment, bewildered, their training keeping them in place even as their instincts told them to move. Then the lead horse turned its head toward Providence Ridge and began to walk. The other two followed, their hooves sucking in the mud as they moved down the road at a tired, steady pace.

"Ride ahead of us," Nolan said as Elizabeth returned. "Go as fast as you can and prepare my room."

Elizabeth mounted the bay and looked at him for a moment. In that look, he saw everything she wasn't saying: the fear and the questions, and the awareness that their home was about to change in ways neither of them could predict. Then she turned the bay and rode hard down the trail toward the homestead.

Nolan watched her go, then turned to the problem of mounting a horse while keeping the injured, unconscious woman from falling off. It took him three attempts. He settled into the saddle behind her, then lifted and adjusted her limp body so he could hold her against his chest.

He gathered the reins in one hand, holding her steady with his other. Cob stepped forward, picking his way carefully up the slope to the muddy trail with careful, deliberate footing.

The cold worked through Nolan's entire body with the steady, patient cruelty of something that had all the time in the world. The woman didn't move. Her breathing stayed shallow, and her body stayed limp.

Boone trotted ahead, checking back every few strides with the alert, worried eyes of a dog who understood that something important was happening and that his job was to keep moving until his master told him to stop.

The woman stirred. Not waking. Just a shift, a small turning of her head against his shoulder, and her lips moved without sound, shaping a word or a prayer he couldn't hear.

Nolan tightened his arm around her and sent up a silent prayer.

Chapter 12

Cob stopped at the porch without being told, the way a horse stops at the end of a trail it knows by heart. The rain had not let up. The cold had worked into Nolan so deeply that his hands felt like they belonged to someone else, stiff and clumsy on the reins. The woman had moaned twice during the ride, low involuntary sounds that surfaced through whatever dark place she had gone.

Boone barked once, a sharp, announcing bark that cut through the rain, and the front door swung open. Elizabeth had changed into dry clothes and pulled her hair back in a fresh braid. Her eyes were wide, and her gaze went straight to the woman he held against his chest.

By the grace of God, Nolan managed to ease himself off the horse with the woman held tightly against his chest. The muscles in his thighs had been clenched for so long against Cob's sides, holding his balance and the woman's, they trembled with weakness. After he steadied himself, he carried her up the porch steps and through the front door. The warmth in the house hit him with a force that almost stopped him in his tracks. Elizabeth had done her work and done it well. The cookstove was radiating a fierce, steady warmth that filled the main room like a living presence.

Nolan crossed the main room and turned sideways through the doorway of his bedroom, careful not to bump the woman's injured leg against the frame. Nolan lowered the woman onto his bed as gently as his trembling arms could manage.

He stepped back and made himself look at the situation the way he would look at a sick animal, assessing what needed doing and in what order. The woman's skin was still that grayish color that meant the cold had settled deep into her core, and her lips had a faint blue tinge that he didn't like. Her breathing was shallow but steadier than it had been at the wreck site.

Elizabeth moved to the other side of the bed. She pressed her hand flat against the woman's forehead, then against her cheek, then lifted one of the woman's hands and held it between both of her own. Her face was calm and focused, but when she looked up at Nolan, he could see the fear written in her eyes.

"She's so cold, Nolan. Her hands feel like they've been packed in snow."

"The cold's what'll kill her if we don't get ahead of it," Nolan said. "The leg can wait. Warm her first, then we'll deal with the broken bone."

He looked at what Elizabeth had assembled on his trunk against the wall: every quilt and blanket they owned, stacked in a thick pile. A pot of hot water, still steaming, with clean cloths draped over the side. A bar of their lye soap. A tin of the salve Elizabeth made each fall from beeswax and tallow and dried yarrow, useful for cuts and scrapes and raw skin. A small drawstring pouch that held their supply of dried willow bark for pain tea. A brown glass bottle of camphor liniment they used on sore muscles and chest colds. And Elizabeth's own nightgown, a plain cotton garment, white and worn soft from years of washing, lay neatly across the top of the blanket stack.

Elizabeth had thought of everything he would have thought of and several things he wouldn't have. The sight of that careful preparation told him something about his sister that he had known for years but had never put into words. She wasn't a girl keeping house for her brother. She was a woman running a household, and she'd done so from a tender age without complaint.

"I need to see to Cob," Nolan said. "I'll be back in a few minutes."

Elizabeth nodded without looking up. She was already reaching for the buttons at the collar of the woman's traveling jacket, her fingers working with quick, purposeful movements. Nolan turned and walked out of the bedroom, pulling the door closed behind him with a quiet click.

The main room felt enormous after the close quarters of his bedroom. The sound of the rain on the roof filled the space with a steady, drumming roar that he had stopped hearing somewhere on the trail and now noticed again. He crossed to the front door, opened it, and stepped out onto the porch, where the cold hit his wet shirt and drove through him with a force that made his teeth clench. Cob stood where Nolan had left him, head low, rain streaming off his flanks. Boone was on the porch with his chin on his paws, watching Nolan with patient, worried eyes.

Nolan gathered Cob's reins and led him across the yard to the barn. The barn door took more effort to open than usual because his arms were shaking with a fine, persistent tremor that had nothing to do with the cold and everything to do with the hours of sustained tension that were only now releasing their grip on his body. He got the door open and led Cob inside, and the warm, close smell of hay and horse and old wood wrapped around them both like a second shelter.

He cross-tied Cob in the aisle and pulled the saddle, which was heavy with rainwater, and carried it to the tack room. Nolan came back to Cob and rubbed the horse down, working in long, firm strokes. Cob leaned into the rubbing the way he always did, his eyes half-closed, his lower lip drooping in the particular expression of equine contentment that meant the work was appreciated. Nolan checked each leg, running his hands from shoulder and hip down to the hoof, feeling for heat or swelling or any sign that the difficult trail had cost the horse more than tiredness. Everything was sound. He gave Cob a measure of oats in his feedbox, forked hay into the stall, and topped the water from the barrel.

The other horses watched with mild interest as Nolan led Cob into his stall. The barn was quiet except for the sound of Cob eating while rain hammered the roof.

Nolan checked on the bay mare that Elizabeth had ridden and saw she was already in her stall, rubbed down and fed.

He then stood in the aisle with his hands at his sides and let the stillness take him.

His hands were shaking. The adrenaline that had carried him through the mile-by-mile effort of keeping the woman safe and warm against his chest on the back of his horse was draining out of him now. What it left behind was a weariness so heavy it felt like something physical pressing down on his shoulders.

He walked back into Cob's stall and leaned his forehead against the gelding's warm flank, resting it there in the curve between the horse's barrel and hip where the heat was deepest. He closed his eyes and let himself breathe deeply.

He didn't know who the woman was. He didn't know her name, or where she had come from, or where she had been going, or why she had been on that road in a storm in Hank Meecham's mail hack. He knew only that she was hurt and lying in his bed and that she was his responsibility now until she was well enough to leave or until someone came looking for her. He knew that Hank Meecham was lying dead on a mountain road in the rain and that the man deserved better than what this day had given him. He knew that the woman's leg was broken badly, and that he was going to have to set it, and that the setting would cause her a kind of pain that he had witnessed several times before. The thought of putting this small woman through that pain sat in his stomach like a swallowed stone.

He stood up straight and opened his eyes. Cob turned his head and looked at him with the calm, uncomplicated regard of an animal. Nolan rubbed the gelding's neck once and walked away.

He moved to the back of the barn, where he kept his lumber scraps and building supplies. He sorted through the pile until he found two flat pieces of pine board, each about eighteen inches long and three inches wide, smooth enough that they wouldn't splinter against skin and sturdy enough to hold a leg immobile.

He tucked the boards under his arm and walked out of the barn into the rain.

The yard between the barn and the house was a stretch of mud and gray light, and he crossed it with his head down and the rain driving against his shoulders.

Nolan opened the door to his home and stepped inside. His bedroom door was still shut. He could hear Elizabeth moving on the other side of it, the soft sounds of cloth and water and the careful, quiet work of a woman tending to someone who couldn't tend to herself. He set the splint boards on the table beside the lamp, pulled out the chair, and sat down.

Nolan bowed his head and folded his hands.

Chapter 13

The bedroom door opened, and Elizabeth stood there, wiping her hands on a cloth, her sleeves pushed past her elbows. "She's ready," she said.

Nolan pushed back from the table and stood. His legs were still stiff from the cold that had settled into his joints during the ride. His shoulders still ached from the hours of holding the woman steady in the saddle, but the trembling in his hands had quieted while he sat.

He followed Elizabeth into the bedroom. The lamp on the nightstand burned with a low, steady flame that threw soft light across the bed and the woman lying beneath the sheet.

The mud and the blood and the rain-soaked traveling suit were gone, and in their place was a woman in Elizabeth's cotton nightgown, her hair washed and spread across the pillow in long, damp waves the color of dark chestnuts. The cut above her eyebrow had been cleaned and showed itself now as a thin red line against pale skin. The bruise along her cheekbone had deepened to a mottled purple that stood out sharply against the pallor of her face. The gray tinge that had frightened Nolan at the wreck site had faded, replaced by a color that was still to off but no longer carried the waxy look of a body giving up its fight with the cold. Elizabeth's work and the home's warmth had pulled her back from whatever edge she had been approaching, and her breathing, while still shallow, came with a steadier rhythm than it had on the ride.

"She didn't wake up," Elizabeth said quietly, moving to the far side of the bed. "Not once. She made sounds a few times, but she never opened her eyes." Elizabeth folded her arms across her chest and looked down at the woman. "I checked her over as best I could. Her ribs seem sound. No other breaks that I can feel. Her arms and shoulders are bruised from the fall, and she's scraped up along her right side where she hit the ground, but the leg is the worst of it. By far."

Nolan looked at the woman's leg. Elizabeth had positioned it on top of the sheet, with rolled cloths packed on either side. Below the knee the swelling had increased since the wreck site, the skin stretched tight and discolored with the deep, angry bruising that comes from a bone displaced beneath the surface. He could see where the break was by the way the lower leg angled slightly inward, a subtle wrongness that would become permanent if the bone wasn't set properly and soon.

"Do we have plenty of willow bark?" he asked.

"Enough to see us through this for quite some time."

Nolan nodded. The willow bark would help with the pain and the swelling, but it would only help if the woman could drink it, and the woman couldn't drink anything in the state she was in.

Which meant the bone had to be set, without anything to dull what was coming.

He set the splint boards on the nightstand beside the lamp and looked at Elizabeth. "I need you to hold her down. Both shoulders, as much of her weight as you can. When I pull the leg, she's going to fight it, whether she's conscious or not. The body reacts on its own, and she'll try to move, and if she moves while I'm working the bone back into line, it could make things worse."

Elizabeth's face went a shade paler, but she didn't hesitate. She positioned herself with her hands on the woman's shoulders, pressing down with a firm, steady pressure. Her jaw was set, and her eyes fixed on Nolan.

Nolan moved to the foot of the bed. He placed his hands on the woman's lower leg, one above the break and one below, and felt the displacement beneath his fingers. The bone had shifted inward during the fall, and the muscle and tissue around it had already begun to tighten in the body's instinctive attempt to protect the injury. He would need to pull the lower leg straight, applying steady traction until the bone ends slid past each other and back into alignment. He had done this several times before, the most memorable being a logger named Pettit, whose forearm had snapped between two rolling timbers near the mill three years ago. Pettit had been conscious and had screamed and bitten through the leather strap they'd given him and then fainted, which had made the rest of the work easier.

He looked at the woman's face one more time. Her lashes lay dark against her cheeks, and her lips were parted slightly. The bruise on her cheekbone gave her face a fragile, damaged look that made his chest tighten around his ribs. She was small and still and completely at his mercy, and the trust that unconsciousness forced upon her, the absolute vulnerability of a woman who couldn't consent to or refuse what was about to be done to her body, was a weight he felt in his hands as surely as he felt the broken bone beneath them.

"Ready?" he asked Elizabeth.

"Ready."

He drew a breath and pulled.

The technique was simple in principle and brutal in practice. He gripped the lower leg firmly below the break with both hands and pulled downward with a steady, sustained traction, drawing the bone ends apart while guiding the angle of the limb back toward straight. The resistance was immediate and fierce. The muscles surrounding the break clenched against the movement, and the swollen tissue fought him with the blind, animal stubbornness of a body trying to protect itself from further damage.

The woman reacted. Her back arched off the mattress, and a cry came out of her that wasn't a scream but something worse, a raw, involuntary sound torn from somewhere deeper than consciousness. It was the kind of sound that a body produces when pain exceeds every threshold the mind has built against it. Her right hand clawed at the sheet beneath her, and her left arm swung outward in a reflexive attempt to stop whatever was causing the agony. Through it all, Elizabeth leaned her full weight across the woman's shoulders, holding her against the bed with a strength that belied her frame.

He felt the bone shift. A grinding, muffled sensation transmitted through his hands and up through his wrists, the nauseating feel of broken ends moving against each other beneath the skin.

He adjusted the angle, corrected the inward drift, and pulled again with steady, relentless pressure until he felt the bone ends slide past each other and seat with a faint, sickening click that he felt more than heard.

The woman's body went limp. The cry cut off as suddenly as it had begun. She let out a shuddering exhalation that seemed to empty her of every tension and pain that had surfaced during those terrible seconds. Her hand released its grip on the sheet. Her head turned to one side on the pillow, and she was still again, her breathing ragged but present, her body retreating back into the deep unconsciousness that was the only mercy available to her.

Elizabeth was breathing hard. She released the woman's shoulders slowly, as if afraid that letting go too quickly might cause something else to break. When she straightened up and looked at Nolan, her eyes were bright with tears and her chin was trembling.

"God be with her," she said, her voice not quite steady.

"Prepare some cloth." Nolan's voice sounded strange to him, rougher than it should have been, and he realized his jaw had been clenched so tight during the procedure that the muscles ached all the way to his temples.

He picked up the two pine boards from the nightstand and positioned them along either side of the woman's lower leg, one on the inside and one on the outside, spanning from just below the knee to past the ankle. Elizabeth was ripping a piece of cloth into long strips with quick, efficient motions that sent small threads floating in the lamplight. She handed the strips to Nolan one at a time, and he wrapped them around the splint boards, working his way from the knee downward. Each wrap was firm enough to hold the boards in place and keep the bone from shifting, but not so tight that it would cut off the blood flow to her foot. He checked the color of her toes when he finished, pressing his thumb against the nail of her big toe and watching the pink return when he released it. Blood was moving. The splint was holding. The bone was set.

He straightened up and stood at the foot of the bed, looking at the woman who lay in his bed with her leg splinted between two pine boards and her face turned to the side on his pillow. Elizabeth gathered the quilts from the trunk and layered them over the woman one at a time. She pulled each one up to her chin and tucked the edges along her sides with the same careful, gentle hands that had washed and dressed her. The last quilt was one their mother had made, a double-wedding-ring pattern in blue and cream that she had pieced during the winter she was carrying Elizabeth. The sight of that quilt spread over a stranger in his bed nearly did him in.

He stood there watching the woman's face. Her breathing had steadied, and the tension that had drawn her features tight during the bone-setting had released, leaving her face soft and slack against the pillow. Her features were fine and even, with high cheekbones and a straight, narrow nose and a mouth that even in unconsciousness held a shape suggesting composure, as though the habit of keeping herself together was so deeply ingrained that it persisted even in the absence of consciousness. Her skin, beneath the bruising and the pallor, had the particular smoothness of a woman who had not spent a significant amount of time outdoors fighting the wind and hard weather.

He wondered what her name was. He wondered where she had come from; what city or town had produced such a fine-featured woman? He wondered who was waiting for her, because a woman didn't travel alone across the territory unless someone was expecting her. He wondered if that someone would come looking when she didn't arrive.

"Nolan."

Elizabeth's voice pulled him back. She was standing beside him, her hand on his arm, looking up at him with an expression that was gentle and knowing and older than eighteen.

"She's going to be all right. The bone is set, and she's warming up, and she's breathing fine." She tugged his arm lightly, the way she had tugged his arm since she was a little girl trying to get his attention at the supper table. "Come on. I'll find us something to eat. You look about as worn through as that woman does."

Nolan looked at the woman one more time. The quilts rose and fell with the slow rhythm of her breathing. The lamplight caught the damp strands of her hair where they lay across the pillow, and her face was peaceful in the way that deep sleep sometimes looks peaceful. Though he knew the peace was borrowed and the pain would come back when she woke.

He let Elizabeth lead him out of the room. They left the door open so the warmth from the stove could fill the room. Nolan sat down at the table while Elizabeth moved to the stove and began pulling together whatever she could find that required the least effort.

Supper was simple, and neither of them pretended otherwise. Elizabeth heated a couple of slices of cured ham. She cut thin slices of cheese and thick slices from the bread she had baked yesterday. They ate across from each other at the table in a silence that was heavier than their usual evenings, weighted with everything the day had brought into their house. Nolan ate without tasting, his body taking in fuel the way a stove takes in wood, mechanically and out of necessity.

"We should take shifts tonight," Elizabeth said after a while. "Someone should be with her, or at least close enough to hear if she wakes up. She'll be confused and in pain, and she shouldn't be alone when that happens."

"I'll take the first watch," Nolan said.

"You've been up since before dawn, you rode through a storm, and you carried a woman off a mountain. You should sleep first."

"I'll take the first watch," he said again, in the tone that Elizabeth knew better than to argue with. Arguing with him when he used that tone was like arguing with the weather. It didn't accomplish anything, and it wore you out.

Elizabeth studied him for a moment with those clear, knowing eyes. Then she nodded. "Wake me at midnight. And I mean midnight, Nolan. Not two in the morning because you decided you weren't tired enough to hand it off."

"Midnight."

"Promise me."

"I'll wake you at midnight."

She held his gaze for another moment, satisfying herself that he meant it. Then she stood and cleared their plates and washed them in the basin with quick, economical motions. She dried her hands on the cloth hanging from the nail on the wall.

"I'm going to check on her one more time, and then I'm going to bed. If she wakes up enough to swallow, prepare some willow bark tea and give her small sips. Not too much at once. And if her skin goes gray again, or if her breathing changes, you come get me. Don't sit there being stoic about it. Come get me."

"I will."

Elizabeth looked at him for a long moment, and in the lamplight her face was tired and young and fierce all at once. Nolan thought, not for the first time, that their mother and father would have been proud of the woman Elizabeth was becoming.

She went into his bedroom. He heard her move around the bed, heard her talking softly to the woman, and then heard the faint rustle of quilts being adjusted. Then she came back out and disappeared into her own small room. Her door closed with a quiet click, and Nolan was alone.

He sat at the table for a while, listening to the rain, the tick of the stove, and the silence. Then he rose, carried the chair from the table into the bedroom, and set it beside the bed where he could see the woman's face and watch the rise and fall of the quilts over her chest.

The chair creaked beneath his weight, and the sound was loud in the quiet room. The lamp on the nightstand had burned low, its flame small and orange. The rain had softened from the driving sheets of the afternoon into a steady, gentler fall that tapped against the window glass with a rhythm that might have been soothing under other circumstances.

The woman breathed in and out; the quilts rising and falling in a slow, steady cadence that Nolan watched with the attentive vigilance of a man who understood that some things couldn't be hurried and that presence was sometimes the only medicine available. Her face was turned toward him on the pillow, and in the low lamplight her lashes lay against her skin like threads of dark silk. She was, he realized with a quiet jolt that he immediately pressed down and set aside, one of the most beautiful women he had ever seen.

He folded his arms across his chest, settled deeper into the chair, and listened to the rain and her breathing.

Chapter 14

The pain found her before the light did. It came from somewhere far below her, rising through layers of darkness the way a sound rises through deep water. At first it wasn't pain so much as a sensation of wrongness, a heavy, pulsing awareness that something in her body had been damaged in a way that sleep could muffle but not erase.

The first thing she became aware of was warmth. Not the warmth of a summer afternoon or a fire at a comfortable distance, but an encompassing, close warmth that pressed against her skin from every direction, heavy and dense. The second thing she noticed was a ceiling she didn't recognize. Rough-hewn timber beams, close and low, lit by the amber glow of a lamp turned down to its smallest flame. The wood was old and darkened, and the spaces between the beams were filled with hand-fitted planking that had been planed smooth but never painted. It wasn't the ceiling of any room she had ever slept in. It wasn't the pressed tin of Mrs. Peabody's boardinghouse in Chicago, and it wasn't the white plaster of her bedroom on Franklin Street, and it wasn't the knotty pine of Mrs. Calloway's room in Livingston. It was a stranger's ceiling in a stranger's room, and the sight of it sent a spike of fear through her chest that was sharp enough to make her draw a breath that caught in her throat.

She tried to move, and the wrongness in her leg became pain.

Not the dull, throbbing ache she had been feeling through the layers of unconsciousness but a bright, screaming, white-edged agony that roared up from her left leg below the knee and flooded her entire body. The force of it made her vision go dark at the edges and pulled a cry from her mouth that she couldn't control. Something was wrong with her leg, catastrophically and undeniably wrong, and the pain was so enormous and so total that for several seconds it was the only thing in the world. A wall of sensation that blotted out the strange ceiling and the quilts and the lamplight and everything else.

She heard quick, light footsteps from somewhere beyond the doorway of this room, and then a figure appeared in the lamplight, and a voice reached her through the pain.

"You're awake. It's all right, you're safe, you're all right. Don't try to move."

The voice was young and female and carried a warmth that was so immediate and so genuine that it cut through her panic the way a hand cuts through water. Opal blinked against the tears that the pain had forced from her eyes and tried to focus on the face above her.

A girl. A young woman, perhaps eighteen, with light-brown hair pulled back in a braid and clear blue eyes that were wide with concern and bright with a gentle, unguarded kindness. Her face was fresh and open, with the particular look of someone who was happy to see her.

"Where..." Opal's voice came out as a rasp, dry and cracked, barely a voice at all. Her throat felt as if it had been scoured with sand, and the effort of pushing a single word through it made her realize how thirsty she was.

"You're in our home," the girl said in a calm, measured tone. "My brother and I found you on the road yesterday. Your wagon wrecked in the storm, and you were hurt. You've been asleep since we brought you here." She paused, and her hand settled on the quilt beside Opal's shoulder. "My name is Elizabeth. Elizabeth Ridgeway. You're at our homestead, about eight miles outside Providence Ridge."

Providence Ridge. The name reached through the fog of pain and disorientation and connected to something in Opal's memory, a town she had passed through, a mercantile where the driver had stopped to swap mail sacks. And then the road had continued toward the pass, and then...

The wreck came back to her in pieces. Not a smooth, ordered memory but a shattered collection of images and sensations that arrived without sequence or mercy. Rain driving sideways into her face. The road turning to clay. The bench tilting beneath her. The crack of wood. The shriek of harness chains. The moment her hands found nothing to hold, and the world shifted sideways, and then the blow to her leg, that single, enormous, world-ending blow that had swallowed everything.

"The driver... Hank," Opal said, and the words scraped against her throat like broken glass.

Elizabeth's hand moved from the quilt to Opal's forearm, resting there with a light, steady pressure. "He didn't make it," she said quietly. "When we reached the wreck, he was already gone."

Hank Meecham. The lean, weathered man who had spoken thirty sentences in a full day of driving, most of them to the horses. The man who had scratched behind the bay's ear with a rough gentleness that had told Opal more about his character than any conversation could have. The man who had looked at the sky the evening before and said the mountains were building something.

"Your leg is broken," Elizabeth continued, her voice gentle but direct. "Below the knee. My brother set it last night and splinted it. The bone went back into place, and the splint is holding, but you're going to be in a good deal of pain for a while, and you won't be able to put weight on it for weeks."

Weeks. The word settled over Opal like another quilt, heavy and suffocating. She was lying in a stranger's bed in a stranger's home, miles from the nearest town, with a broken leg. The man who had been driving her to Silver Springs was dead. The wagon that had held her trunks and everything she owned was overturned on a mountain road in the rain.

The enormity of her situation opened within her like a trapdoor, and for a moment she felt the falling sensation of absolute helplessness. The sensation of being trapped by circumstances so far beyond her control that no amount of planning or intelligence or faith could alter them.

Her eyes burned, and she blinked hard against the tears.

"Can I get you some water?" Elizabeth asked. The question was so simple and so kind and so perfectly timed that Opal understood this girl had seen the tears building and had chosen to give her a reason to look away rather than an audience for her pain.

"Yes," Opal managed. "Please."

Elizabeth moved to the nightstand, where a pitcher and cup sat beside the lamp. After pouring some water, she slid one hand beneath Opal's shoulders and lifted her just enough to bring the cup to her lips, supporting her weight with an arm that was stronger than it looked. The water was cool and refreshing, and she drank until Elizabeth gently pulled the cup away.

"Not too much at once," Elizabeth said, easing her back onto the pillow. "You haven't had anything in your stomach since before the wreck, and too much water on an empty stomach could make you sick. I'll bring you broth when you're ready. I have willow bark tea I can make to help with the pain. It won't make it go away, but it'll take the worst edge off, and it'll help you sleep."

Opal lay against the pillow and looked around the room. It was small. A log-walled room with a single window that showed nothing but darkness. A nightstand. A trunk against the wall with a stack of folded cloth on top, a brown glass bottle, and a tin that might have held salve. A row of pegs on the wall holding a heavy shirt, a pair of work trousers, and a leather belt.

Men's clothing. This was a man's room.

The realization moved through her slowly, with the careful, measuring awareness of a woman who had learned to assess her surroundings before reacting to them. She was wearing a nightgown that wasn't hers, a soft, worn cotton garment. She was lying in a bed that she assumed belonged to a man, in a house she had never seen, and someone had undressed her, washed her, and changed her clothing while she was unconscious.

"How did I get here?" Opal asked as Elizabeth settled into a chair beside the bed.

"Nolan, my brother, and I were riding the upper pastures, bringing the cattle down ahead of the storm. He saw the wreck from the ridge above the road. We rode down together." She paused. "He carried you back on his horse. It was raining hard, and you were cold, very cold. He held you in the saddle the whole way home." Her voice softened. "And I'm the one who cleaned you up and changed your clothes."

The quiet specificity of that last detail, offered without being asked, told Opal two things about Elizabeth Ridgeway. First, that she was perceptive enough to anticipate the question that a woman in Opal's position would need answered. And second, that the answer mattered to her, that the propriety of what had happened in this house was something she wanted Opal to know had been preserved.

"Thank you," Opal said, and the words felt impossibly small against the weight of what this girl and her brother had done. They had found her on a road in a rainstorm, carried her miles through the cold, brought her into their home, undressed and washed and warmed her, and set her broken bone. They had done all of this for a stranger. The cost of that kindness was a debt so large that two words couldn't begin to approach it, but they were the only words she had.

"You don't need to thank me," Elizabeth said.

"Opal. My name is Opal."

Elizabeth leaned forward in the chair, her elbows on her knees, her face open and expectant.

"Opal," Elizabeth repeated. "That's a lovely name."

The pain in Opal's leg had settled into a deep, steady throb that pulsed in time with her heartbeat. A rhythm she could feel from her knee to her ankle and back again with each beat. It wasn't the sharp, screaming agony that had greeted her when she first tried to move, but it was relentless, a presence that couldn't be ignored or reasoned with or prayed away. It consumed her energy and her focus, and left less of both with every passing minute.

"I'm going to make you some willow bark tea. I promise you it will help with the pain you are feeling." She paused in the doorway and looked back with a small, lopsided smile that transformed her whole face from the serious, capable young woman who had delivered difficult news into the warm, bright girl who lived beneath the competence. "Or would you prefer a cup of coffee that could strip paint off a fence post?"

Opal almost smiled. Her mouth didn't quite complete the expression because the pain pulled it back before it reached its full shape, but the intent was there.

"Tea it is then," she said before disappearing through the doorway.

She lay in the quiet room and let her gaze settle on the ceiling above her while the rain tapped steadily against the window glass and the quilts pressed their heavy warmth against her body. Her leg throbbed in excruciating pain, and she breathed around it the way she had learned to breathe around grief and fear and all the other things that were too large to hold and too constant to set down. Careful, measured pulls that kept the worst of it from rising into her throat.

She was in a stranger's home. She was in a stranger's bed. Furthermore, she was wearing a stranger's nightgown. Her broken leg had been set by a stranger's hands. Hank was dead. The future she had been riding toward had shattered in the blink of an eye.

And yet.

She was alive.

She was warm.

She was in a bed with clean quilts pulled to her chin, and a girl named Elizabeth had washed her and dressed her. A man she had not yet met had held her on his horse for miles and given up his room so that she could lie in his bed while her broken body tried to remember how to heal. These people hadn't known who she was. They didn't know where she came from, or what she was running from, or what she carried in her heart. They had helped her anyway, with a completeness and a lack of hesitation that Opal recognized as something rare, something she had seen in her own parents and in Mrs. Jennings and in very few other people in her twenty-two years of living, the kind of goodness that does not calculate the cost before it acts.

Elizabeth returned carrying a cup that steamed in her hands. She slid her arm beneath Opal's shoulders again with the same easy strength she had shown before, lifting her just enough to drink. The tea was bitter and earthy and tasted of bark and something vaguely mineral. Opal drank it in slow, steady sips while Elizabeth held the cup and watched her with attentive patience.

"All of it," Elizabeth said when Opal tried to stop halfway. "I know it's terrible. Drink it all, and I won't make you have another cup for at least a few hours, which is the closest thing to mercy I can offer."

Opal drank the rest. The bitterness spread through her mouth, down her throat, and settled in her stomach.

"There," Elizabeth said softly, easing her back against the pillow. "That'll start working soon. You'll get sleepy, and that's all right. Sleep is the best thing for you right now. Your body needs it more than anything else I can give you."

Within minutes she could feel it working at the edges of the pain. Not removing it but softening its grip, blurring the sharp, bright edges into something duller and more bearable. Her muscles began to loosen, and a heaviness crept into her limbs.

Opal's eyelids grew heavy, the willow bark pulling her down toward sleep with a gentle, insistent tug that she didn't have the strength or the desire to fight. The room softened around her, the sharp edges of the log walls and the lamplight and the rain on the window blurring into a warm, indistinct wash of color and sound. Elizabeth's face above her was steady and kind, and her hand rested on Opal's forearm with light, anchoring pressure.

"Elizabeth," Opal said, and her voice was fading, the words coming from further and further away.

"I'm here."

"Thank you for..." The sentence drifted, unfinished, because sleep was pulling her down.

"Shh," Elizabeth said, and her thumb moved in a small, slow circle on Opal's forearm. "I'm right here. You sleep now."

Opal closed her eyes. The pain receded to a distant shore, still present but no longer touching her. She felt the quilts around her and the pillow beneath her head and Elizabeth's hand on her arm. She thought of her mother, who used to sit beside her bed during childhood fevers and stroke her hair and sing hymns so softly that the words blurred into the melody and the melody blurred into sleep.

She carried that thought down with her into the dark, and the dark was warm, and she wasn't alone in it.

Chapter 15

Opal's first conscious act the next time she woke up was to clench her jaw against the grinding throb below her left knee and hold perfectly still while her body remembered where it was and why everything hurt. Her leg had its own pulse now, a deep, structural ache that lived in the center of the bone and radiated outward with every beat of her heart.

Through the open doorway, she heard voices. Elizabeth's came first, light and clear.

Then another voice.

A man's voice. Low and unhurried, with a roughness to it.

Elizabeth's brother. She had heard his voice once before, she thought, thin and far away, during the ride through the rain. Or perhaps she had imagined it. The memories from that day were broken glass, scattered and sharp-edged and impossible to assemble into anything whole.

Opal lay still and listened.

He was talking about his plans for the day, and the structure of what he said told her something about the man saying it. He moved through a list the way a person moves through familiar ground, each item placed in order, each one practical. He would bring a cord of firewood around to the front porch before tomorrow evening. The weather concerned him. The temperature had dropped further overnight, and the sky had a quality he didn't like.

"I expect snow by tomorrow evening," he said. "Maybe sooner."

Snow. The word landed in Opal's mind and sat there, heavy and foreign. It was October. Early October. In Virginia, October meant the last warm afternoons and the first soft color creeping into the maples along Franklin Street. October meant light shawls and open windows. Snow was a December word in Richmond.

Snow by tomorrow evening. In October.

The man continued talking; he would take the wagon to town this morning and stop and speak with the marshal, and then ride to the wreck site afterward and see if he could find any of the woman's belongings.

Her belongings. Everything she owned in the world was in her two trunks, her carpetbag, and her satchel. Her clothing. Her father's Bible. The books she'd brought. The thought of her things lying in the mud at the wreck site, soaked through, produced a spike of urgency that cut through everything else.

"Elizabeth?" Her voice came out rough and thin, scraped to almost nothing by disuse. She swallowed against the dryness in her throat and tried again, louder. "Elizabeth?"

The conversation in the main room stopped. A chair scraped against the floorboards. Quick, light footsteps crossed the room, and Elizabeth appeared in the doorway with her sleeves pushed past her elbows and a cloth over one shoulder.

"Good morning." Elizabeth came to the bedside and sat in the chair beside her. "How are you feeling?"

Opal considered offering something polite and measured. The kind of answer a Richmond woman would give to a social inquiry about her health: Quite well, thank you. But politeness felt absurd in this room, in this bed, with this pain grinding through her leg like a millstone.

"The pain is considerable. Worse than anything I've experienced. It doesn't stop."

Elizabeth nodded. "The first week is the hardest. The bone is trying to knit, and your body doesn't know what to do with itself except hurt. The willow bark helps, but it only takes the edge off. It won't take it away."

"I understand."

Opal's stomach chose that moment to announce itself. The growl rose through the quilts with a volume and rudeness that would have sent every etiquette instructor she'd ever had reaching for smelling salts. Heat climbed into Opal's cheeks, and she pressed her lips together in a failed attempt at composure.

Elizabeth's face broke into a grin so genuine and so delighted that it transformed her entire bearing, and despite the pain and the embarrassment, Opal smiled. She couldn't help it. The girl's pleasure was that infectious.

"Well... I'd say you're hungry."

"I am," Opal admitted. "I'm also sorry. That was hardly lady-like."

"That was the best sound I've heard all morning." Elizabeth leaned forward in the chair with her elbows on her knees. "I'll heat some broth for you. You shouldn't have solid food just yet; maybe tomorrow. But the broth is good. I made it yesterday from the last of the ham bone."

"Thank you. The voice I heard. That was your brother?"

"That's Nolan. I'm sorry if we were talking too loud... did we wake you?"

Opal opened her mouth to respond, but a shadow shifted in the doorway, and the words left her.

He filled the doorway. Not crowded it, not leaned against it. Filled it, the way a man fills a space when his shoulders are broad enough and the doorframe is narrow enough that there isn't much room left over. He wore buckskin and dark pants. His hat was in his hand, held against his thigh.

He was tall. Considerably taller than any man she'd known, and built with the thick, long-limbed solidity of someone whose body had been shaped by years of hard labor rather than leisure. The men in Opal's experience, her father's business associates and the young men at Richmond gatherings, and Edward Hawthorne with his tailored coats, were built for parlors and offices and carriage seats. This man was built for the country. His hands were large and rough, and across the left one she noticed a clean white scar that caught the light from the window. His face was strong-boned and weathered to a quality that had nothing to do with age and everything to do with wind and cold and sun and the kind of life that doesn't happen indoors. His beard was thick and brown.

His eyes were blue. Not pale, but deep, a quiet, steady shade of blue. They met hers for a moment. Direct. Assessing. Then they moved to Elizabeth.

Elizabeth looked from her brother to Opal and back again. "Nolan, this is Opal. Opal, this is my brother, Nolan Ridgeway."

Opal looked at the man in the doorway again. "Mr. Ridgeway. I owe you and your sister a debt I cannot adequately express. You saved my life, and I am more grateful than I know how to say."

He studied her for a moment. His expression didn't change. Then he nodded, a single, brief motion.

"You needed help." He shifted the hat in his hand. "I saw two trunks strapped inside the wrecked wagon bed. Both yours?"

"Yes. Both are mine." Opal pressed her palms flat against the quilt. "And if you could look for a carpetbag. Dark floral tapestry with leather handles. And a leather satchel, brown, with a shoulder strap."

"I'll look for them," he said, and then he looked at Elizabeth. "Anything you need from town?"

"Coffee," Elizabeth said without hesitation. "We have plenty for now, but with snow coming, I don't want to go without if we can't make it to town for some time."

"I'll stop at the mercantile."

He turned and walked out of the doorway. His boots were quiet on the floorboards for a man his size, and Opal listened to the sound of him crossing the main room until the front door opened. Cold air pushed through the house in a single sharp breath.

Elizabeth rose from the chair. "I'll heat your broth and make some willow bark tea."

"Elizabeth."

The girl paused in the doorway.

"The weather," Opal said. "What your brother said about snow. Is that truly possible? In October?"

Elizabeth's expression held a gentle humor that carried no mockery. "Not just possible. Likely. We've had snow in September some years, though it doesn't usually stick. October snow is different. October snow can settle in and mean business." She tilted her head, studying Opal's face. "Quite a different world, I suspect, from where you come from?"

"Yes. Quite different."

"And where might that be?" Elizabeth leaned one shoulder against the doorframe, her posture easy and curious.

"Virginia," Opal said. "Richmond."

Elizabeth's eyebrows lifted, and genuine fascination moved across her face. "Richmond. I've never met anyone from Virginia before." She came half a step back into the room, as if the pull of curiosity had a physical weight. "And what brought you all the way out here to Montana Territory? Traveling on the Star Route toward Silver Springs?"

The question was logical. Opal had known it was coming from the moment she'd said the word Virginia. But knowing a question is coming and being ready to answer it are different things, and Opal wasn't ready. Not because Elizabeth would judge her. She was increasingly certain Elizabeth wouldn't. But because the truth involved a newspaper advertisement, a stranger named Callahan, and a series of decisions that, spoken aloud in this small bedroom to a girl she'd known for two days, might sound reckless or desperate. And Opal was neither. She had made her choice with prayer and open eyes and the steadiest courage she possessed. But explaining that required a kind of trust she hadn't had time to build.

"I'd rather talk about that another time, if you don't mind," Opal said. She kept her voice gentle because the last thing she wanted was for Elizabeth to feel rebuffed. "I promise you I had good reason for being on that road. I wasn't doing anything wrong. I'm just not quite ready to tell the whole of it yet."

Elizabeth studied her for a moment. Her head tilted to one side, and something moved behind her eyes that was both accepting and quietly amused. The expression of a girl who had spent her life reading the moods of animals and weather and a taciturn older brother and had developed an instinct for when to press and when to wait.

"That's all right," Elizabeth said. "I expect when you're ready, it'll be a good story. And I'm a patient woman." The corner of her mouth curved upward. "Well. Patient enough. Nolan would disagree, but Nolan thinks everyone talks too much, so his opinion on the matter is suspect."

She disappeared through the doorway, and Opal heard her moving in the kitchen. The clank of an iron pot. The soft thud of a stove lid being lifted. Small, purposeful sounds that filled the house with the particular music of a home being tended.

Opal stared at the ceiling while the pain in her leg throbbed its steady, punishing rhythm.

She should tell them. Not everything. Not Richmond in its fullness, not the Bennett name or the inheritance or the man who controlled both. But the rest of it. The mail-order bride situation. If she was going to live under this roof for weeks until her leg healed enough to travel, she owed them at least the shape of the truth.

Why she'd been on that road. Where she'd been going. Who she'd been going to meet.

A prickle of uncertainty rose as she thought about admitting to complete strangers what had brought her here. A refined woman answering a matrimonial advertisement in a newspaper. A Virginia heiress sitting in a boardinghouse in Chicago writing a letter to a stranger because of a feeling she couldn't explain that had pointed her west. What would these people think of her?

She tested that uncertainty against what she'd seen of Elizabeth and found it didn't hold. Elizabeth Ridgeway was not a woman who judged. She was a woman who washed a stranger's hair and grinned at the sound of a hungry stomach and carried difficult news with gentleness and humor in equal measure.

When the time was right, she would be honest. Not today. But soon.

The front door opened again. Nolan's voice carried from the main room, low and brief. He was telling Elizabeth he was leaving now.

"Be safe," Elizabeth called back. "And don't forget the coffee. If you come home without it, I'll be less kind than usual."

Opal heard something that might have been a short breath of laughter from him. Then the door closed. Then she heard the creak of a wagon. The heavy, patient clop of a horse. The sounds moved away from the house, growing smaller and thinner until they dissolved into the quiet. The homestead settled into a stillness so complete that she could hear the stove ticking in the other room and the wind pressing against the log walls outside.

Her thoughts returned to the man in the doorway.

She turned over what she'd observed, examining each piece with careful, attentive curiosity. He was not polished, not practiced, and not performing. There had been no social calculation in how he stood or what he said. No effort to impress, no false modesty, no charm deployed as currency. He was like his house: built for function and solid all the way through. When he'd said, "You needed help," it was the most unadorned act of grace she'd encountered since Mrs. Jennings' hands on her face in the dark kitchen on Franklin Street.

She turned her head toward the small window. The light outside had shifted from the flat blue-gray of early morning into something brighter. Through the glass, she could see a stretch of sky above a ridgeline thick with timber, and beyond that, further and higher, the upper peaks of the mountains. The sight of them took her breath away. They were enormous. White-capped and ancient and so close in the clear air that she could see the individual folds and ridgelines cut into the rock, and so far away that they belonged to a world she couldn't reach.

A month ago she couldn't have found this place on a map.

And here she was with a broken leg and a broken plan. Under two hundred dollars to her name, assuming her money was still pinned inside her petticoat pocket, which reminded her she'd need to ask Elizabeth about the clothing she'd been wearing when they found her. Her pockets, pinned to her underskirts, one holding her remaining banknotes and the other holding her mother's jewelry. She needed to know they were safe.

She should be terrified. Part of her was. The part that had spent two years under Charles Hawthorne's evil thumb knew what it meant to be powerless and understood exactly how vulnerable she was right now.

But another part of her, the part that had written a letter to a stranger, sold her mother's jewelry, and boarded a train into the unknown, felt something else. Something quiet and adventurous and stubbornly present, like a candle flame in a room where the windows won't quite shut. She was alive. She was in pain, yes, a great deal of it, but she was alive and breathing and lying in a clean bed in a warm house where a girl had washed her hair. A man she'd never met had given up his room without being asked.

She closed her eyes.

Lord, I don't understand this place You've brought me to. Not fully. Not yet. I don't understand these people or this country or why I'm lying in this bed instead of arriving in Silver Springs the way I planned. But I'm alive, and I'm grateful, so truly grateful. The girl who washed my hair is kind. And the man who carried me through the rain is riding to find my trunks today because he said he would, and I believe him. I don't know what comes next. I'm here. And for right now, that's enough. Thank You for this journey and for the peace You've placed in my heart even when nothing around me makes sense.

She paused. The prayer sat there, warm and unfinished.

And Lord... help me to be worthy of the kindness Elizabeth and Nolan have shown me. Help me to be honest when the time comes. I'm ready for whatever You have planned for me.

Chapter 16

The wagon rocked along the ruts of the valley road. Nolan kept his eyes on the team and his mind on the work that still waited at home. Behind him in the wagon bed, the woman's belongings shifted with each deep rut. The sound of brass fittings scraping against wood was the only noise besides the team, the wind, and the steady grind of iron-rimmed wheels over hard ground.

The sunlight had thinned to that pale, slanting quality that came an hour before dusk, and the shadows of the surrounding trees stretched long across the road. The world was settling into the particular quiet that preceded a hard frost. By morning the grass would be white and brittle, and the water troughs for his livestock would have a skin of ice that he'd need to break before they could drink.

He'd reported the wreck to Marshal Sutter in town that morning. Told him about Hank Meecham's death and the woman they'd found alive with a broken leg. The marshal had listened without interruption, his face settling into the grim, businesslike expression of a man who'd seen enough frontier accidents to know how quickly the territory could take a life. Nolan had asked that if anyone came looking for the woman, they be sent his way. The marshal had organized men to ride out to the wreck site for Hank's body and the scattered mail. Nolan had stopped at the mercantile for the coffee Elizabeth wanted, then ridden out to meet them.

Hank had deserved better than the end he'd gotten, but the best Nolan could do for him now was see that the marshal handled the recovery with the dignity a man who'd driven the Star Route for years had earned. The rest—the paperwork, the county report, the arrangements—would happen without him.

But his mind wasn't on Hank anymore. It was on the trunks sitting behind him in his wagon and the woman who owned them.

He'd handled them at the wreck site, unstrapping them from the overturned wagon bed with the marshal's help. They were well-built trunks, wood-framed, leather-covered, with brass hardware. Quality that a rancher recognized even if he couldn't name the maker. One trunk had taken weather along the exposed side where the torn canvas had failed to cover it. The leather was darkened there, stained by rain, and the brass fittings were a bit tarnished. The other was in better shape but showed the same marks of hard travel: dents in the corners, scrapes along the edges, the kind of damage that came from being loaded and unloaded from trains and freight wagons and stagecoaches across a thousand miles.

The carpet bag had been wedged against a cracked sideboard when he'd found it. Floral-patterned fabric, clearly Eastern, the kind of thing a woman carried when she traveled through cities and stayed in hotels with carpeted stairs and gaslights in the hallways. It had gotten damp where the rain had found its way through the torn canvas, and the fabric showed water stains along one side. The satchel had been beneath a fold of canvas and was in better condition, though it too had taken some weather.

Brass fittings. Quality leather. Quality fabric. The kind of belongings a woman brought when she came from somewhere with brick streets and parlors and a life that didn't include hauling water from a creek or chopping wood to keep from freezing.

He'd been engaged once to a woman accustomed to finer things. The engagement lasted three months. Catherine was the daughter of a lumber baron, educated, delicate, and accustomed to a world where hands stayed clean and winters were something you watched through glass. Her family had come to Providence Ridge while her father considered expanding his business west. He had spoken of opportunity the way men like him always did, as if the land were waiting to be claimed by money and men with maps.

Nolan had believed he could give Catherine a decent life. That she might see beyond the isolation and the hard work and decide the quiet was worth it. He'd even started planning an addition to the house in his head during those three months, sketching out an extension onto the back of the house to expand the living space in the center of his home and his bedroom which he assumed he would share with his bride. He'd been a fool, making plans in his mind for a woman who was already looking for the door.

Catherine had come to his homestead twice during their engagement.

The second time, she and her parents had stayed for supper. Elizabeth served venison stew and fresh bread, and Catherine had done what a well-bred woman was meant to do. She smiled at the right moments, praised the meal, and asked careful questions that sounded as if she were interested in Nolan's life. Elizabeth had gone quiet that evening, the way she did when she was listening to someone she didn't trust.

Afterward, she lingered on the porch while her parents waited in their carriage, looking out at the valley and the mountains beyond. Nolan had watched her take it in, her gloved hands folded, her posture perfect.

She'd been quiet for a long moment. Then she turned to him and offered the word that had stayed lodged under his ribs ever since.

"Charming."

Not beautiful. Not peaceful. Not honest enough to be called hard. Charming—the word a woman used when she meant quaint. Small. Something to look at once, smile politely, and then return to a life with afternoon tea served in china teacups while sitting in a parlor.

Then she had asked, gently, as if she were discussing curtain fabric, whether he'd reconsidered her father's offer to buy his land and accept the job he had been proposed. Good pay, steady work, a position in the new operation. A chance, she implied, to leave this place behind. He could build them a nice home in town where they could live after they married, where life would be smoother and softer and never require a person to carry water with aching arms.

He told her no. He would never sell his land and had no desire to move into town. His parents had built this homestead with their hands, their faith, and their labor.

A week later, her father's letter arrived via a young boy he had hired in Providence Ridge to deliver it. The letter had explained that Catherine and his wife had returned home because they'd "missed the finer things." He added, almost as an afterthought, that his plans in Providence Ridge were moving forward. A timber operation would open here soon. He had offered a slightly higher price for Nolan's land and extended the offer of a job once again. Nolan could come work for him, manage the operation, earn a handsome salary, and live a life that was much easier than what he currently had.

Catherine's own note was shorter, the ink neat and controlled, as if even her refusal had been trained.

I cannot marry you. I am not built for your lifestyle. Come work for my father, and I will consider your proposal again.

Not come to me. Not let us build a life together. Just step into my world, and I might choose you after all.

There was no explanation beyond the words themselves, and none was needed. She'd seen his life and decided it wasn't enough.

He had been foolish enough to think he could make her happy. He thought she genuinely had liked him and wanted to be his wife. He'd replayed every conversation, every smile, every moment she'd leaned closer to listen to him talk about the horses or the land, and he'd tried to find the seam where the performance ended and the real woman began. He never found it. Maybe there hadn't been one. Maybe everything she'd shown him had been exactly what it appeared to be: a well-mannered woman doing her part in a transaction her father had arranged.

Nolan had learned his lesson. Refined women didn't belong in his world. He was certain that he had basically been blind the entire length of their engagement. He had been so mesmerized by Catherine's beauty at the time and the desire to have a wife, a companion to share his life with, that he missed all the signs as they were: Catherine had played her part and was a pawn in her father's desire to purchase his land. Land full of rich timber that he was absolutely certain her father's greedy hands had wanted.

The road curved, and the homestead came into view: the barn first, then the house, both structures dark against the golden grass. Smoke rose from the chimney in a thin, steady column that leaned slightly south in the wind. The lamplight hadn't been lit yet in the windows, but it would be soon. Elizabeth would be starting supper. The chickens would be settling into their roost. The evening routine would unfold the way it always did, familiar and predictable, and his.

Except it wasn't just his anymore.

There was a woman in his bed. A woman with a Southern voice and hazel eyes and belongings that didn't match this country any better than Catherine's had. And he was bringing her fine trunks and a floral carpetbag to a house she hadn't chosen and a situation she'd leave the moment her leg healed enough to carry her away.

He pulled the wagon up near the front porch and set the brake. Cob shifted in the corral and nickered at the mare, and Boone came around the corner of the barn at a trot, tail swinging, to inspect the wagon the way he inspected everything that arrived on his property. The light was fading fast now; the sky deepening to violet in the east while the western horizon still burned pale gold above the ridge.

The front door opened, and Elizabeth stepped out, wiping her hands on her apron. Her braid had come loose on one side, the way it did when she'd been bending over the cookstove, and there was flour on her left sleeve.

"I'm glad you made it home before dark," she said, and there was relief in her voice that went deeper than the words. She'd been worried. She always worried when he was gone longer than expected, though she'd sooner eat raw flour than admit it. "How was town?

"Fine. Reported the wreck. Marshal's handling Hank's body and the mail." He gestured toward the wagon bed. "Got her things."

Elizabeth moved to the side of the wagon and looked at the trunks, her expression shifting from curiosity to something more thoughtful as she took in the brass fittings and the quality of the leather. "Those are nice," she said, her voice low enough that it wouldn't carry through the walls. "Real nice."

"They took some weather," Nolan said. "One more than the other. The carpetbag and satchel got damp."

Elizabeth reached into the wagon bed and ran her hand along the edge of one trunk. "Bring Opal's carpetbag and satchel inside first," Elizabeth said. "She's awake, and we'll see if she wants her trunks inside the house or if we should store them in the barn."

Nolan gathered the carpetbag and satchel from the wagon bed, tucking one under his arm and carrying the other by its handle.

Elizabeth led the way inside, moving ahead of him through the main room toward the bedroom. The house was warm with the heat from the cookstove, and the air held the rich, savory smell of whatever she'd been cooking. Something with onions and salt pork.

Opal was sitting up, propped against the pillow, and when she saw her carpetbag and satchel, she smiled. It was a real smile, not the polished, careful expression he'd grown accustomed to seeing on well-bred women when they were being gracious. This one started in her eyes and reached her mouth a half second later, as if the relief arrived before the manners could arrange it into something more composed.

"Your trunks are in the wagon. Both are sound. One took some weather along one side where the canvas tore. Your carpetbag and satchel were in the wreckage, partially covered. They got damp," he said as he set the bags on the bed near her.

She reached for the satchel, and he saw the wince that crossed her face when the movement pulled at her injured leg. She opened the satchel and looked inside, her hands moving through the contents with the kind of careful urgency that meant she was searching for something specific.

He watched her face as she searched. The anxiety was plain in the set of her jaw and the quick, focused movements of her fingers. Then her hand stilled, and something in her expression changed. Her shoulders dropped a fraction of an inch, and the tension that had been pulling her features tight released so suddenly that he could see the exact moment the worry left her body. Whatever she'd been looking for, she'd found it.

"Thank you," she said. "My personal documents received only minor damage from getting wet, and for that I'm grateful."

He nodded. "I'll bring the trunks inside if you'd like. Or I can store them in the barn for now and bring them in when you're ready."

"I'd like them inside, if it's not too much trouble," Opal said. "My Bible is in one of them. And some books I brought with me. I'd very much like something to read."

"No trouble," Nolan said, and turned to go.

He made two trips. The first trunk was the heavier of the two, and he carried it through the main room and into the bedroom, angling it through the doorway to keep the brass corners from catching the frame. He set it against the wall near the window, lowering it carefully so the weight didn't drop the last few inches and shake the floor beneath her bed. Then he went back for the second. Elizabeth directed him where to place it, and he followed her instructions without comment, setting the trunk down with the same deliberate care.

When he straightened, Opal was watching him.

She was alert and present in a way she hadn't been before. The fog of pain and willow bark and exhaustion that had softened her features during their previous encounter had lifted, and what remained was a woman looking at him with clear, focused attention. The color in her face had fully returned. Her hazel eyes were bright and steady, with flecks of green and amber that caught the lamplight in a way he hadn't noticed before and wished he hadn't noticed now. Her hair fell over her shoulder in a long braid Elizabeth must've plaited for her, dark and thick against the white cotton of the nightgown.

She was beautiful.

The thought arrived uninvited and unwelcome, and he shoved it aside before it could take root. He'd done the same thing before, noticing a woman's features and letting that noticing become something more, and he knew where that road ended. It ended with a letter in neat handwriting.

"Elizabeth," Opal said, her attention shifting to his sister. "Would you mind searching through my trunks? I'd like my Bible, please. And perhaps a book or two."

Elizabeth moved to the trunk near the window and knelt beside it, working the latches. They opened with a metallic click, and she lifted the lid. Nolan saw the contents from where he stood: clothing, neatly folded and layered with the kind of precision that spoke of a woman who'd been taught to pack properly, each garment placed with care and intention. The fabrics were fine, even from a distance. Cotton and wool in colors that belonged in a life that took place in the city, not a Montana homestead. Elizabeth's hands moved through the top layer, lifting a shawl of soft blue wool and setting it aside, then a folded dress in dark green.

"I found your Bible," Elizabeth said, as she pulled it out. The cover was dark leather, worn smooth at the corners from years of handling, the spine creased in the particular way that came from a book that had been opened thousands of times to the same familiar passages. Even from across the room, Nolan recognized the quality of the Bible. Elizabeth handed it to Opal, who took it with both hands and held it the way a person holds something irreplaceable, her fingers curving around the edges with tenderness.

"This was my father's. It means the world to me," Opal said, her voice catching just enough on the word father's that Nolan heard the loss beneath the composure. She set the Bible on the quilt beside her and smoothed her hand across the cover in a slow, deliberate stroke, as if she were reassuring herself that it was real and solid and here. "I wrapped some books in cloth. There should be several in there. Just whatever you find is fine."

Elizabeth reached in again and pulled out a bundle wrapped in linen. She unwrapped it carefully, revealing three books stacked together, their spines showing titles Nolan couldn't read from where he stood. She held them up. "Will these be okay?"

"Yes, those will be fine."

Elizabeth brought them to the bed and set them beside the Bible. Opal reached for the top book, looking at the cover with a smile.

"I love to read," she said as she looked up at him. "Do you enjoy reading, Mr. Ridgeway?"

The question caught him off guard. Not the question itself, which was simple enough, but the way she asked it. There was genuine curiosity behind the words, the kind that came from a person who cared about the answer rather than one who was making conversation to fill silence.

"When there's time for it," he said.

"And is there time for it?"

"Not often."

She nodded, her expression thoughtful, and for a moment he thought that was the end of it. Then she said, "If you'd like to borrow any of these, you're welcome to them. I'd be happy to share."

"I appreciate it," he said, and the words came out stiffer than he'd intended.

"What sort of books do you enjoy?" she asked. "When you do find the time that is."

"History, mostly. Accounts of the Lewis and Clark Expedition. Anything about the territory."

Her face brightened, and the change was so immediate and so genuine that he didn't know what to think. "I brought a volume of Washington Irving's western writings. Astoria, about the fur trade expedition. If you'd care to read it, it's yours for as long as I'm here."

"That's generous of you," he said. "I should tend the animals."

He turned and left before she could respond, before the warmth in her voice and the brightness in her eyes could settle into any place inside him where it might take hold. Elizabeth's voice followed him from the kitchen, light and unbothered. "Supper will be ready shortly."

He pushed through the front door into the cold, and the relief of it hit him like water. The air was sharp and clean, stripped of the warmth and the smell of cooking and the faint floral scent of a woman's belongings and the sound of a Southern voice asking questions he didn't know how to answer safely.

He moved the wagon to the barn. The last of the daylight barely reached through the open doors, and he worked by feel as much as sight as he unhitched the mare from the wagon. She stood patiently while he loosened the traces and backed her out of the shafts, her breath steaming in the cold air. He led her to her stall and removed the harness, hanging each piece on its peg with the automatic precision of a task he'd done ten thousand times.

The mare lowered her head to the water trough and drank, and Nolan picked up the brush and began working through her coat, loosening the sweat and dirt from the day's work. The rhythm of it settled him: the pull of the brush, the mare's warmth beneath his hands, the familiar smell of hay and horse and leather. This was his world. Solid. Predictable. A world where a man knew what was expected of him and how to meet it. A world where a kind word from a pretty woman didn't send cracks through walls he'd spent two years building.

But his mind wouldn't stay on the work.

It kept circling back to the woman in his house. To the way she'd opened that satchel with careful urgency and the relief that had crossed her face when she'd found her things within. To the books she'd offered to share. To the question she'd asked, Do you enjoy reading?, as though his answer mattered to her. To the way she'd held her father's Bible with both hands, and the way her voice had caught on a single word, and the loss he'd heard in that small, controlled break. She'd lost her father. He understood that kind of loss. He understood what it felt like to hold something that belonged to a person who was gone and feel the absence in the weight of it.

Catherine had asked polite questions too. She'd smiled and complimented and inquired about the ranch and the livestock, and every word had been the kind of thing a woman said when she was being gracious.

But Opal's question hadn't felt like that. It hadn't felt practiced or strategic or designed to fill a silence. It had felt like a woman lying in a strange bed in a strange house, in pain and far from home, reaching for the one thing that was familiar to her: conversation with another person about something that mattered. She'd offered her books the way a person offers a piece of themselves, and the offer had been real.

That was worse, somehow. A polished woman being polished was something he knew how to resist. A genuine woman being genuine was something else entirely.

She was educated, he would guess. Refined. A woman who packed books in her trunk and carried a family Bible from wherever she had come from. A woman who spoke with a Southern accent and had belongings that didn't belong in a place like this. She'd leave. Of course she'd leave. Women like her didn't stay in rough-hewn houses on isolated homesteads where winter meant months of snow and cold and nothing but work to fill the days.

Catherine had left. This woman would too. The moment her leg healed, and the pass reopened, and she had somewhere else to go.

The smart thing, the only sensible thing, was to keep his distance. Tend her injury and provide for her until she recovered enough to move on, because that was the decent thing to do, because a man didn't leave someone to suffer when he had the means to help. But providing for someone and caring about someone were two different things, and the line between them was thinner than he liked.

He hung the brush on its peg and gave the mare a final pat on the shoulder. She swung her head around and nosed his coat pocket where he sometimes kept an apple, and he pushed her muzzle away gently. "Not tonight," he told her, and the sound of his own voice in the quiet barn reminded him of how easily he spoke to animals and how difficult it was to speak to the woman whose hazel eyes had watched him carry her trunks as though the act itself meant something.

He stood in the barn doorway, looking across the yard toward the house. Lamplight glowed in the windows now, warm and amber against the deepening dusk. Elizabeth would've set the table by now. Supper would be ready soon.

He'd have to go back inside. Sit at his table, share a meal with his sister, and pretend that everything was the same as it had been three days ago. Pretend that a sweet, Southern, refined woman wasn't lying in his bed with her father's Bible on the quilt beside her and a voice that made simple questions feel like invitations to a conversation he wasn't brave enough to have.

"Nolan!" Elizabeth's voice carried across the yard, clear and strong. "Supper's ready!"

He pulled the barn doors shut and crossed the yard toward the house. He told himself it would be fine. He'd get through this the way he got through everything: by working, by staying steady, by keeping his hands busy and his mouth shut.

He'd do what needed doing for the woman in his home, and he'd keep his distance while he did it.

It was the only safe course. And Nolan Ridgeway had learned, at considerable cost, that safe was the only course worth taking.

Chapter 17

The warmth of the kitchen wrapped around him the moment he stepped through the door. The smell had thickened since he'd last come through: salt pork and onions and the deep, slow richness of beans that had been on the stove long enough to earn their flavor. The stove radiated a steady, deep heat that pushed against the cold still clinging to him.

Elizabeth stood at the stove with a wooden spoon in one hand and a plate in the other. She turned when the door closed behind him and smiled.

"Here." She held the plate out to him. Beans and salt pork, a thick slice of bread balanced on the rim, a fork laid across the top. "We're eating in the room with Opal tonight. I thought the company would be good for her."

Nolan took the plate.

"She's already got hers," Elizabeth continued, turning back to the stove to fix her own plate. "I brought it in a few minutes ago. Go on in, and I'll be right behind you."

He didn't go in. He stood in the kitchen holding a plate of beans and salt pork and watching his sister ladle food onto her own plate with the efficient movements of a woman who considered the matter closed.

Elizabeth glanced over her shoulder. "Nolan. Go."

"I'm waiting for you."

"I can see that." She set the ladle down and picked up her plate. "Fine. We'll go together, since apparently you need an escort to enter your own bedroom."

He didn't respond to that because there was nothing to say that wouldn't prove her right.

They walked together through the main room toward the bedroom. Lamplight spilled through the doorway in a warm, uneven wash. Opal was propped against the pillows with her plate balanced on a folded quilt across her lap. A second chair had already been brought in, and the room, which had always felt adequate when it held nothing but his bed, his trunk, and his few belongings, now felt considerably smaller.

Elizabeth settled herself into a chair, arranging her plate on her lap. Nolan took the remaining chair. He set his plate on his knees and his hat on the floor beside the chair leg.

"Opal, would you like to say grace or should Nolan?" Elizabeth asked.

"I'd be glad to," Opal said.

She bowed her head, and Nolan bowed his, and Elizabeth followed.

"Lord, we thank You for this meal and for the hands that prepared it with such care. We thank You for your mercy, and for the goodness of people who open their homes to someone in need. We ask Your blessing on this household and on the days ahead. Amen."

"Amen," Elizabeth said.

"Amen," Nolan said.

Nolan did his best to keep his focus on his dinner and avoid eye contact with Opal. The beans were good, seasoned with salt pork and onions and a trace of molasses. The bread was yesterday's, sliced thick and warmed on the stove so it was soft enough to soak up the broth at the bottom of the plate.

"Elizabeth, this is wonderful," Opal said after her first several bites. "How did you learn to cook like this?"

"My mother taught me when I was young. I've been doing it on my own since I was fourteen, so I've had plenty of time to practice." She took a bite of her bread and chewed thoughtfully. "And plenty of time to get it wrong. You should have seen my first attempt at biscuits. Nolan teased me something awful for a week."

"I did not."

"You absolutely did."

"I have to confess," Opal said, "I know almost nothing about cooking. In my family's home, the kitchen was run by our house-keeper. She was extraordinary at what she did, but I never learned from her. I can sew a straight seam. I can balance a household ledger. I can write correspondence that would satisfy the most exacting schoolmaster." She paused, and the honesty in her expression deepened into something that was neither ashamed nor apologetic but simply true. "But I've never made a pot of beans in my life."

Elizabeth set down her fork and stared at Opal with an expression of such pure, unconcealed delight that Nolan recognized it instantly. It was the same face she'd made when their father had brought home the barn cat, as if something she'd wanted for a long time had just walked through the door on its own legs.

"Well," Elizabeth said, and the word carried the weight of a woman who had just been given a project she intended to enjoy thoroughly. "That is going to change."

"I would welcome it," she said.

"I'll teach you everything. Biscuits first, because biscuits are the foundation of everything in my kitchen. Then bread. Then, how to make a simple pot of beans. Then stew, then pie crust, then preserves when the season's right." She ticked each item off with a tap of her fork against the edge of her plate.

"Oh... I would love that so very much," Opal said.

The conversation moved easily after that, carried by Elizabeth's natural warmth and Opal's genuine curiosity. Elizabeth talked about the daily rhythm of the homestead, and Opal listened with an attentiveness that went beyond polite interest. She asked questions. Not the careful, socially calibrated questions of a woman making conversation at a dinner party, but practical ones. What time did the day begin? How did they store food through the winter months? What kind of work filled the hours between morning and evening? Each question built on the last, drawing a picture of a life that was clearly unfamiliar to her, but which she seemed intent on understanding rather than merely hearing about.

Elizabeth answered all of it with enthusiasm, and her answers revealed, without her intending it, the particular quality of her loneliness. She talked the way a person talks who has been holding words inside for a long time and has finally found someone willing to receive them. Not desperately, not with the urgency of someone pouring out a confession, but with the steady, grateful relief of a girl who had been carrying conversations alone for years and suddenly didn't have to.

Nolan ate his supper and let them talk. This was how meals had always worked in this house since his parents had passed. Elizabeth talked. Nolan ate. The arrangement suited them both, and it had suited them for years.

Opal turned to him. "Nolan... the horse that you rode while you carried me here from the wreckage. What's his name?"

The question was directed at him, and the politeness of ignoring it wasn't available without being rude.

"Cob," he said.

"Is he yours?"

"Raised him from a foal. He's eight years old. Quarter horse cross, out of a mare my father bred from range stock."

She waited, her attention steady, as if she trusted that there was more coming and she was willing to be patient until it arrived.

"He's a good horse," Nolan said. "Steady in bad weather. Doesn't spook at things that send most horses sideways. I've ridden him through thunderstorms, through river crossings running fast enough to pull a man off a saddle, and through brush thick enough to tear the coat off your back. He goes where I point him and does what I ask." He paused. "He's the best horse I've ever sat on . My father would have said the same."

Across the room, Elizabeth had gone still. He'd said more in the last thirty seconds about Cob than he typically said about any subject in the course of an entire meal.

He picked up his bread and took a bite, which gave his mouth something to do besides talk.

"He sounds remarkable," Opal said. "I don't remember the ride here from the wreckage at all. Everything is so jumbled from that day. The last thing I remember is hitting the ground and then darkness. I've had a few things flash through my mind the past day... but I'm not sure if those flashes were real or if my mind is playing tricks on me." She looked at him with an expression that was quiet and direct and stripped of every social veneer. "I am indebted to you and your sister. Thank you for saving me."

He nodded. "We did what anyone would have done. Cob did the hard work... he carried us both through the storm and got us home safely."

"Then please give Cob my regards."

"Will do," he said as he ducked his head and resumed eating.

The conversation settled after that into an easier rhythm between Opal and Elizabeth.

"You mentioned before that you're from Richmond," Elizabeth said, tucking one leg beneath her in the chair. "I've been thinking about that ever since you told me. Tell me what it's like there?"

Opal tilted her head, considering the question with the careful attention of someone who wanted to give it an honest answer rather than a quick one. "Richmond is old and full of rich history. The city has been there for nearly a hundred and fifty years, and you can feel that age in the streets and in the buildings. The houses in the better neighborhoods are brick, with columns and iron fences, and gardens. There are shade trees along the avenues that have been growing since before anyone alive can remember, and in the autumn, the maples turn the most extraordinary colors. Gold and crimson and a deep, burnished orange that looks like the entire city has caught fire."

Elizabeth leaned forward. "It sounds beautiful."

"It is. Or it was, to me." Opal paused, and something in her expression shifted, settling into fondness. "There's a river that runs through the city, the James River, wide and so beautiful. My mother painted it once, a watercolor from a spot along the bank where we used to walk on Sunday afternoons after church. She captured the light on the water so perfectly that I kept the painting hanging in my bedroom for years." She smoothed the edge of the quilt across her lap. "Richmond is a city that cares very much about how things appear. About propriety and social standing and who your family is and how long they've been there. It can be a very gracious place if you fit inside its expectations."

Nolan heard the careful way she framed that last sentence and filed it away without comment.

"And you had a pleasant home there?" Elizabeth asked.

"I did. My parents' home was comfortable and warm and so lovely. My father was a businessman, a textile manufacturer, and my mother was active in church charities and community work. They were good people." The simplicity of the statement carried a depth of feeling that needed no elaboration. "We had a housekeeper, Mrs. Jennings, who had been with us since before I was born. She ran the household with an efficiency that bordered on military precision, and she made the best ginger cake I've ever tasted in my life."

Elizabeth smiled at that. "What about school?"

"I attended a ladies' academy. Literature, composition, needlework, French, and music, though I was better at reading and writing than I ever was at the piano. My mother tried very hard not to wince during my recitals." A faint, self-deprecating humor crossed Opal's face. "She was kind about it, but I could always tell."

Elizabeth laughed, and the sound was bright and unguarded in the small room. "I can't play a single instrument. Nolan tried to teach me the harmonica once when I was twelve, and it sounded so awful that even the dog left the front porch and hid in the barn."

"I don't recall owning a harmonica," Nolan said.

"It was Uncle Josiah's. You borrowed it."

"I don't recall that either."

"You have a very selective memory when it suits you. But we were very young at the time, so I forgive you." Elizabeth turned back to Opal with the quick, conspiratorial warmth of a girl who had been waiting a long time for someone to share these kinds of exchanges with. "What was it like when you first arrived here in Montana? It must have been so different from everything you knew."

Opal was quiet for a moment, and when she spoke, her voice carried the particular tone of someone revisiting a memory that still had the power to surprise her. "I arrived in Livingston by train, and I remember stepping off onto the platform and just... standing there. The sky was the first thing. In Virginia, the sky is something you see in pieces, between rooftops and tree canopies, and church steeples. It's always framed by something. In Livingston, I stepped off the train, and the sky was everywhere. And the mountains were right there, enormous and snow-touched, and I had the strangest feeling that the world had suddenly gotten much, much larger and I had gotten much, much smaller."

Nolan glanced at her. The way she described it wasn't the way most people talked about Montana when they first saw it. Most people said it was big, or wild, or empty, and left it at that. Opal described it as if the landscape had rearranged something inside her, and she was still working out what had shifted.

"Livingston is nothing like Richmond," Opal continued. "Everything was newer, more rustic, built from raw timber, and the streets were hard-packed dirt. The buildings had false fronts to make them look taller than they were. Everyone moved with this tremendous sense of purpose, as though there was never quite enough daylight to get everything done." She looked at Elizabeth. "And the women, they moved differently than the women I'd known. They carried themselves with a kind of practical briskness that I found admirable. They looked like happy women who had work to do and no patience for anything that didn't matter."

"And the air." Opal drew a breath as if tasting the memory of it. "The air in Richmond is thick, especially in summer. Heavy and warm and damp. The air in Livingston was so thin and so clean that it almost hurt to breathe. I could smell pine trees and something mineral... very unique... it was a fresh, earthy scent, something that smelled like open space, if open space had a scent."

The observation was so quietly perceptive, and Nolan watched his sister as she listened to Opal. Elizabeth had never been anywhere but Montana. She'd never left the Territory, never boarded a train, never seen a city with brick houses and shade trees and a river running through it. Everything she knew about the world beyond this valley came from conversations with travelers passing through Providence Ridge, from the occasional newspaper Nolan brought back from town, and from the stories their mother had told about Tennessee before she'd come west with their father.

He wondered, not for the first time, whether the life he'd built for Elizabeth was enough. Whether a girl of eighteen, sharp and warm and hungry for the world the way she was, deserved more than a homestead eight miles from a town that barely qualified as one and a brother who talked less in a week than most men talked in an afternoon. He didn't feel badly about it, exactly. It was the life their parents had built and the one he'd kept standing through sheer stubbornness and hard work. But watching Elizabeth lean toward Opal with that eager, almost reverent attentiveness, he could see the shape of what had been missing. Not a thing he'd failed to provide. A thing that simply couldn't be provided by a brother and a homestead and the same four walls through every season. She needed this. Another voice. Another woman's company. Someone to talk to who talked back with more than grunts and one-word answers over supper.

"Elizabeth," Opal said, "have you ever been on a train?"

Elizabeth shook her head. "I've never been farther than Livingston. Nolan takes the wagon for supply runs when we need things the mercantile in town doesn't carry, and I've gone along with him three times. I've seen the trains at the depot, though. They're magnificent up close. The noise they make is something else."

"The noise is extraordinary," Opal agreed. "The whistle blowing and the sound of metal groaning and wheels finding their rhythm—it's hard to explain. The wheels have this steady, repeating pulse as they cross the joints in the rail, and after a while, it stops being noise and becomes something almost like a heartbeat. The train's heartbeat."

"What did you see from the window?" Elizabeth asked. "What does the country look like between here and Virginia?"

Opal settled more comfortably against the pillows. "Virginia is green," she began. "Rolling hills and farmland and old forests with trees so tall and so close together that the light comes through in slants and patches. Then the Blue Ridge Mountains... but they are very different from what is here in Montana. The train moves through it all so quickly, and the landscape outside the window is so constant that after a little while it feels like the whole world looks the same. Then you cross into the Midwest, and everything changes."

She paused, choosing her words. "The farmland in the Midwest is flat. Not gently rolling the way Virginia is, but truly, deeply flat, as if someone had taken a great hand and pressed the earth smooth. The fields go on and on, wheat and corn in enormous squares that stretch to the horizon, and the horizon itself is just a line where the land meets the sky with nothing in between. No hills, no trees, no buildings. Just land and sky, repeating themselves in every direction until you start to wonder whether the earth and the sky simply ran out of ideas and decided to keep going, anyway."

Elizabeth laughed softly at that. "That sounds terrifying."

"It was a little. I'd never seen a landscape with nothing vertical in it. In Richmond, there's always something between you and the distance: a building or a hill, or a row of trees. On the plains, there's nothing. You can see weather coming from fifty miles away. I watched a thunderstorm build on the horizon for nearly an hour before it reached us, and when it did, the rain hit the train windows so hard it sounded like gravel."

"And then... what else did you see beyond the Midwest?" Elizabeth prompted.

"A vast new landscape like nothing I've ever seen before. The view was amazing. The mountains were amazing. I'd been watching the flat land for so long that I'd almost stopped looking. And then I glanced up from the book I was reading, and there they were. Just... there. Rising out of the plains as if someone had built a wall across the entire western sky. I pressed my face to the glass like a child." She smiled at the memory, and the smile was honest and a little embarrassed. "A woman across the aisle gave me the most peculiar look, and I didn't care at all, because I had never seen anything so enormous in my life. The scale of them... no painting or photograph prepared me for what I saw. They don't sit on the landscape the way hills do. They command it."

Elizabeth laughed at the image of Opal with her face pressed to the train window, and Opal laughed with her, and the sound of two women laughing in his bedroom was so foreign to Nolan's experience that it took him a moment to identify what it was doing to the room. It was making it warmer. Not in temperature, but in something less measurable that he had no proper word for.

"I want to ride a train someday," Elizabeth said, and the words carried the quiet, fierce sincerity of a wish that had been held for a long time and rarely spoken aloud.

"You will," Opal said. "You'll ride one, and you'll see the plains and the farmland and the cities, and you'll come home and tell Nolan all about it, and he'll listen to every word and then say something like, 'Sounds fine.'"

Elizabeth turned to Nolan with a grin that was equal parts affection and accusation. "She's known you for little more than a day, and she already has you figured out."

Nolan took a bite of his bread and said nothing, which proved the point so thoroughly that both women laughed again.

He noticed Opal had cleared her own plate thoroughly. She'd eaten everything Elizabeth had given her. Hunger meant healing. A body that wanted food was a body that was doing its work.

"I've been meaning to ask," Elizabeth said, setting her empty plate on the floor beside her chair. "The trunk that took the water damage. I'd like to go through it with you if you're willing. Any clothing that got damp needs to be pulled out and washed."

"That would be very kind," Opal said. "I didn't want to ask, but I've been worrying about what the water might have reached."

"It's not a problem at all."

Nolan watched Opal as Elizabeth spoke about the trunk, and he saw it then. The shift had been building for the last several minutes, so gradual that only someone who was watching closely would have caught it. Her posture had changed. The alertness that had carried her through the meal, the engaged, upright attentiveness she'd maintained throughout, was softening at the edges. She held herself more carefully now, as if the simple act of sitting propped against the pillows had accumulated a cost that she was trying to manage without announcing it. Her responses to Elizabeth came a beat slower than they had at the beginning of the meal, and there was a tightness around her mouth that hadn't been there half an hour ago. The pain was returning, or it had never left and she'd been overriding it with conversation and willpower, and both were running low.

"Elizabeth," he said.

His sister looked at him.

"Maybe the trunk can wait until tomorrow. Let her rest."

Elizabeth's glance moved from Nolan to Opal and back, and he saw the understanding arrive on her face.

"He's right. You've been sitting up for well over an hour. The trunk will keep until morning."

"I think that might be wise," Opal admitted.

"I'll make you some willow bark tea," Elizabeth said, already rising from her chair. "Tomorrow we'll tackle the trunk," she gathered her plate and Opal's and stacked them neatly.

"Something to look forward to," Opal said, and the faint smile that accompanied the words was thin with exhaustion.

Opal settled back against the pillows with the slow, measured care of someone negotiating with pain, and Nolan stood to leave.

"Mr. Ridgeway… thank you for going out to the wreck site today and for bringing my things back. You didn't have to do that, and I'm grateful."

"You're welcome, Miss Opal," he said, and then he left the room.

In the kitchen, he set his plate beside the washbasin and then he filled the water bucket from the barrel by the back door and set it on the counter for Elizabeth. He started a fire in the fireplace and then carried an armload of firewood from the stack on the porch to the box beside it.

He pulled his bedroll from the shelf where he'd stored it that morning and laid it out on the floor near the fireplace, the same spot he'd slept last night. The floor was hard, but he'd slept on worse.

Elizabeth emerged a few minutes later, and she worked quickly to make a cup of tea for Opal. "Goodnight, Nolan."

"Night, sis."

Eventually the house settled into its nighttime sounds after Elizabeth had given Opal her tea and then retreated to her own room to sleep. Wind pressing against the north wall of the house with a low, steady insistence that promised weather was still building somewhere in the mountains.

From behind his bedroom door, silence. Opal had either fallen asleep or was lying in the dark with her own thoughts, and he had no business wondering which one it was.

Nolan pulled the blanket to his chest, turned onto his side, and closed his eyes.

Sleep, when it finally found him, was a long time coming.

Chapter 18

Opal turned the thin Bible page carefully, smoothing it flat with her fingertips before settling into the next verse. She'd been reading from Isaiah since she'd woken, and the familiar language had wrapped itself around the quiet of the morning the way a well-loved hymn fills a room without crowding it.

The world beyond the bedroom window had changed overnight in a way so complete and so quiet that it seemed less like weather and more like a decision the sky had reached while she slept. The ground was white. The fence posts she could see from this angle wore caps of snow that sat thick and rounded on their flat tops, and the sky above them was a pale blue.

The smell of breakfast being cooked in the kitchen was making Opal's mouth water. She was hungry in a way that felt almost aggressive; her body demanding fuel. Hunger, she was learning, was not polite. Hunger while a body was on the mend was something closer to righteous.

The front door opened with a gust of cold air that she felt even from the bedroom. Boots on the floorboards, heavy and measured, a tread she'd learned to recognize over the past several days.

"Morning, sis."

"You look half-frozen," Elizabeth said. "Come stand by the stove before you sit down."

"I'm all right."

"You're dripping snow on my floor is what you are. How bad is it out there?"

"Four inches, maybe a little more. Still coming down, but it's slowing. The wind shifted north about an hour ago, so it should taper off by midday."

"And the cattle?"

"Rode out to the western herd at first light. They're all accounted for. They've moved themselves down to the lower meadow near the treeline. The creek they're watering from hasn't frozen yet, but the edges are starting to ice up. I'd give it another day, maybe two, before it freezes through."

Opal lay still and listened. She'd been doing this more than she would have admitted to anyone, listening to Nolan talk to Elizabeth through the walls of this house, gathering the shape of his days from the reports he gave his sister at various times of the day. He spoke about his land and his animals with a specificity that revealed something about the man that conversation alone might never have shown her. He knew each herd by its location and habits. He tracked the creek levels and the wind direction, and the movement of his cattle with the quiet attentiveness of someone whose livelihood depended on reading the details correctly. It wasn't boasting. It was simply the language of a man whose world was measured in weather and water and the welfare of things that depended on him.

"Nolan... Opal and I talked about it last night before she fell asleep. She'd like to eat with us at the table this morning, if you'd carry her out."

A pause. "Her leg's only been splinted a few days. Moving her isn't something I want to rush."

"I'm not asking you to take her dancing, Nolan. I'm asking you to carry her twenty feet to the table and set her on the bench. She can stretch her leg out along the length of it and prop it up while she eats. She wants to sit at a table and eat a meal with people instead of balancing a plate on a quilt by herself."

"You talked to her about this?"

"I just told you we did."

"And she thinks she's up to it?"

"She's the one who asked. And I agree with it."

A brief silence. "All right. Let me wash up."

Water poured into a basin. Then his boots crossed the main room toward the bedroom, and his shadow arrived in the doorway a moment before he did.

He filled it the way he always did: tall and broad-shouldered and unhurried. His face was reddened from the cold, a raw flush across his cheekbones that hadn't had time to fade, and his dark hair was damp at the temples where the snow had melted. He'd taken off his buckskin but still wore his heavy wool shirt.

"Morning, Miss Opal."

"Good morning, Nolan."

"Elizabeth tells me you'd like to come to the table."

"If it's not too much trouble."

"No trouble." He stepped into the room and stopped beside the bed, studying the logistics of the task. She could see him calculating the angle, the placement of his arms, how to account for the splint that held her left leg rigid from below the knee to past her ankle.

"I'm going to put one arm behind your back and one under your knees," he said. "I'll be careful with the leg. Tell me if anything hurts."

She nodded and set the Bible on the nightstand. Then she reached up and put her left arm around his neck as he bent down toward her, and she felt the muscles of his shoulder tighten beneath her arm. His right arm slid behind her back, warm and steady, and his left arm came beneath her knees with a gentleness that seemed almost incompatible with the size of his hands. He lifted her in a single, smooth motion that made her weight feel like nothing at all.

She was close to him. Closer than she'd been to any man since hugging her father. The wool of his shirt was rough against her arm. She could feel the warmth of him through the fabric, a living heat entirely different from quilts and cookstoves. His jaw was inches from her temple. He smelled of fresh air and leather and something underneath both that was simply him, warm and particular, the scent of a man who worked outdoors.

He walked carefully through the doorway and into the main room, adjusting his stride so that each step was measured and even, absorbing the motion in his own body so it wouldn't transfer to hers. He held her with a controlled strength that was all the more noticeable for how deliberately it was restrained.

The main room opened around her.

It was smaller than she'd imagined. The main room served as kitchen and dining area, and sitting room all at once, beneath a low ceiling of rough-sawn planks that couldn't have been more than seven feet above the floor. The cookstove dominated the kitchen end, a large cast-iron box on legs with a flat cooking surface and a stovepipe that angled upward through the ceiling, radiating a heat she could feel from across the room. Shelves lined the wall behind it, holding earthenware plates and tin cups and a few pieces of what appeared to be china that sat apart from the rest. Cooking implements hung from nails driven into the exposed wall studs — a cast-iron skillet, a Dutch oven, a ladle. Beneath the shelves, sacks of flour and tins of coffee and dried beans stood in orderly rows, and a dry sink with a zinc-lined basin held a water bucket and a dipper.

The table sat near the center, a handmade thing of rough-hewn timber. A long bench ran along one side, and chairs occupied the other side. A Bible lay open near one end, beside a tin cup.

Beyond the table, at the far end of the room, two rocking chairs and a straight-backed chair faced each other near a small side table that held an oil lamp. A stone fireplace occupied the wall opposite the chairs; its face built from rounded fieldstones in shades of gray and rust, and a low fire burned in its grate. On the mantel, a tintype photograph in a simple frame. Nearby on the wall, a calendar was hanging from a nail.

Nolan set her down on a long bench with the same care he'd used to lift her, lowering her slowly until her weight settled onto the smooth, worn wood. Elizabeth was already there with a folded quilt, which she tucked beneath Opal's splinted leg to cushion and elevate it along the length of the bench.

"Comfortable?" Elizabeth asked.

"Yes. Thank you."

Nolan took his seat across the table. Elizabeth returned to the stove, where the skillet was still popping with rendered fat.

Opal let her eyes wander around the living space. She'd grown up in a home with twelve-foot ceilings and carved molding and wallpaper imported from England. She'd eaten her meals at a mahogany table that seated ten, set with bone china and crystal and silver that the housekeeper polished every Thursday. Every room in the Bennett house had been furnished with taste, maintained with precision, and arranged to communicate something about the people who lived in it.

This room communicated nothing except itself. It was plain and honest and built entirely for the purpose of keeping people alive and warm and fed. There was no ornament that didn't serve a function, and the beauty it possessed came not from what had been added to it but from what had been worn into it. The smooth paths on the floorboards where feet had walked the same routes for years. The dark seasoning on the cast-iron skillet. The soft, curled edges of the Bible's pages. The quilt folded over the rocking chair's arm; its colors faded from washing.

It felt more like a home than the one she'd lived in on Franklin Street had felt in a very long time.

Elizabeth set plates on the table. Ham sliced thick and fried until the edges crisped. Eggs cooked in the ham's rendered fat, their yolks bright and trembling. Biscuits split and stacked on a separate plate, golden brown and steaming. A crock of butter and a small jar of berry preserves that caught the light from the window in a deep, jeweled red.

"I'll say grace," Nolan said.

They bowed their heads.

"Lord, we thank You for this food, for the hands that made it, and for the company at this table. Watch over this household and those in it. Amen."

"Amen," Elizabeth said.

"Amen," Opal said.

She opened her eyes and found Nolan looking at her across the table. It wasn't a lingering look, and it carried no particular expression she could name, but for the space of a single breath their eyes held, and something moved between them that was too quiet and too unformed to be called anything at all. Then his gaze dropped to his plate, and the tips of his ears went a shade darker than the cold had already painted them, and he picked up his fork.

Opal soon discovered that the ham was excellent, salted and cured and fried to the point where the fat had gone translucent and the lean had taken on a deep, caramelized sweetness. The eggs were rich, their yolks breaking in a warm, golden spill that she soaked up with a piece of biscuit. The biscuit itself was tender and flaky and still warm enough to melt the butter she spread across it.

"Elizabeth, these biscuits are extraordinary," she said.

Elizabeth smiled. "I've had a lot of practice. Biscuits were the first thing our mother taught me, and I must have made a thousand batches before I got them right. The trick is keeping the lard cold and not overworking the dough."

"My mother's housekeeper made biscuits every Sunday morning," Opal said. "I remember them being wonderful, but I never once thought to ask her how she did it. I simply ate them and assumed they appeared by some form of domestic magic."

Elizabeth laughed. "That's what biscuits are. Domestic magic. You should hear Nolan when I run out of flour and can't make them. You'd think the world had ended."

Nolan did not confirm or deny this. He ate his breakfast with steady, methodical attention, but there was a softening at the corner of his mouth that suggested he'd heard the accusation and found it not entirely inaccurate.

"The chickens are starting to lay less," Elizabeth said after a few minutes. "We had six eggs this morning. I imagine in a few more days, we'll be lucky to get three or four a day."

"Is there anything to be done about it?" Opal asked.

"Not much. Some people hang a lantern in the coop to give the hens extra light, and I've done that in past years when we could spare the kerosene. It helps a little. But mostly you just eat fewer eggs in winter and make do with what you have. We have plenty of ham and salt pork and beans, and the root cellar is well stocked." She paused and gave Nolan a look that carried a sisterly authority. "Though somebody eats enough for two people from November through March."

"Hard work in the cold burns through a man," Nolan said.

"Speaking of the cold," Opal said, turning toward him, "is your work here much harder when there's snow on the ground?"

He set down his fork. "It's harder in some ways. The cattle need more looking after. In summer, they graze and water themselves and mostly just need to be kept together and moved to fresh grass. In winter, the grass is buried and the creeks freeze, so I'm hauling hay to them every day and break ice so they can drink. That's the heaviest work. A man can spend three or four hours a day just on feeding and watering."

"You haul the hay on the wagon?"

"When the snow's not too deep for it. When it is, I use a sled, or I carry it on Cob's back in bundles. Depends on the herd and how far they are from the barn."

"And the horses?"

"Horses are easier in some respects. They'll paw through snow to get at the grass underneath, which cattle won't do. But they still need supplemental hay and water, and their hooves need checking more often in winter because ice and packed snow can cause problems. The milk cow stays in the barn through the worst of it, and she needs milking twice a day, regardless."

"Every day," Opal said.

"Every day. The animals don't care what day of the week it is, and they don't much care whether a man's tired or sore or would rather stay in bed."

"Interesting. I imagine there are many days when you are completely worn out from all your responsibilities. Elizabeth, tell me more about these preserves... they're delicious. Did you make them yourself?"

Elizabeth told her about the preserves she puts up every year and about the vegetables lining the root cellar shelves, and how the winter supply always looked sufficient in October and considerably less so by February. Nolan mentioned wanting to ride out and check the herd in the south pasture before the snow accumulated further. Opal listened and asked questions and absorbed the rhythms of a life so different from anything she'd known that it sometimes felt as though she'd crossed not merely a continent but a border into an entirely different understanding of what it meant to sustain a household.

She lifted her cup and found it empty.

Nolan was on his feet before she'd set it back down. He went to the stove, brought the percolator to the table, and filled her cup without a word. Then he filled his own, returned the pot to the stove, and sat back down.

"Thank you," she said.

He nodded once and went back to his biscuit.

They finished the meal together with the comfortable, unhurried quality of a table where no one was expected elsewhere, and the warmth of the room conspired to hold people in their chairs a few minutes longer than necessary. For Opal it simply felt good to be sitting in a room surrounded by good people.

"Opal," Elizabeth said as she stood to gather their breakfast plates, "would you like to stay out here with me this morning? I've got mending to do, and the company would be welcome."

The bench was solid enough for the duration of a meal, but the thought of sitting there for hours, her leg stretched out along its length and her back unsupported, presented a challenge her body wasn't ready for. She could feel the effort of sitting upright beginning to accumulate, a slow tightening in her lower back that reminded her how little she'd been upright unsupported the past few days.

"I would love the company," she said, "but I think the bench might be difficult for very long. Could we sit in the bedroom instead? I could prop myself up against the pillows, and if you bring your mending basket, I could help. I'm a fair hand with a needle, though I should warn you my experience runs more toward embroidery than patching."

Elizabeth brightened. "That would be wonderful. I'll bring everything in."

Nolan stood. "Ready?"

She put her arm around his neck again when he bent to lift her, and he carefully carried her back to the bedroom. He set her down on the bed and helped arrange the pillows behind her back. When she was settled, he straightened.

"Give it another week or so," he said. "You'll be able to tolerate sitting up longer. There's rocking chairs by the fireplace that are comfortable, and once you can manage it, you can sit out there during the day and keep Elizabeth company." The corner of his quirked up into a grin. "She'll talk your ear off, but at least you won't be staring at these four walls."

From the kitchen: "I heard that."

"Thank you," Opal said. "For carrying me. For breakfast. For all of it."

He nodded and turned toward the door.

"Nolan."

He stopped and turned back toward her.

"I noticed something," she said. "While we were eating. Your home has two bedrooms. Yours and Elizabeth's." She paused. "Where have you been sleeping?"

Something in his posture shifted, a faint settling of his shoulders. "I lay a bedroll out by the fireplace. Floor's a little hard, but I've slept on worse."

"Nolan, you've given me your bed. You've been sleeping on the floor."

"It's not a problem."

"It's your home. Your bed. I've taken your room, and you're sleeping on the floor because of me."

"You're sleeping in a bed because you've got a broken leg, and the floor isn't an option for you. The arrangement makes sense, and it's no hardship." His voice carried the same plain, final quality she'd heard him use when reporting on weather. "Don't worry about it, Miss Opal."

He left the room. She heard his boots cross the main room and heard the front door open and close.

Opal pressed her hands flat against the quilt she had pulled up over her lap.

He'd been sleeping on his own floor. It had been two days since he'd carried her out of a wrecked wagon in a rainstorm and brought her here and given her his room and his bed and the care of his sister, and in all of that time, he hadn't mentioned it. Not once. He'd simply done it, the way he did everything, without announcement and without expectation, and if she hadn't noticed the two bedrooms this morning and asked directly, she suspected he would have gone on sleeping on that floor for as many weeks as her recovery required and never said a word.

The men she'd known in Richmond had not been like this. Her father had been generous and good, but even her father's generosity had operated within a world that recognized and rewarded it. And the men who had come after, the men in Hawthorne's circle, those men kept careful accounts. Every courtesy extended was a line in a ledger. Every favor was an investment that expected a return.

Nolan Ridgeway slept on his own floor and said, *"don't worry about it"* with the same inflection another man might use to describe the weather.

She picked up her father's Bible from the nightstand, held it against her chest, and closed her eyes.

Thank You, Lord, for bringing me to good people.

From the kitchen, she heard Elizabeth gathering her mending basket, and the sounds of the morning continued around her, steady and warm.

Chapter 19

Elizabeth walked into the bedroom with a mending basket balanced on her hip and a smile on her face.

The basket was a wide, flat-bottomed thing woven from willow, its sides darkened and smooth from years of handling, and it was full nearly to overflowing. Opal could see the contents as Elizabeth set it on the bed beside her and began sorting through the pile. A pair of thick wool socks with holes worn through the heels. A cotton work shirt missing two buttons from its front placket. One of Elizabeth's own dresses with a tear along the side seam that ran a good four inches. A second shirt, this one heavier flannel, with a frayed collar. And at the bottom, folded neatly, a pair of Nolan's canvas trousers with a hole worn clean through the left knee, the edges of the fabric thinned and soft from use.

"This pile of work never seems to end," Elizabeth said, settling into the straight-backed chair she'd pulled close to the bedside. "I mend through it, get to the bottom of the basket, and by the time I look up there's a fresh stack waiting. Nolan is particularly hard on socks and trousers. I think he kneels on rocks for sport and walks around in his stocking feet outside when I'm not looking. "

Opal smiled. "Where would you like me to start?"

Elizabeth held up the shirt with the missing buttons. "Can you sew a button?"

"I can sew on a button."

"Then you've got a job." She fished two bone buttons from a small tin at the bottom of the basket, along with a needle and a length of heavy thread. "These won't match the others perfectly, but they'll hold. Matching buttons is a luxury we gave up about years ago."

Opal took the shirt and spread it across her lap, examining the placket where the buttons had pulled free. The fabric was worn but clean, laundered so many times that the original blue had faded to a soft, dusty color that was neither blue nor gray but something in between. She threaded the needle on her first attempt and positioned the first button where the thread marks showed its former place.

"I should tell you," Opal said, pushing the needle through the fabric, "my experience with needlework is almost entirely decorative. I can do a French knot and a satin stitch and several varieties of cross-stitch that would look very handsome on a pillow, but I've never darned a sock in my life."

Elizabeth's face lit up. "You can do embroidery stitches? I've learned a few before my mamma passed, and Mrs. Colquitt, who owns the mercantile in town with her husband, has taught me a few as well, but I'd love to learn more. Maybe you could teach me? I can mend a sock in my sleep, but if you asked me to make something pretty…" She paused and grinned. "Well, my knowledge of pretty stitches is pretty small."

"I'd be happy to teach you whatever I know," Opal said. "Though I suspect what you know is considerably more useful than what I know."

"We'll trade, then. I'll teach you to darn and you'll teach me to make pretty flowers out of thread. That seems fair to me." Elizabeth picked up one of the holey socks and turned it inside out over her fist, the worn spot stretched taut across her knuckles. "Watch what I do. This is the easiest mend there is once you learn the trick of it."

Opal set the shirt aside and leaned forward as Elizabeth demonstrated. She worked a blunt-tipped darning needle threaded with wool yarn, running a series of parallel stitches across the hole and slightly beyond its edges into the sound fabric on either side, leaving small loops at the end of each pass rather than pulling the thread tight.

"You're building a foundation," Elizabeth explained, her fingers moving with the easy rhythm of long repetition. "These go one direction first, across the hole like the rungs of a tiny ladder. You want them close together, but not bunched. Then once you've got your ladder built, you turn the sock and weave back through them the other way, over and under, over and under, until you've filled the hole with a little patch of woven thread. It won't be pretty, and it won't feel like the rest of the sock, but it'll hold for another few months, and that's all a sock needs to do."

She handed the sock and the darning needle to Opal.

The wool yarn was coarser than anything Opal had worked with before, rough between her fingers and resistant to the delicate control she was accustomed to exercising over silk floss and fine cotton. The darning needle was thick and blunt, where her embroidery needles had been slender and sharp. She made her first pass across the hole and pulled the yarn too taut, puckering the fabric around the edges.

"Looser," Elizabeth said. "You want a little slack in each row. If you pull it tight, the darn will bunch up inside the shoe and give him a blister, and then we'll never hear the end of it."

Opal loosened her tension and tried again. The second row lay better, and by the third she'd found something close to the right feel, though her stitches were uneven compared to Elizabeth's effortless spacing. When she'd laid enough rows to span the hole, she turned the sock as Elizabeth had shown her and began the weaving, threading the needle over and under the foundation rows in alternating passes.

It was tedious work, nothing like the satisfaction of watching a pattern emerge beneath an embroidery needle. There was no beauty in it, no artistry, only the slow, painstaking business of reconstructing something that had worn away. Her fingers, trained for precision but not for this particular kind of precision, fumbled twice, and she had to unpick a row where she'd woven two passes in the same direction.

"You're doing fine," Elizabeth said, glancing over from the dress seam she was repairing. "Better than fine, actually. Your stitches are more even than mine were when I started, and I had my mamma standing over me correcting every pass."

"Your mother taught you?"

"She taught me nearly everything. Mending, cooking, preserving, how to keep a kitchen garden, how to dress a chicken." Elizabeth's needle paused for a moment, held still in the air while the memory passed through her. "She was practical to her bones, my mamma was. She used to say that a woman who couldn't keep her household running with what she had on hand wasn't trying hard enough, and she meant it kindly, not harshly. She just believed in competence the way some people believe in luck."

"She sounds wonderful."

"She was." Elizabeth resumed her stitching with the quiet acceptance of someone who had carried a loss long enough to know its exact weight. "I think about her every time I sit and stitch. She'd be pleased to know I kept up with the mending. She'd be less pleased about the state of Nolan's trousers, but I can only do so much with a man who thinks fences are for climbing over instead of walking around."

They worked in the companionable rhythm that needlework creates between two women, the small sounds of thread pulled through fabric and scissors snipping loose ends filling the spaces between conversation. Outside the window, the snow continued to fall in a light, unhurried descent, and the warmth from the main room's cookstove reached the bedroom in slow, steady waves.

"Elizabeth," Opal said, tying off the last weave of her darning and holding the sock up to examine it, "most of my clothing is in those trunks your brother brought in from the wreck. I packed quite a lot before I left Virginia. Probably more than I'll ever need out here, if I'm being honest with myself." She smoothed the finished darn with her thumb, feeling the bumpy texture of her work. "I've been thinking. I have several dresses that could be altered. Would you let me give you a few? We could take them in or let them out, adjust the hems, whatever's needed to make them fit you properly."

Elizabeth looked up from her sewing. "Oh, I couldn't take your dresses, Opal. You'll need them yourself."

"I have more than I need. Truly. I packed as if I were going to attend a social season, not live in a land such as Montana, and some of them are entirely wrong for the life I'll be living here. They'll sit in a trunk doing nothing. Please, let's rework a few of my dresses for yourself." She met Elizabeth's gaze steadily. "You've been feeding me and caring for me, and I'm lying here in your brother's bed wearing borrowed nightclothes. Let me do this one thing."

Elizabeth's resistance wavered visibly, the way a candle flame leans in a draft before righting itself. "Are you sure? I imagine your dresses must be very fine."

"Some of them are. And they'd look lovely on you." Opal smiled. "Once my leg heals up enough that I can sit up for longer stretches, we'll go through the trunks together. We can sit in those rocking chairs by the fireplace, and you can pick whichever ones you'd like, and we'll alter them to fit. I'm sure between the two of us, we could manage quite well altering a few dresses."

The delight that spread across Elizabeth's face was so unguarded and so complete that Opal felt something catch in her chest, a quick, sweet ache that had nothing to do with pain and everything to do with the simple pleasure of making someone happy.

"I'd love that," Elizabeth said. "I truly would. But only if you're certain you can spare them."

"I'm certain."

"Then yes. And we need to look through that water-damaged trunk today, too, after we finish here. Some of your things may need to be washed before they're ruined, if they aren't already."

"I've been worrying about that," Opal admitted. "I don't know what condition they'll be in."

"We'll see what can be saved. I've rescued worse than wet fabric in my time." Elizabeth bit off a length of thread with her teeth, a gesture so unconscious and practical that it made Opal aware, with a small, interior jolt, of how many of her own habits had been shaped by the expectation that someone was always watching. In Richmond, she'd been taught to use scissors. Always scissors. Biting thread was simply something a lady did not do.

She was beginning to suspect that common and capable were closer cousins than she'd been raised to believe.

Elizabeth reached over and took the finished sock from Opal's lap, turning it right side out and stretching the darned section flat between her hands. She examined it closely, running her fingertip across the weave, testing the tension and the evenness of the rows. "This is good work, Opal. Your first darn and it's solid. The weave's a little tight in the middle, but that'll loosen with washing, and it'll hold. Nolan won't even notice it's there."

Opal looked at the sock in Elizabeth's hands, the small, bumpy patch of rewoven wool where a hole had been, and felt a satisfaction that settled into her chest, warm and heavy and earned. It was a sock. A mended sock, done imperfectly by a beginner's hands, and it would be worn inside a boot by a man who would never think twice about it. It was the smallest possible contribution to this household that had taken her in, fed her, and given her a bed and the steady, uncomplaining company of two people who had no obligation to her beyond basic human kindness.

And yet it mattered to her in a way she hadn't expected. She'd done something with her hands that served someone else's home. Not something decorative, not a pillow or a sampler or a piece of needlework meant to demonstrate her refinement to guests who would admire it from across a parlor. Something useful. Something that would be worn and washed and worn again until it needed mending once more, at which point someone would sit down with a needle and yarn and do the work again, because that was how things were maintained out here. Not by replacing them with something new, but by repairing what you had with whatever you could find and making it last another season.

In Richmond, Opal's value had been measured in drawing rooms. In the things she could display: her manners, her education, her appearance, her father's name, and later, her compliance. She'd been ornamental in a world that prized ornament, and the few times she'd tried to be something more, the effort had been redirected back toward its proper decorative purpose with a firmness she hadn't always recognized as control.

Here, in this small bedroom with snow falling past the window and a mending basket between them, she'd darned a sock. And the feeling it gave her, the quiet, grounded sense of having contributed something real to a household that needed real things, was more satisfying than any compliment she'd ever received in a ballroom.

"Shall I try the trousers next?" she asked.

Elizabeth laughed. "Let's not get ahead of ourselves. The trousers need a proper patch, and that's a different skill entirely. Here." She handed Opal the second shirt, the flannel one with the frayed collar. "See if you can turn that collar so the worn edge is folded under. I'll show you how."

Opal took the shirt, and Elizabeth leaned close to demonstrate the technique.

The morning continued in this way: the two of them bent over their work while the snow fell quietly outside and the smell of the cookstove's banked coals drifted through the open doorway. They talked about fabric and stitches, about the mercantile in town where Elizabeth bought her thread and the bolts of calico that came in twice a year on the freight wagon. Elizabeth described the process of making her own dresses from patterns cut out of newspaper, and Opal told her about the dressmaker on Grace Street in Richmond who'd made her gowns, a tiny Frenchwoman with silver-rimmed spectacles and opinions about sleeves that she held with the conviction of a preacher discussing Scripture.

Elizabeth asked what kind of dresses Opal had brought, and Opal described a few of them, watching Elizabeth's face cycle through expressions of wonder and delight and something very close to hunger at the mention of velvet trim and covered buttons. Opal made a mental note to insist that Elizabeth deserved the prettiest of the dresses she could spare, the ones with the details that would make Elizabeth's eyes go wide, because this girl who mended socks and bit her thread with her teeth and wore the same few dresses in rotation deserved something beautiful, and Opal had beautiful things she could give.

The mending basket slowly emptied as the morning wore on. Buttons were reattached, seams were closed, the frayed collar was turned under and stitched down flat. Elizabeth finished patching a spot on the elbow of one of Nolan's shirts with a square of fabric cut from an old flour sack, and Opal watched the efficiency of her hands and thought about how many hundreds of hours of small, invisible labor were represented in every piece of clothing in this household, every sock and shirt and patched pair of trousers that kept two people dressed and warm through seasons that would have defeated anyone less stubborn or less skilled.

"There," Elizabeth said, folding the last mended piece and stacking it on the chair beside her. "That's the pile done. For today, anyway. It'll be back by next week."

"Thank you for teaching me," Opal said. "I mean that."

"And I thank you for the company." Elizabeth stood and stretched, pressing her hands against the small of her back. "I'm going to put some coffee on and then we should look at that damaged trunk. The longer wet fabric sits folded, the harder it is to save."

"I'll be ready."

Elizabeth paused in the doorway and turned back. "Opal? I'm glad you're here. I know the circumstances aren't what anyone would have chosen, but I'm glad." She said it simply, the way she said everything, without performance or decoration, and then she was gone, her footsteps moving toward the kitchen and the sound of the stove lid being lifted.

Opal sat with the warmth of those words settling into a place she hadn't known was waiting for them. She looked down at her hands resting on the quilt, hands that still bore the softness of a life lived indoors but that had, this morning, done work that mattered to someone, and she folded them together and held still for a moment in the quiet of the room.

Outside, the snow kept falling. Inside, the coffee began to warm on the stove, and the morning held its shape around her like something she was being given permission to keep.

Chapter 20

The barn was warmer than the yard by twenty degrees, and the difference hit him the moment he pulled the door shut behind him. Not warm in the way the house was warm, with its cookstove and its fireplace, but the dense, animal warmth of a building that held living things. The cold outside was sharp and bright and carried the sharp edge of more snow coming, but in here the air was close and still and the sounds were the sounds Nolan knew better than any others: the shuffle of hooves on straw, the rhythmic pull of a horse working at its hay, the low, contented lowing of the cow in her stanchion.

Cob lifted his head as Nolan came down the aisle, ears forward, nostrils working. The buckskin gelding had the easy, unhurried manner of a horse who knew his person's footsteps and didn't need to be alarmed by them.

"Mornin'," Nolan said.

Cob blew once through his nose and went back to his hay.

Nolan started with the water. He checked each bucket in the stalls, dumping and refilling from the barrel he'd filled the night before and hauled in on the small sledge. The bay mare, Nell, had drained hers to the bottom overnight and stood watching him fill it with the air of a woman who'd been waiting and wanted him to know it. The sorrel, a younger horse with more opinions than sense, tried to drink before Nolan had finished pouring and got his muzzle pushed aside for the trouble.

"Wait," Nolan told him.

The sorrel waited. Barely.

He forked fresh hay into each stall from the stack he kept at the barn's near end, pulling from the supply he'd already brought down from the loft. The hay was good this year, cut in late July when the weather had cooperated and dried thoroughly before he'd stacked it. It smelled of summer even now, the ghost of warm grass and long days trapped in the dried stems, and the horses buried their faces in it the moment it hit the manger.

The milk cow came next. Nolan settled the three-legged stool beside her and pressed his forehead against her warm flank as he worked, his hands moving with the steady, rhythmic pull that emptied the udder into the pail. The milk hit the tin in a thin, ringing stream that thickened and deepened as the pail filled. The cow stood patiently and chewed her cud, tolerating him the way she always did, with the bovine indifference of an animal who understood the transaction and found it acceptable.

"Good girl," he said when the last quarter was stripped. He set the pail aside, covered it, and gave her a measure of grain in her feedbox.

He mucked the stalls one by one, forking the soiled straw into the wheelbarrow and replacing it with clean bedding from the pile near the door. It was the kind of work that occupied the body completely and left the mind to go where it wanted, and this morning Nolan's mind went exactly where he'd been trying not to send it since he'd walked out the front door of the house over an hour ago.

He'd carried her.

The thought arrived the way most unwelcome thoughts did: without permission and with no intention of leaving. He'd carried her from the bed to the table and from the table back to the bed, and in the space between those two trips his awareness of Opal Bennett had rearranged itself into something he wasn't prepared to examine.

She'd weighed almost nothing. That was the first thing, the thing his body kept returning to like a tongue to a sore tooth. She was a small woman; he'd known that from the moment he'd pulled her out of the wreckage, but carrying her conscious and carrying her unconscious were two different experiences entirely. When she'd been limp in the rain, the weight of her had been simple physics. She was a body that needed to be moved, and he'd moved her, and the urgency of the situation had crowded out everything else.

This morning had been different. She'd been awake and looking at him with those hazel eyes, and when he'd told her where he'd put his arms, she'd nodded and reached up and put her arm around his neck. She'd held on. Not desperately, not the way a frightened person grabs, but with a deliberate trust that said she believed he wouldn't drop her and didn't need to worry about it. Her fingers had curled against the back of his collar, and the warmth of her hand through the fabric had been a specific, located thing, a point of heat he could still feel if he let himself think about it.

He shouldn't let himself think about it.

He forked a load of dirty straw into the wheelbarrow and pushed it toward the barn door with more force than the task required.

She'd looked at his house. That was the second thing. He'd set her on the bench and stepped back and watched her eyes move across the room, and what he'd seen in her face wasn't what he'd expected to see. He'd watched a very different woman look around his home before. He'd watched Catherine's gaze travel across the same surfaces: the same rough-sawn ceiling, the same handmade table, the same cookstove and earthenware plates and tin cups, and what Catherine's eyes had done was inventory. They'd moved across the room the way a person's eyes move across a list of deficiencies, cataloging what was absent rather than what was present, measuring the distance between what she was accustomed to and what she was being asked to accept.

Opal had looked around that room and smiled.

Not a polite smile. Not the mannered, measured expression of a woman being gracious about difficult circumstances. She'd looked at the stone fireplace and the rocking chairs and the handmade table, and the quilt folded over the chair arm, and her face had opened in a way that he'd only seen happen to people encountering something that genuinely pleased them. She'd studied his house with the interest and warmth of a woman visiting a place she found remarkable, and there'd been nothing in her expression that even faintly resembled Catherine's careful, appraising distance.

He dumped the wheelbarrow outside the back barn door and stood for a moment in the cold, his breath clouding in front of him, the snow falling in a thin, steady curtain that was already beginning to taper as the wind shifted.

He didn't know what to do with this. He didn't know what to do with a woman who looked at his plain, honest house and seemed to find it worth looking at. He didn't know what to do with the way she'd asked about his work over breakfast, not with the surface curiosity of a person making polite conversation but with genuine interest, her questions specific enough that he'd found himself answering at length before he'd realized how much he was talking.

Cob was watching him from the stall with the patient, vaguely judgmental expression the gelding reserved for moments when Nolan was standing still for no productive reason.

"I know," Nolan said. He wheeled the barrow back inside and got back to work.

He checked hooves next, starting with Cob because Cob was the most cooperative and the best model for the younger horses. He worked his way around each foot, cleaning the frog and sole with the pick, checking for cracks in the hoof wall, feeling for heat that would indicate a bruise or abscess. Cob stood like a gentleman for the entire process. Nell required two attempts on the left hind and a firm word. The sorrel required three attempts, a firm word, and a look that communicated exactly how Nolan felt about horses who couldn't stand still for five minutes.

"You could learn something from him," Nolan told the sorrel, nodding toward Cob.

The sorrel looked unrepentant.

His mind, freed again by the routine of the work, circled back to breakfast. Not to Opal this time, but to Elizabeth. He'd watched his sister this morning with the peripheral attention of a man who'd been looking after her for so long that monitoring her mood was as automatic as checking the weather. And what he'd seen had caught at something in him that he'd been filing away for years in the place where he kept the things he couldn't fix.

Elizabeth had been animated. She'd chattered through breakfast with a lightness he hadn't heard in quite some time, talking about the preserves and the chickens and the winter stores, leaning forward across the table to tell Opal about the berry picking and the canning and the root cellar shelves, her hands moving with the particular emphasis she used when she was excited about what she was saying. He'd noticed, between bites of his own breakfast, how Opal listened. She hadn't just been polite about it. She'd asked questions that led Elizabeth deeper into whatever she was describing, the kind of questions that told a person their subject was interesting and their knowledge worth sharing. Elizabeth had expanded under that attention the way a plant leans toward a window, and by the end of the meal she'd been laughing with an ease Nolan hadn't seen in her since before their parents had died.

His sister had been lonely. He'd known it. He'd known it the way he knew most things he couldn't remedy, by acknowledging the fact in the back of his mind and then turning his attention to what he could control. He couldn't give Elizabeth the company she needed. Their days were full of work done separately, his in the barn and the pastures and the timber and hers in the house and the garden and the chicken coop, and when they came together at meals, the conversation between them ran along tracks worn so smooth by repetition that they could have had most of their exchanges in their sleep. He loved his sister completely and would lay down his life for her without a second's hesitation, but he couldn't be what she actually needed, which was another woman. Someone to talk to the way women talked to each other, in that particular register of shared experience and easy intimacy that men couldn't replicate no matter how much they cared.

Opal, sitting at his table this morning with a borrowed nightgown, and a splinted leg and those hazel eyes that seemed to take in everything they landed on, had given Elizabeth something in the space of a single meal that he hadn't been able to provide in four years. And that pleased him. It pleased him more than he'd have admitted to anyone, the knowledge that this small, quiet woman who'd come into their lives through a wrecked hack wagon and a rainstorm was proving to be a kind of unexpected grace.

He finished with the horses and hung the hoof pick back on its nail in the tack room. The barn was settled now; the animals fed and watered and cleaned, the stalls fresh, the milk covered and waiting to be carried to the house. He should bring the milk in. He should check the woodpile. He should ride out to the south pasture and look in on the herd there before the snow picked up again.

Instead, he stood in the aisle and thought about the way Opal had sat on that bench this morning during breakfast.

She'd been uncomfortable. He was certain of it, though she hadn't complained and he kind of sensed she wouldn't have. He'd watched her shift twice during the meal, small adjustments of her weight and her splinted leg that she'd made as unobtrusively as she could, trying to find a position that didn't pull at whatever was hurting her. The bench was flat and hard and offered no support for her back, and her leg had been extended along its length at an angle that forced her to sit with her body slightly twisted toward the table. She'd managed. She'd eaten her breakfast and talked and smiled and never once said she was in pain. But he'd seen it in the way she'd braced her hand against the bench when she thought no one was looking, and in the slight tightening around her eyes when she'd turned her body too quickly.

She couldn't sit on the bench for any length of time, and the bed would drive her mad if she spent another week staring at the same four walls. Elizabeth had mentioned the rocking chairs by the fireplace, and that was the right idea; a rocking chair would support her back and let her sit upright without the strain the bench demanded. But the splinted leg would need to be elevated, propped on something at the right height to keep it level and take the weight off her knee.

He could build a stool. Low enough that her leg could rest on it comfortably from a seated position in the rocking chair or even on the bench if she preferred. Wide enough on top that the splint would sit stable without sliding off. Sturdy enough to take the weight without wobbling. Nothing fancy. Four legs, a flat top, maybe a slight dish carved into the surface so the splint wouldn't roll. A couple of hours' worth of work if the wood cooperated.

He walked to the back of the barn where he kept his lumber scraps and building supplies, the same stockpile he'd pulled the splint boards from when he'd set her leg. His eyes wandered over rough-cut pine boards of various widths stacked on edge against the log wall. A few pieces of oak salvaged from a wagon bed that had cracked beyond repair. Short lengths of lodgepole pine, peeled and dried, useful for legs and braces. A small keg of cut nails. A tin of wood screws he'd bought at Colquitt's mercantile last spring.

He selected a wide pine board for the top, measured it by eye against the span of his two hands, and marked it with a pencil stub he kept in the coffee can with his other marking tools. For the legs he chose four pieces of dried lodgepole, straight-grained and sound, each about fourteen inches long. He'd trim them to final length once he had the top shaped and could judge the height needed.

He set up at the workbench near the barn's side wall, a heavy plank table scarred with saw marks and chisel cuts. The hand saw bit into the pine board with the familiar rasping sound that meant the teeth were still sharp, and he worked the cut slowly, following his pencil line with the patient accuracy of a man who'd been cutting wood since he was old enough to hold a saw steady. The board separated cleanly. He smoothed the cut edges with the drawknife, taking long, controlled passes that peeled thin curls of pale wood from the surface and let them fall to the floor in coils.

The legs he shaped with the same drawknife, rounding the square edges into a comfortable taper and cutting a shallow tenon on each end that would seat into holes he'd bore in the underside of the top with the brace and bit. He worked without hurrying, letting his hands find the rhythm they always found when he was making something, that particular pace of careful attention that wasn't fast and wasn't slow but was simply the speed at which good work got done.

There was a satisfaction in building something for a specific person. He'd built some of the furniture in the house: the bench and the bedframes, and the shelves. The bench Opal had sat on this morning was one he'd built three years ago, when the old one split. He'd built it for durability and function.

This stool he was building for a woman with a broken leg and hazel eyes who'd looked at his house this morning as though it were something worth seeing. He didn't examine the feeling that gave him. He simply let it sit in his chest while his hands worked.

He bored the leg holes with the brace and bit, angling each one slightly outward so the legs would splay for stability. He seated the tenons with firm taps of the mallet, testing each joint for snugness before driving a single nail through the side of each to pin it. He flipped the stool upright and set it on the barn floor, pressing down on the top with both hands to test the joints. It held firm, no wobble, no give. He sat on it himself, and the legs took his full weight without complaint, which meant they'd carry Opal's splinted leg without question.

He ran his hand across the top surface and found a rough spot near one edge where the grain had torn slightly against the drawknife. He smoothed it with a scrap of sandstone he kept near the workbench, working the grit across the wood in small circles until the surface was even and wouldn't catch on fabric or skin. He checked the legs for splinters and found one, which he shaved off with his pocketknife.

The finished stool was a plain thing. Four legs, a flat top, no decoration of any kind. It looked like what it was: a piece of furniture built by a man who valued function over ornament and who measured quality by whether something did its job without complaint. It would do its job.

Nolan picked it up in one hand, grabbed the pail of milk in the other, and walked out of the barn.

The snow had nearly stopped. A few last flakes drifted down through air that had gone still and cold and sharp in the way that meant the temperature was dropping now that the clouds were thinning.

As he neared the house, he could hear the sound of his sister laughing.

Chapter 21

Elizabeth had brought two cups in from the kitchen and settled back into her chair beside Opal. The conversation had drifted from needlework to fabric to whether calico or muslin wore better through a Montana winter, a subject on which Elizabeth held strong opinions and Opal held none at all but was content to listen. The mending basket sat empty on the floor, its former contents folded and stacked on the seat of the other straight-backed chair. The bedroom had taken on the particular liveliness that comes from two people occupying a small space for long enough that their presence becomes part of the room's atmosphere, as natural as the quilts on the bed and the Bible on the nightstand.

The front door opened and closed. Elizabeth's head came up, her cup halfway to her mouth.

"That's Nolan." She frowned. "He shouldn't be back yet. He said he was riding out to the south pasture."

Boots crossed the main room, steady and unhurried. Then he was standing in the doorway and in his right hand he carried a small wooden stool.

"Built you something," he said.

He said it the way he said everything, plainly and without ceremony, as though the statement required no further elaboration and the object in his hand was explanation enough. He stepped into the room and set the stool on the floor beside the bed.

"For your leg," he said. "When you're ready to sit in one of the rockers, or one of the other chairs, you can prop the splint on this and take the weight off. It'll work with the bench, too, if you'd rather sit on it."

Opal looked at the stool. It was a simple thing: four legs and a flat top. The surface had been smoothed until it was free of any roughness, and the legs splayed slightly outward in a way that spoke of deliberate craftsmanship rather than accident. There was no decoration on it, no carving, nothing that existed for any reason other than function. It was built the way everything on this homestead was built: to do its job and to last.

"You made this?" she asked, though she already knew the answer.

"I did."

Two words. He stood there with his hands at his sides, his face carrying the same neutral expression he wore when reporting on weather or cattle, as though building a piece of furniture for a woman he'd known for a matter of a couple of days was the most unremarkable thing a person could do with a morning.

"Nolan, thank you," she said. "That's incredibly thoughtful."

He nodded once. "Should be the right height. If it's not, I can cut the legs down."

"I'm sure it's perfect."

He turned to Elizabeth. "I'm gonna bring in firewood so you don't have to step out into the cold and then ride out to the south pasture. More snow is sure to come."

"Be careful," Elizabeth said. "We'll see you at supper."

He left. The front door opened and closed again, and then the sound of firewood being moved on the front porch. The door opened again and closed. Opal heard the firewood being stacked in the box she'd noticed that resided by the fireplace. Then the front door opened and closed again, the muffled sound of his boots on the porch, and then nothing.

Opal looked at the stool for a long moment. She reached down and ran her fingertips across the top, feeling the smooth grain of the wood where he'd sanded it even. The surface was warm to the touch, or perhaps that was only her imagination investing the object with a quality it didn't possess. It didn't matter. What mattered was that this man had built her a piece of furniture because he'd thought it would help her. He hadn't asked whether she wanted it. He hadn't mentioned he was going to do it. He'd simply observed a problem, solved it with his hands, and delivered the result with a few words of explanation and no expectation of anything in return.

This was how Nolan Ridgeway communicated. She was beginning to understand it now more and more: the grammar of a man who spoke through what he did rather than what he said. The bed she slept in was his, given without announcement. The floor he slept on was his choice, made without complaint. And now this stool.

She pulled her hand back from the wood and folded both hands in her lap.

"He's never done that before," Elizabeth said.

Opal looked up. Elizabeth was watching her with an expression that held something more complicated than surprise, a kind of quiet recognition, the look of a woman seeing something she'd been waiting to see for a long time.

"Done what?"

"Built something for someone." Elizabeth paused, as though choosing her words with unusual care. "He builds for the homestead. He builds for the ranch. Furniture, fences, gates, shelves—whatever needs building, he builds it because it needs to be built and there's no one else to do it. But he's never..." She trailed off and then started again. "He doesn't build things for people. He builds things for a purpose. That stool isn't for the house, Opal. He built it for you."

The distinction landed in a place Opal hadn't known was listening. She looked at the stool again, at the plain pine surface and the splayed legs and the careful, unadorned craftsmanship of a man who measured quality by whether something did what it was supposed to do, and she felt the weight of what Elizabeth was telling her settle into her understanding of Nolan Ridgeway with a quiet, rearranging force.

"He's a good man," Opal said. It was inadequate, but it was true.

"He's the best man I know. He just doesn't know how to show it with words. Never has. Even when our parents were alive, Nolan was the one who'd fix your broken chair instead of telling you he was sorry it broke. Papa used to say that Nolan's love language was through his actions."

The phrase was so unexpectedly tender that Opal felt her throat tighten.

"From what you've told me so far about your parents... I wish I could have met them. It would be such an honor to meet the people who raised two good human beings."

Elizabeth smiled, the kind of smile that carries loss inside it without being consumed by it. "Mama was the talker. Papa and Nolan are cut from the same cloth. Were. Are." She shook her head slightly at the tangle of tenses that death created. "You know what I mean."

Opal did.

They sat for a moment in the quiet that follows when two people have touched something real and need a breath before continuing. Elizabeth lifted her coffee cup, found it empty, and set it back down. Outside the window, the snow had nearly stopped, and the light coming through the glass had shifted from the flat white of heavy cloud cover to something thinner and brighter as the sky began to clear.

"Opal... can I ask you something personal?"

"Of course."

"Did you have a beau back in Virginia? Before you came west?"

The question was delivered with the guileless curiosity of an eighteen-year-old girl who had been starved for this exact kind of conversation, and Opal recognized in it the hunger of a young woman who had no one to talk to about the things young women wanted to talk about most. There was no calculation in the question, no probing for advantage. Elizabeth simply wanted to know, the way she wanted to know everything about Opal, with an open and uncomplicated interest that made dishonesty feel not just wrong but unnecessary.

"No," Opal said. "I didn't."

"Not ever?"

"There were young men I was introduced to at social gatherings when I was younger, when my parents were alive. Richmond has a social season, parties and dances and dinners where families with eligible sons and daughters bring them together in hopes that something will develop. I attended several of those." She paused, remembering the parlors and the punch bowls and the young men in their pressed suits who'd asked her to dance with the careful formality of boys fulfilling an obligation their mothers had arranged. "But nothing ever came of any of it. I was told I was too quiet and too bookish, which in Richmond's social circles was another way of saying I wasn't lively enough to hold a young man's interest across the length of a waltz."

Elizabeth's brow furrowed. "That's ridiculous. You're wonderful company."

Opal smiled. "Thank you, Elizabeth. I think the problem was less about me and more about what Richmond expected a young woman to be. And after my parents passed, I fell into a deep melancholy that lasted the better part of a year. I wasn't attending gatherings or accepting invitations or doing any of the things a woman does when she's open to being courted." She smoothed the quilt across her lap, a small, anchoring gesture. "And after the melancholy lifted, my circumstances changed in ways that made courting impossible. I wasn't in a position to entertain the idea, even if I'd wanted to."

She left it there. The shape of what she'd said was honest without being complete, a doorframe without the room behind it, and she could see Elizabeth registering the boundary with the quiet instinct of a young woman who understood, perhaps from her own losses, that some stories opened only when the person telling them was ready.

"I'm sorry," Elizabeth said. "About your parents. About all of it."

"Thank you." Opal held Elizabeth's gaze and let the sincerity of the girl's sympathy reach her without deflecting it. It was a harder thing to do than it should have been. She'd spent two years deflecting kindness, treating it as currency that would eventually be called in, and learning to receive it simply, as a gift with no strings, was a discipline she was still practicing. "And you, Elizabeth? Have you ever had a beau?"

The color that rose in Elizabeth's cheeks was immediate and thorough, a flush that started at her collar and climbed to her hairline.

"No," she said. "I haven't."

"Never?"

"Never. Not even close." She laughed, but the sound had a rueful edge. "It's hard to have a beau when there's no one around to be one. The nearest families with sons anywhere near my age are in town or miles and miles away. I don't get to town more than once a month when the weather's good, less than that in winter. And when I do go, it's for supplies; there's just not much time for socializing. Nolan and I load the wagon, buy what we need, and come home." She picked at a loose thread on the cuff of her dress, a gesture that betrayed more than her voice did. "I've met a few

young men when we gather for church during warmer months…
mind you, we don't have a formal church building here yet. Usually in the warmer months, one of the families in the community will
host a Sunday gathering if a traveling preacher happens to be in the
area. Sometimes we have no preacher and some of the elders will
simply take turns reading the good book and sharing their wisdom.
I met a nice boy once while at the Hadley ranch, and there are boys
in town who seem decent enough that I've gotten to meet. But
meeting someone at a Sunday service once a month isn't exactly
courting, and none of them has ever shown particular interest, and
I've never had the chance to show any either."

She said it plainly, the way she said most things, without self-pity
or complaint. But Opal heard what lived underneath the plainness,
the longing of a young woman who'd spent her girlhood on a
homestead miles from town with a brother she loved and no one
else, who cooked and cleaned and mended and tended chickens
and put up preserves and did the work of a woman twice her age
without any of the companionship that should have come with it.

"Do you want that?" Opal asked. "A beau? Marriage?"

Elizabeth's face changed. The embarrassment softened into
something more honest, more vulnerable, and Opal saw in her
expression the same cautious hopefulness she recognized in herself
when she let herself think about the future she wanted rather than
the past she'd fled.

"More than almost anything," Elizabeth said. "I want a home
like this one, with a husband and children to fill it. I dream about
a kitchen with more than two people at the table enjoying what
I cook. I want a house full of noise and laughter and children
arguing over who gets the last biscuit." She smiled, and it was the

most unguarded smile Opal had seen from her, wide and wistful and aching with a longing she'd clearly been carrying for years without anyone to share it with. "Lots of children. I want a big family. I want what my parents had before they died: the two of them working side by side and raising us together, and sitting on the porch in the evenings. I remember that so clearly... the love between my parents... it was such a beautiful thing to witness."

"That's a beautiful dream, Elizabeth."

"What about you?" Elizabeth leaned forward, her elbows on her knees, her eyes bright with the particular intensity of a young woman who had finally found someone she could ask. "What do you want? In a marriage, I mean. What matters to you?"

Opal considered the question. It deserved more than a quick answer, and the woman asking it deserved more than a polished one. Elizabeth had given her the truth, raw and unadorned, and Opal owed her the same.

"I want a partnership," she said. "A love built on honesty and respect. I want a man who sees me clearly, who knows who I am and not just what I look like, or what my family name means, or what I can do for his household. Someone who wants me... just for me. I want a marriage where my voice matters. Where I'm consulted, not managed. Where disagreements are settled through conversation and not through someone deciding they know better and overriding what I think."

She paused. She was treading close to the edges of things she wasn't ready to explain, and she could feel the border the way a person feels the edge of a step in the dark.

"I want to be chosen," she said more quietly. "Not acquired. There's a difference, and it matters to me more than I can say. I want to be loved."

Elizabeth was watching her with an attention that was older than her eighteen years, the kind of listening that comes from a girl who'd lost her parents young and learned to hear what people meant beneath what they said.

"That doesn't sound like too much to ask," Elizabeth said.

"It shouldn't be. But in my experience, it has been."

Elizabeth reached across the space between them and took Opal's hand. She held it briefly, firmly, the way one woman holds another's hand when words aren't sufficient and the gesture has to carry what language can't, and then she let go and sat back.

"You'll find it," Elizabeth said. "I believe that. God doesn't bring a person this far to leave them wanting."

Opal felt the sting behind her eyes that preceded tears and blinked them back. Not because she was unwilling to cry in front of Elizabeth, but because the tears, if they came, would carry more truth than she was prepared to explain. The truth that she'd traveled across a continent looking for exactly what Elizabeth had just described. The truth that she'd left everything she'd ever known on the faith that God was leading her toward something better. And the truth, still new and still frightening in its specificity, that the man who'd just walked out of this room carrying sawdust on his sleeves had built her a stool because he'd noticed she was uncomfortable, and the feeling that had given her was closer to what she'd been searching for than anything she'd encountered in twenty-two years of living.

"I hope you find it too," Opal said. "You deserve it, Elizabeth. A husband who sees how remarkable you are. Children who grow up in a home as warm as the one you've made here."

"Wouldn't that be something?" Elizabeth's smile was luminous. "The two of us, with husbands and babies and kitchens full of noise. Maybe we'd even live close enough to visit."

"I'd like that very much."

"We could teach each other's children. You'd teach mine embroidery, and I'd teach yours to darn socks."

Opal laughed, and the sound of it surprised her, the way laughter sometimes does when it rises from a place deeper than amusement. "And make biscuits."

"Goodness, yes. The biscuits are non-negotiable... which reminds me... that may just be what I teach you next."

They laughed together, and the sound filled the small bedroom with a warmth that had nothing to do with the cookstove in the other room and everything to do with two women who'd been lonely in different ways and for different reasons and who had, on a Friday morning in October with snow on the ground and a mending basket sitting empty on the floor, found in each other something they'd both been missing.

Elizabeth had been lonely for companionship. For another woman's voice in a house that held only her brother's silence and the sounds of her own labor. For someone to sit with and talk to about the things that mattered to her, the dreams she carried and the life she hoped was coming, the ordinary, essential conversation that women had shared across kitchen tables and mending baskets for as long as women had existed.

Opal had been lonely for something harder to name. For someone who saw her. Not the heiress, or the orphan, or the ward, or the problem to be managed, but the woman underneath all of those labels, the woman who wanted to be known and valued for nothing more complicated than who she was. She'd found pieces of it with Mrs. Jennings, who'd loved her enough to help her disappear. She'd found pieces of it in the prayers she'd offered on trains and in boarding houses and in a hack wagon that carried her toward a life she couldn't yet see.

And she was finding it here, in this room, with this girl whose hands were rough from work and whose heart was wide enough to welcome a stranger as though she'd been expected all along.

Elizabeth stood and gathered their empty cups. "I'm going to warm up the coffee. And then we really should look at that trunk before the dampness sets in any deeper. Back in a minute."

She left, and Opal sat in the quiet she'd left behind, listening to the sounds of Elizabeth moving in the kitchen, the clink of the percolator lid, the soft scrape of the stove being stoked.

She looked at the stool beside her bed. She reached down and rested her hand on it again, her palm flat against the smooth pine surface, and held it there for a moment, feeling the wood that Nolan Ridgeway had shaped and sanded with his own hands.

From the kitchen, Elizabeth called something cheerful about the coffee being almost ready, and Opal called back that she was looking forward to it, and the morning went on, held together by the small, ordinary sounds of two women making a home of each other's company.

Chapter 22

Nolan had been up since before five, stoking the cookstove until the iron ticked with heat, readying it for Elizabeth to cook on.

He sat at the table with his Bible and a cup of coffee now. Elizabeth was at the stove behind him. The soft scrape of the skillet being set on the cooking surface. The hiss of rendered fat meeting the hot iron.

This was Nolan's time. The only part of the day that belonged entirely to him, the narrow space between waking and the first demand of the homestead, when the coffee was hot and the Bible was open and the world outside hadn't yet required his attention. He read most mornings, though not always for long. Some mornings he managed a full chapter. Others he read three verses before the day pulled him away. Either way, the habit mattered to him. His mother had taught him to start the day in Scripture.

He'd opened to Psalm 37 this morning, drawn to it the way he was sometimes drawn to passages without quite knowing why, his hand finding the page before his mind had settled on a reason.

Trust in the Lord, and do good; so shalt thou dwell in the land, and verily thou shalt be fed.

He read slowly, the way he did everything, giving each verse the same measured attention he gave a fence post or a hoof. The language of the Psalms suited him. David wrote like a man who understood work and weather and the particular loneliness of being responsible for things that depended on him. There was comfort in that, the knowledge that the God who'd watched over a shepherd on a Judean hillside was the same God who watched over a rancher on a Montana homestead, and that the instructions hadn't changed much in the intervening centuries. Trust. Do good. Dwell in the land. Be fed.

Rest in the Lord and wait patiently for him.

He turned the page. The lamp on the table threw a small circle of warm light across the open Bible and the surface of his coffee.

The scream cut through the house like a blade.

It came from the bedroom, sharp and ragged and so saturated with terror that Nolan was on his feet and moving before the sound had finished leaving his ears. His chair scraped backward across the floorboards and he crossed the main room in four strides, his body operating on an instinct that bypassed thought entirely, the same instinct that moved him toward a spooked horse or a downed calf or any living thing that was frightened and needed to be reached.

Elizabeth was right behind him. He heard her grab something from the table as she moved, and when he reached the bedroom doorway she was at his shoulder with the oil lamp held high, its flame throwing unsteady light into the dark room.

Opal was tangled in the quilts. She'd thrashed in her sleep, and the bedding was twisted around her legs and torso in a way that must have been agonizing against the splint. Her face was wet with tears, and her eyes were open but unfocused, staring at something that wasn't in the room, and her breathing came in ragged, shallow pulls that sounded like a person who'd been running.

"Opal," Elizabeth moved past him and set the lamp on the nightstand, then sat on the edge of the bed and took Opal's hand. "Opal, you're safe. You're in our house. It's Elizabeth."

Opal blinked. Her eyes found Elizabeth's face and fixed on it, and Nolan watched the nightmare release her in stages, the wild, unfocused terror narrowing into confusion and then recognition and then the particular expression of a person who realized they'd been screaming and couldn't take it back.

She lifted her free hand and touched her cheek. Found the tears. Wiped them with the heel of her palm in a gesture so self-conscious.

"I'm sorry," she said. Her voice was hoarse and unsteady. "I'm so sorry. It was just a bad memory. From the past. I didn't mean to frighten you."

A bad memory. The words were doing the work of a hundred words, and Nolan knew it. He'd heard men talk about their nightmares with the same careful understatement, offering the smallest possible description of the largest possible pain, and the phrase bad memory told him nothing about what she'd seen in her sleep and everything about the fact that whatever it was had been bad enough to produce the sound he'd just heard.

"Nothing to be sorry for," he said from the doorway. His voice came out low and steady, which was what he'd intended, the same tone he used with frightened animals because it was the only tone he trusted not to make things worse.

Elizabeth had already moved to the pitcher on the nightstand and was pouring water into a cup. She brought it to Opal and held it while Opal drank, her other hand resting on Opal's forearm with a naturalness that spoke of the bond these two women had built in the span of a few days.

Opal drank half the cup, and the color began to return to her face. She was steadier now, her breathing evening out, the panic receding like a tide drawing back from shore. But her eyes were still too bright, and the set of her mouth carried a fragility he hadn't seen from her before, as though the composure she usually wore had been stripped away and what was underneath was thinner than anyone would have guessed.

"Can you help me sit up a bit more?" she asked.

Nolan stepped into the room. He moved to the bedside and reached behind her, sliding his arm between her back and the pillows, and she leaned forward as he adjusted the pillows to prop her higher. The cotton of the nightgown was thin under his arm, and through it he could feel the fine architecture of her shoulder blades and the small, specific warmth of a body that weighed almost nothing and contained, he was beginning to understand, more courage than most men he'd met.

He settled her back against the pillows and stepped away.

"Thank you," she said, and the steadiness was returning to her voice.

Elizabeth studied her for a moment. "Are you hungry? Breakfast is almost ready. Would you like to come eat with us?"

Opal drew a breath and released it slowly. "Yes. I'd like that."

Nolan bent and lifted her the way he'd done before, one arm behind her back and one beneath her knees, careful with the splint, careful with everything. She put her arm around his neck, and he carried her through the doorway and into the main room, and the familiarity of the motion registered in his body with a quiet clarity that he noted and didn't examine. He was developing the muscle memory of her shape. The specific distribution of her weight in his arms. The way she held her injured leg rigid and braced her right hand against his shoulder for balance. The way she smelled, faintly, of clean cotton and the lavender water Elizabeth had used when she'd washed her hair. His body was learning the mechanics of carrying this woman, and the learning felt less like repetition and more like something settling into place.

He set her on the bench and went back to the bedroom for the stool. He brought it to the table and positioned it beneath, then lifted her splinted leg with both hands, gentle and deliberate, and settled it on the flat pine surface.

"Is that all right?" he asked.

"Yes. Thank you."

He sat in his chair across from her. His Bible was still open on the table where he'd left it, and Elizabeth returned to the stove.

Opal's eyes moved to the open Bible. She looked at the page for a moment, then up at him.

"Would you read aloud?" she asked. "If you don't mind. I heard you reading from Isaiah to me. I'm not sure when it was... I was fading in and out. Your voice was..." She paused, searching for the word. "It was a comfort. Perhaps... Matthew 5."

He hadn't known she'd heard that. He'd read to her on the first night, when he'd sat beside the bed and taken first watch so that Elizabeth could get some rest. He'd read because he hadn't known what else to do, and because the sound of Scripture in a quiet room had always seemed to him like a kind of medicine that worked whether the patient was awake or not.

"I don't mind," he said.

He turned to Matthew and found the fifth chapter.

"Blessed are the poor in spirit, for theirs is the kingdom of heaven."

His voice carried the passage the way his hands carried wood, steadily and without embellishment, letting the weight of the material speak for itself. He read through the Beatitudes one by one.

"Blessed are the meek, for they shall inherit the earth."

He glanced up briefly and found Opal listening with her hands folded on the table and her eyes closed, her face carrying an expression he couldn't name but recognized—the look of a person receiving something they'd been hungry for. Elizabeth had paused at the stove, a plate in one hand and a serving spoon in the other, and was watching her brother with the particular tenderness she reserved for moments when she caught him being something other than the blunt, practical man the world saw.

He read on. Through the verses about salt and light, about the law and the prophets, about anger and reconciliation, and the requirements of a heart that sought to be righteous not in letter but in truth.

Elizabeth set plates of food on the table while he read. Ham and eggs and biscuits and coffee, arranged within reach without interrupting the reading, and the image of it, a table being laid while Scripture was spoken, carried a warmth that settled into the room like heat from the stove.

He finished. Closed the Bible gently and set it aside.

"Thank you," Opal said. Her eyes were open now, and they were bright, but not with tears. With something steadier. "That was exactly what I needed this morning."

"Let's say grace," Elizabeth said as she sat down.

Nolan bowed his head. "Lord, we thank You for this food and for this morning and for the peace You offer to those who seek it. Watch over this table and the people at it. Amen."

"Amen," Elizabeth said.

"Amen," Opal said.

They ate. The ham was good, thick-cut and fried crisp, and the eggs were rich.

Several minutes into the meal, Opal set down her fork. "Elizabeth," she said. "I owe you an honest answer to a question you asked me earlier this week. You asked me what brought me to Montana. What I was doing on that wagon traveling toward Silver Springs." She paused. "I told you I'd rather talk about it another time. That I had good reason for being on that road, but I wasn't ready to tell the whole of it yet."

Elizabeth had gone still, her biscuit halfway to her mouth.

"I'm ready now," Opal said.

She looked at Elizabeth, and then at Nolan, and something in her expression settled, as though she'd made a decision that had been building for days, and the relief of finally arriving at it was stronger than the fear of what came next.

"My parents died two years ago," she said. "A stagecoach accident in Virginia. They were traveling to visit family, and the coach overturned on a bridge. They were both killed instantly. My father was Thomas Bennett. He was a textile manufacturer in Richmond. He owned half of a company called Hawthorne and Bennett, and his partner was a man named Charles Hawthorne."

"When my parents died, I was twenty years old and entirely alone. I had no brothers or sisters, no aunts or uncles, no family of any kind nearby. My father's will left me his share of the company, but the inheritance was placed in trust until my twenty-fifth birthday. The executor and trustee of that trust was Charles Hawthorne." She drew a breath. "My father trusted him. He believed Hawthorne was his friend. He named him in the will because he believed Hawthorne would protect me and manage my inheritance honestly if it was ever needed."

Nolan watched her hands. They were resting on the table on either side of her plate, and they were still, deliberately so, held in place by the same composure that kept her voice level and her gaze direct.

"At first, Hawthorne was attentive. He visited the house regularly. He expressed concern for my welfare. He offered guidance on financial matters and household management. It seemed, in the beginning, like the behavior of a man honoring his obligation to his late partner's daughter." She paused. "It wasn't. It took me months to see it, but what Hawthorne was doing, slowly and carefully, was taking control. Not just of the company and the finances, but of me. Of my daily life. Of everything."

Elizabeth had lowered her biscuit to her plate, untouched.

"He controlled my stipend. Every penny I received from my own father's estate passed through Hawthorne's hands, and the amount gradually decreased. He replaced the household servants, one by one, with people who reported to him rather than to me. He reviewed every household expense. He opened my mail. I was living in my parents' home, the home I'd grown up in, and yet it no longer felt like mine. It felt like his. I was a guest in my own house, and my welcome depended on my willingness to cooperate with whatever Hawthorne decided was best for me."

Her voice was steady, but Nolan could hear the effort the steadiness required. This wasn't a story she'd told before. She was choosing each word, laying each piece of the truth down on the table between them with the care of a woman who understood that once these words were spoken they couldn't be taken back.

"What Hawthorne wanted," Opal said, "was for me to marry his son. Edward Hawthorne. The marriage would give the Hawthorne family permanent control of my shares in the company. And it would give him legal authority over me through his son that went beyond what he already held as trustee."

"He wanted to marry you off to keep control of your money?" Elizabeth asked.

"Yes. And the pressure was relentless. It began as social expectation, the kind of gentle suggestion that everyone around me seemed to echo, as though the entire city of Richmond had agreed that Opal Bennett marrying Edward Hawthorne was the sensible, natural, obvious thing to do. Then it became financial. Hawthorne told me my stipend would be reduced to mere pennies if I continued refusing Edward. Then it became something worse."

Opal's hands moved for the first time, a small adjustment of her fingers against the tabletop, as though she were steadying herself against what came next.

"Three years ago, Hawthorne had his own wife committed to an asylum. Adelaide Hawthorne. I'd known her my whole life. She was a quiet woman, gentle, not a woman anyone would have called unstable. But Hawthorne arranged it. A doctor's signature, a concerned husband's testimony, and Adelaide was removed from her own home and placed in an institution. No one in Richmond questioned it. No one objected. The community accepted it with sympathetic nods and moved on, because Charles Hawthorne was a respected man and if he said his wife needed care, then his wife needed care."

The silence in the room had a weight to it now that Nolan could feel pressing against his ribs.

"Hawthorne never said directly that he would do the same to me. He didn't need to. He said only that he'd been observing concerning patterns in my behavior. That my withdrawal from society and my refusal to attend social functions suggested emotional instability. That he would hate to see a similar pattern in someone he cared for so deeply." Her voice didn't break, but it thinned, the way a wire thins under sustained tension. "I understood what he meant. An unmarried woman with no family, no legal standing, no allies, exhibiting signs of what a doctor might be persuaded to call nervous distress. It would take so little. A few quiet conversations. A few papers signed. And Opal Bennett would follow Adelaide

Hawthorne into the kind of care from which women do not return."

Elizabeth's hand had come to her mouth. Her eyes were wide and bright and filled with something that was not merely sympathy but a fierce, protective fury that Nolan recognized because he could feel the same thing building in his own chest, deep and slow and structural, like a foundation being laid.

"I decided to leave," Opal said. "Not to negotiate. Not to wait. Not to appeal to courts or lawyers or anyone in a city where Hawthorne's word carried more weight than mine ever would. I decided to disappear. My housekeeper, Mrs. Jennings, the woman who'd been with our family since before I was born, helped me. She helped me pack what I could carry. On Friday, August 12th, I walked out of that house before dawn and went to the train station and bought my first ticket to freedom."

She stopped. She picked up her coffee cup, drank from it, and set it down again.

"My plan was simple. Get as far from Richmond as I could. Find a city where I could work and live anonymously. Start over." A brief pause. "Then, on the train, I read the newspaper I had purchased. In it, there was an advertisement. A man in Silver Springs, Montana Territory, a Mr. E. Callahan, had placed a notice seeking a wife. The advertisement was thoughtful and sincere, and spoke of faith and partnership and an honest life. I read it several times. I prayed about it. And I felt, through those prayers, a peace so clear and so specific that I trusted it the way I trust very little else in this world."

"You answered a mail-order bride advertisement," Elizabeth said.

"I did. I wrote a letter at a boarding house in Chicago and posted it to the address listed. I didn't include my surname. I didn't include a return address. I simply told him my name was Opal, that I was a Christian woman of good character, and that I was willing to share the life he'd described." She met Elizabeth's eyes. "Then I boarded a train to Montana. I traveled to Livingston by rail, and from Livingston I made my way here. And you know the rest."

"The wreck," Elizabeth said softly.

"The wreck."

The room was very still. Nolan sat with his hands flat on the table on either side of his plate, and inside him two things were happening at once, pulling in opposite directions like a team of horses hitched to different loads.

The first was anger. Not the explosive kind, not the kind that sent a man's fist through a wall or his voice across a room. The kind that settled. The kind that sank into the bedrock of a man's understanding of right and wrong and became part of the foundation. A man had used his legal authority and his social standing to control and coerce a woman who'd been placed in his protection. He'd isolated her. Manipulated her. Replaced her allies with his own people. Threatened her with the same institutional erasure he'd already inflicted on his own wife. And he'd done all of it behind the face of a concerned guardian.

Nolan would likely never meet this Charles Hawthorne. But something settled in him as he listened to Opal speak, something quiet and permanent that arranged itself in his chest the way a keystone arranges itself in an arch, bearing weight it would never set down. He didn't articulate it. He didn't need to. The decision was already made, the same way his decision to pull her from the wreckage had been made, not through deliberation but through the instant, structural recognition that a thing needed to be done and he was the man standing closest to it. Help and protection.

The second thing was more complicated, and it arrived at the end of Opal's story like a stone dropped into the river after the surface had already gone still.

She'd been traveling to marry someone.

She'd answered an advertisement in a newspaper, written a letter to a stranger, and boarded a train bound for a man she'd never met in a town she'd never seen, on nothing but faith and the conviction that God was leading her where she was meant to go. The depth of that trust staggered him. The courage it required to stake everything—her safety, her future, her life—on a peace she'd felt in prayer and a handful of words printed in a newspaper. It was the kind of faith he admired and wasn't certain he possessed, the kind that moved forward into darkness without demanding to see the ground first.

And underneath that admiration, in a place he couldn't quite reach and didn't want to examine, there was something else. There was a man in Silver Springs. A man named Callahan, who'd placed an advertisement and might or might not have received a letter. A man who might, at this very moment, be waiting for a woman who'd never arrived. Or he could have married another by now. Opal had been traveling toward that man's house, that man's table, that man's life. She'd crossed part of a continent for him, or for the possibility of him, and the only reason she was sitting at Nolan's table this morning instead of Callahan's was a rainstorm and a wrecked mail wagon and the particular geography of the place where the accident had happened to occur.

He felt something about that, something sharp and specific that lodged itself beneath his ribs the way Catherine's charm had lodged there two years ago, except this feeling pointed in the opposite direction. Catherine's word had been a wound. This was something else. Something that burned with a low, persistent heat he couldn't name and didn't want to, because naming it would mean admitting that the woman across his table had come to matter to him in a way that had nothing to do with duty and everything to do with the fact that she was sitting in his house, eating his food, wearing his sister's borrowed nightgown, and the thought of her sitting in someone else's house, at someone else's table, produced a reaction in him that no amount of practical thinking could quiet.

He buried it. The way he buried everything. He set it down in the deep place where he kept the things he couldn't afford to feel during daylight hours, and he picked up his coffee cup and drank.

"The pass to Silver Springs," Nolan said after a moment. "It's most likely closed by now. That first snow we had would have been enough to make the upper road dangerous, and the second round of snow would have sealed it. It won't open again until spring."

Opal nodded slowly. "I'd thought as much."

"And the man," Elizabeth said, leaning forward with the intensity of a young woman whose mind was already working three steps ahead. "Mr. Callahan. Would he have received your letter?"

"I don't know," Opal said. "I posted it from Chicago days after I had left Richmond. Whether it arrived before I did, or after, or at all, I have no way of knowing."

"But if he did receive it," Elizabeth pressed, "he'd have been expecting you."

"He'd have been expecting a woman named Opal, traveling from the east, arriving sometime in late September. When no one arrived..." she trailed off. "There's simply no way to know."

"You could send a letter," Elizabeth said. "Explaining what happened? We could post it at the mercantile in town. It would go by the postal route, the long way around, through Livingston and back around the mountains in another direction. It might take weeks, but it would get there eventually... maybe."

Opal was quiet for a moment, then looked directly at Nolan. "I suppose I could. The question is whether I should."

He held her gaze and didn't know how to respond.

"We should eat," Elizabeth said after a moment, looking down at the plates that had gone neglected during the telling. "The food's getting cold."

They continued eating, and the conversation that followed was practical rather than emotional, carried by Elizabeth's instinct for keeping things moving forward when the weight of what had been said threatened to settle the room into silence.

Nolan ate his breakfast, listened, and said very little. The anger about Hawthorne had settled into a permanent place in his understanding of the woman across from him, reshaping everything he'd observed since the moment he'd pulled her from the wreckage. Her composure wasn't merely good breeding. It was armor, forged in a house where showing weakness meant inviting control. Her gratitude wasn't mere politeness. It was the bewildered relief of a woman who'd spent two years in a place where every kindness came with conditions, discovering a household where kindness came free. Her insistence on being useful, on contributing, on never asking for more than she absolutely needed, wasn't merely character. It was survival, the deeply learned habit of a woman who'd been taught that her welcome depended on what she could provide.

He saw her differently now. Not more clearly, because he'd been seeing her clearly from the beginning, but more completely. The picture had been there all along, but whole sections of it had been in shadow, and what she'd told them this morning had moved the light.

She was braver than he'd known. She was more alone than he'd guessed. And the faith that had carried her across half a continent to answer a stranger's advertisement wasn't naive or desperate. It was the hardest, most deliberate kind of trust there was, the kind that steps forward when every reasonable voice says stay where you are.

The meal ended. Elizabeth cleared the plates. Opal sat on the bench with her leg propped on the stool and her hands folded on the table, and the quiet that settled over the room was not empty but full, crowded with questions that none of them had answered and weren't ready to answer, because the answers depended on the weather and the pass and the healing of a broken leg and the unknowable intentions of a man in Silver Springs and on other things, harder things, things that lived in the spaces between what people felt and what they were willing to say.

"I need to see to the horses," he said as he stood and made his way to the front door. He grabbed his buckskin and hat off the nails in the wall and walked out into the frigid cold. He stood there and breathed it in, sharp and clarifying, and looked out at the white that covered his land and the mountains beyond, and he let himself feel, for just a moment, the full pain of everything he'd heard and everything he couldn't say.

Then he put on his hat and walked to the barn.

Chapter 23

The bread dough was alive under her hands, and Opal didn't trust it.

She sat in the ladder-back chair Elizabeth had helped her move to after breakfast; her splinted leg propped on the pine stool Nolan had built, and worked the mass of flour and milk and yeast on the table's floured surface with the uncertain concentration of a woman learning a language she hadn't known existed. Her hands knew needle and thread. They knew ink pens and piano keys and the smooth leather spines of books lined on a shelf. They didn't know bread dough, and the dough seemed aware of this, resisting her efforts with a sticky, formless stubbornness that made her feel as though she were wrestling something that refused to be shaped into anything useful.

"Push with the heel of your palm," Elizabeth said from beside her, demonstrating on her own portion with the ease of long practice. She stood at the table, leaning her weight into the motion, and the dough flattened and folded under her hands with a rhythm that looked effortless and was, Opal was discovering, anything but. "Then fold it back toward you. Push and fold. Push and fold. You'll feel it change."

Opal pushed. The dough stuck to the heel of her palm and came up with her hand when she tried to fold it, trailing a web of sticky strands between her skin and the table.

"More flour?" she asked.

"A pinch. Not too much, or it'll turn tough." Elizabeth dusted a small handful across Opal's section. "There. Try again."

Opal tried again. The push was harder than it looked, particularly from a seated position where she couldn't lean her body weight forward the way Elizabeth did. The muscles in her forearms protested, a soreness that seemed disproportionate to the task. She'd lifted heavier things than this lump of dough. But kneading required a specific, sustained pressure that worked muscles she apparently hadn't known she possessed, and by the time she'd managed a dozen repetitions, her wrists ached and the dough still looked more like a lopsided pile of wet plaster than anything a person would want to eat.

"Is it supposed to look like that?" she asked.

Elizabeth glanced over. A grin broke across her face, quick and bright and entirely unhelpful. "Not exactly."

"What does 'not exactly' mean?"

"It means keep going. It'll come together. The dough knows what it wants to be. You just have to convince it you're serious."

Opal looked down at the misshapen lump beneath her flour-dusted hands. "I'm not entirely certain it believes me."

Elizabeth laughed, the sound warm and easy in the quiet kitchen. "It doesn't yet. That's the point. You have to earn its respect. Like a horse."

"I've never earned a horse's respect either."

"Well," Elizabeth said, still grinning, "you'll have plenty of time to practice both."

Opal pushed and folded. Pushed and folded. The rhythm began to find her after a while, not gracefully but persistently, the way a stumbling walk eventually smooths into something that passes for a stride. The dough resisted, then softened, then resisted again, and she learned to adjust her pressure, to read the tension in the mass under her palms and respond to it rather than fight against it. It was, she realized, not unlike learning to knit a difficult stitch; the initial clumsiness giving way, by small and frustrating degrees, to something approaching competence.

Elizabeth talked while they worked. She talked the way she always did, in a steady, comfortable current that moved from one subject to the next without requiring much response, and Opal had come to understand that this was Elizabeth in her purest form. She filled the silence the way her brother guarded it, instinctively and without effort. She talked about the sourdough starter she kept in a crock on the back of the stove, how their mother had begun it years ago and Elizabeth had maintained it ever since, feeding it flour and water every few days like a pet that required tending. She talked about the time she'd made bread alone, after their parents died, how she'd over-kneaded the dough in frustration until it was dense as a river stone and Nolan had eaten it without a word of complaint.

"He didn't say anything?" Opal asked.

"Not one word. He ate it with butter and looked at me like I'd made the finest bread in Montana Territory." Elizabeth shook her head with affectionate exasperation. "That's Nolan. He'd eat a boot if I served it to him and tell me it was good."

Opal smiled. Something in the image of a younger Nolan eating terrible bread and saying nothing caught in her chest with a tenderness that was becoming harder to set aside.

The dough was changing. She could feel it under her hands, the texture shifting from rough and shaggy to something smoother, more elastic, a surface that pushed back against her palms with a gentle springiness that hadn't been there ten minutes ago. She pressed her thumb into the center and the indentation filled slowly back; the dough rising to meet the shape of where her thumb had been.

"There ya go," Elizabeth said, watching. "That's what you're looking for. That's ready."

Opal looked at the smooth, rounded mass beneath her hands. It wasn't beautiful. It was lopsided and slightly smaller than Elizabeth's, and there was flour all around her on the table, on her borrowed dress and on her left cheek. But the dough was warm and alive, and she'd made it into something that might, with patience and the heat of the oven, become bread.

The satisfaction of it surprised her. She'd embroidered linens that took weeks of painstaking work. She'd composed letters in flawless penmanship on cream stationery. She'd written poetry in her journal and loved the flow of the words that had come so naturally to her. None of those accomplishments had produced quite this feeling, this particular pleasure of having transformed raw ingredients into something that would feed people. It was humbler work than any she'd been trained for, and it mattered more.

"Now we let it rise," Elizabeth said. She covered both portions in separate bowls with clean cloths and set them on the back of the stove where the warmth from the firebox would do its quiet work. "An hour, maybe a bit longer. Then we'll shape it, put it in pans and let them rise again."

She washed her hands in the basin and then dunked a towel in the water and handed it to Opal so she could clean her own as well. Elizabeth refilled the kettle and set it on the stove for tea, and Opal wiped the flour from the table with a damp cloth, working carefully around the edges from her seated position.

Elizabeth brought two cups of tea to the table eventually and sat down across from Opal. She wrapped her hands around her cup and looked at Opal for a moment with an expression that was quieter than her usual brightness, more considered, as though she'd been holding a thought all afternoon and was only now deciding it was time to let it out.

"This morning," she said. "Everything you told us."

She paused for a moment and looked down as if she were hesitant about what she wanted to say next.

"I've been thinking about it," Elizabeth continued. "About all of it. And I keep coming back to the advertisement." She set her teacup down. "What did it say? Do you remember the words? Please tell me if you do… I'm ever so curious."

"I have it," Opal said. "The newspaper. It's in my satchel, and if you'll go get it, I'll let you read it for yourself."

Elizabeth retrieved the leather from beside the bed and brought it to the table. Opal opened it and found the newspaper, folded to the same page it had been folded to since a boardinghouse room in Chicago that already felt like another lifetime. She smoothed it flat on the table and turned it so Elizabeth could read it.

Elizabeth leaned forward and read the advertisement in silence, her lips moving slightly with the words. When she finished, she read it again. Then she looked up at Opal with an expression that held both admiration and something closer to wonder.

"He sounds like a good man," she said.

"He sounds like a man who chose his words carefully," Opal said. "That's what drew me. Every other advertisement on that page described the kind of wife the man wanted. Mr. Callahan described the kind of life he was offering and asked if someone wanted to share it. He didn't list requirements. He extended an invitation."

"And you answered because of that and your faith."

"I did. From Chicago. I sat at a table in a boardinghouse and wrote a letter on stationery I had brought with me." She could see the letter in her mind as clearly as if it were still in front of her, each word chosen with the care of a woman who understood that she was committing her future to nine sentences on a sheet of cream paper. "I wrote, 'Dear Mr. Callahan. My name is Opal. I am a Christian woman, educated and of good character. I have read your advertisement, and I am writing because your words describe a life I believe I could share with earnest willingness and honest labor. I am capable of hard work and eager to learn what I do not yet know. I value faith, honesty, and mutual respect above all else in any partnership, and I would bring those qualities to yours without reservation. I expect to travel from Chicago to St. Paul by rail and from there by the Northern Pacific Railway to Livingston, Montana Territory. From Livingston, I will seek passage to Silver Springs. Weather and connections permitting, I hope to arrive by the end of September. If you have already made other arrangements, I ask only that you leave word at the post office in Silver Springs so that I may know upon arrival. Respectfully yours, Opal."

Elizabeth was quiet for a moment. "No surname."

"No surname. No return address. Nine sentences. I mailed it and walked to a jeweler's shop and sold two pieces of my mother's jewelry so that I had extra funds just in case." Opal touched the edge of the newspaper. "I'd prayed about it for two days. I read his advertisement on the train leaving Virginia and it followed me to Chicago, and I read it again in that boardinghouse room and I prayed and I felt..." She paused, looking for language precise enough to carry the truth of what she'd experienced. "I felt a peace. Not excitement, not certainty in the way the world means certainty, but a quiet, specific peace that I've learned to recognize as the Lord speaking to me. He kept bringing me back to that advertisement. Every time I tried to plan something else, to think about taking a position as a seamstress or a governess, my heart returned to those words. I knew. I can't explain it better than that. I simply knew."

"So you trusted it."

"I trusted it with everything I had, which wasn't much." Opal folded the newspaper along its worn crease and set it on the table between them. "Two trunks of clothes and books, a satchel, a carpetbag, less than two hundred dollars, and a peace I was staking my life on. That was the whole of my resources when I boarded the train to Montana."

Elizabeth was quiet again. She turned her teacup in her hands. "What will you do now?"

The question Opal had been turning over all afternoon. The question she'd carried with her through the bread kneading, through the quiet domestic rhythm of this kitchen, through the complicated hours since she'd sat at this same table and told two people her whole truth and watched it land.

"I don't know. I feel I owe Mr. Callahan something. Not a legal obligation, but a moral one. I told him I was coming. I gave my word, such as it was, in a letter with no surname and no return address. He may have received it. He may not. He may be waiting for me. He may have married someone else. There's no way to know." She drew a breath. "Sending a letter is possible as you suggested this morning. The postal route through Livingston could carry it around to Silver Springs eventually. But the pass is closed for now, and that's the reality I have. By the time my leg has healed and the road opens again in spring, months will have gone by. Whether it would even be worth the expense of traveling to Silver Springs at that point, I can't say."

"And if it's not worth it?" Elizabeth asked. "What then?"

"Then I'll need to find work. When I'm healed and able to move about, I could travel back to Livingston and seek a position. Or even here, in Providence Ridge, if there's work to be had. I can sew. I can teach. I can learn whatever else needs learning." She met Elizabeth's eyes. "For now, I'm fine with where God has put me. That's the truest thing I can say. I prayed my way onto a train in Richmond and across several states, and prayed while I sat beside Hank before we wrecked on a mountain road, and when I opened my eyes, I was here. In this house. With you and your brother.

And I've stopped trying to tell God that the way His plan has unfolded... well, I'm not sure what's next... but I do know I have to have faith. There is a reason and a purpose for my being brought here."

The words were steady, but the feelings beneath them were not. Because the truth Opal couldn't bring herself to say, the truth that pressed against the inside of her ribs with an ache that prayer hadn't eased, was that the idea of leaving this homestead produced something in her that she hadn't expected and she wanted to live every moment fully and cherish them long after she left.

She'd sat at this table that morning and looked directly at Nolan and said, The question is whether I should, and she'd meant it, every word of it. She'd watched his face when she said it, watched the stillness settle over him, and he hadn't responded. He'd held her gaze and hadn't said a word, and she didn't know what that silence meant. She didn't know if it was the silence of a man who wanted something he couldn't say or the silence of a man who had nothing to say.

Both possibilities hurt. One more than the other.

What she knew, what she could hold in her hands and turn over and look at honestly the way she'd looked at the raw bread dough moments ago, was this: she'd been in this house for less than a week. She'd arrived unconscious and broken, and entirely dependent on strangers. And in that short span, Elizabeth Ridgeway had become the closest thing to a sister Opal had ever known, and this simple home had become the closest thing to home she'd felt since the night her parents died.

That was not nothing. That was enormous.

"I'm glad you're here, Opal. I know the circumstances were awful. I know you were headed somewhere else, and you never meant to end up on our doorstep. But I'm glad you did. I'm glad you're here."

Opal's throat tightened. She pressed her hands flat against the table the way she did when she needed to steady herself, and the flour still dusted in the grain of the wood felt fine and soft under her palms.

"I'm glad too," she said. "More than I know how to tell you."

Elizabeth smiled. Then the smile shifted, turning from warm to something sharper, something that carried the unmistakable glint of an eighteen-year-old girl who had arrived at an idea and intended to deliver it whether anyone was prepared for it or not.

"You know," Elizabeth said, leaning back in her chair with studied casualness, "I have a very simple solution to your whole predicament."

Opal looked at her. "Do tell."

Elizabeth's grin widened. "Marry my brother."

The heat rose into Opal's face so fast and so completely that she felt it in her ears. She opened her mouth and nothing came out. She closed it. Opened it again. Her hands, which had been resting on the table, moved to her teacup and then away from it and then to the edge of the table as though they were looking for something to hold on to and couldn't find it.

"Elizabeth—" she managed.

"What? It solves everything. You need a place to stay. He needs a wife. You're already here. You already know he can read Scripture and loves the good Lord, and he can carry you around the house without dropping you. That's more than most brides know about their husbands before the wedding."

"Elizabeth, I—" Opal's cheeks were burning. She could feel the flush spreading down her neck, and she pressed her palms against her face as if she could push it back through sheer force of will. "That's—you can't just—"

"I'm being practical," Elizabeth said, looking supremely pleased with herself. "Someone has to be."

The front door opened.

Nolan stepped inside carrying the milk pail, his coat dusted with a fine layer of snow and his hat pulled low against the cold. He stopped just inside the threshold. His eyes moved from Elizabeth, who was grinning with the particular satisfaction of a young woman who had just detonated something, to Opal, whose face was the color of a ripe apple and whose hands were pressed against her cheeks in a posture that communicated nothing whatsoever except total and absolute mortification.

He stood there for a moment. The milk pail hung from his right hand. A curl of cold air followed him through the door and dissipated into the warmth of the kitchen.

"I have no idea what I just walked into," he said. He set the pail on the bench by the door. "Here's the milk. I'm heading back out to the barn."

He turned, pulled his hat lower, and walked back out into the cold.

The door closed behind him.

Opal and Elizabeth looked at each other across the table. Elizabeth's grin was enormous. Opal's flush hadn't receded a single degree. The silence held for two seconds, three, and then Elizabeth laughed, a bright, helpless burst of it that she tried to muffle behind her hand, and Opal, despite every effort she made to maintain her composure, despite the heat in her cheeks and the chaos in her chest and the fact that she still hadn't produced a coherent response to the most audacious suggestion anyone had ever made to her in her entire life, felt the laughter rising in her own throat and couldn't stop it.

They laughed together. It was the kind of laughter that fed on itself, that calmed for a moment and then surged again when they caught each other's eyes, the kind that left Opal breathless and aching in her ribs and wiping tears from her face. Elizabeth put her forehead on the table and shook with it, and Opal pressed her hand over her mouth and tried to breathe and couldn't, and every time she thought she'd regained control, she saw Nolan's bewildered face and the milk pail and his measured retreat back through the door, and the laughter took her again.

When it finally subsided, leaving them both spent and bright-eyed and breathing in careful, hiccupping pulls, Elizabeth lifted her head from the table and wiped her eyes.

"You didn't say no," she observed.

Opal pressed her lips together. The flush that had nearly faded came roaring back. "I didn't say anything. I... I didn't have a chance."

Elizabeth's expression softened into something gentler, something that was still teasing but held underneath it a sincerity that couldn't be laughed away. "Think about it."

Opal didn't answer. She didn't need to. They both knew she'd been thinking about very little else.

Elizabeth stood and moved to check the dough on the back of the stove, lifting the cloth to peer at the risen mounds beneath. "These are ready to shape," she said, and the shift back to practical matters was graceful enough that Opal recognized it as mercy.

They shaped the loaves together, Elizabeth's hands working with confident, practiced motions while Opal followed her lead, forming her dough into something that approximated the right shape if one was generous about definitions. Elizabeth set the loaves in the greased pans and covered them again, then turned her attention to the soup they would create for dinner.

Opal helped where she could. Elizabeth brought her a cutting board and a small pile of root vegetables from the cellar, carrots, turnips, potatoes, and an onion, and Opal peeled and chopped them slowly and carefully from her seated position, the knife moving in small, deliberate strokes that turned rough roots into ncat, even pieces. It was careful work, the kind of work that occupied the hands and let the mind settle, and she was grateful for it.

Chapter 24

His home had changed, and Nolan wasn't sure when it happened. The walls were the same rough-sawn timber his father and uncle had cut and framed thirty years ago. The fireplace held the same creek stones Samuel Ridgeway had hauled up the bank in a canvas sling, stone by stone, through the better part of a July. The floorboards still creaked in the same places they'd creaked when Nolan was a boy walking to the kitchen in his socks. The north wind still pressed against the same north wall with the same low insistence it had shown every October since before he was born.

Three days had passed since the bread-making incident when Nolan had walked in with the milk pail and walked back out again without learning what he'd interrupted. In those three days, the household had settled into a rhythm that felt less like accommodation and more like something that had always been there, waiting to be discovered beneath the surface of the life he and Elizabeth had been living.

Opal sat at the table for every meal now with her splinted leg propped on the stool. She helped with all the cooking when she could, peeling vegetables and rolling biscuit dough with hands that were learning the work a little better each day. She washed dishes in the basin by balancing her weight on her good leg without complaint.

Nolan noticed these things the way he noticed the weather. Opal Bennett was in front of him at every meal, every evening. Every morning when he came through the door, stamping snow from his boots, ready to eat breakfast, the smell of fresh coffee met him—coffee that she had made. She helped Elizabeth make breakfast every morning as much as she could while leaning on the counter to keep her weight off her bad leg.

He'd stopped being startled by the sound of a third voice in the kitchen. A week and a half ago, the only voice he expected to hear when he opened the front door was Elizabeth's. Now there were two, layered over each other in the easy cadence of women who'd been talking long enough to have developed their own rhythms, their own private references. Their own way of falling silent when they heard his boots on the porch.

He'd stopped noticing it the way a man stops noticing a creek that runs past his house. It was simply there. Part of the landscape.

On this particular evening, the supper dishes had been cleared and washed, and the three of them had migrated from the kitchen table to the fireplace the way they'd begun doing after the evening meal. Elizabeth occupied one of the rocking chairs with her mending in her lap, a pair of Nolan's work trousers draped across her knees and a needle threaded with heavy cotton between her fingers. Nolan sat on a chair he'd pulled closer to the hearth, his legs stretched toward the fire. Opal was in the other rocking chair, the one nearest the lamp, with her splinted leg resting on the footrest he'd built. A quilt was tucked around her waist against the chill that crept along the floor no matter how well the fire burned.

In her hands she held a book, a small cloth-bound volume with a worn spine and gilt lettering that caught the lamplight when she turned it in her hands.

"Elizabeth mentioned she'd like to hear some of it," Opal said, looking across at him with the particular expression she wore when she was about to ask for something and wasn't sure of the answer. "Would you mind if I read aloud for a while?"

"Go ahead," he said.

She opened the book to a place she'd marked with a thin ribbon and began to read.

Her voice was clear and unhurried, the kind of voice that had been trained for parlors and drawing rooms. She read the way a person reads who loves what they're reading, not performing the words but offering them, letting the sentences move at their own pace without rushing toward the next page. The story was something English, a novel with characters whose lives were quieter, the kind of book where nothing much happened on the surface and everything happened underneath, and Nolan followed the thread of it more easily than he'd expected.

Elizabeth's needle moved in steady pulls through the fabric of his trousers. The fire crackled and sent a scatter of sparks up the chimney. Outside, the wind worked its way along the eaves with a sound like breath drawn through a narrow space. Inside Opal's voice filled the room the way lamplight filled it, reaching the walls and the corners and the spaces between things.

Nolan listened. He was aware of the picture the three of them made, the kind of picture a man passing by a window would see and mistake for a family. Two women. A fire. A man listening.

Opal read for the better part of an hour. She paused between chapters to rest her voice, and during those pauses the conversation surfaced briefly, Elizabeth asking a question about a character's motives, Opal answering with a thoughtfulness that suggested she'd considered the same question herself. Nolan offered nothing to these exchanges. He was content to listen, and the contentment itself was notable because contentment was not a thing he associated with evenings. Evenings were the hours after the work was done, the hours he endured until sleep came, necessary but rarely pleasant. Tonight was different, and he was not examining why.

Elizabeth finished the trouser seam, bit the thread, and folded the mending into the basket on the floor. She covered a yawn with the back of her hand.

"I'm turning in," she said. She stood and stretched, her shoulders rolling back with the ease of a woman who'd been sitting too long. "That's a lovely book, Opal. I want to know what happens next, so don't you dare read ahead without me."

"I wouldn't dream of it."

"Good. Goodnight, both of you."

"Night, sis."

"Goodnight, Elizabeth."

Elizabeth disappeared into her bedroom and pulled the door closed behind her.

Opal closed the book and rested it on her lap. The fire had burned down to a bed of coals that glowed orange and white beneath a lattice of charred wood. The lamplight on the side table between them had become the room's primary source of illumination, casting its circle of amber across the quilts and the rockers and the floor between them.

"Your home is beautiful," she said.

Nolan looked at her. Beautiful wasn't a word anyone had used to describe this house. Solid, maybe. Warm on good days. Small, certainly. But beautiful was a word for other things, other places.

"My father built it," he said. "Most of it. Felled the logs from the hillside above the barn and skidded them down with a team of horses. Took him the better part of two years, working between everything else that needed doing."

"He built it alone?"

"Mostly. A neighbor from the next valley helped him raise the ridgepole. Two men can't lift a ridgepole alone, not one that spans a house this size. But the walls, the floor, the roof—that was my father's work, mostly. My uncle Josiah came out from Tennessee to help him for about a month as well."

Nolan watched her as her gaze traveled around the room. "The fireplace," she said. "Those stones."

"Hauled from the creek. My father carried them up the bank in a canvas sling, one or two at a time, and laid them himself. He wasn't a mason by trade, but he'd watched one work and he had a good eye." Nolan looked at the fireplace, at the irregular shapes of river-rounded stone fitted and mortared into something that had held heat for three decades without cracking. "Took him most of a summer just to get enough of the right size and shape. He was particular about it. My mother used to say he chose those stones more carefully than he chose her."

"Opal has told me a lot about your mother; she sounds like she was an amazing woman."

"She was."

"Will you tell me more about her?"

He should have said no. Or he should have offered a sentence, two at most, the kind of answer that acknowledged the question without opening the door behind it. Instead, he told her about Ruth Ridgeway.

He told her that his mother had been a minister's daughter from Kentucky who followed his father west because she believed God had plans for them in the mountains. She'd arrived in Montana Territory with a Bible, a cast-iron skillet, and a conviction that any house with Scripture and a warm stove could be made into a home. He told her that Ruth had taught him to read at this very table, tracing letters in flour on the surface because paper was dear. He told her about the garden his mother had kept, the rows of carrots and turnips and potatoes that she'd tended with the same steady attention she'd given to everything, and how she'd sung hymns while she worked in it.

He told her that Ruth had loved this valley. That she'd stood on the porch in every season and looked at the mountains with an expression that combined reverence and familiarity, the way a person looks at something holy that also happens to be home. He told her that his mother had prayed every night at that table, her hands folded and her voice low, and that the words she'd used were never grand or formal but plain and specific, the prayers of a woman who talked to God the way she talked to her children, with directness and trust and the occasional note of exasperation when the weather or the woodpile or the stubbornness of men refused to cooperate with her plans.

He told her more than he'd told anyone in years. The words came without eloquence, in the plain, careful sentences of a man who measured language the way he measured lumber, cutting to the length required and no more. But there were more of them than he'd expected, and they carried more weight than he'd realized they held. Somewhere in the telling, he stopped being aware of how much he was saying and became aware only of the woman listening.

Opal didn't interrupt. She didn't fill his pauses with words the way people sometimes did when they were uncomfortable with silence or eager to demonstrate their sympathy. She listened the way the valley listened to weather, with a stillness that was not empty but receiving, taking in what was offered and holding it without trying to reshape it into something more comfortable or familiar.

When he finished, the fire had gone quiet. The coals glowed with a deep, steady heat that would last another hour if he didn't add wood, and the lamp had burned lower, its circle of light tightening around them.

"Thank you," she said. "For telling me."

He nodded. "It's late," he said after a moment. "I should get you to bed."

She nodded.

He stood and crossed the space between his bench and her rocking chair. She'd been doing this long enough to know the sequence and leaned forward slightly as he bent to her. His left arm went behind her back, and his right slid beneath her knees, and she reached up and put her arm around his neck.

He lifted her. She weighed so little that the effort of it never announced itself in his muscles, only in his awareness, which sharpened every time he held her.

The lamp threw their combined shadow across the floor in a single shape that moved with them as he carried her into the bedroom. Fifteen steps, maybe fewer, through the main room and across the threshold of the bedroom door, and in each of those steps, the silence between them was full in a way he didn't have a word for. Not the absence of speech. Something closer to the presence of everything speech would have said if either of them had known how to say it.

Her hand rested against the back of his neck. Her fingers were still, and the warmth of them reached through the fabric of his shirt to the skin beneath.

He set her on the bed. Carefully. The way he always did, lowering her so the splinted leg settled without jarring, keeping his arm behind her back until she was steady. She drew her arm from around his neck and folded her hands in her lap.

He straightened. The space between them widened as he stepped back, and the air that replaced her warmth against his chest was cool and thin and carried the particular emptiness of a thing that had been there and then wasn't.

"Goodnight, Opal."

"Goodnight, Nolan."

He pulled the door mostly closed and walked back through the main room. He added two logs to the coals and watched them catch, the dry wood curling with flame at the edges, the fresh heat pushing outward into the room. He positioned them so they'd burn slow and steady through the night, holding the cold at a distance.

The room was quiet, the way rooms are quiet when someone has just left them.

He looked at the rocking chair, the book, the quilt and the footrest, and what he thought, with the plain, unflinching honesty that was the only kind of honesty he knew, was that this house had been his and Elizabeth's alone for four years. He'd never once noticed how much empty space it held until someone came along and filled it.

Chapter 25

Two weeks had passed since the evening Nolan told her about his mother, and in those days the household had settled into rhythms so natural that Opal sometimes forgot she hadn't always been part of them. Mornings began with Elizabeth's knock on the bedroom door, soft and cheerful, followed by the business of getting Opal upright and mobile. She'd learned to swing her good leg off the bed first and stand balanced on it while Elizabeth or Nolan steadied her, one arm around her waist or gripping her elbow, and then she'd hop the short distance from the bedroom to the kitchen. She was faster now. Less hesitant. She'd learned which floorboards gave the best footing and which ones listed slightly underweight, and she navigated them with a confidence that would've seemed impossible weeks ago.

She'd learned the cookstove. That was the accomplishment she carried with a quiet, private pride. The massive cast-iron box that had once intimidated her with its dampers and its moods and its tendency to run hot on the left side and cool on the right had become, through repetition and Elizabeth's patient instruction, something she understood. She could gauge the firebox temperature by holding her hand six inches above the cooking surface. She could adjust the damper to bring the heat up or bank it down without overshooting in either direction. Her bread was consistent now, the loaves rising evenly and baking to a crust that was golden and firm, and her biscuits had progressed from the dense, lopsided objects of her first attempts to something that actually flaked when you pulled them apart and held butter the way biscuits were meant to.

She cooked. She cleaned. She stood at the counter on her good leg with her hip braced against the edge for balance and peeled potatoes and chopped onions and stirred pots while Elizabeth worked beside her, and the kitchen had become their shared territory in a way that felt less like accommodation and more like partnership. They planned the day's meals over morning coffee, and the conversations were practical and warm and occasionally punctuated by laughter when one of them suggested a combination of ingredients that the other deemed either inspired or criminal.

The evenings were the best. She looked forward to them the way she'd once looked forward to the quiet hour before bed when her parents had been alive. Nolan had begun staying inside after supper. He no longer retreated to the barn or to whatever chore he could manufacture to keep himself occupied and absent. He sat with them by the fireplace, sometimes reading from the Bible in that low, unhurried voice of his, sometimes listening while Opal read from her novel, sometimes simply present in the way that a man is present when he has decided that where he is, is where he wants to be.

He'd started making her laugh. That was new, and it undid her a little more each time it happened. His humor was so dry and so buried beneath his usual reserve that she missed it entirely the first few times, only recognizing the joke seconds later when Elizabeth was already shaking with laughter and Nolan's face carried nothing but the faintest suggestion of satisfaction at the corner of his mouth. She'd learned to listen for it now, the slight shift in his tone that signaled something unexpected was coming, and catching it felt like discovering a room in a house she'd thought she already knew.

Tonight the blizzard had them all safely tucked in the house, listening as the storm raged..

Opal had never heard or seen weather like this. She'd experienced storms in Virginia, the heavy summer rains that turned Richmond's streets to rivers and the occasional ice storm that sheathed the trees in glass. But nothing in her experience had prepared her for the sound that a Montana blizzard made against the walls of a house. The wind didn't gust. It pressed, a continuous, unbroken force that leaned against the north side of the house with a weight she could almost feel through the timber, and the sound it produced was not a howl so much as a voice, low and enormous, as though the valley itself were drawing a breath that wouldn't end. Snow drove against the windows in a hiss that rose and fell with the wind's shifting pressure, and the glass rattled in its frames with each surge.

Nolan had done his barn chores early, and when he'd come through the front door, the cold had come with him like a living thing, sharp and immediate, filling the room for the seconds it took him to pull the door shut and latch it. Snow had clung to his coat, hat, and the tops of his boots. His beard had carried a fine dusting of white that made him look older and wilder than usual. He'd stamped his boots and hung his coat and stood by the cookstove for a long moment with his hands extended toward its heat, saying nothing, letting the warmth work its way back into his fingers.

Now the three of them were settled by the fireplace, and the storm outside kept pressing on. The fire burned steady and hot, the logs Nolan had added moments ago throwing good heat, and the oil lamp on the side table cast its circle of light across the two women and the dress spread between them.

Opal held a seam ripper in her right hand and worked it carefully along the stitching of a bodice seam on one of her dresses from Richmond. The dress was a deep blue wool, well-made, with lace at the collar and cuffs and covered buttons running down the front. It was beautiful and entirely useless on a Montana homestead, a garment designed for receiving visitors in a parlor, and Opal had offered it to Elizabeth with the suggestion that the fabric could be reworked into something practical. Elizabeth had protested. Opal had insisted. Elizabeth had protested less convincingly. And now they sat with the dress between them, carefully dismantling it seam by seam, saving the lace and the ribbon and the buttons in a small tin, and discussing what the fabric could become.

"The skirt panels alone could make a proper winter bodice," Elizabeth said, turning a length of the wool over in her hands and examining the weave. "The fabric's heavier than anything I've got. If we cut it right, there's enough for a bodice and sleeves with material left over for a collar."

"Take what you need," Opal said. "I've got several other dresses in that trunk that are just as useless to me here, and I'm glad to put them to good use."

"You're sure? This wool alone would cost more than we spend on supplies in a month."

"I'm sure. I'd rather see it worn than folded in a trunk gathering dust."

Elizabeth smoothed the fabric across her lap with the expression of a woman who was already designing the finished garment in her mind. Opal continued working the seam ripper along the bodice, the small blade catching each stitch and releasing it with a quiet pop that was almost inaudible beneath the wind.

Across the room, Nolan sat in his chair with a book open on his knee.

He wasn't reading it. Opal knew this because she'd glanced over twice in the past ten minutes and both times his eyes had been on the scene in front of him rather than the page beneath his hand. He sat with the book angled toward the lamp as though the light mattered, and he turned a page now and then with the unhurried motion of a man maintaining an appearance he wasn't fully committed to. His attention was on the room. On the fabric and the lamplight and the two women bent over their work with their heads close and their voices low and the particular absorption that comes from shared labor done with care.

She caught him on the third glance. When she looked up, their gazes met across the six feet of fire lit space between them and held for a count of two before he dropped his attention to the book.

He had the most extraordinary eyes. She'd noticed them the first time she'd seen him clearly, standing in the bedroom doorway on the morning Elizabeth had introduced them, but noticing was different from knowing, and she knew them now the way she knew the floorboards and the cookstove and the particular sound the wind made when it found the gap beneath the front door. They were blue, deep and steady, the color of the sky above the mountains on the coldest mornings when the air was so clear it seemed like glass. There was nothing sharp about them. They were quiet eyes, watchful without being guarded now, and when they rested on her, which they did more and more often, she felt the attention the way she felt the fire's warmth, not as something directed at her but as something that simply existed in the space she occupied.

He was handsome. She'd known that for weeks, though she'd been careful about how much room she gave the thought. But tonight, with the firelight catching the angle of his jaw and the lamplight picking out the threads of copper in his beard, she let herself look. He was built the way the homestead was built, solid and strong and made for the work the land required, and there was something in the steadiness of him, in the way he sat in his chair with his legs crossed at the ankle and his shoulders settled against the back of it, that made her feel as though the storm outside were simply weather and not a threat. He made everything feel like that. Safe. Grounded. As though the world beyond these walls could do its worst and the walls would hold because he'd made sure of it.

"Nolan," she said, and his eyes came up from the book immediately. "This storm. How do you manage your work in weather like this?"

He set the book aside. "Depends on how long it lasts."

"What do you mean?"

"A blizzard that blows through in a day is one thing. You hunker down, keep the fires going, and check the stock when the wind lets up enough to see the barn. A blizzard that sets in for three or four days is something else." He leaned forward slightly, his forearms on his knees. "The cattle are the biggest concern. They'll drift with the wind. They'll turn their backs to it and walk, and they'll keep walking until they hit a fence line or a draw or a creek bank, and if they hit something that stops them, they'll pile up against it. If the snow buries them before it's over, they'll die there."

"That happens?"

"It happens. Not often if a man's doing his job, but it happens. The big die-ups back in '81 and '82 killed thousands of head across the territory because the storms came too fast and the ranchers couldn't get to their herds in time. I lost three heads in '82. Cattle that drifted into a coulee during a storm and the snow filled it in over them before I could ride out." His voice carried no drama when he said this. He reported it the way he reported fence posts and feed calculations, as a fact of the life he lived. "So when a storm like this one comes, I've already pushed the herd down to the lower pastures where I can reach them. I'll ride out at first light when the wind drops and check their position, break the ice up in the creek so they can drink, and haul hay out on the sled if the snow's too deep for the wagon."

"Tell me more about the sled."

"Flat-bottomed work sled. Cob pulls it. It rides on top of deep snow where wagon wheels would sink and stick." He glanced toward the window, where the glass was white with driven snow. "The hay's the calculation that matters most. I put up enough last summer to carry the herd through to April if the winter's average.

A hard winter eats into that margin. Every storm like this one means the cattle burn more energy staying warm, which means they need more feed, which means the supply gets shorter faster. By February, I'm counting bales and watching the weather and doing arithmetic in my head every morning before I saddle up."

"And the horses, tell me about them again."

"Horses are smarter about it. They'll paw through snow to get at the grass underneath, which cattle won't do. They still need supplemental hay and water, and their hooves need attention because ice and packed snow can ball up in the frog and cause trouble. But they manage better. The milk cow stays in the barn through the worst of it, and Bessie's not particular about weather as long as she's fed and milked on schedule. She's got opinions about the schedule."

Elizabeth looked up from her fabric. "She does. She'll let you know if you're late."

"How?" Opal asked.

"Lowing," Nolan said. "Loud and persistent. She can keep it up for an hour if she's got a grievance."

Opal smiled. She liked learning things like this. She liked the specificity of it, the practical details that built a picture of what his days actually contained, the weight and scope of the work he carried without complaint and largely without witness. Every conversation like this one added another layer to her understanding of who he was, and each layer made the whole of him more vivid, more real, more impossible to set aside.

She watched him as he talked. The way his hands moved when he described something spatial, the sled's runners, the angle of a coulee where cattle might drift. The way his voice dropped lower when he talked about loss, those three heads buried in snow, and rose slightly when he talked about the work itself, the satisfaction of a full hay shed, a herd accounted for, a winter survived. He loved this life. She could hear it beneath every practical sentence, an affection for the land and the labor that ran so deep it had become indistinguishable from who he was.

Elizabeth watched the conversation with her fabric in her lap and her needle still, and the expression on her face was the one she wore when she was pleased about something and trying not to show it.

The evening wound down the way their evenings did now, by slow and reluctant degrees, the fire burning lower and the lamp burning steadier and the pauses between words growing longer until the silence was more comfortable than the conversation. Elizabeth set aside her sewing and stretched.

"I'm turning in." She kissed Opal on the cheek and squeezed her hand. "Goodnight, you two."

Nolan banked the fire. He laid a large log at the back of the grate where it would burn slowly and hold coals through the night, and he adjusted the damper until the draw was just enough to keep the flame alive without consuming the wood too quickly. Opal watched his hands while he worked, the sureness of them, the way they moved through tasks his body knew by memory.

"Ready?" he asked.

She stood on her good foot, one hand braced on the arm of the rocking chair. He came to her, and she slipped her arm around his waist. His arm settled across her back, his hand gripping her arm just above the elbow to keep her balanced, and she hopped beside him through the main room and across the threshold into the bedroom. His body was warm against her side, solid and close, and his grip was steady without being tight. She could feel the fabric of his shirt beneath her palm where her hand rested against his ribs, and the warmth of his skin beneath the fabric, and the slow, even rhythm of his breathing.

He helped her sit on the edge of the bed and stepped back.

"Thank you," she said. "Goodnight, Nolan."

"Goodnight, Opal. See ya in the mornin'."

He pulled the door partially closed, and she listened to his footsteps cross the main room and heard him spread out his bedroll near the fireplace.

She lay in the dark and listened to the storm. The wind had not eased. It pressed against the house with the same relentless patience it had shown all evening, and the snow hissed against the window glass in a rhythm that rose and fell like breathing. The quilts were heavy and warm around her.

She thought about the evening. The fabric in her hands. The lamplight. The way Nolan's voice had filled the room when he talked about his work, low and unhurried, the voice of a man who trusted what he was saying because he'd lived every word of it. She thought about his eyes meeting hers across the firelight and the way the contact had felt, not startling but steady, a warmth that arrived and stayed.

She thought about Elizabeth's words from weeks ago. Marry my brother. The suggestion that had turned her face the color of a ripe apple and sent her hands searching for something to hold on to. She pressed her palm flat against her sternum now, against the place where the thought of Nolan Ridgeway had taken up residence and showed no sign of departing.

She was attracted to him. The word felt too small for what she meant, too clinical for the particular ache that lived beneath her ribs when he looked at her with those quiet blue eyes or when his hand steadied her waist or when she heard him laugh, that rare, low sound that seemed to surprise him as much as it surprised her. She'd never felt this for anyone. The young men at Richmond's socials had been pleasant enough, polite in their pressed suits with their rehearsed conversation, but none of them had produced anything in her beyond a mild and forgettable interest. None of them had made her aware of herself the way Nolan did, aware of her own skin and her own breath and the exact distance between her body and his in any room they shared.

She didn't know if he felt the same. She knew he watched her. She knew he'd started staying after supper when he used to leave, and she knew his book went unread when she was in the room. But knowing these things was different from understanding them, because Nolan Ridgeway kept his heart behind the same quiet walls he kept everything else, and she couldn't tell whether what she saw in his eyes when he looked at her was the beginning of something or simply the steady kindness of a good man caring for a woman under his roof.

She wanted it to be the beginning. She wanted it with a fierceness that startled her, this woman who'd crossed several states to meet a stranger because a newspaper advertisement had offered her a life of honest partnership. She hadn't known what she was looking for then. She was beginning to know now.

Chapter 26

November had come in quietly. The snow that had fallen in late October hadn't melted. It had settled, packed itself down under its own weight, and then accepted the next snowfall on top of it and the next after that until the valley floor carried a permanent white that made distances harder to judge. The mountains above the homestead had disappeared into the overcast and hadn't fully reappeared in days. The heart of winter had arrived not as an event but as a condition.

Cob's hooves broke through the top crust with each step, dropping four inches into the packed snow beneath, and the empty hay sled dragged behind them with a low rasp that was the only sound in the valley besides the horse's breathing and the creak of cold leather. Nolan sat easy in the saddle, his collar turned up against the wind that came steady and sharp from the northwest, his gloves stiff with cold where he held the reins. The buckskin he wore kept the worst of it off his chest and back, but the cold found the gaps: his wrists between the gloves and the sleeves, his neck above the collar, the bridge of his nose beneath the brim of his hat. He'd been out since dawn, hauling hay to the cattle in the south pasture and breaking ice on the section of creek where they watered.

The ice had been thicker this morning. He'd used an ax to crack through it as he normally did, standing on the bank and swinging down into a surface that had gone from a skin of ice to nearly three inches solid, and the creek beneath it moved slow and dark, reluctant in the cold. The cattle had gathered to drink when the hole opened, their breath rising in clouds around their lowered heads, and he'd counted them while they drank. All accounted for. None drifting, none limping, none showing the pinched flanks that meant they weren't getting enough feed. The hay was holding for now.

He rode Cob through the barn doors and swung down. The barn was warmer than the air outside by enough degrees to feel like mercy. He unsaddled Cob and rubbed him down, working the dried sweat and snow from the buckskin's shoulders and barrel with long, firm strokes. He checked each hoof, picking out the packed snow that had balled in the frogs, and gave the gelding a measure of grain and fresh hay.

The other horses watched from their stalls. The bay mare, Nell, nickered when he passed, and he ran his hand down her neck without stopping. The sorrel stamped once and looked at him with the particular expectation of a young horse who believed that every human visit should involve food.

"You already ate," Nolan told him.

The sorrel did not appear convinced.

He milked Bessie, the familiar rhythm of his hands producing the thin ring of milk against the pail that thickened and deepened as the pail filled. Bessie chewed her cud and tolerated him. When the milking was done, he covered the pail and set it near the door where the cold would keep it until he carried it to the house.

Then he stood in the barn aisle and looked at the workbench.

He'd been thinking about this for three days. Longer, if he was honest, though the idea hadn't taken its final shape until yesterday morning when he'd watched Opal hop from the bedroom doorway to the kitchen table with her hand trailing along the wall for balance. She'd made it. She was strong enough now and stubborn enough that she made most of the short distances in the house under her own power, hopping on her good foot with a concentration on her face that bordered on ferocious. But he'd watched her stumble twice in the past week, catching herself on the counter's edge once and on the back of a chair once, and both times Elizabeth had lunged toward her and both times Opal had waved her off with a breathless insistence that she was fine, she'd simply misjudged the distance, she was fine.

She wasn't going to stop. That much was clear. She was going to keep hopping and leaning and reaching for whatever surface was nearest, because Opal Bennett did not accept limitation as a permanent state. He admired this about her.

Walking sticks. A pair of them, the right height and the right weight, with grips that fit her hands, would give her freedom with less risk. She could move through the house, bear her weight on her arms instead of hopping, and keep her balance over uneven ground. She could get to the porch when the weather allowed. To the privy without Elizabeth escorting her.

He walked to the back of the barn where his lumber was stored and sorted through the pieces leaning against the wall. He needed ash. Pine was plentiful and easy to work, but it was brittle under sustained pressure and would crack at the worst moment. Ash was harder to find and harder to shape, but it flexed without breaking and could carry weight. He had a few pieces of ash salvaged from a blown-down tree he'd dragged off the upper pasture two summers ago, set aside because ash was too useful to waste. He selected two that were close to the right diameter and length, straight-grained and free of knots, and carried them to the workbench.

He measured by eye, the way he always did. The sticks needed to reach from the floor to a point just below her armpit, with enough length above the grip for her hand to close around it and enough below for the base to clear the floor with room to spare.

He cut the ash to length with the handsaw, working the blade in steady, patient pulls that followed the pencil line he'd drawn. The saw teeth bit into the dense grain, and the cut opened clean. He trimmed both pieces to the same length, checked them against each other, and found them true to within a quarter inch, which he corrected with three strokes of the drawknife.

The shaping took time. He worked with the drawknife first, peeling the rough outer layer from each stick in long curls that fell to the barn floor and filled the air with the clean, sharp scent of fresh-cut ash. The wood was cream-colored and smooth-grained, and it came alive under the knife's edge, the surface emerging with a satin quality that would only improve with sanding. He rounded the shafts into a comfortable taper, thicker at the top where the grip would be and narrowing gradually toward the base, following the natural taper of the wood rather than fighting against it.

The grips required the most attention. He carved each one from the thick shaft of wood, shaping a horizontal crosspiece that would sit in her palm and give her something to push down on when she bore her weight. The crosspiece had to be wide enough to distribute the pressure across her hand and contoured enough to fit the natural curl of her fingers. He worked it with the small carving knife his uncle Josiah had given him, the one with the walnut handle worn smooth from years of use, taking thin shavings and testing the shape against his own hand and then adjusting because his hand was twice the size of hers and the grip needed to be smaller, narrower, more refined.

The leather wrapping came next. He cut two strips from a piece of soft deerskin he kept in the tack room, the same leather he used for replacing worn bridle cheekpieces and mending harness straps. He wound the strips around each crosspiece in tight, overlapping turns, securing the ends with small tacks driven into the wood beneath the leather's edge. The wrapping would keep the wood from blistering her palms during extended use and would give her a better grip; the soft texture of the deerskin holding against her skin instead of slipping the way bare wood would when her hands grew warm.

While the walking sticks took shape under his hands, his mind did what it always did when his hands were occupied with careful work. It wandered to memories or fussed over things that were bothering him.

His father had built the rocking chairs in the house. Both of them. They were his mother's most treasured possessions in the house, more valued than the cookstove, because Samuel had made them with his own hands for her and she'd said once, that a woman who had a chair her husband built for her had a home, and everything else was just furniture. Samuel had built the table, too, and the ladder-back chairs that surrounded it.

Nolan was building walking sticks for a woman who read aloud by his fire.

He didn't examine the parallel. He didn't need to. It was there in the grain of the wood and the care of the leather wrapping and the fact that he'd measured the height from memory, from the knowledge his arms carried of how tall she was when he held her, and that kind of knowledge didn't come from building something for a guest. It came from building something for someone who mattered, and the distinction was one he'd been avoiding for weeks and could no longer avoid while his hands shaped ash wood into a gift she hadn't asked for and wouldn't refuse and would understand, the way she understood the footrest and the way she understood his silence, as the language of a man who showed what he couldn't say.

He also knew what these walking sticks would change.

Once she had them, she wouldn't need him to help her as much. She wouldn't need Elizabeth bracing her through the kitchen. She wouldn't need his arm around her waist or his hand on her elbow or the brief, electric proximity of his body beside hers as she hopped through the main room, leaning into him for balance. She'd walk on her own. She'd navigate the house under her own power, and the practical necessity that had put his hands on her every morning and every evening would evaporate like breath in cold air, and what would remain was the question he'd been holding at arm's length since the night he'd told her about his mother and she'd listened as though his memories were something worth keeping.

What remained when the necessity was gone was whether he'd still find reasons to be near her.

He sanded the sticks with the sandstone block, working every inch of the surface in small circles until the wood was glass-smooth beneath his fingers. He checked the grips, the leather wrapping, the base of each shaft where it would meet the floor. He tested the balance by holding each one at the grip point and letting it hang, watching the shaft settle into a vertical that told him the weight was distributed evenly. He set the base of each one on the barn floor and pressed down with his full weight, and the ash held without a creak, without a flex, as solid and reliable as the wood knew how to be.

He held the finished pair up in front of him. Two sticks of ash, shaped and sanded and wrapped in soft deerskin, the best work he'd done since the footrest, and better than the footrest, because more of himself had gone into them.

Chapter 27

The venison had been simmering since mid-day, and the kitchen smelled of it, rich and deep and layered with the onions and wild thyme Elizabeth had added after lunch. Opal stood at the counter on her good leg with her hip braced against the edge, stirring the pot with slow, even strokes while Elizabeth pulled the sourdough from the oven. The loaf came out with a crust that was dark and crackling and exactly right, and Elizabeth set it on the counter to cool.

"That's a beautiful loaf," Opal said.

"It is. I think the trick was letting the starter sit an extra couple of days. It might be a bit tangier, but the rise in it was better."

Opal gave the stew another stir. Chunks of venison floated thick in the broth alongside carrots and potatoes, and turnips she'd peeled and chopped earlier; the knife work still slower than Elizabeth's but neater than it had been a month ago. The stew had reached the point where it would hold without attention, and she set the spoon across the rim of the pot and shifted her weight against the counter, the familiar ache settling into her good hip from standing too long on one leg.

The front door opened. Cold air pushed into the main room in a visible wave, and Nolan came through it carrying the milk pail in one hand and something else in the other. Two somethings. Long, slender, upright, gripped together at the middle like a pair of fence posts that had been polished into something far too fine for fencing.

He set the milk pail on the table and stood there holding the two sticks, and Opal could see that they were shaped. Smoothed. The tops were wrapped in something pale and soft, and the shafts tapered from thick to thin with a symmetry that spoke of hours, not minutes.

"Made these," Nolan said. He held them out slightly, the way a man might hold out a tool he was returning. "Walking sticks. For you. They should be the right height, but I can adjust them if they're not."

He said it the way he said most things. Plainly. Without ceremony. As if he'd built a shelf or mended a gate latch and was simply reporting the fact of it.

Opal looked at the walking sticks.

The crosspieces were carved to fit a hand, her hand, contoured and wrapped in soft leather that had been wound in tight, careful spirals and tacked beneath the edge so no sharp point would press against her palm. The shafts were pale, cream-colored wood sanded to a smoothness. They were beautiful. They were practical and thoughtful.

The tears came before she could stop them. They weren't the polite, manageable kind. They rose from somewhere below her ribs and filled her eyes and spilled over before she'd drawn a full breath, and the sound that came with them was small and broken and completely involuntary, a single hitched gasp that she pressed her hand against her mouth to contain and failed.

She wasn't crying about walking sticks.

She was crying because this man had sat in his barn in the cold and had made something for her.

Nolan's expression shifted from neutral to something that looked very much like alarm. He glanced at Elizabeth and then back at Opal, and the walking sticks lowered an inch in his grip as though he was considering taking them back and pretending he'd never brought them inside.

"I didn't mean to..." he started.

"Nolan." Elizabeth's voice was gentle, amused, and very patient. "She's not upset."

He looked at Elizabeth with the expression of a man who could see tears and hear crying and was being told these things didn't indicate sadness, and who found this information deeply unconvincing.

"She's happy," Elizabeth said. "You did something that means something to her, and she's happy about it, and sometimes when women are that kind of happy the tears just come whether we want them to or not."

Nolan looked back at Opal. She was still crying. She was also nodding.

"Oh," he said.

He stood there holding the walking sticks and looking at her with an uncertainty she'd never seen on him before, this man who approached every physical task with a quiet sureness that never wavered, standing in his own kitchen looking entirely at a loss because a woman was crying over something he'd made with his hands. The contradiction of it, his competence and his bewilderment occupying the same broad-shouldered frame, broke something loose in her chest that wasn't grief and not gratitude but something larger than both. She hopped toward him, her hand running along the counter to steady herself, and then she wrapped her arms around him.

She heard the walking sticks clatter against the floor where he dropped them. She felt the solid, startled stillness of his body against hers, the width of his chest beneath her cheek, the warmth of him through his buckskin that was so immediate and so real that it made her breath catch for a reason that had nothing to do with crying. Her arms tightened around his waist and she held on with the fierceness of a woman who had spent weeks being carefully and devotedly looked after by a man who never asked for a single thing in return, and this was the only language she had right now that matched his.

He didn't move. For several seconds he stood with his arms at his sides and his chin above her head and his whole body held in the rigid posture of a man who had not been embraced in a very long time and didn't know what to do with the fact that it was happening now.

Then his arms came up.

They settled around her slowly, carefully, the way his hands did everything, with a deliberateness that wasn't hesitation but something closer to reverence. One arm across her back. The other higher, his hand resting between her shoulder blades with a gentleness that belied the size and roughness of it. He held her the way he held everything that mattered to him, as if the holding itself were an act of faith, and Opal felt the tension leave his body in a single, long exhale that stirred the hair at her temple.

She caught a glimpse of Elizabeth bending to pick up the walking sticks with the biggest, most triumphant grin Opal had ever seen on a human face. Elizabeth straightened with a stick in each hand and said nothing, which was a feat of restraint that probably cost her physically.

Reality returned in degrees. Opal became aware of the stew simmering behind her, the cold still rolling off Nolan's buckskin, the impropriety of what she was doing, and the fact that she couldn't bring herself to care about propriety when his arms were around her.

Slowly she loosened her arms. She stepped back, balancing on her good foot, and felt the absence of his warmth.

Her face was wet. Her cheeks burned. She swiped at her eyes with the back of her hand and took a steadying breath, and looked up at him, and the expression on his face was one she'd remember for the rest of her life. It was open. Unguarded. A man caught in the act of feeling something he hadn't been prepared to feel, and the look in his eyes was so tender and so startled and so entirely undefended that she had to look away from it before it undid her completely.

"Nolan," she said. Her voice was rough and thick and not at all composed. "Thank you."

He cleared his throat. "You're welcome."

Elizabeth appeared at her elbow with the walking sticks, still grinning. "All right. Let's see how these work."

She positioned the sticks on either side of Opal and showed her how to grip the crosspieces, thumbs over the top, fingers curled beneath, weight pressing down through her arms rather than pulling against the grip.

"Push down, don't lean," Elizabeth said. "The sticks hold you up. You're not hanging from them."

Opal gripped the crosspieces. The leather was soft and warm against her palms. She pushed down and felt her weight transfer from her good leg to her arms, and the sticks held her, steady and even, one on each side like a pair of hands she could carry with her.

She took a step.

Her arms shook. Her good leg did the work of moving forward while the splinted one hung between the sticks bearing nothing, and the motion was shuffling and graceless and required a concentration so complete that she couldn't think about anything else, which was probably a mercy given what had just happened against Nolan Ridgeway's chest.

"Good," Elizabeth said from her left side. "Take another one."

She took another one. The sticks thudded softly against the floor, her good foot followed, and she advanced perhaps eight inches with the athletic elegance of a newborn foal.

"That's it," Elizabeth said. "You're doing it, Opal."

Nolan was on her right. He hadn't touched her, but she could feel him there the way she could feel the stove's heat from across the kitchen. His hands were at his sides, ready, and she knew without looking that if she faltered he'd catch her.

She took another step. Then another. The rhythm began to organize itself: sticks forward, weight down, foot forward, and each repetition was slightly less unsteady than the last, her arms learning the motion, her balance finding its center between the two points of contact. Elizabeth kept pace beside her with vocal encouragement, and Nolan kept pace beside her with quiet readiness, and together the three of them moved across the kitchen into the main sitting room in a procession that was slow and shuffling and, to Opal, as significant as any distance she'd ever covered.

Her arms burned. Her good leg trembled with the effort of bearing weight and moving and balancing all at once, and her breath came in short, controlled pulls.

She turned slightly and made her way to the fireplace. She stopped, breathing hard, her arms quivering against the crosspieces, her whole body alive with exertion and triumph.

She turned again, which took a careful, deliberate rearrangement of sticks and weight and balance, and looked toward Nolan, who had stopped a few feet away, watching her. He hadn't followed. He'd let her go. She held his gaze, and everything she felt was in that look, and everything he wouldn't say was in his, and neither of them spoke because the silence said it more clearly than words could have.

"All right, you two," Elizabeth said with the cheerful practicality of a young woman who knew exactly what she was interrupting and was choosing mercy over mischief. "That stew is going to turn to leather if we don't eat it soon, and I didn't spend all day on that bread to let it sit on the counter and look pretty."

Opal laughed. The sound came out breathless and shaky and warm, and then she used the walking sticks with more confidence than before and made her way to the washbasin.

Elizabeth ladled the stew into bowls. She sliced the sourdough into thick, even pieces and arranged them on the board, then set the butter crock beside it and stepped back to survey the table with a nod of approval.

Opal reached her place on the bench. She leaned the walking sticks against the wall where she could reach them, and Elizabeth was there with a steady hand on her elbow as she lowered herself onto the seat and settled her splinted leg along the bench.

Nolan hung his buckskin on the peg by the door, washed his hands at the basin, and took his place across from her. He bowed his head when Elizabeth asked him to say grace, and his voice was low and steady and unhurried as he thanked the Lord for the food and for the hands that had prepared it and for the strength that had been given where it was needed, and Opal kept her head bowed and her eyes closed and felt the meaning of that last phrase settle into her chest.

Amen.

Chapter 28

The first several days of Opal using her new walking sticks had left her arms burning and her grip aching until the muscles in her forearms learned what was being asked of them. By the end of the first week her muscles were getting the hang of it. The sticks had become what Nolan had built them to be, a tool, and her body had absorbed them into its vocabulary of motion the way it had once absorbed the rhythms of a drawing room, without conscious thought.

She could get to the privy on her own now. That particular independence was worth more than she'd have been able to explain to anyone who hadn't spent weeks relying on another person for the most private necessities of living.

Now, she wanted to go outside and explore.

She'd said so twice, dropping little hints. Once to Elizabeth while they were washing dishes, a quiet mention that the air through the cracked window smelled so clean she could taste it, and once at the supper table where Nolan sat across from her and heard her say that she missed the feel of cold air on her face and the openness of a sky that wasn't framed by glass. Neither time had anyone said no. But neither time had anyone said yes, or even caught on to what she desired.

This morning after the breakfast dishes were cleaned and put away, she looked at Elizabeth and said, "I can't stand it any longer. I must get outside. We're going on an adventure."

Elizabeth studied her for a moment, and then she nodded and grinned.

Bundling up against the cold was quite an ordeal. Elizabeth brought one of Nolan's old work coats, heavy brown canvas lined with wool, and held it open while Opal slid her arms in. The coat hung past her hips, and the sleeves swallowed her hands. Elizabeth rolled the cuffs twice and buttoned the front and then wrapped a knitted scarf around Opal's neck and the lower half of her face, tucking the ends into the collar with the efficient care of a woman who had dressed for Montana winters her entire life. Gloves came last, Elizabeth's own, wool-lined leather that were slightly too large but would keep the cold from reaching her fingers.

"Ready?" Elizabeth asked after she had herself bundled up.

"I've been ready for a month."

Elizabeth laughed and opened the front door.

The cold hit her hard. It came through the scarf and filled her lungs with a sharpness that made her eyes water and her chest expand with something that wasn't pain but wasn't comfortable either, a bright, stinging clarity that tasted of fresh air and snow. She breathed it in and smiled against the wool of the scarf.

The porch was several planks wide and swept free of snow from the door to the edge. Opal planted the walking sticks and moved across it carefully, each placement deliberate, the wood thudding solid against the boards. The steps at the porch's edge were the first real test. Two steps down, each one a negotiation of balance and gravity that required her to lower herself on her good leg while the sticks took the angle and the splinted leg hung suspended between them. Elizabeth stayed one step below her, hands hovering near Opal's hips, ready to catch.

Opal made it down both steps without falling, which felt like a victory worth celebrating, and she celebrated by looking up.

The world opened.

The snow covered everything in a single unbroken white that ran from the base of the porch to the tree line and beyond, and the sky above it was a blue so deep and so clear it looked like something poured from a height. The sun was high and threw a light across the snow that made the surface glitter with a brilliance that stung her eyes, and she didn't care. She was outside, and the air was so cold it burned and so clean it tasted like fresh water, and the world was enormous and beautiful, and she was standing in the middle of it on two sticks.

"Oh, Elizabeth," she breathed.

"I know," Elizabeth whispered. "It's something, isn't it?"

The path to the barn was shoveled to a width of about three feet, the packed snow on either side rising to mid-calf height where Nolan had thrown it with the shovel. Opal planted the walking sticks and moved forward. The tips sank a little into the packed surface before catching, and the footing was harder to read than the flat floors inside, the texture uneven where boot prints had frozen into shallow ridges. She adjusted. She placed each stick more firmly, pressing down until she felt the resistance hold, and then she swung her good foot forward and repeated it.

Elizabeth walked behind her with both hands near Opal's hips, steadying her whenever a stick slipped or her balance shifted too far to one side. They moved at the pace of a slow walk, and it took them a good five minutes to cover a distance that Nolan probably crossed in a minute, and neither of them cared. Halfway to the barn, Opal's left stick caught an ice ridge, and she wobbled, and Elizabeth's hands clamped onto her hips and held her steady, and they both laughed, the sound bright and startled in the still cold air. Something about the wobble and the catching and the laughter stripped the last of the caution away, and they giggled like school-girls the rest of the way, Elizabeth narrating the journey in the dramatic tones of an explorer's dispatch. "The brave adventurer encounters treacherous terrain. Her faithful companion maintains the rear guard."

"Stop," Opal gasped, laughing so hard her arms shook on the crosspieces. "I'll fall if you make me laugh."

"Then fall. I'll catch you."

They reached the barn door, flushed and breathless and grin-ning. Elizabeth pulled the heavy door open, and the warmth inside rolled over them in a wave that smelled of hay and horses and animal heat, and Opal stepped across the threshold into a world she'd never entered before.

Nolan was halfway down the aisle with a pitchfork in his hands, mid-stride between stalls, and his head came up at the sound of the door. The expression on his face moved through surprise to confu-sion to something that arrived too fast for him to catch and smooth away, a flash of open, unguarded pleasure that transformed his features for the half-second before he mastered it.

He grinned. An actual grin, wide enough to show his teeth, and on Nolan Ridgeway's face it was so rare and so unexpectedly warm that Opal felt it.

"What is this?" he said.

"A mutiny," Elizabeth announced. "We couldn't stand another day inside those walls, so we staged an expedition. We made it alive and only nearly fell once."

"Twice," Opal corrected.

"The second one doesn't count. That was a controlled wobble."

Nolan looked at Opal. His eyes moved to the walking sticks planted on the barn floor, to the oversized coat she wore, to the flush on her cheeks and the brightness in her eyes.

"I can't believe you walked out here," he said.

"Believe it."

The barn was larger than she'd imagined. It was a long, open structure with a center aisle flanked by stalls on both sides and a hayloft above that was stacked deep with hay. The air was warm and close and rich with the smell of animals and dried grass, and the light that came through the gaps in the plank walls fell in narrow lines across the straw-covered floor. Tack hung along one wall: bridles and halters, and coils of rope. A workbench sat against the far wall beneath a window, its surface scarred with the marks of tools and scattered with wood shavings.

Cob was in the first stall. The buckskin gelding lifted his head from his hay when Opal approached, his ears swiveling forward, his dark eyes regarding her with the calm, intelligent appraisal of a horse who had seen enough of the world to be unbothered by most of it. Opal stopped at the stall door and looked at him.

"Hello. You must be Cob," she said quietly. She removed one of her gloves and reached out her hand.

Cob lowered his head to her palm. His muzzle was velvet-soft and warm. He breathed against her fingers with a slow, measured exhale that fogged in the cold air between them. She stroked the flat plane of his face, feeling the ridge of bone beneath the short, coarse hair, and the gelding stood perfectly still and let her.

"Thank you," she told him. "You carried us both through that storm, and I never got to thank you properly."

Cob blinked at her with an expression of benign disinterest.

Nolan was watching as he stood beside her.

"This is Nell," he said as he moved to the next stall. The bay mare pushed her nose over the stall door and investigated Opal's coat with enthusiastic curiosity, her nostrils flaring as she cataloged every unfamiliar scent. "She's the best-tempered horse on the place. Good under a saddle and good in a harness."

"She's beautiful." Opal said as she stroked Nell's neck.

"And this one." Nolan nodded toward the third stall, where a young sorrel mare stood at the back, watching them with the wary, suspicious eye of an animal who hadn't yet decided whether newcomers were worth approaching. "She's green. Still learning. Got opinions about everything and experience about nothing."

"She doesn't have a name?" Opal asked.

"Haven't given her one yet."

Elizabeth appeared at Opal's elbow. "You should name her."

Opal looked at the sorrel. The mare was a warm copper color, her coat thick with winter growth, and her mane was beautiful. She was young and wary and full of the cautious energy that came from wanting to trust and not quite knowing how. Opal recognized something in the stance.

"Copper," she said.

Nolan looked at the mare. Looked at Opal. "Copper," he repeated, as if testing the word against the animal.

"It suits her."

"It does."

The milk cow, Bessie, occupied a stanchion near the far end, chewing her cud with the philosophical patience of an animal whose chief concern was whether the hay would keep coming. Opal greeted her too, and Bessie regarded her with the mild, bovine indifference of a creature who had opinions about very little and expressed none of them.

A bark from the barn door announced Boone, who'd evidently been making his rounds outside and had returned to discover that his barn contained unexpected visitors. The dog trotted down the aisle with his tail moving in cautious, investigative sweeps, his thick coat rimed with frost along the shoulders. He sniffed Opal's walking sticks, sniffed the hem of the borrowed coat, and then sat down at her feet and looked up at her with an expression that suggested he'd been aware of her existence for some time and had been waiting for her to come to him rather than the other way around.

"Boone remembers you," Elizabeth said.

Opal leaned carefully on her sticks and reached down to scratch behind his ears. The dog's tail swept the straw floor in wide, approving arcs.

Then Opal started asking questions. She couldn't help it. Everything in this barn was new and fascinating to a woman who'd grown up in a house where the closest thing to livestock was a carriage horse kept at a livery three blocks away. She asked about the hay in the loft and how much the horses ate in a day. She asked about the tack on the wall and what each piece was for. She asked about the workbench and the tools arranged along its back edge, and Nolan answered each question in his plain, unhurried way, and she listened and stored each answer the way she stored everything he gave her, carefully and completely.

Opal turned to face them both at one point, her cheeks still bright from the cold. "Could we go for a ride? On the sled... the one used to haul the hay? Just a short one?"

Elizabeth's face lit up. She turned to Nolan and grinned.

Nolan hesitated. His eyes went to Opal's splinted leg, to the walking sticks, to the barn door and the snow beyond it.

"Please?" Opal said. "Just a short one. I'll hold on to Elizabeth the whole time. We'll be fine."

He looked between them, and Opal watched him weigh the risk the way he weighed everything, carefully, practically, with the quiet calculation of a man who understood consequences. Then something in his expression softened, the way it did when Elizabeth asked for something he'd already decided to give her, and he set the pitchfork against the wall and went to get Cob's harness.

While he worked, leading Cob from his stall and backing him between the traces of the flat-bottomed work sled that sat along the barn's far wall, Elizabeth pulled Opal aside. They stood near the stalls in the warm, hay-scented air, close enough to hear the jingle of harness buckles and Nolan's low murmur as he talked Cob through the hitching.

"Your brother is a remarkable man," Opal said quietly, watching him work. "The walking sticks. The footrest. Everything he does, he does with such care." She paused. "I'm surprised he hasn't married."

Elizabeth's expression shifted. The brightness didn't leave her face, but something more careful moved behind it.

"He was engaged once. About two years ago. To a woman named Catherine Ellsworth."

Opal waited.

"Her father was a lumber baron from Livingston. He'd come out to Providence Ridge to consider expanding his operation. Catherine came with her parents. She was pretty and proper, and she seemed like she wanted this life." Elizabeth glanced toward the far end of the barn where Nolan was adjusting the traces. "She visited the homestead twice during the engagement. We had her family for supper the second time. I cooked venison stew and fresh bread, and she smiled and praised the meal and said all the right things."

"After that second visit, she broke off the engagement. By letter. Through the mail." Elizabeth met Opal's eyes. "A few sentences. She said she couldn't marry him. And then she told him that if he'd sell this land to her father and come work for his operation and build her a house in town, she'd consider his proposal again."

The words settled into the quiet of the barn. A horse shifted in its stall. Hay rustled.

"I hurt for my brother watching him go through that," Elizabeth said softly. "I promise you... I don't believe for one second that she cared a bit for my brother. She was her daddy's right hand and the only thing she wanted was our land for her precious daddy to profit from. Please forgive me... I know that sounds terrible of me to say."

Opal's hands tightened on the crosspieces of the walking sticks.

"He doesn't talk about it," Elizabeth continued. "He's never said her name to me more than twice since the letter came. But I watched what it did to him. He thought she loved him. He'd started planning an addition to the house in his head, making it bigger for her. And she looked at everything he was and everything he'd built and she called it charming, and then she walked away."

"I'm telling you this," Elizabeth said, and her voice dropped to something quieter and more deliberate, "because I think you should understand him. Why he's careful. Why he shows what he means instead of saying it. Why he builds things for people instead of telling them how he feels." She held Opal's gaze. "He offered his heart to someone who found it wasn't enough. That's not something a man like my brother recovers from quickly."

Opal stood very and considered what she'd just learned about this caring man.

His silences. The way he watched her when he thought she wasn't looking and glanced away when she turned her head. The footrest carved to the exact angle her splinted leg needed. The walking sticks. The restraint in his touch, the care in every gesture, the way he gave and gave and gave and never once asked for anything in return. She'd read all of it as the language of a man who felt things deeply and expressed them through his hands. She'd been right. But she hadn't known the rest of it—the reason the language existed at all.

He spoke through action because his words had been returned to him. He built because building was safer than asking. He showed love instead of speaking it because the last time he'd spoken it, the woman he'd loved had weighed his life against her comfort and found it wanting.

Of course, he was careful. Of course, he was guarded. He'd been brave enough to offer everything he had, and a woman had looked at everything he had and decided it wasn't enough, and she'd walked away without even the courage to say it to his face.

Opal looked down the barn aisle to where Nolan was checking the harness one final time, his broad hands moving over the leather with the same steady care he brought to everything. She couldn't see his face. She could see the set of his shoulders, the unhurried confidence of his movements, the way Cob stood calm and trusting beside him because the horse knew what Opal was only now fully understanding, that this man poured himself into everything he did and asked for nothing back and would never, not once, tell you how much it cost him.

She didn't pity him. Pity was the wrong word for what she felt, and she knew that Nolan Ridgeway would recoil from it if she offered it. What she felt was recognition, bone-deep and immediate.

"Thank you for telling me," she said to Elizabeth.

Elizabeth nodded once. Her eyes were bright and steady and held the quiet fierceness of a sister who loved her brother well enough to give another woman the map to his heart.

"Sled's ready," Nolan called.

Nolan helped Elizabeth up onto the sled first, and then he turned to Opal. She handed him the walking sticks one at a time, and he leaned them against the barn wall. Then he offered his hand.

She took it, and he guided her onto the flat wooden bed of the sled beside Elizabeth, his grip firm and warm even through the gloves, and he held on until she was seated and steady with her splinted leg stretched before her and Elizabeth's arm linked through hers.

He climbed into the saddle. A click of his tongue, and Cob leaned into the traces, and the sled moved.

Nolan kept Cob at a slow pace, the gelding's hooves breaking the snow crust in a steady rhythm while the sled runners hissed over the packed surface behind him. The flat ground near the homestead spread out around them in a white expanse that caught the low sun and threw it back in a brilliance that made Opal squint, and didn't stop her from looking. The mountains rose on every side, enormous against the sky, and the timber on the lower slopes stood dark and still beneath its burden of snow. The air was so cold it made her teeth ache and so clear she could see individual trees on ridges that must have been a mile away.

Elizabeth laughed beside her, her cheeks red, her breath clouding, and Opal laughed too because the sled was moving and the snow was glittering. The sky was the deepest blue she'd ever seen, and she was outside. She was finally outside, and the world was so vast and so beautiful it made her chest hurt in the best way she could imagine.

The sun was warm on her face. That was the strangest part: the contradiction of bitter cold against her lungs and bright warmth against her skin, as if the world couldn't decide what season it wanted and had settled for both at once. She tipped her face toward it and closed her eyes for a moment and let the warmth soak into her.

She opened her eyes and looked back at the homestead.

She'd never seen it from a distance. From inside, it was close walls and low ceilings and the smell of the cookstove and the creak of floorboards she'd memorized. From here, it was small and solid and settled into the landscape as if it had grown from the ground rather than been built on it, the house and the barn and the outbuildings holding their place against the white valley and the mountain wall behind them with a stubbornness that matched the man who kept them standing.

It was beautiful. Not the way her father's house in Richmond had been beautiful, with its columns and its manicured grounds and its air of studied permanence. Beautiful, the way a living thing is beautiful, worn, and real and exactly what it needed to be.

Lord, thank You for this. For these people. For this place. For whatever purpose You had in bringing me here, even if I don't fully understand it yet. Thank You.

Nolan turned Cob back toward the barn, and the sled followed in a wide, gentle arc. Elizabeth squeezed her arm, and Opal squeezed back, and neither of them needed to say what they were both thinking because the cold air and the bright snow and the laughter still warm in their chests said it well enough.

Nolan helped them off the sled when they had returned to the barn.

Elizabeth brushed the snow from her skirt and clapped her hands together. "All right. We need to get inside Miss Opal and start supper, or we'll be eating cold bread and apologies tonight."

"I'm going to milk Bessie and then I'll come inside shortly," Nolan said.

Opal looked at the milk cow in her stanchion. At the three-legged stool beside her and the tin pail hanging on its nail.

"I'd like to stay," she said as she turned to look at Nolan. "Will you teach me to milk her?"

Nolan looked at her and tilted his head. "All right."

Chapter 29

Opal was sitting on his milking stool beside Bessie, bundled up in his old work coat, and he couldn't help but think that she was the most beautiful thing he had ever seen..

Nolan set the pail beneath Bessie. "First... you'll need to take your gloves off."

She looked at the gloves, then at the cow, then back at him with an expression that was half amusement and half apprehension. "Both of them?"

"Both."

She pulled the gloves off and tucked them into the coat pockets. Her hands were small and pale in the barn light, her fingers slender, the skin fine enough that he could see the blue thread of veins at her wrists.

"Bessie won't kick," he said. "She'll stand patient as long as you're steady with her. If you jerk or grab, she'll let you know about it."

"How will she let me know?"

"She'll move. And you'll have milk on your skirt instead of in the pail."

Opal looked at Bessie. Bessie looked back with the mild, untroubled gaze of a cow.

"All right," Opal said. "Show me."

He crouched beside her, which put him close enough to see the concentration already gathering in her face as she studied the cow's udder with the earnest focus of a woman who intended to master this task or exhaust herself trying.

"Wrap your hand around the teat," he said. "Thumb and forefinger first, then close the rest down in order. Squeeze, don't pull. The milk's already there. You're just telling it where to go."

She reached out and wrapped her fingers around the nearest teat with the cautious precision of someone handling an unfamiliar instrument. Her grip was too high and too tight, and when she squeezed, nothing happened.

Bessie turned her head and regarded Opal with an expression that conveyed, with remarkable clarity for a creature without words, that this was not how things were done.

"She's judging me," Opal said.

"She's patient."

"She's judging me, Nolan."

He almost laughed. He kept it to a breath through his nose, but the effort cost him, because her voice carried that warm, self-aware humor that surfaced when she was failing at something and knew it and refused to be defeated by it, and it was the most disarming sound he'd ever heard from a woman.

"Lower," he said. "Start your grip lower and close your fingers one at a time. Like this."

He reached out and placed his hands over hers.

Her fingers were cold beneath his. Small and cold and precise, and his hands covered them completely, his rough, calloused palms against the backs of her hands, his fingers guiding hers into the correct position around the teat. He could feel the fine bones of her knuckles and the tension in her tendons as she adjusted her grip, and he was close enough now to see the flush on her cheek nearest him and the slight catch in her breathing when his hands settled over hers. He was aware of all of it, the way a man is aware of a fire in a dark room, completely and from every direction at once.

"One at a time," he said. "Top to bottom. Squeeze and release."

He guided her hands through the motion. Squeeze. A thin, hesitant stream of milk hit the pail with a sound that was barely audible above Bessie's breathing. Opal's fingers moved again under his, and a second stream followed the first, stronger this time, the milk ringing against the tin.

"There," he said, and took his hands away.

The absence of her skin against his registered like stepping out of a warm home into cold air. He straightened and moved back a half step.

Opal tried again on her own. Her first attempt produced a weak, stuttering stream that went sideways and hit the inside of the pail's rim. The second was better. The third found its rhythm, and the milk began hitting the bottom of the pail in the thin, high ring that would deepen as the pail filled. She looked up at him with an expression of such unguarded triumph that he had to look away from it.

He looked at the far wall of the barn and breathed deeply through his nose and thought about fence posts and hay quantities and the ice on the creek that would need breaking again tomorrow. Because looking at Opal's face when it held that particular brightness was like looking at something he shouldn't want, and if he stared at it too long, he'd start believing it was meant for him.

Her skin was as fine as a piece of delicate china. That was the thought he couldn't shake. A woman built like porcelain, with hands that should've been holding a teacup in a drawing room. Yet here she was sitting on a rough wooden stool in his barn learning to milk his cow and looking at him as though he'd given her something precious by teaching her a chore that every girl in the territory learned by age eight.

He didn't understand what God was doing. He'd asked, more than once in his evening prayers, what purpose this woman served in his life beyond the obvious obligation of care, and the answer he kept getting wasn't the answer he expected. The answer he kept getting was the feeling in his chest when she laughed, the pull in his ribs when she looked at him, the way his whole body oriented toward her in a room the way a compass needle finds north, not by choice but by nature, by the essential design of the thing.

He loved her. The admission had stopped startling him a week ago and had settled instead into something structural, something load-bearing, like a beam set into the frame of a house. He loved her the way he loved this land, not because it was easy but because it was true, and he'd never felt anything like it for another living soul. Catherine had stirred something in him: want and hope and the picture of a future, but it had been thin, he knew that now. It had been the idea of love rather than the thing itself. What he felt for Opal wasn't an idea. It was bone and blood and breath, and it terrified him.

"Am I doing it right?" she asked.

"You're doing fine."

She milked. Slowly, unevenly, with pauses to adjust her grip and shift her weight on the stool, the pail was filling, and the rhythm was finding her. Bessie stood in her stanchion, chewed her cud, and tolerated the lesson.

"Will you teach me to ride?" Opal asked, her eyes on the pail. "A horse. I've never been on one. Only behind one in a carriage."

He stared at her. "You've never ridden a horse."

"Never."

It was the kind of fact that didn't fit anywhere in his understanding of how a person moved through the world. In his life, everyone rode. Men, women, children old enough to grip a mane. Elizabeth had been on a horse before she could walk, propped in the saddle in front of their mother while the mare grazed the home pasture. The idea of a grown woman who had never sat a horse was as foreign to him as a parlor with wallpaper imported from England, which, he reminded himself, was exactly where she'd come from.

"When your leg's healed," he said. "I'll teach you."

She smiled. "I'll hold you to that."

"I expect you will."

The milk continued to hit the pail in a steady, thickening rhythm. Cob shifted in his stall and sighed the long, contented sigh of a horse who'd had his grain and wanted nothing. Boone had settled near the barn door with his chin on his paws, watching them with the drowsy attention of a dog who considered all human activity mildly interesting but not worth standing for.

"Did you build this barn?" she asked.

"My father built the bones of it. The center aisle and the first four stalls. My uncle Josiah and I added the rest: the hayloft, the tack room, the stalls on the east side. We did it the summer before he died."

"You and your uncle were close."

"Yes. After my parents passed, he came from Tennessee and stayed to help me and my sister." Nolan leaned against the stall rail and crossed his arms. "He was a good man. He taught me as much about building and woodworking as my father did."

"What do you love most about this life?" she asked.

The question was simple. The answer wasn't.

"The mornings," he said. "Before anyone else is up. I walk out the front door and there's nothing but the sky and the creek and the whole valley stretched out, and everything I can see is mine to look after. The horses. The cattle. The land. Elizabeth." He paused. His eyes found the barn wall, the tack hanging in its careful order, the tools his uncle had taught him to use, and the tools his father had left behind. "Most people think of responsibility as something heavy. Something you carry because you have to. But when it's yours, when you chose it and built it and it matters to you, it doesn't feel like an obligation. It feels like standing on solid ground."

He'd said more than he meant to. He could feel it the way a man feels he's walked farther from camp than he intended, the slight disorientation of looking back and realizing the distance.

Opal had stopped milking. Her hands rested still around the teat, and she was looking up at him with those hazel eyes, and the expression on her face was quiet and full.

"That's beautiful," she said.

He didn't know what to do with that. No one had ever called the way he felt about chores and cattle and cold mornings beautiful. He cleared his throat and nodded toward the pail. "You've still got about a quarter left."

She laughed softly and turned back to Bessie, and her hands found the rhythm again.

She finished the milking. It took her three times longer than it took him, and the last quarter was a negotiation between her tiring hands and Bessie's thinning patience. She stripped the udder dry and sat back on the stool with her fingers curled in her lap and an expression of tired, radiant satisfaction that he knew would stay with him long after this evening was over.

He covered the milk pail and then gave Bessie her grain. He helped Opal to her feet, which meant offering his arm and taking her weight while she found her balance and reached for the walking sticks.

His mind flashed to Catherine for a moment as he watched Opal. Catherine had refused to even step foot in the barn. She'd stood outside and said, "That is no place for a lady." She'd never sat on the milking stool. She'd never touched Cob's muzzle or asked how the loft was built or wanted to know what he loved about his life. She'd looked at his world from a careful distance and decided it wasn't worth entering.

Opal had entered it, seemed a part of it, and he wondered if she would stay.

He pushed the thoughts aside and picked up the milk pail. He looked at Opal, who was watching him closely. "Ready to head inside?"

"I am."

He walked ahead of her and pushed the barn door open. The cold met them, sharper now than it had been an hour ago, the air carrying the particular bite of a late afternoon turning toward evening. The sky was still bright, but the light had thinned, and the shadows from the barn and the house stretched long and blue across the snow.

Opal planted the walking sticks on the shoveled path and started forward. Her pace was slow; the exhaustion of the day showing in the careful placement of each stick and the slight tremor in her arms as they took her weight. Nolan walked beside her with the milk pail in his left hand and his right hand open at his side, close enough to catch her if she stumbled. He shortened his stride until it matched hers, and they moved together across the packed snow toward the house, and he didn't rush her.

The house had lights in the windows where Elizabeth had the lamps going. Smoke from the chimney rose thin and straight in the still air. Elizabeth's shape moving behind the kitchen curtain, and the whole picture of it, the light and the smoke and the small solid house against the snow and the mountains, was a thing he'd seen ten thousand times and was seeing now as if for the first time. Opal was walking toward it beside him, and her presence beside him changed what it meant.

"Wait. Let me help you," he said as they reached the porch. He set the milk pail down and stepped behind her. He placed his hands on either side of her waist and lifted her.

She's so tiny and fragile. That was the thought that went through him, vivid and immediate. This woman, he'd watched wrestle a milking stool and a stubborn cow with a broken leg stretched out before her, weighed nothing at all in his hands. He held onto her as if she were a fine crystal lamp and was more valuable than he had the right to touch.

He kept his hands on her waist until her walking sticks were planted and her balance was sure.

She turned toward him so quickly it startled him. They were eye to eye. So close that he could see tiny freckles on her nose and twinkles of amber in her hazel eyes. She didn't say a word. She didn't have to because those eyes told him everything.

Then she smiled.

Nolan stood in the snow below her with his hands at his sides, and the cold deepening around him, and he felt his entire world expand.

Chapter 30

December had settled over the valley like a hand pressing down. The days had shortened to a window of gray light that opened around eight in the morning and closed by four in the afternoon, and the hours between were cold and bright and still in a way that made the homestead feel like the only inhabited place on earth. The mountains above the treeline had disappeared entirely, buried in the permanent overcast that sat above the valley like a lid, and the world beneath it was white and close and quiet.

Opal had learned to read this quiet the way Elizabeth read a cookstove and Nolan read the sky. She knew the difference between the silence that meant clear cold weather and the silence that meant snow was coming. She also knew the particular quality of stillness that settled over the homestead in the long evenings when the three of them sat by the fireplace and enjoyed this time together immensely. The only sounds were the crackle of the fire and Nolan's voice reading aloud from the Bible or from one of her novels, unhurried and low, while she and Elizabeth worked their embroidery and the lamplight made the room feel small and cozy.

Opal arose in the mornings, sometimes even before Elizabeth did. She dressed in the cold bedroom with the quick efficiency she'd learned from weeks of practice, and she sat with Nolan and drank coffee and talked about what he had planned for the day. He would leave and tend to his morning chores. She and Elizabeth would prepare breakfast, and Opal always made sure there was coffee ready on the back of the stove by the time he came in from morning chores, his coat frosted at the shoulders, his cheeks raw from the cold.

Her splint was off. It had come off four days ago. Elizabeth had unwound the binding and carefully removed the boards, and the leg beneath had emerged pale and thinner than the other, the muscles diminished from weeks of disuse. Opal had stood on it for the first time with both hands gripping the kitchen table's edge and her jaw set against the tenderness that flared from ankle to knee, a deep, structural soreness that told her the bone was mended but the body around it needed time. She still used the walking sticks. She still favored the good leg. But each day she tested the healing one a little more, bearing a fraction of weight and then a fraction more, and the soreness retreated in increments so small they could only be measured across days, not hours.

She milked Bessie every morning and every evening now. She'd claimed the task with a quiet firmness that neither Ridgeway had contested, partly because she was competent at it and partly because the look on her face when anyone suggested helping her with it carried the particular steel of a woman who had found a thing that was hers and intended to keep it. The milking had become her meditation: the rhythmic squeeze and release, the warm flank against her forehead, the sound of milk filling the pail with only the horses, Bessie, and the dog for company. She talked to Bessie during the milking the way Nolan talked to Cob, in a low, easy murmur that was more for herself than for the cow, though Bessie seemed to approve.

She'd started writing again. The journal had been packed in the bottom of her trunk, a leather-bound book with cream pages she'd brought from Virginia, and she'd pulled it out one evening after the fire had burned low and Elizabeth had gone to bed and the house was quiet. She wrote by lamplight in the rocking chair with a quilt across her lap and her pen moving in the small, precise hand her mother had taught her. She wrote about the homestead. About the chickens and their ridiculous personalities and the way Copper had finally let her touch the white blaze on her forehead. About the bread she could make now without measuring, the biscuits that rose properly, and the feeling of flour beneath her hands. She wrote about the valley in winter, the silence and the stark whiteness of it all, and the way the sky looked at four in the afternoon when the light was going and the mountains turned to shadow. She wrote poems again, short and careful and full of images she gathered during the day and shaped into lines during the quiet evenings. The writing brought her a joy she hadn't felt in years, the private, sustaining pleasure of putting the world into words and finding that the words held.

She and Elizabeth had started embroidering pillowcases. Elizabeth had known the basic stitches, but Opal knew the finer work, the satin stitch and the French knots and the feathered chain that her own mother had shown her in the parlor of their Richmond home when Opal was ten and the world was still whole. Teaching Elizabeth these stitches had become their evening occupation, the two of them working side by side in the rocking chairs with their hoops in their laps while Nolan read, and the domesticity of it, the three of them in the lamplight with their separate tasks and their shared quiet, had settled into something that felt less like an arrangement and more like a life.

Nolan spoke more easily now. That was the change Opal held closest, the one she turned over in her mind late at night when the house was dark and the fire was low and she could hear his breathing from the bedroll in front of the hearth. The silences between them had shifted from guarded to companionable, and the conversations came more readily, about the cattle, the weather, the book she was reading, the horse she would learn to ride when spring came. He told her about the creek in summer, how the water ran clear and fast over smooth stones and the trout held in the pools behind the boulders. He told her about the wildflowers that covered the upper meadows in July: lupine and Indian paintbrush and a dozen others he knew by sight but not always by name. He was giving her his world in pieces, and she collected each one the way she collected the images she wrote into her journal, carefully and with the awareness that what she was being given was rare.

On a Friday morning, the second week into December, Nolan had eaten his breakfast quickly. He'd been watching the sky for two days, and whatever he saw in it had tightened the set of his jaw in a way Opal had learned to recognize as concern. Over breakfast he had told them he needed to ride out to the south pasture and the upper range to check both herds because weather was coming, something worse than the ordinary snowfall. He wanted to make sure the cattle were where they needed to be before it hit. He'd be gone most of the day.

Opal and Elizabeth packed his saddlebag with biscuits and cheese and dried venison wrapped in cloth, and he'd taken it with a nod and pulled on his heavy buckskin and his gloves and his hat and gone out into the cold. Opal had watched from the kitchen window as he rode Cob out past the barn and into the white expanse until horse and rider were small against the snow and then gone.

The morning passed quietly. Opal washed the breakfast dishes while Elizabeth swept the floors. They worked in the easy, practiced rhythm they'd developed over weeks of shared labor, talking intermittently.

Elizabeth had been quieter than usual this morning. Not silent, because Elizabeth was never silent, but the brightness in her voice had been operating at a lower register, as if the energy that usually powered her cheerfulness was being drawn from a reserve that was running thin. She'd eaten half her breakfast and pushed the rest around her plate. She'd swept the same section of floor twice without seeming to realize it.

Now, standing at the counter wiping down the surface she'd already wiped, Elizabeth paused. She set the cloth down and pressed the heel of her hand against her forehead, and Opal saw the flush.

It wasn't the flush of warmth from the cookstove or exertion from sweeping. It was higher in her cheeks and more vivid, a bloom of color that sat on her skin like paint on porcelain, and above it her eyes had gone bright in a way that had nothing to do with laughter. They were glassy. Opal recognized the glassiness. She'd seen it in her own mirror before when she was coming down with a fever, that particular wet sheen that meant the body was fighting something and losing.

"Elizabeth." Opal set the dish she'd been drying on the counter. "Are you all right?"

Elizabeth lowered her hand and attempted a smile that didn't quite arrive. "I feel a bit off," she said. "A little light-headed. I'm not sure what's wrong. Probably just tired."

"You're flushed."

"Am I?" Elizabeth touched her cheek with her fingertips, as if she could diagnose herself by touch. "It might be the stove. I've been standing near it all morning."

She hadn't. She'd been sweeping on the far side of the room. Opal didn't correct her.

"Come sit down," Opal said. She reached for her walking sticks and moved toward the rocking chairs. "We'll work on the pillowcases. Take an easy afternoon. I think we've both earned it."

Elizabeth nodded. The nod was slower than it should have been, as if the motion required thought rather than reflex, and she untied her apron and hung it on its hook and turned toward the main room.

She made it four steps.

Opal heard it before she saw it, a soft sound, almost a sigh, and then the heavier sound that followed, the particular weighted thud of a body meeting the floor. She turned on her walking sticks and Elizabeth was down, crumpled beside the table with one arm still extended as if she'd reached for the table's edge and missed, her cheek against the plank floor, her braid fallen across her face, and her body utterly still.

"Elizabeth!"

Opal's walking sticks hit the floor before she'd finished saying the name. She dropped them and took two steps on her own legs, both of them, the healing one flaring with a pain she registered and dismissed in the same instant because Elizabeth was on the floor and nothing else mattered. Her third step buckled. Her knee folded, and she went down hard beside Elizabeth, catching herself on her hands, the impact jolting through her wrists and up into her shoulders.

She reached for Elizabeth's face. Turned her head gently, brushing the braid aside. Elizabeth's skin was burning. The heat of it against Opal's palm was immediate and alarming, not the warmth of exertion or a too-hot room but the dry, fierce heat of a fever that had been building for hours. It had just announced itself with the subtlety of a collapsing wall.

"Elizabeth. Elizabeth, can you hear me?"

Nothing. Elizabeth's eyelids fluttered once, a quick tremor beneath closed lids, but she didn't open her eyes and she didn't speak. Her breathing was shallow and rapid and carried a faint rasp at the bottom of each exhale.

Opal didn't know what to do. She couldn't lift her. Elizabeth was a sturdy young woman, taller than Opal and solidly built from years of frontier work, and Opal was kneeling on a leg that had been broken three months ago and was four days out of a splint. She couldn't carry her to a bed. She couldn't drag her without risking injury to both of them. Nolan was hours away on horseback in the south pasture or the upper range, and the sky outside the window was already thickening with the weather he'd ridden out to prepare for.

She was alone.

The fear came in a single cold wave that washed through her chest and receded. What it left behind wasn't panic but clarity, the bright, focused awareness that arrived when there was no one else to act and the person on the floor needed her to act now.

Pillow first. She crawled to the bedroom, her healing leg protesting with every movement, and pulled the pillow from Elizabeth's bed. She crawled back and lifted Elizabeth's head with both hands, gently, carefully, feeling the heat radiating from her scalp, and slid the pillow beneath it. Elizabeth's head settled into the pillow, and her breathing didn't change, still shallow, still rapid, still carrying that rasp.

Quilts. She pulled two from the back of the rocking chair and spread them over Elizabeth's body, tucking them around her shoulders and along her sides the way Elizabeth had tucked quilts around Opal in those first terrible days after the wreck, when Opal had been the one lying still and someone else had been the one doing the caring.

Water. She pulled herself up using the table's edge and stood on both legs, the healing one trembling beneath her weight, and made her way to the basin. She soaked a cloth in the water bucket, wrung it until it was damp and not dripping, and brought it back to the floor beside Elizabeth. She pressed the cool cloth against Elizabeth's forehead, against her temples, along the sides of her neck where the fever burned hottest, and Elizabeth stirred for the first time, a small, restless turning of her head against the pillow and a sound that was almost a word but wasn't.

"I'm here," Opal said. "I'm right here, Elizabeth."

She kept the cloth moving. Forehead, temples, neck. She dipped it again when it grew warm, wrung it, and returned to the steady, repetitive work of trying to draw heat from a body that was producing more of it by the minute. Elizabeth's breathing hadn't worsened, but it hadn't improved either. The rasp at the bottom of each exhale was a sound Opal's father had made during the pneumonia that had kept him in bed for two weeks when she was twelve. Her mother had sat beside him through every night of it with a damp cloth and a basin of cool water, doing exactly what Opal was doing now.

She thought about willow bark. Elizabeth kept the dried bark in a tin on the shelf above the cookstove, beside the elderflower and the camphor and the small brown bottle of the tallow remedy she used for chest complaints.

But Elizabeth was unconscious. She couldn't swallow tea. The willow bark would have to wait until she woke. And would it do her any good?

Opal sat on the kitchen floor with her back against the table leg and Elizabeth's head on the pillow beside her and the damp cloth in her hands, and the house quiet around her, and she prayed.

Lord, please. Please watch over her. She took care of me when I couldn't take care of myself. She sat beside my bed and held my hand and brewed tea she knew I hated and made me drink every drop. She washed my hair and mended my clothes, and laughed with me when I needed laughter more than medicine. Please don't take her. Please don't take this good, bright, precious girl who loves You and serves You and makes every room she walks into warmer than it was before she entered. I can't lose her. Nolan can't lose her. Please, Lord. Please.

The prayer didn't end so much as it opened into a continuous, wordless plea that ran beneath every other thought like water beneath ice. She kept the cloth cool, and the quilts tucked, and she watched the rise and fall of Elizabeth's breathing and counted the seconds between each exhale. She told herself that as long as the breathing continued and the count stayed steady, there was time. There was still time.

The light shifted. The short December afternoon was already turning toward evening, the gray outside the windows deepening by degrees, and the cookstove needed wood. Opal stood, her body stiff from sitting on the floor, her healing leg aching in a dull, persistent complaint that she acknowledged and overruled. She fed the cookstove from the wood box and checked the fire in the fireplace and added two logs because the house had to stay warm. Elizabeth had to stay warm.

She returned to the floor beside Elizabeth and pressed the cloth to her forehead again. Elizabeth stirred. Her eyes opened, unfocused and bright with fever, and she looked at Opal without recognition for a long, terrible moment before something cleared behind the glassiness and she said, in a voice that was rough and thin and nothing like her own, "Opal?"

"I'm here."

"What happened?"

"You fainted. You have a fever. You're on the kitchen floor because I couldn't move you, and I'm sorry about that."

Elizabeth's mouth attempted something that might have been a smile. "How long?"

"A few hours. Don't try to get up."

"Nolan?"

"He's not back yet. He'll be home soon."

Elizabeth's eyes closed. The brief window of consciousness had cost her something visible, a withdrawal of energy she didn't have to spare, and her breathing settled back into that shallow, rapid rhythm with the rasp at the bottom.

Opal dipped the cloth and pressed it to her temples and waited.

The door opened just after dusk fell.

The rush of cold air so sharp it made Opal's eyes water from across the room. Then Nolan filled her line of vision, broad-shouldered and frosted with snow, stamping his boots, already pulling his gloves off, already starting to speak.

He stopped.

His eyes found the floor. Found Elizabeth. Found Opal kneeling beside her with a damp cloth in one hand and the other resting on Elizabeth's shoulder. Found the pillow and the quilts and the basin of water and the picture they made: his sister unconscious on the kitchen floor.

She watched his face change.

She'd seen Nolan steady in a storm, quiet under pressure, composed in every situation she'd witnessed since the day she'd woken in his bed with his sister at her side. She'd never seen him afraid. She saw it now. It came and went in the space of a breath, a fracture in the steadiness that ran through the center of him, there and then controlled, but not before she'd seen it and understood what it meant.

"She collapsed around midday," Opal said. "Fever. It came on fast. She was conscious briefly about an hour ago but went back under. Her breathing has a rasp. I've been keeping her cool with a damp cloth. I couldn't move her."

Nolan crossed the room in three strides. He knelt beside Elizabeth and laid his hand against her forehead, and Opal saw his jaw tighten at the heat he found there.

"How high did it get?" he asked.

"This high. It hasn't broken."

He slid his arms beneath Elizabeth, one under her knees and one behind her shoulders, and lifted her from the floor in a single motion as if she weighed no more than a sack of grain. Elizabeth's head fell against his shoulder, and her arm hung limp, and the quilts trailed from her body as he carried her toward the bedroom. Opal pulled herself up using the table's edge and followed, the walking sticks forgotten on the floor, both legs carrying her because they had to.

He laid Elizabeth on the bed, and Opal arranged the quilts around her while Nolan stood at the bedside and looked down at his sister and didn't speak. His hands were at his sides. His shoulders rose and fell with controlled breaths.

"Willow bark tea," Opal said. "I know where she keeps it. I'll make it. When she wakes again, we'll get her to drink."

He didn't respond, and his eyes didn't leave Elizabeth.

Outside, the first flakes of the blizzard Nolan had been preparing for began to fall, thick and silent and steady.

Chapter 31

The cough woke Opal in the wee hours of the morning, and she was on her feet before her eyes were fully open, her hands reaching for the cloth in the basin beside Elizabeth's bed, her body moving through the motions it had learned over four days of nursing without waiting for her mind to catch up. She wrung the cloth, pressed it to Elizabeth's forehead, and held it there while the cough tore through Elizabeth's chest with the deep, wet, rattling sound that Opal had come to dread more than anything she'd ever heard in her life.

It was the sound of fluid. Nolan had told her that on the second night.

Elizabeth's eyes opened. They were glassy and unfocused, the fever painting a vivid flush across her cheekbones that made her look almost healthy until you saw the rest of her, the sunken quality around her temples, the way her lips had gone dry and cracked despite the water Opal pressed on her every hour. She looked at Opal without recognition, her gaze drifting past Opal's face toward the ceiling, and then her eyes closed again and her head turned on the pillow and she was gone, pulled back under by the fever that held her like a current.

"I'm here," Opal said, though she had no clue if Elizabeth heard her. She said it anyway. She'd been saying it for days, a refrain that had become as automatic as the wringing of the cloth and the checking of the fire and the steady, repetitive work of trying to cool a body that wouldn't cool.

She'd lost track of the days for a while, but she'd counted backward this morning while feeding the cookstove and arrived at Tuesday, December sixteenth. Four days since Elizabeth had collapsed on the kitchen floor. Four days since the blizzard had sealed the valley in white. The snow had stopped falling sometime on Sunday, but the drifts were taller than she was, and the world beyond the homestead was buried and still and impossibly far from any help that might have mattered.

Opal tucked the quilts tighter around Elizabeth's shoulders and stood, her healing leg stiff from hours on the floor. She'd been sleeping on a pallet of folded quilts on one side of Elizabeth's bed, and Nolan slept on his bedroll on the other side, and between them Elizabeth breathed her shallow, rattling breaths through the long nights while neither of them truly slept. They dozed in shifts. They listened for changes in the rhythm of her breathing the way sailors listen for changes in the wind.

She made her way to the kitchen and fed the cookstove until the iron ticked with heat, then filled the kettle and set it on to boil. She pulled the pot of broth from the back of the stove where she kept it warm through the night and checked its level. She'd made it yesterday from the last of the venison bones she'd brought up from the cellar. It was rich in vitamins and exactly the kind of nourishment Elizabeth needed if only Elizabeth would stay conscious long enough to swallow more than a few spoonfuls at a time.

She set out two cups for coffee and then stood at the counter with her hands flat on the wood and her head bowed and allowed herself thirty seconds of something that wasn't quite despair but lived in the same country. She was so tired. The exhaustion had moved past the ordinary weariness of too little sleep and settled into her bones, a heaviness that made her movements deliberate and her thoughts slow, and her emotions closer to the surface than she liked. She'd cried twice in the past four days, both times in the root cellar where no one could hear her, brief and fierce and over quickly because there wasn't time for more.

She made coffee, strong and black, and she drank her first cup standing at the counter, watching the dark kitchen windows.

Nolan came in from morning chores with snow on his shoulders and ice in his eyebrows and the particular set to his jaw that meant the cold was brutal. He'd been out since before she'd risen, tending the cattle he'd moved down closer to the house and the barn before the blizzard hit, breaking ice on the water troughs, feeding the horses, mucking stalls. The work that kept the homestead alive didn't pause for illness, and he did it all now with the compressed efficiency of a man racing the clock, getting through in two hours what normally took three so he could be back inside near Elizabeth.

He hung his buckskin on the hook and pulled off his gloves and accepted the cup she handed him without a word. He drank half of it in two long swallows, and the warmth of the kitchen put color back into his face.

"How is she?" he asked.

"The same. The cough woke her a little while ago, but she didn't know me."

He nodded.

"I need to show you something," he said. He set the cup down. "Other remedies. Elizabeth keeps them in the cellar. We need to try other things than what we have been doing. I'm almost certain Elizabeth has pneumonia."

"Show me," Opal said.

They went out the back door and across the short distance to the root cellar, Nolan walking ahead to break a path through the snow that had drifted against the heavy plank door set into the hillside. The cold hit Opal's face like a slap, and she pulled Elizabeth's shawl tighter around her shoulders—the shawl she'd been wearing for days because wearing it felt like keeping Elizabeth close.

The cellar was dark and cool and smelled of earth and stored vegetables and the faintly sweet mustiness of dried herbs. Nolan lit the lantern that hung on a nail just inside the door, and the light found the wooden shelves lining the walls, the crocks of pickled beets and preserves, the bins of potatoes and carrots and turnips layered in sand, and, on the highest shelf against the back wall, a row of tins and jars and small bundles wrapped in cloth that Opal had never looked at closely.

Nolan reached for the shelf and began setting things on the narrow work surface that ran along one wall.

"Willow bark. You know this one." He set the tin down.

"Elderflower." A jar of dried, pale blossoms. "Tincture for congestion. Elizabeth makes it every fall from the bushes along the creek. You can brew it as tea or mix it with honey. It loosens what's tight in the chest."

"Yarrow." A bundle of dried stalks bound with string. "Good for bringing a fever down. You brew it strong, stronger than the willow bark, and it makes them sweat. Our mother used to say that a yarrow sweat was the body's way of burning the sickness out."

"Peppermint." Another bundle, this one still carrying a faint, sharp scent even dried. "Settles the stomach when the fever makes them sick. Elizabeth mixes it with the elderflower sometimes."

He reached for a jar filled with soft, gray-green leaves, large and faintly fuzzy even dried. "Mullein leaf." He turned the jar in his hands. "There was an Apsáalooke woman who lived a few miles north of here when we were young. Her name was Makes Good Fire. Our parents traded with her family and had become friends over the years. She was a healer, and she taught our mother things, and our mother taught Elizabeth."

"Makes Good Fire used mullein for the lungs. You brew the leaves into a tea, strain it through cloth so the little hairs don't get into the liquid, and it soothes the cough and helps them breathe easier. She told our mother it opened the chest the way a window opens a room."

He set the jar down and reached for the next. "Coltsfoot. Same purpose, similar to mullein. Lung remedy. You can brew it alone or with the mullein."

"Licorice root." A handful of dried, woody pieces in a small tin. "Elizabeth chews on this when she has a sore throat, but you can steep it too. It coats the throat and eases the rawness."

"Horehound." Another bundle of dried leaves, darker than the mullein. "Cough remedy. Elizabeth makes horehound drops from this in the fall, boils it down with honey and lets it harden. There should be a jar of them somewhere." He looked along the shelf and found a small crock with a lid. "Here. These'll help if we can get her conscious enough to let one dissolve in her mouth."

"Sage." The last bundle. "Good for sore throats and fever both. I remember Makes Good Fire saying sage tea is the remedy that does a little bit of everything and none of it spectacularly, but sometimes a little bit of everything is what you need."

Opal had been committing each one to memory as he spoke, fixing the name to the jar or tin or bundle. She looked at the row of remedies on the work surface. Nolan was giving her knowledge. His mother's knowledge and the knowledge that an Apsáalooke healer had shared with them across the boundary of culture and language because sickness didn't observe boundaries and healing shouldn't either.

"The mullein tea," she said. "I strain it through cloth. How long do I steep it?"

"Until the water turns the color of weak coffee. Ten minutes, maybe twelve. Not longer, or it gets too strong and turns the stomach."

"And the elderflower tincture. How much honey?"

"A spoonful to a cup. Elizabeth uses the darkest honey we have.
"

"The yarrow sweat. How do I know when to stop? How long do I let her sweat before I cool her down again?"

"When the fever breaks. You'll feel it. The skin changes, goes from that dry heat to damp. When she starts to sweat on her own, that's the fever letting go. Then you cool her gradually, not all at once. Change the bedding, put a fresh nightgown on her, keep the room warm."

She repeated each instruction back to him, and he nodded at each repetition, and the exchange had the steady, focused rhythm of two people doing necessary work with no room for anything wasted.

"There's one more thing," he said. "A mustard plaster. For the chest congestion. It draws the fluid up and helps them breathe."

He gathered what he needed from the cellar shelves and they carried everything back to the kitchen, where the warmth of the cookstove met them at the door. Nolan set a tin of mustard powder on the table beside a sack of flour and a bowl.

"One part mustard to three parts flour," he said. He measured with his hands, scooping mustard powder into the bowl, then flour. "You mix them dry first, then add warm water, just enough to make a paste. Not too thick, not too thin."

He stirred the mixture with a wooden spoon while Opal watched his hands. The paste came together, yellow-brown and pungent, the sharp bite of mustard rising from the bowl.

"You spread it on a piece of cloth. Thin, about the thickness of a knife blade." He laid a square of flannel on the table and spread the paste across it with the back of the spoon, working it evenly to the edges. "Then you fold the cloth over so the paste is between two layers. Never put the mustard directly on the skin. It'll burn."

"How long does it stay on?"

"Fifteen minutes the first time. You check the skin underneath every five minutes. If it's going red, that's normal, that's the draw working. If it starts to blister or she says it's burning, you take it off."

"And this draws the fluid from the lungs?"

"It draws the congestion toward the surface. Opens the chest." He paused, his hands still on the cloth. "Makes Good Fire showed our mother this. Said her people had used mustard and other poultices for generations. Elizabeth watched our mother make them for our father when he'd get a winter cough, and she kept making them after."

They applied the first plaster together. Nolan carried it to the bedroom, and Opal unbuttoned the top of Elizabeth's nightgown enough to lay the folded cloth against her upper chest. The smell of mustard filled the small room, sharp and medicinal. Elizabeth stirred at the warmth of it, her head turning on the pillow, and a cough broke loose from somewhere deep in her lungs, wet and rattling, and for a terrible moment Opal thought she might choke on whatever was loosening inside her.

But the cough spent itself and Elizabeth's breathing settled, and when Opal pressed her ear close she thought, perhaps, that the rasp at the bottom of each exhale was fractionally less thick than it had been that morning. Perhaps. She didn't trust herself to be sure. Hope was a dangerous thing when you were this tired, capable of turning shadows into shapes that weren't there.

They removed the plaster after fifteen minutes and checked the skin beneath, pink and warm, and Nolan nodded and said, "Good. We'll do that again in a few hours."

The afternoon passed in the relentless rhythm the days had taken on. Opal brewed mullein tea, straining it through a piece of cheesecloth until the liquid ran clear and golden. She mixed elderflower with honey and set it near the fire to stay warm. She made willow bark tea, the bitter, familiar smell of it filling the kitchen. When Elizabeth surfaced briefly around noon, her eyes open but confused, Opal got three spoonfuls of broth into her and half a cup of the mullein tea before Elizabeth's eyes glazed and she slipped under again.

Nolan went out to check the cattle and came back an hour later with fresh snow on his coat and a grimness in his expression.

They sat at the kitchen table in the late afternoon, both of them holding cups of coffee, and the quiet between them was the quiet of two people who were exhausted, mentally drained, and worried.

"The Apsáalooke healer," Opal said. "Makes Good Fire. Does she still live nearby?"

Nolan turned his cup in his hands. "She moved north with her family about two years ago. Government kept pushing them onto the reservation lands. She was a good woman. She knew things about healing that I've never seen anyone else know. She'd look at a person and tell you what was wrong before they'd finished describing it."

"Do you think she could help Elizabeth? If we could reach her?"

"I don't know where she is. And even if I did, the snow's too deep to ride any distance. The closest doctor is in Livingston, and that's a full day and a half ride in good weather. We're doing everything I know to do. If the fever doesn't break in the next day or two..."

He didn't finish. He didn't need to.

Opal reached across the table and laid her hand over his. His fingers were rough and cold as they closed around hers with a pressure that was careful and firm. Then he released her hand and stood and went to check on Elizabeth. Opal stood and added another piece of wood to the cookstove.

Darkness came early and completely, the way December nights did in the valley, the light draining from the sky by four o'clock and night settling in with the finality of a door being closed. Opal heated broth and carried it to Elizabeth's bedside and managed to get several spoonfuls into her during a brief, groggy waking. She applied a third mustard plaster, checking the skin every few minutes.

Nolan ate the supper Opal set before him: biscuits and salt pork and potatoes she'd fried in lard. She ate without tasting any of it. Food had become fuel, nothing more, something you put into your body so your body would keep working because the work couldn't stop.

They settled into their positions for the night. Nolan on his bedroll on one side of Elizabeth's bed, Opal on her pallet of quilts on the other, the lamp turned down to a thin, amber glow that barely reached the corners of the room. Elizabeth lay between them, her breathing the only sound, that shallow, rattling rhythm that Opal had memorized against her will, every catch and rasp and pause mapped in her mind so precisely that any deviation would wake her from whatever thin sleep she managed.

Eventually, after not being able to fall asleep, Opal got up quietly and sat on the edge of Elizabeth's bed with her back against the headboard, her legs drawn up beneath a quilt, and she prayed.

The prayers came without structure or formality, the way water comes when a dam breaks, in a rush that carried everything with it.

Lord, I've already lost my mother and my father. I've carried that grief like a stone in my chest for two years, and I've borne it because

You gave me the strength to bear it and because I believed, I still believe, that You don't leave us alone in our suffering. But I'm asking You now, Lord, please. Please don't take Elizabeth. She's eighteen years old. She has so much life ahead of her, so much joy she hasn't had yet, and she deserves every bit of it. She deserves to fall in love and be married and have children who inherit her laugh and her stubborn goodness and her way of walking into a room and making it brighter just by being in it.

She took care of me when I was broken and helpless and a stranger in her home. She washed my hair and held my hand, and made me willow bark tea I didn't want to drink, and sat beside my bed through the worst nights of my life and never once complained. She called me her friend. She called me her sister. She gave me a place in her home and in her heart without asking for anything in return, and I love her, Lord. I love her so much it terrifies me because loving people means you can lose them, and I've already learned that lesson, and I can't learn it again. Not with her. Please, not with her.

Elizabeth's breathing hitched, and Opal froze. She counted the seconds of silence, one, two, three, her own breath held in her throat, and then the exhale came, rattling but steady, and the rhythm resumed, and Opal's held breath released in a shudder she felt all the way to her fingers.

And Nolan. Lord, please give him peace. He's carrying so much. He's lost his mother and his father and his uncle, and he's held this homestead and this family on his shoulders since he was barely more than a boy, and Elizabeth is all he has left. He loves her the way I loved my parents, with everything in him, and if he loses her, I don't know what it will do to him. I know You see him. I know You see the good in him, the faithfulness, the quiet way he serves and works and gives without ever counting the cost to himself. Please protect his heart. Please protect his sister. Please give us the strength to get through this night and the next one and the one after that until this fever breaks, because I believe it will break. I have to believe it will break.

She pressed a cool cloth to Elizabeth's forehead and listened to her breathe. Her prayers continued, a river of asking that ran beneath every thought and every action, and every moment of watching.

Across the room, Nolan turned on his bedroll. She could hear the restlessness in his movement, the shifting and resettling of a body that wanted sleep and a mind that wouldn't permit it. He turned again, and then a third time.

She saw his silhouette in the dim lamplight as he stood up, the broad line of his shoulders and the shadow of exhaustion in the way he moved, slower than usual, as if the weight he carried had settled into his muscles and bones. He came around to her side of the bed and sat on the edge of the mattress opposite her. She could see his face in the thin amber light. What she saw there just about broke her.

He was so tired. The skin beneath his eyes was bruised with sleeplessness, and the lines around his mouth had deepened into furrows that hadn't been there a week ago. But it was his eyes that held her, the rawness in them, the unguarded quality of a man who was exhausted and worried.

He reached out and laid his hand on Elizabeth's forehead. His fingers rested there for a long moment, reading the heat he felt, searching for any sign of change. His jaw worked once, a small, involuntary tightening. He withdrew his hand and looked at Opal.

"I love her so much," he said. His voice was low and rough and stripped of everything except the truth. "I can't lose her too."

"Thank you," he continued. "For caring for her and loving her as much as I do."

Opal's eyes never left his. She saw the man who had carried her through a storm. The man who had given her his room and slept on the floor in his own home. The man who showed love through every action but rarely, so rarely, spoke it aloud. And she understood what these words had cost him.

She nodded.

Nolan held her gaze for a moment longer. Then he reached over and pulled the quilt higher around Elizabeth's shoulders with the same gentleness he used with everything he loved, and he returned to his bedroll on the other side of the bed, and the room settled back into its vigil.

Opal dipped the cloth. Pressed it to Elizabeth's temples. Listened to her breathe.

Outside, the December cold held the valley in its grip, and the stars above the homestead were sharp and countless in the clear black sky, and inside the small bedroom three people who had become a family weathered the long night the only way they knew how: with faith, and with love, and with the stubborn refusal to let go of either one.

Chapter 32

The sixth cow was dead when Nolan found her. She was lying on her side in the lee of the hayrick where the rest of the herd had clustered against the wind. A young heifer, second winter, one of the Hereford crosses he'd been building the herd around. He stood over her with snow driving sideways into his face and the wind tearing at his buckskin, and he didn't feel anything. Six heads in two days. The blizzard, the cold, the relentless accumulation of loss that a Montana winter exacted from everything it touched.

He tied a rope around the heifer's hind legs and used Cob to drag her away from the herd because a dead animal among live ones bred panic and disease. The snow was deep, and the effort of trying to walk through it left him winded and shaking in a way that had less to do with exertion than with the fact that he'd slept six hours in the past three days and eaten only what Opal put directly in front of him.

He broke the ice in the creek with his ax. The ice was thick, and it took several swings, each one jarring up through his arms and into his shoulders. When the water opened up dark and still beneath the shattered surface, the cattle moved toward it with the heavy, deliberate patience of animals that had learned not to waste energy.

The blizzard had no ceiling and no walls, just a continuous, howling press of snow and wind that reduced the world to the twenty feet of visibility directly in front of him and erased everything else.

He went back to the barn, and he worked. It was what he knew how to do when everything else was failing. He checked the stalls, checked the water, and ran his hands along Copper's flank and down each of Cob's legs because a lame horse in this weather was a catastrophe he couldn't afford.

He milked Bessie. Opal had been doing it morning and evening since she'd claimed the task weeks ago, but he'd taken it back yesterday during the worst of this latest storm because the walk between the house and the barn was treacherous. The milk steamed as it hit the pail, and Bessie chewed her cud.

He carried the milk pail to the barrel near the barn door and set it down. He'd take it to the house when he went in. He should go in now. He should check on Elizabeth. He should eat something. He should relieve Opal, who'd been at Elizabeth's bedside since he left the house hours ago.

He walked to Cob's stall instead. The big gelding was standing hip-shot in the straw, one hind hoof tipped, his head low and his eyes half-closed in the drowsy contentment of a horse that had been fed and watered and had nowhere to be. Nolan unlatched the stall door, stepped inside, and closed it behind him. He stood there with one hand on Cob's shoulder, and the last of whatever had been holding him upright gave way.

His back hit the stall wall, and he slid to the straw-covered floor. His legs went out in front of him, and his head dropped. He pressed the heels of his hands against his eyes because if he didn't press them there; he was going to lose the hold on himself he'd kept for days, and he wasn't sure he could get it back.

He feared Elizabeth was dying.

"Lord." His voice was rough and cracked, and the word came out broken. "Lord, I don't know what else to do."

"I've done everything I know. Everything our mother taught us and everything Makes Good Fire showed us. I've kept the house warm and the fires burning, and I've watched Opal tend Elizabeth with care and devotion... and it isn't enough. None of it is enough, and I'm sitting here in a barn asking You for something I don't deserve because I've already asked for so much from You. You've given me more than most men get in a lifetime, but Lord, I am begging You."

The words tore loose from a place deeper than his chest, deeper than his bones, from the foundation of him where grief, fear, and love were all tangled in a knot so tight he couldn't separate them.

"She's eighteen, Lord. Eighteen. She's kind and brave, and good. I've built my entire life around keeping her safe, and I am failing. I am failing her, Lord, and I don't want to bury another person I love. I can't. I can't do it again."

His voice broke on the last word, and the silence that followed was enormous, filling the stall, filling the barn, filling the gap between his asking and whatever answer might come. He sat in the straw with his hands over his face and his shoulders tight against the wall, and he waited. He didn't know what he was waiting for.

A sign. A voice. The sudden lifting of a weight he'd been carrying so long he'd forgotten what it felt like to stand without it.

What came instead was Cob's nose.

The gelding lowered his head and pushed his muzzle against Nolan's shoulder, a firm, insistent nudge. Then Cob nudged him again, harder, and Nolan's hand came up and found the broad, flat of the gelding's jaw and held it. His throat seized, and his eyes burned, and he pressed his forehead against Cob's face and held there, trembling, for a long moment that he would never speak of to anyone.

He breathed in deeply. He let the shaking pass through him. He breathed in deeply again. The tightness in his chest loosened by a fraction, not much, barely enough to notice.

He stood. He brushed the straw off his clothes. He walked to the barrel of water near the barn door, cupped his hands, and splashed the cold water over his face. Once, twice, and the shock of it drove the rawness back behind his eyes where it belonged. He dried his face against the sleeve of his buckskin and cleared his throat.

"Lord, give me the strength to walk back into that house," he said quietly. "That's all I'm asking for myself."

He picked up the milk pail, opened the barn door, and the storm hit him full in the face, and he walked into it.

The wall of heat that met him as he opened the front door wrapped around him like two strong hands. The cookstove was radiating steadily, fed and tended, and a lamp burned on the kitchen table. The broth pot sat on the back of the stove with steam curling from beneath its lid. The kitchen was clean. The floor had been swept. A plate sat on the counter covered with a cloth, and beneath it he knew without looking there would be food she'd set aside for him.

He hung his buckskin, pulled off his boots, and walked to Elizabeth's room. The lamp inside was turned low, and in its glow he saw Opal sitting in the chair beside Elizabeth's bed with her Bible open in her lap, reading aloud in a voice that was quiet and steady.

"Fear thou not; for I am with thee: be not dismayed; for I am thy God: I will strengthen thee; yea, I will help thee; yea, I will uphold thee with the right hand of my righteousness."

Elizabeth's face was flushed with fever, her breathing a shallow, rattling sound. Her hair was freshly braided, her nightgown clean, and the quilts tucked neatly around her shoulders.

He stepped into the room, and Opal's eyes lifted from the page and found him. Her gaze held his for a moment, steady and calm, and then her eyes returned to the Bible and her voice continued.

"For I the Lord thy God will hold thy right hand, saying unto thee, Fear not; I will help thee."

He sat in the chair on the opposite side of the bed. He reached out and laid his hand on Elizabeth's forehead, a gesture he'd repeated a hundred times in the past several days, and the heat was still there, steady and fierce. It had cracked briefly yesterday morning, and then it had climbed again by evening. The hope that had opened in him during those few hours during the day had closed again like a fist.

Opal closed the Bible with her finger marking the page and looked at him across the bed.

"She was awake for a few minutes about an hour ago," she said. "She knew me. She asked for water, and I got a full cup into her and some broth. The cough is still deep, but I think the mullein is helping. She's breathing a little easier."

He nodded. He wanted to believe her. He wanted the fractional improvement she described to be the beginning of something rather than one of the fever's tricks.

"I've been considering combining yarrow with elderflower," Opal said. "The yarrow to push the fever and the elderflower for the congestion, both at once instead of spacing them apart. If we could get the fever to break and her chest to loosen at the same time, it might give her body a chance to gain some ground."

"Elizabeth never mixed those two," he said.

"But we've tried them separately, and the fever keeps coming back. I thought if we brought both to bear at once, it might be what pushes it over."

He looked at Elizabeth's face on the pillow. The flush on her cheeks. The cracked lips. The faint blue shadows beneath her eyes. "Try it," he said.

Chapter 33

The needle pulled the thread through in a long, even draw, and Opal watched the pale blue floss lay itself against the white cotton in the shape of a petal she'd been working on for the better part of an hour. Her embroidery hoop rested in her lap, the pillowcase stretched taut within its wooden circle, and the stitches she'd laid down over the past several nights had begun to form a spray of forget-me-nots along the pillowcase's edge. The work was slow and required a focus that had nothing to do with artistry and everything to do with keeping her hands occupied while the rest of her listened.

She listened constantly now. Every breath Elizabeth drew was a sound Opal tracked the way a mother tracked the breathing of a newborn, with a vigilance so deep it had become a condition of her body rather than a choice of her mind. The shallow, rattling rhythm filled the bedroom with its fragile metronome, and Opal's needle moved in counterpoint to it, rising and falling between the fabric.

The lamp on the bedside table was turned low, its flame barely more than a tongue of light behind the glass chimney. The bedroom was warm from the fire Nolan had built up before he'd laid down, and the air carried the faint, lingering sharpness of the mustard poultice they'd applied to Elizabeth's chest earlier that evening. The quilts rose and fell with Elizabeth's breathing. Her face on the pillow was flushed and thin, the bones of her cheeks more prominent than they'd been a week ago, and her braided hair lay across the pillow in a rope that Opal had re-plaited that afternoon because caring for Elizabeth's hair had become one of the small, tender rituals that gave structure to the formless days.

Nolan slept on his bedroll on the opposite side of the room. He'd come in from the barn hours ago with exhaustion carved into the lines around his eyes. He'd sat with Elizabeth for a long while, his hand on her forehead. She had told him to sleep. He'd resisted. She'd told him again, and he'd finally unrolled the bedroll and laid down, and within minutes the steady rhythm of his breathing had joined Elizabeth's in the quiet room.

Opal set another stitch. The forget-me-not took shape beneath her needle, five small petals surrounding a center of yellow French knots, and the delicacy of the work was absurd in this context, a Virginia parlor skill practiced beside a sickbed in a Montana cabin while a blizzard buried the valley outside. But her mother had taught her that needlework was prayer for the hands, and tonight Opal needed every form of prayer she could find.

A sound broke the rhythm.

It wasn't a cough. It was softer than that, a murmur that rose from somewhere beneath the fever's surface like a bubble rising through deep water. Elizabeth's head turned on the pillow. Her lips moved, shaping something that might have been a word, and then the sound came again, stronger this time. A low, confused vocalization that carried the unmistakable quality of a person trying to surface from a place that had held them under for a very long time.

Opal's embroidery hoop hit the floor. She was on her feet and at the bedside with her hand on Elizabeth's forehead before the hoop had finished rolling, and what she felt beneath her palm stopped the breath in her chest.

The skin was warm. Still warm, still carrying fever. But the fierce, dry heat that had burned beneath her hand for days, the heat that had made Elizabeth's forehead feel like a stone left in the sun, had receded. The difference was subtle, perhaps a degree or two, the kind of change that could have been wishful thinking from a woman who'd been praying for exactly this.

She reached for the basin on the bedside table, wrung the cloth in the cool water, and pressed it to Elizabeth's forehead with a care that trembled in her fingers. She folded a second cloth and laid it along the side of Elizabeth's neck where the blood ran close beneath the skin.

"Elizabeth," she said softly. "Elizabeth, can you hear me?"

Elizabeth's eyes opened. They were glassy and unfocused, the pupils wide in the low lamplight, and they moved across Opal's face without settling, as though Opal were a shape seen through water rather than a person. Her lips parted, and a sound came out that was rough and thin and bore no resemblance to the bright, warm voice that had filled this house previously.

"Where..." Elizabeth's brow furrowed. Her gaze drifted past Opal toward the ceiling and then back, and something flickered behind the glassiness, a struggle to organize what she was seeing into a world that made sense. "What... Opal?"

"I'm here." Opal pressed the cloth gently against her temple. "You're in your bed. You've been very ill. You're safe."

Elizabeth's mouth moved again, but the words that came were tangled and incomplete, broken syllables that started toward meaning and collapsed before they arrived. She tried to lift her head, and the effort produced a tremor that ran through her neck and into her shoulders, and Opal placed her hand gently on Elizabeth's collarbone and said, "Don't try to move. Just stay still. I'm right here."

From across the room came the sound of Nolan coming awake. Not gradually. All at once, passing from sleep to full awareness in the space of a single breath. Opal heard the bedroll shift, heard his boots on the floor, and then he was beside her, standing over the bed, and the look on his face when he saw Elizabeth's open eyes was something Opal would carry with her for the rest of her life. It was hope, raw and undisguised, breaking through the exhaustion and fear.

"She's conscious," Opal said. "The fever's dropped. Not broken, but lower than it's been."

Nolan knelt beside the bed. His hand found Elizabeth's and closed around it, and his sister's fingers twitched weakly inside his grip. He didn't speak. He held her hand and looked at her face, and the stillness in him was different from the stillness of the past week. This wasn't the stillness of a man holding himself together. This was the stillness of a man afraid to move in case the thing he was seeing turned out not to be real.

"Nolan..." Elizabeth's voice was a whisper scraped across sandpaper. Her eyes found him and this time they focused, narrowing with the effortful concentration of someone pulling a distant object into clarity. "Nolan."

"I'm here, Beth."

The name slipped out of him, soft and unguarded, and Opal realized she'd never heard him call his sister anything but Elizabeth. The tenderness of the shortened name in his rough voice nearly brought tears to her eyes.

Opal refreshed the cloth and pressed it along Elizabeth's neck again. "She needs fluids. Broth if we can get it into her, and water."

"I'll heat the broth." He stood. His hand released Elizabeth's slowly, as though letting go required a conscious act of will, and then he was moving toward the kitchen.

Opal turned back to Elizabeth. The girl's eyes had drifted closed again, and for a terrible instant Opal thought she'd lost her, thought the fever had pulled her back under the way it had so many times before. But Elizabeth's lips moved, and a sound came out, garbled and confused, and her eyes opened again with the heavy, bewildered effort of a person fighting a current that wanted to drag her down.

"Stay with me," Opal said. She took Elizabeth's hand. "Keep your eyes open, Elizabeth. Talk to me. Tell me something. Anything."

"I... cold." The word came out slurred and effortful. Elizabeth's brow creased. "My... everything hurts."

"I know it does. You've been fighting a fever for days and your body is tired, but you're doing so well. You're coming back to us,"

Opal squeezed her hand gently. "What else? Can you tell me where you are?"

Elizabeth's gaze traveled slowly around the room, taking in the lamp, the quilts, the familiar walls of her own bedroom as though she were cataloging them from a great distance. "Home," she said. The word cost her something visible. "I'm... home."

"That's right. You're home and safe, and Nolan and I are right here."

"How..." Elizabeth swallowed with difficulty, her throat working against the dryness. "How long?"

"Several days. Don't worry about that now."

Elizabeth's eyes found Opal's face again, and something that wasn't confusion moved behind them. It was recognition, not just of Opal's features but of something deeper, an awareness of what Opal's presence at her bedside at this hour in these clothes with those shadows beneath her eyes actually meant. Her fingers tightened around Opal's hand with a strength that surprised them both.

"You stayed," Elizabeth said. The words were barely audible, but they were clear.

Opal's throat closed. She pressed her lips together and nodded because her voice had deserted her, and she held Elizabeth's hand and willed herself not to cry.

She bowed her head. Elizabeth's hand was still in hers, thin and warm, and Opal closed her eyes and let the words come the way they'd been coming for days.

"Lord, I am begging You. I am begging You to spare this girl. She is kind and brave and good, and she has so much life ahead of her, and I love her, Lord. I love her the way I would love a sister of my own blood, and I am asking You, I am pleading with You, show her mercy. Show us all mercy. Let this fever break. Let her body heal. Let her stay."

The words ran out, and the silence that followed was not empty. It was full in the way that a room is full after music stops, the resonance of what had been spoken still vibrating in the air. Opal kept her head bowed and her eyes closed, and she held Elizabeth's hand and breathed, and the breathing itself became the prayer, each inhale an asking and each exhale a surrender.

Nolan came through the doorway carrying a steaming cup of broth, and Opal raised her head and wiped her eyes with the back of her free hand.

"Elizabeth," Opal leaned close. "Your brother's brought you some broth. We need you to drink it. Can you sit up a little?"

Elizabeth's attempt to rise produced a tremor in her arms that collapsed almost immediately, her body too depleted by days of fever to support even the simplest effort. Opal shifted onto the bed beside her and slid her arm beneath Elizabeth's shoulders, gathering the girl's weight against her own body and lifting her to a half-sitting position. Elizabeth's head lolled against Opal's shoulder, and the frailty of her, the lightness, the way her bones felt close beneath the cotton of her nightgown, sent a wave of protectiveness through Opal so fierce it startled her.

Nolan brought the cup to Elizabeth's lips. He tipped it carefully, watching her face, letting the warm broth reach her mouth in small, measured amounts. Elizabeth swallowed. The effort of it moved through her throat, visible and labored, but the broth went down. By the third swallow, Nolan's jaw eased.

Elizabeth drank the entire cup. It took several minutes, Nolan patient with each small tilt and pause, Opal holding her steady. When the cup was empty, Elizabeth turned her head slightly, and her voice came out in a whisper that was barely a breath.

"Water."

Nolan set the cup down and reached for the pitcher on the bedside table. He poured water into the cup and brought it to her lips, and Elizabeth drank with the slow, careful swallows of a body remembering what it needed. When she'd had enough, she turned her head away.

Opal lowered her gently back onto the pillow. She smoothed the quilts around Elizabeth's shoulders and placed a cloth on her forehead. Elizabeth looked up at the two of them from the pillow with an expression that was exhausted and confused, and grateful all at once. She tried to speak. The words came in fragments that didn't quite connect, broken pieces of thoughts that the fever had scattered, but her eyes moved between Opal's face and Nolan's with a clarity that hadn't been there moments ago.

Then she smiled.

It was small and weak, and it barely lifted the corners of her cracked lips, but it was unmistakably Elizabeth's smile. Opal felt the knot in her chest that she'd been carrying since the afternoon Elizabeth had collapsed on the kitchen floor.

Elizabeth's eyes closed. Her breathing settled into a rhythm that was slower and deeper than the shallow, rapid pattern of the past week, and the rasp at the bottom of each exhale was still there but slightly diminished, as though something inside her chest had loosened its grip.

Nolan was kneeling beside the bed. He looked at Opal across his sleeping sister, and his expression held fear and hope, and exhaustion, yet it was tender and unguarded.

"She's turning," Opal said quietly. "The fever is dropping. I can feel it."

He nodded. His hand rested on the quilt near Elizabeth's shoulder, and Opal watched his fingers press into the fabric.

"Stay with her," Opal said. "I'm going to make a fresh mustard poultice while she's resting. If we can keep drawing the congestion out while the fever drops, it'll give her lungs a chance to clear, I'm sure of it."

He nodded, and Opal rose from the bed carefully, testing her weight on her healing leg as she stood. The stiffness was there, the deep ache that lived in the bone and flared when she'd been sitting too long, but she gathered her walking stick from where it leaned against the wall and made her way out of the bedroom.

The cookstove radiated its steady warmth. The broth pot sat on the back burner, and the kettle held water she'd boiled earlier that evening. She set the walking stick against the counter and reached for the tin of mustard powder on the shelf, the flour sack beside it, and the mixing bowl she'd used before.

One part mustard. Three parts flour. Mix dry ingredients, then add warm water to form a paste.

Her hands knew the motions now. She'd made this poultice several times by now, following the instructions Nolan had taught her. She scooped the powder and the flour with a precision that had become routine. She reached for the kettle and tipped warm water into the bowl, and the sharp, pungent smell of mustard rose into the kitchen air.

The wind pressed against the north wall of the house with its low, relentless voice, and the fire ticked softly inside the cookstove as she stirred the paste.

Elizabeth was alive. Elizabeth had opened her eyes, spoken, smiled, and taken broth. The fever was dropping, and there was hope, genuine hope...

The sound that came out of her was not a sob. It was something larger than that, something that had been building in her body for a week, compressed and contained behind the composure she'd maintained. She'd held herself together through the long nights and the terrifying days and the moments when Elizabeth's breathing had grown so shallow that Opal had pressed her ear to the girl's chest to confirm there was still a heartbeat beneath the rattling of her lungs. She'd held herself together through the fear and the exhaustion and the sight of Nolan's face each time he came in from the barn with his jaw set. She'd held herself together because falling apart was a luxury she couldn't afford while there was work to be done and a girl to be saved.

The poultice was half-mixed in the bowl, and Opal stood at the counter with mustard paste on her fingers and her shoulders folded inward, and she wept.

Her weeping came fast and violent from the place where her love for Elizabeth lived alongside her terror of losing her. It came from the exhaustion that had moved past tiredness into something that felt structural, as though the framework of her body had been held at tension for so long that the release of it was itself a kind of collapse. She pressed her hand over her mouth, but the sound came through her fingers, a ragged, broken sound that filled the kitchen and wouldn't stop.

She didn't hear him come in, but she felt his hands on her shoulders, turning her, and then his arms were around her and he pulled her against his chest with a firmness that left no room for resistance. He held her the way a man holds something he is unwilling to let go of, one arm low across her back and the other high between her shoulder blades, his hand spread wide and steady against the fabric of her dress. The solidity of him, the sheer physical fact of him surrounding her, was so immediate and so complete that the last of her composure broke apart and she let it.

She cried against his chest. She cried with her face pressed into the worn cotton of his shirt and her hands gripping the fabric at his sides. The sound of it was ugly and honest and human, and his arms didn't loosen. His chin rested above her head and his hands held her and he said nothing, because he was a man who had never needed words to say what mattered, and what mattered right now was that she was falling apart in his kitchen and he was not going to let her fall.

She could feel his heartbeat against her cheek. Steady. Strong. The rhythm of it came through the cotton of his shirt and into her skin and settled there, a counterpoint to the ragged pattern of her breathing. She pressed closer because closer was where the steadiness was. His arms tightened.

They stood there long enough for her breathing to slow and the crying to spend itself and the trembling in her shoulders to quiet to a stillness.

He continued to hold her, and she let him.

Chapter 34

The rope was stiff in his hands, frozen where it had hung coiled on the side of the house since autumn. Nolan worked the hemp between his gloves, bending it joint by joint until it softened enough to handle, and the cold bit through the leather into his fingers while he tied the first knot around the porch post. A bowline, the same knot his father had taught him when he was eight years old.

He couldn't see the barn. He knew where it was the way he knew where his own hands were in the dark, by knowledge that lived in his body rather than his eyes, but the blizzard had erased it. The snow drove horizontally across the yard in sheets so dense and so white that the air itself had become a solid thing, a wall of moving ice that pressed against his face and chest and filled his mouth when he turned the wrong way. The wind came from the north and it didn't gust. It sustained itself at a pitch that was less a sound than a pressure, a constant, tremendous force that leaned against him like a man trying to push him off his feet.

He stepped off the porch and entered a world of white.

The rope paid out behind him through his left hand while his right arm shielded his face. He walked in the direction he knew the barn to be, each step a negotiation with snow that reached past his knees and drifted higher against anything vertical. The cold was absolute. It found the gaps at his wrists and his collar and the seam where his hat met his forehead, and it occupied those spaces with an efficiency that left no room for warmth. His eyes watered and the tears froze against his lashes.

The barn was over a hundred yards from the house, a distance he'd walked numerous times without thought, and now each step was an act of faith in its most literal form. He couldn't see what was ahead of him. He couldn't see what was behind. The rope in his left hand was the only proof that the house still existed.

His boot caught on something beneath the snow, and he stumbled forward, catching himself with his free hand against the drift, and the snow swallowed his arm to the elbow. He pulled free and kept walking. The rope slid through his glove, rough and steady, paying out from the coil he'd slung across his chest.

Lord, be with me. Guide me, Lord.

His shoulder hit something solid and the shock of it ran through his arm and into his chest. His hand came up and found rough-sawn planking beneath a skin of ice, and the relief that moved through him was so profound it weakened his knees. The barn wall.

He followed the wall to the door, his hand tracing the planks, and he hauled the door open against the drift that had built up against it and stepped inside. The wind cut off so abruptly that the silence felt like a sound of its own. Snow swirled in behind him before he got the door shut.

He tied the rope off to the post beside the barn door. A second bowline, pulled tight, tested with his full weight. The line between the house and the barn was taut now, a thread of hemp stretched through a complete whiteout. He'd heard stories from men who hadn't strung a rope. Men who'd stepped off their own porches in a blizzard and walked past their barns and kept walking because in a whiteout there was no past and no future and no sideways, only the direction your body was pointed. If that direction was wrong by even a few degrees, the next thing you found was open ground, and the next thing after that was the death.

He pulled off his gloves and flexed his fingers until the feeling came back in sharp, needling waves. The barn was cold, but it was sheltered, and the difference between cold and wind-driven cold was the difference between discomfort and danger. Copper stamped in her stall and blew through her nostrils, and Cob turned his big head toward Nolan with the patient, unsurprised expression of a horse who'd seen a great many storms and expected to see a great many more.

"Mornin'," Nolan said, and Cob blinked at him.

He worked. He broke the ice that had formed on the water trough inside the barn and checked the level. He mucked the stalls with the methodical, unhurried rhythm of a man who understood that this work, today, was the only work within his reach. The cattle were beyond him. He'd moved the herd closer before the worst of the storm, pushed them down to the lower pasture near the creek where the tree line broke the wind. The hay he'd sledged out two days ago would hold them for a while longer. But he couldn't reach them now. The blizzard had sealed the valley so completely that the world beyond this barn might as well have been another country.

He'd lost six head so far. The number would climb. He knew it the way he knew weather, in his bones. A storm this fierce, this prolonged, killed cattle. It killed them by cold and by drift and by suffocation when the snow buried them where they'd huddled.

He'd rebuild. He'd done it before, after the bad winter of '82. God had provided then and would provide again.

He milked Bessie. She stood patient and warm in her stall, her bag heavy, and the milk came down in steady streams that rang against the pail. The sound was regular and ordinary and allowed his mind to go where it wanted to go.

Where it wanted to go was the kitchen. Last night. The feel of her against his chest.

He'd heard her crying. He'd found her at the counter with mustard paste on her fingers and her shoulders curving inward. The sound coming out of her had cracked something fierce open within himself. He'd crossed the kitchen and turned her and put his arms around her because there was nothing else to do. The woman he loved was falling apart, so he held her.

She'd fit against him as though the space between his chin and his chest had been built for her. The top of her head had come just beneath his jaw, and her hands had gripped the fabric at his sides. He'd felt her breathe against him in ragged, broken pulls that gradually lengthened and slowed until the trembling in her shoulders went still. He'd held her through all of it. The smallness of her had stunned him again, as it had in the past. The realization that this woman who carried herself with such composure, who'd nursed his sister through a fever that would have broken most people, and read Scripture aloud in the lamplight as though her voice alone could hold death at the door, was a small, slight woman whose shoulders fit entirely inside the span of his arms.

The milk pail was full. Nolan set it aside and rested his forearms across his knees.

He wasn't fighting the memory. That was the thing he noticed about himself, sitting in this barn with the storm howling against the walls. He wasn't pushing the feeling away or measuring it against Catherine or telling himself to be careful. The prayer he'd spoken in this barn the other night had opened something in him that he couldn't close, and he didn't want to close it. He'd asked God to give him the strength to walk back into that house, and God had given him something larger than strength. God had given him clarity.

He loved her. He loved the way she tucked Elizabeth's hair behind her ear when she braided it. He loved the steadiness of her hands when she changed a poultice. He loved that she'd learned to milk a cow and to build up a fire, and to make broth from bones because the work needed doing and she refused to be a woman who watched while others worked. He loved the careful way she held her embroidery hoop. The quiet way she read aloud and the look on her face when she stood at the kitchen window watching the snow fall, an expression that was both longing and contentment, as though the landscape she saw was a country she'd been traveling toward without knowing its name.

And she loved him. He knew that now too, not from anything she'd said but from the way she'd pressed her face into his shirt and held on. A woman didn't weep like that in a man's arms unless she trusted him with something deeper than friendship. The trust she'd shown him last night, the complete, unguarded surrender of her composure, had told him everything.

He stood and picked up the pail and carried it to the barrel near the door. He checked the rope's knot one final time, pulled on his gloves, and opened the barn door.

The storm hit him fresh. He took the rope in his right hand and the milk pail in his left, and he walked, leaning into the wind. The porch post appeared out of the blizzard like something surfacing from deep water, and he found the steps with his boot and climbed them and opened the front door and stepped inside.

The cookstove radiated its deep, steady heat, and the air smelled of fresh coffee.

He hung his buckskin on the hook beside the door and worked the knot on his boots with fingers that were clumsy from the cold. The boots came off, and he set them on the hearth near the fireplace where the heat would dry the leather. The fire was burning low, a bed of coals beneath a single log that had nearly spent itself, and he took two lengths of split pine from the wood box and laid them across the coals, and watched the bark catch and curl. The new flames climbed, and the fire settled into its work. The warmth of it reached his stockinged feet and began the slow process of returning feeling to his toes.

He stood at the fireplace with his hands extended toward the heat, turning them palm-up to let the warmth find the places the cold had gone deepest. He turned so the direct heat hit his backside.

He noticed a pillowcase on the chair near the hearth, the one Opal had been embroidering beside Elizabeth's bed. He could see the forget-me-nots from here, pale blue stitches against white cotton, delicate and precise and entirely out of place in a bachelor's cabin in the Montana foothills. But the out-of-placeness was exactly what made them matter. She'd brought something fine into a rough house.

He walked to the kitchen and poured himself a cup of coffee. The coffee was strong and hot, and exactly right.

Opal came out of Elizabeth's room with a basin of water in her hands and a cloth over her shoulder. She'd pinned her hair back and her sleeves were rolled to the elbow. The shadows beneath her eyes were darker than they'd been yesterday, but her face when she saw him carried a warmth that reached across the kitchen and settled against his chest.

"She ate this morning," Opal said. "Two cups of broth and a few sips of water. She asked where you were."

"What'd you tell her?"

"That you were tending the animals and that the storm was keeping you longer than usual. She said to tell you Bessie probably has opinions about the cold." A small, tired smile. "Her words."

"The rope's up," he said. "Between here and the barn. Visibility's nothing out there. I'll use it every trip until this breaks."

Opal set the basin on the counter and wrung the cloth into it. "How bad is it?"

"Bad. I can't check the herd until the wind lets up. The horses and Bessie are fine. Everything's watered and fed."

She nodded. She poured the basin water out and set it aside, and then she stood at the counter across from him. They looked at each other in the quiet kitchen with the fire ticking in the stove and the wind leaning against the walls.

There it was. The thing that lived between them now, unspoken and undeniable. The memory of her face against his shirt and his arms around her and the long, still minutes they'd stood in this kitchen after her crying had stopped, when neither of them had moved and neither of them had spoken. The silence had said more than any words he knew. She knew it was there. He knew it was there. The knowledge sat in the room with them like a third presence, warm and tentative and so new that neither of them seemed willing to touch it directly for fear it might not survive the handling.

She was small. He kept returning to that: the way her frame contained so much resolve and tenderness and strength in a body that was slight enough that he'd held her entirely inside his arms. The petiteness of her struck him not as fragility but as a kind of concentrated grace, the same way a well-made tool carried all its purpose in a compact form. God had put this woman in his path. God had brought her to his door broken and stranded and had asked him to tend her the way he tended everything entrusted to his care, and somewhere in the tending, the caretaking had become something holy.

He didn't feel worthy of her. The thought arrived without drama, a quiet recognition that the woman standing across from him had left a life of wealth and refinement and education. She had ended up in a cabin in Montana with a man whose hands were rough and whose vocabulary was spare. His entire estate amounted to a hundred and sixty acres and a herd that was shrinking by the day. She'd had parlors and gas lamps and a library with books, and here she was making broth from bones and sleeping in a chair beside his sister's sickbed. She'd never once, not in all the weeks she'd been here, made him feel beneath her.

That was the thing. That was the piece of it that made him feel like a man who'd been given more than he'd asked for. She saw this life clearly, saw the roughness and the labor and the isolation and the cold, and she'd not fought it.

He wanted to say something. The wanting was a physical thing, a pressure in his chest that pushed against the silence. But the words didn't come, because they never came easily for him, and the ones that mattered most were the ones that cost the most to speak. So he held her gaze across the kitchen and he let the silence carry what it could.

"I should check on her again," Opal said softly. She picked up a clean cloth from the counter and turned toward the bedroom.

"Opal."

She stopped. She turned back. Her eyes found his and held.

"You should rest," he said. "I'll sit with her. You haven't slept much in days."

"Neither have you."

"I slept enough last night. You didn't."

She opened her mouth to argue, and he watched the argument form and then dissolve, replaced by weariness and gratitude.

"Two hours," she said. "Wake me in two hours."

"I will."

Nolan poured himself a second cup of coffee as she went back into Elizabeth's room. He checked the broth pot and added water from the kettle to keep the level steady. He carried his cup to Elizabeth's room and settled into the chair beside her bed. His sister was sleeping. Her breathing was slow and even. The rasp at the bottom of each exhale had softened further. The flush on her cheeks was the flush of healing now, not fever.

The blizzard pressed on and the fire burned in the fireplace. Nolan Ridgeway sat beside his sister's bed and drank his coffee and thought about the woman sleeping on the pallet of quilts on the floor on the other side of the bed. He felt like a man whose life was not merely endured but blessed.

Chapter 35

Elizabeth ate the porridge one careful spoonful at a time, her hand trembling with the effort of lifting each bite to her own mouth, and Opal let her do it. The instinct to take the spoon and feed her was strong, but Elizabeth had asked to hold it herself, and the asking had been the most Elizabeth-like thing she'd done in days.

The porridge was thin, more milk than oat, sweetened with a spoonful of the honey Nolan had brought up from the cellar. Elizabeth managed half the bowl and then leaned back against the pillows Opal had stacked behind her. The tiredness of a body doing the hard work of mending rather than the terrible exhaustion of a body losing its fight.

"That was good, Opal. Did you put honey in it?"

"I did."

"Nolan hates honey in porridge. He thinks it's frivolous."

"Then Nolan can make his own porridge."

Elizabeth smiled. It was small and tired, but it was real, and Opal carried it with her like a coin in her pocket for the rest of the morning.

The blizzard had eased overnight from its worst fury into something that was merely relentless; the wind no longer howling but pressing steadily against the walls in a sustained, low moan that had become so constant Opal sometimes forgot to hear it.

Eventually, Nolan came in from the barn. Opal heard the front door and by the time he appeared in the bedroom doorway with his face reddened from the cold and his hair pressed flat from his hat, Elizabeth had dozed off again. He looked at his sister sleeping against the stacked pillows.

"She fed herself," Opal said quietly. "Half a bowl of porridge."

He nodded as he walked to the chair on the other side of the bed and sat down. For a while neither of them spoke. They watched Elizabeth sleep the way they'd been watching her breathe for days, with a vigilance that had become a shared habit so deeply ingrained that the absence of crisis felt almost disorienting. The rhythm of her breathing was slow and even now. The rasp diminished to a faint catch at the bottom of each exhale. The color in her face was the warm flush of life returning rather than the fierce, dry heat of fever burning it away.

"She'll need several more days of rest," Opal said. "Perhaps longer. The pneumonia weakened her more than she'll want to admit, and she'll try to do too much too soon."

"She will." The corner of his mouth moved, not quite a smile but the suggestion of one. "She's stubborn."

"I can't imagine where she gets that."

He glanced at her. The look held for a moment, warm and brief, and then he turned back to Elizabeth as she stirred and opened her eyes.

"You're both here," she said.

"Where else would we be?" Nolan said.

Elizabeth considered this with the careful deliberation of a mind still moving at half its usual speed. "What day is it?"

Opal and Nolan looked at each other. The question was so ordinary and the answer so uncertain that it exposed something neither of them had acknowledged until that moment. The days of Elizabeth's fever had collapsed into a single, unbroken stretch in which time had stopped keeping its usual shape.

"Saturday," Nolan said after a pause. "December twentieth. No." He stopped. "Twenty-second."

"The twenty-second," Opal confirmed, and the number surprised her. "That means Christmas is in three days."

Elizabeth's brow furrowed. "Three days?"

"Three days."

Christmas had approached while they weren't looking, advancing through the blizzard with its quiet, ancient inevitability. Now it stood three days away in a house where the tree wasn't cut and the woman who usually organized such things was lying in bed.

"Well," Elizabeth said, "I suppose we'll have a quiet one this year."

"Quiet suits me fine," Nolan said.

"Quiet always suits you fine. You'd celebrate Christmas with a handshake and a cup of coffee if I let you." Elizabeth's gaze shifted to Opal. "What was Christmas like for you? In Virginia?"

The question opened a door Opal hadn't expected, and behind it stood a room full of memories so vivid she could smell the pine boughs and the cinnamon and the beeswax candles her mother had ordered from the chandler on Broad Street every December without fail.

"It was my mother's favorite time of year," she said. "She started planning weeks in advance. The house would be decorated with garlands of holly and cedar, and she'd arrange the mantelpiece herself because she had very particular ideas about how the greenery should drape. My father would bring home the tree the week before Christmas, and the three of us would trim it together after supper. We had glass ornaments that had belonged to my grandmother, and paper angels I'd made as a child that my mother kept in a box lined with tissue." She paused. The memories were warm and they hurt, the way touching something beautiful that you'd lost always hurt. "On Christmas morning we'd attend services at St. Paul's, and the church would be full of candles and hymns, and then we'd come home to a dinner my mother had spent two days preparing. She cooked the important things herself, the things her own mother had taught her. The rest she left to Mrs. Jennings and the kitchen."

"It sounds lovely," Elizabeth said softly.

"It was." Opal smoothed the fabric in her lap. "After my parents died, Christmas became something to survive rather than celebrate."

Nolan was watching her with quiet, focused attention.

"Ours has always been simple," he said. "Elizabeth cuts the tree. I haul it in. We've got a box of ornaments our mother made from scraps of fabric and ribbon, and Elizabeth adds something new every year. We read the nativity from Luke. Elizabeth makes spice cake, and that's Christmas." He glanced at his sister. "It's enough."

"It's more than enough," Elizabeth said. "It's what Christmas is supposed to be."

The conviction in her voice, thin as it was, made Opal's eyes sting.

The conversation settled into a quiet, natural rhythm after that, drifting the way conversations do between people who are tired and relieved and sitting in a warm room while the weather keeps them honest about how small their world has become. They talked about the cattle. Nolan was direct about it, the way he was direct about everything, and Opal listened. He expected to lose half the herd by the time this current storm broke.

"Half?" Opal said.

"Maybe more. I won't know until I can ride out and check. But a storm this bad, this long..." He shook his head. "The Hereford crosses handle cold well, but there's a limit. And the ones that probably drifted somewhere they shouldn't... I'm sure I've lost several."

His words sat in the room, enormous and practical and utterly without self-pity. Half his herd. Half the foundation of his liveli-hood. Opal watched his face and saw the cost registered there not as anguish but as the steady, clear-eyed acceptance of a man who understood that loss was woven into the fabric of this life and that the thread of recovery ran through the same cloth.

"You'll rebuild," she said.

"I will. God provided before. He'll provide again. He'll show me the way."

Elizabeth had closed her eyes again, her breathing settling into the slow, steady rhythm of a sleep her body demanded. Opal watched her for a moment and then looked at Nolan across the bed.

"I've been thinking about what comes next. For me," Opal said quietly.

Nolan went still.

"I'm not going to Silver Springs. That door closed the night of the wreck, and I've known it for some time. Mr. Callahan was a stranger, and whatever I was looking for when I answered that advertisement, I don't think it's waiting for me in Silver Springs." She paused. "I believe God led me here for a reason, and that reason wasn't Mr. Callahan."

He watched her, and she held his gaze without flinching. She could see him absorbing what she was saying with the careful, thorough attention he gave to everything.

"I want to stay in Providence Ridge. When Elizabeth is well and the weather breaks. I intend to find work. Teaching, if there's a school that needs someone. Sewing, if there isn't. Whatever honest work is available. I want to build a life here."

The room was quiet except for Elizabeth's breathing and the snow hitting the window.

"Providence Ridge could use a schoolteacher," he said. His voice was measured and careful. "There's no proper school building yet, but there's been talk of one. And Mrs. Colquitt at the mercantile, she takes in sewing and mending. She's mentioned more than once that she could use help." He paused. "Elizabeth will be glad. Having you nearby."

The words landed in Opal's chest with a precision that took her breath, not because they were cruel but because they were kind. He was being practical and genuinely supportive, and every word he spoke sorted her neatly into a category she recognized, with a familiarity so deep it lived in her bones. Providence Ridge could use a school teacher. The town could use her. Elizabeth would be glad to have her nearby. She was an asset to the community. She was a comfort to his sister. She was useful.

She waited. She gave him the space of three full breaths to say something else, something that had nothing to do with the town or Elizabeth. Something that was just about him and just about her and just about what had happened in this kitchen two nights ago when he'd held her against his chest and hadn't let go. The silence stretched between them. He sat with his hands resting on his knees and his eyes steady on her face, and she could see that he meant every word he'd said and that he believed he'd said enough.

"I'd need to find a place to board," she said. Her voice was composed and clear, the voice of a woman who'd spent two years under Hawthorne's thumb learning to absorb a blow without letting it show on her face. "I have enough funds to establish myself modestly. I wouldn't need to depend on anyone."

"There's a boardinghouse in town. Leora Hanscombe runs it. She's particular about who she takes in, but she'd take you."

"That sounds suitable."

"I could introduce you when we're able to get to town. She'll want to meet you properly."

"Thank you, Nolan. That's kind."

The smile she gave him was genuine, and it reached her eyes because she'd meant what she said about staying. She was grateful for his support, and none of those things were false. What was false was the composure beneath the smile, the smooth, practiced surface that held its shape because she'd built it to hold under conditions far worse than this. Hawthorne had taught her that. He'd taught her that a woman who let the wound show gave the world permission to press on it, and she'd learned that lesson so thoroughly that the skill had become part of her architecture. A load-bearing wall she could erect in the space between one breath and the next.

"I should check the broth," she said, and rose from the chair.

She walked to the kitchen. She lifted the lid on the broth pot and stirred it. Then she set the lid back in place and stood at the counter with her hands flat on the wood and breathed.

He hadn't said I want you to stay.

He hadn't said, stay here.

He had said Elizabeth will be glad.

She went back to the bedroom. Nolan looked up when she entered, and she gave him the same warm, composed smile and sat down and picked up her embroidery hoop and threaded her needle. They talked a while longer about small things: the wood supply, the state of the cellar stores, whether the snow would ease enough by Christmas for Nolan to cut a tree. The conversation was easy and natural. Opal participated in it with the full warmth of her attention because she was genuinely fond of this man and grateful for everything he'd done for her.

Eventually, Nolan stood and stretched, and told her he'd be back in an hour.

The front door closed. The sound of it carried through the house with a soft, final thud.

Opal looked down at the forget-me-nots. The pale blue petals were nearly finished. Tiny flowers arranged along the pillowcase edge in a spray that was delicate and lovely. She'd made them here in this house for a bed she'd been sleeping in that wasn't hers, beside a girl she loved who wasn't her sister and across from a man she loved who'd just told her the town would be glad to have her.

Chapter 36

Elizabeth was sitting in a rocking chair by the fireplace when Nolan came through the front door. A quilt covered her lap, and a cup of tea sat cradled between her hands. The sight of her upright, out of bed, sitting in the main room with color in her cheeks and her eyes open and clear, stopped him in his tracks.

"What are you doing out here?" he said. "I expected you'd be in your room."

Elizabeth smiled, "Opal helped me. I needed out of that bed for a little while."

Opal sat in the other rocking chair beside Elizabeth, her embroidery hoop in her lap, her needle moving through the fabric in slow, even pulls. She didn't meet his eyes across the room the way she'd been meeting them for weeks.

She rose from the chair, crossed to the kitchen, poured him a cup of coffee and set it on the table. She sat back down in the rocking chair and picked up her embroidery hoop and resumed her stitching without having looked at him once.

Nolan pulled the buckskin from his back and hung it on the peg, then sat on the bench beside the door and worked the frozen laces on his boots. His fingers were stiff and clumsy from the cold, and the laces fought him, but the boots came off eventually.

He picked up the cup of coffee and sat in a chair at the end of the table where he could see both of them by the fire. Then he proceeded to tell them about his morning's work. The snow had eased to a light, steady fall, and from the yard he'd been able to see the tree line and the lower pasture for the first time in days. He'd spotted eight head of cattle standing at the far edge near the creek, which was more than he'd dared hope for. The horses were sound. Bessie was milked. The water troughs were clear.

Elizabeth asked questions. She wanted to know about the cattle, about the hay supply, about whether the guide rope was holding. Her voice was thin, and she tired quickly between sentences, but the sharpness of her mind was coming back in pieces.

Opal stitched. She listened. When Nolan mentioned the eight head of cattle, she gave a small nod. When Elizabeth asked about the hay, Opal glanced up briefly and then returned to her work. She offered nothing. She didn't ask a single question. She sat in her rocking chair and moved her needle through the fabric, and her silence was polite and complete and entirely unlike the woman he'd come to know.

"Opal." He set his coffee cup down. "Are you all right?"

She looked up. Her eyes found his and held for a moment, composed and clear. "I'm fine. Just a little tired." She set the embroidery hoop in her lap. "I think I'll lie down for a bit and try to nap, if you don't mind sitting with Elizabeth."

"Of course."

She stood, smoothed her skirt, and gave Elizabeth's shoulder a gentle squeeze. Then she walked across the main room and into the bedroom and closed the door behind her.

The sound of the latch catching hit Nolan in his chest like a nail.

He stared at the closed door. Elizabeth's teacup clinked against the saucer in her lap, and the fire popped in the hearth. Nolan sat at the kitchen table with his coffee going cold and tried to understand what had just happened.

"Nolan."

He turned from the closed bedroom door.

Elizabeth was looking at him with an expression he recognized from their mother: patient and perceptive, and gently relentless. "Is everything all right? Between you and Opal?"

"Everything's fine."

"She's different," Elizabeth said. "Since yesterday. She's being..." She paused, searching for the word with the careful effort of a mind still convalescing. "Careful."

He didn't answer.

Elizabeth's gaze moved to the fire and then back to him. "It's like she's closed a door and she's standing on the other side of it being perfectly pleasant."

The accuracy of it hit him like a fist in the chest. That was exactly what it was. A closed door with Opal standing on the other side, perfectly pleasant, perfectly composed, perfectly unreachable.

"I don't know what happened," he said.

Elizabeth studied him for a long moment. Her eyes were tired, but they missed nothing, and the look she gave him held something that wasn't quite accusation and wasn't quite sympathy but lived in the country between the two.

"Maybe you do know," she said quietly. "Maybe you just haven't let yourself hear it yet."

She turned back to the fire and closed her eyes, and the quiet she left behind was louder than anything she could have said.

Nolan sat at the table with his cold coffee and the closed bedroom door, and his sister's words.

Later, when he looked up, Elizabeth had dozed off. He stood and put another log on the fire. Then sat down in the rocking chair where Opal had been sitting. He reached for the Bible and opened it to Joshua and began reading.

Have not I commanded thee? Be strong and of a good courage; be not afraid, neither be thou dismayed: for the Lord thy God is with thee whithersoever thou goest.

He closed the Bible and held it against his chest, and bowed his head.

Lord, I think I hurt Opal in some way. I haven't figured out exactly how I did it, but I'm certain I did something. This morning she acted differently... not like the woman I've come to know. She's holding herself back. I know what I want to do. I've known it for a while, and I've been too afraid, and the cost of that fear is sitting in my house right now treating me like a stranger. I don't have fine words like she does. But I've got honest ones, and I'm asking You for the courage to speak them before I lose her.

Chapter 37

Elizabeth and Nolan were already seated at the kitchen table when Opal set the last dish down. The small ham glistened in its pan, sliced and arranged in overlapping rounds that she'd glazed with a spoonful of the molasses from the back of the cupboard. Beside it sat the fried potatoes, browned and salted in the ham's rendered fat, and a bowl of pickled corn that Elizabeth had put up last summer, the kernels still bright and sharp with vinegar. Opal placed the plate of biscuits between the preserves and the butter crock and stepped back to look at the table.

It was Christmas Eve. There was no tree, no gifts, no garlands of holly and cedar draped along a mantelpiece. There were no glass ornaments that had belonged to someone's grandmother and no paper angels kept in a box lined with tissue. There was a kitchen table set with three plates, three cups, and food that a woman who'd learned to cook only weeks ago had prepared.

Elizabeth had walked from the bedroom to the kitchen on Nolan's arm, moving slowly but under her own strength. The color in her face was the warm, living pink of a body that had turned a corner and intended to keep going. She wore a clean dress that Opal had pressed for her that morning with the sadiron heated on the cookstove. Her hair was braided and pinned in a simple arrangement that Opal had done for her while she sat on the edge of the bed and protested that it wasn't necessary.

Nolan sat in his usual place. He'd washed and changed his shirt, and his hair was combed, and the effort of it, the fact that he'd taken the time, told Opal that the evening meant something to him even if he'd never say so.

"Who'll say grace?" Elizabeth asked.

Nolan looked at Opal. She met his eyes for the first time that day and held them for a moment.

"Please," she said. "You say grace."

They bowed their heads.

"Lord, we come to this table on Christmas Eve with grateful hearts. We thank You for this food and for the hands that prepared it. We thank You for bringing Elizabeth through her illness and for giving us the strength to tend to her when she needed us most. We thank You for the people You've placed in our lives. For the ones we were born to and the ones You brought to us in ways we didn't expect and couldn't have planned. We ask for Your guidance in the days ahead, and for the courage to follow where You lead, even when the path isn't clear to us yet. We ask these things in the name of Your Son, whose birth we honor tonight. Amen."

"Amen," Elizabeth said softly.

"Amen," Opal said.

She looked up at him and found his eyes already on her. "That was a lovely prayer, Nolan."

She quickly looked away and busied herself by helping Elizabeth fill her plate with food.

The ham was good, tender, and salt-sweet from the cure, and Opal was quietly pleased with it. She'd chosen the smaller of the two hams from the cellar, and she'd cooked it the way Elizabeth had described to her weeks ago during one of their kitchen lessons. Low and slow in the oven with the molasses glaze brushed on in the last hour.

"How are the animals?" Elizabeth asked between bites.

"Sound," Nolan said. "The horses are holding up well. Bessie's still producing, though not as much as she was before the storm. Boone's been sleeping in the barn, and he's fine, just restless."

"And the cattle? How many do you think you've lost?"

Nolan set his fork down. "Best I can tell, a little more than half the herd made it. I counted eight heads at the creek two days ago, and I've spotted a few more since the snow let up. But I fear some drifted south into the draws..." He shook his head. "I won't know the full count until I can ride out properly. I'd say we kept somewhere around half. Maybe a bit more than that."

"Well... all we can do now is pray on it."

"I agree."

"How's our food supply holding?" Elizabeth looked at Opal.

"We're managing," Opal said. "The chickens haven't been lay-ing, so we've no eggs. The parsnips are running low. But I should tell you honestly that while you were ill, neither of us had much of an appetite. We ate mostly bread or biscuits and soup beans or salt pork." She glanced at Nolan and then back to Elizabeth. "I wasn't concerned with proper meals as much when you were so sick. I was concerned with keeping you alive."

"You did," Elizabeth said. "Both of you."

"These potatoes are good, Opal," Nolan said. "And the ham. You did well with it."

"Thank you."

They finished eating. Elizabeth set her fork on her plate and leaned back in her chair with the careful, measured movement of a woman whose body was still negotiating the terms of its recovery.

"Nolan, would you help me to my room? I'd like to sit in bed where it's comfortable, and then perhaps we could all sit together and you can read the Nativity from the Bible."

"Of course."

Opal began stacking plates. "I'll be along shortly. Let me wash the supper dishes and cover what's left of the food."

Nolan pushed back from the table and came around to Elizabeth's chair. She took his arm and rose slowly, and they made their way toward the bedroom. Opal watched them go and then began clearing the table.

She scraped the plates and set them in the washbasin. She covered the remaining ham with a cloth and set it in the cool corner of the cupboard, wrapped the leftover biscuits, and put the butter crock back on its shelf. She was reaching for the kettle to pour hot water over the dishes when she heard his footsteps behind her.

She turned, and Nolan stood at the edge of the kitchen, his sleeves rolled to his elbows.

"Let me help you with those," he said.

He crossed to the counter, took the kettle from the stove and poured the hot water into the basin himself. Then he stood beside her, and they washed the supper dishes together in silence.

When they'd finished, Opal dried her hands and then handed the towel to Nolan. He dried his hands and hung it on the nail on the wall, and then he turned to her and held his arm out.

"Ready to go sit?" he asked.

She looked from his offered arm up to his eyes. They were steady and blue and watching her with an attentiveness that went beyond the simple question he'd asked, and she took his arm and let him lead her into Elizabeth's bedroom.

Elizabeth was propped against her pillows with a quilt pulled to her waist and the lamp lit on the nightstand beside her.

Opal released Nolan's arm and sat down in her normal chair beside the bed and watched as Nolan picked up his chair from the opposite side of Elizabeth's bed and grabbed the Bible off the nightstand. Then he carried both back around to her side, set the chair down beside hers, and sat.

The distance between their chairs was less than a foot. She could feel the warmth of him along her arm. Elizabeth's gaze moved from Nolan to Opal and back again, and the look on her face was the most dumbfounded expression she'd ever seen her do.

Nolan opened the Bible to the Gospel of Luke and began to read.

"And it came to pass in those days, that there went out a decree from Caesar Augustus that all the world should be taxed. And this taxing was first made when Cyrenius was governor of Syria. And all went to be taxed, every one into his own city. And Joseph also went up from Galilee, out of the city of Nazareth, into Judaea, unto the city of David, which is called Bethlehem; because he was of the house and lineage of David: To be taxed with Mary his espoused wife, being great with child."

His voice carried the words the way it always carried Scripture, low and steady and without embellishment, letting the weight of the passage speak for itself. Opal closed her eyes and listened.

"And so it was, that while they were there, the days were accomplished that she should be delivered. And she brought forth her firstborn son, and wrapped him in swaddling clothes, and laid him in a manger; because there was no room for them in the inn."

"And there were in the same country shepherds abiding in the field, keeping watch over their flock by night. And, lo, the angel of the Lord came upon them, and the glory of the Lord shone round about them: and they were sore afraid. And the angel said unto them, Fear not: for, behold, I bring you good tidings of great joy, which shall be to all people. For unto you is born this day in the city of David a Saviour, which is Christ the Lord. And this shall be a sign unto you; Ye shall find the babe wrapped in swaddling clothes, lying in a manger."

"And suddenly there was with the angel a multitude of the heavenly host praising God, and saying, Glory to God in the highest, and on earth peace, good will toward men. And it came to pass, as the angels were gone away from them into heaven, the shepherds said one to another, Let us now go even unto Bethlehem, and see this thing which is come to pass, which the Lord hath made known unto us. And they came with haste, and found Mary, and Joseph, and the babe lying in a manger."

He read on, and Opal listened with her eyes closed and her hands folded in her lap, and the ancient story settled into the room the way warmth settled into cold wood, slowly and completely and all the way through.

"And when they had seen it, they made known abroad the saying which was told them concerning this child. And all they that heard it wondered at those things which were told them by the shepherds. But Mary kept all these things and pondered them in her heart. And the shepherds returned, glorifying and praising God for all the things that they had heard and seen, as it was told unto them."

He closed the Bible.

The silence that followed was the kind that belongs to sacred things, full and unhurried, carrying the story inside it the way a river carries the shape of the land.

"That was lovely," Opal said. She opened her eyes and looked at him. "Those passages are among my favorites in all of Scripture. My mother used to read them aloud on Christmas Day, and my father would sit beside her in his chair and listen the same way we just did, and it always felt to me like the truest part of the whole season."

As she spoke, something changed in Nolan's face. A shift she couldn't name at first, a gathering, as though every thought he'd carried was converging on a single point behind his eyes. The tips of his ears began to color, a slow, deep red that spread upward from beneath his collar, and his hands tightened on the Bible in his lap.

"Are you all right?" she asked.

He set the Bible on the bed. Then he reached for her hand.

His fingers closed around hers with a firm pressure, the grip of a man who was holding on to something he was afraid of dropping. His palm was rough and warm against hers.

"Opal." His voice was low and not entirely steady. "I need to say something to you, and I'm probably going to do a poor job of it.

But I've been quiet too long already, and the cost of staying quiet is more than I'm willing to pay."

She didn't move.

"I don't want you to go."

He stopped. He looked down at their joined hands and then back up at her face, and the flush that had climbed past his ears had now settled across his cheekbones.

"I'm not a rich man. I can't give you what you had in Virginia." He paused. "But I can promise you that I'll provide for you. I'll work as hard as any man alive to give you a good life, and I'll do it gladly because..." His voice caught. He cleared his throat and pressed forward. "Because I love you."

Opal sat in the chair beside him with her hand in his and her vision blurring.

"I'm asking you to stay," he said. "Here. With me. As my wife. And if that's too much or too soon, or if I've misread everything between us, then I'll drive you to Leora's boardinghouse when you tell me to, and I'll never speak of it again. But I couldn't let another day go by without telling you. I should have said it a long time ago."

The room was quiet. Elizabeth lay against her pillows with tears running down her cheeks, and she was watching her brother with an expression of such fierce, luminous pride that it transformed her face entirely.

Opal looked at this man. This quiet, stubborn, profoundly good man, who showed love through carved footrests and walking sticks. Who'd sat across from her for weeks and loved her in a hundred silent ways, was now, on Christmas Eve, in a bedroom with his recovering sister as his only witness, offering her the one thing she'd crossed a continent to find.

"Yes," she said. "Yes, Nolan. I want to stay. Here. With you."

His face broke open. There was no other way to describe it. The careful, guarded expression he wore like armor simply fell away, and what was beneath it was a man who'd just been given something he'd been afraid to ask for. The joy of it was so raw and so undefended that Opal felt it in her chest like a second heartbeat.

He raised her hand to his mouth and pressed his lips against her knuckles, a slow, deliberate kiss that lingered there against her skin.

"Oh, thank the Lord," Elizabeth said from the bed, and her voice was thick with tears and laughter at the same time. "Thank the Lord."

Nolan hadn't released her hand. He was looking at her with those blue eyes that she loved, and what she saw in them now was the expression of a man who'd stopped being afraid.

He reached across the bed with his free hand, and Elizabeth took it. Elizabeth reached for Opal's other hand, and Opal gave it to her. The three of them sat linked together in the lamplight on Christmas Eve, a circle made of joined hands and the quiet wonder of what had just changed in this room.

"Let me pray," Nolan said.

They bowed their heads.

"Lord, I don't have the words for what I'm feeling right now, and You know I've never been good at finding them. But You brought this woman into our lives through a wreck on a mountain road, and I've spent months trying to understand why, and now I do." His voice was rough with emotion and stripped of every pretense, the voice of a man talking to his God the way he talked to his horses in the barn when no one was listening, honest, unguarded, and true. "Thank You. Thank You for Opal. Thank You for saving

Elizabeth. Thank You for giving me the courage to speak tonight instead of staying silent and losing what You gave me. Watch over this family, Lord. The family we are now and the family we're becoming. Guide us through the winter and into the spring, and help me be the man she deserves. I ask it in Jesus' name. Amen."

"Amen," Elizabeth said.

"Amen," Opal said.

She lifted her head and looked at him. Tears were streaming down her face, and she didn't wipe them away. She reached up and touched his cheek with her fingertips. His skin was warm and rough beneath her hand, and he turned his face into her palm and closed his eyes. The three of them sat together in the lamplight while the snow lay still and deep outside the window and the fire burned low in the hearth.

Christmas Eve in a house in the mountains of Montana. No tree, no gifts, no garlands. A Bible on the bed, a table cleared of dishes in the next room, and the smell of ham and biscuits still hanging in the warm air. A girl recovering in her bed. A man who'd finally found the courage to say what he felt. And a woman who'd traveled a thousand miles to answer a stranger's advertisement and found, instead, a home.

Love arriving in the humblest possible form.

Leave A Review

If you enjoyed this book, please consider leaving an honest review on Amazon

Visit Our Website:

www.vivianbelle.com

Visit Our Amazon Author Page HERE

Find Us On Social Media:

Facebook

Facebook Author Page

Instagram

About Vivian

Vivian Belle is a talented author known for her sweeping **Historical Christian Romance** novels set against the untamed beauty of the American frontier. With a deep love for history and storytelling, she brings to life **resilient heroines, steadfast heroes, and faith-filled journeys** in the vast, rugged landscapes of the past.

Nestled in the **majestic mountains of northern West Virginia,** Vivian finds endless inspiration in the rolling hills, winding rivers, and boundless sky that mirror the spirit of her stories. When she's not writing, she enjoys **kayaking on tranquil waters, hiking through breathtaking mountain trails, and, of course, getting lost in a good book.**

Vivian's novels capture the heart of **faith, love, and perseverance**—where strong women and honorable men overcome life's trials to find hope, home, and happily-ever-after. Whether she's exploring the great outdoors or crafting her next frontier romance,

Vivian's passion for adventure and storytelling shines through in every word she writes.

Visit Vivian on the web: www.vivianbelle.com

Also by Vivian

Where the Heart Finds Home
Faith on the Frontier
Love in Hopewell Creek
Abigail's Promise
Beneath Montana Skies
Rocky Mountain Promise
Hearts Unbroken
Beneath the Oregon Pines
Journey's of the Heart

Providence Ridge Series

Bride Worth Keeping

A Bride Worth Keeping
A Bride Worth Keeping
Stronger Than the River
Tender Mercies
Sanctuary in Providence Ridge

The Heart She Trusted
A Place for Grace
A Bride Worth Keeping
Stronger Than the River
Tender Mercies
Sanctuary in Providence Ridge
The Heart She Trusted
A Place for Grace